The House in the Hedge

Melanie Leavey

Three Ravens Press

Contents

Dedication	VI
Author's note	VII
Chapter One	1
Chapter Two	12
Chapter Three	25
Chapter Four	35
Chapter Five	46
Chapter Six	62
Chapter Seven	79
Chapter Eight	93
Chapter Nine	106
Chapter Ten	120
Chapter Eleven	136
Chapter Twelve	148

Chapter Thirteen   169

Chapter Fourteen   179

Chapter Fifteen   187

Chapter Sixteen   204

Chapter Seventeen   215

Chapter Eighteen   226

Chapter Nineteen   245

Chapter Twenty   262

Chapter Twenty-One   275

Chapter Twenty-Two   291

Chapter Twenty-Three   306

Chapter Twenty-Four   313

Chapter Twenty-Five   320

Chapter Twenty-Six   326

Chapter Twenty-Seven   342

Chapter Twenty-Eight   355

Chapter Twenty-Nine   371

Chapter Thirty   384

Chapter Thirty-One   395

Chapter Thirty-Two   403

Chapter Thirty-Three   418

Chapter Thirty-Four   432

Chapter Thirty-Five   446

Chapter Thirty-Six   457

Chapter Thirty-Seven   468

Wait! Don't go yet...   481

Acknowledgements   482

About the author   483

in loving memory...
of my grandparents,
for everything you taught me about belonging, safety
and the perfect cup of tea.

I really miss you.

Author's note

I wrote this story as an homage to all of the books that have brought me comfort over the years...from Enid Blyton in childhood, to Miss Read and Rosamund Pilcher (and so, so many others) in adulthood. It was started in 2017 as I struggled with grief and loss and continued to carry me as things got steadily more difficult into 2019, when I set it aside to focus on other stories.

It's been a hard book to come back to, bound as it is in so much that was sorrowful, but I felt it was time to let it find its place in the world, time to offer back some gentleness and delight.

Whatever else you may find between these pages, dear reader, I hope you find shelter from your cares and a place to rest your heart for a while as world rages on.

~m. xo

Chapter One

"This is the last of 'em."

The burly, red-faced man with an unlit cigarette dangling from his lips stood looking expectantly at me in the kitchen doorway.

I ran a hand through my hair, snagging my fingers on the wild tangle I'd attempted to contain under a blue-spotted scarf. As I tried to disengage them without pulling the whole lot out from beneath it's precarious containment, I could feel the beginnings of a headache menacing from somewhere at the base of my skull. Moving men of varying degrees of boisterousness had been traipsing to and fro for the last hour and their energy was incredibly jarring. Their apparent delight in carting my belongings up the narrow, winding staircase bewildered me and they seemed to be at their most cheerful (and shouty) when finding themselves, and my possessions, wedged between door-frames.

"Just in the sitting room with the others," I said, giving up entirely on having the boxes placed in the appropriate rooms. My mother had instructed me to direct the moving men accordingly, to minimize the need for my own fetching and carrying and despite being set against my moving to the cottage in the first place, had made sure all of the boxes were properly labeled. It seemed a marvelously sensible idea in theory, but I was struggling with the uncomfortable level of bossiness required to coordinate things. The crew were enjoying themselves far too much to bother with my mother's neatly labeled boxes and I couldn't summon the nerve to interrupt their joviality. After all, my entire life had been lived, thus far, with the aim of making as little fuss as possible.

"Are ye sure, pet?" asked the man, whose name, according to the embroidered patch on his shirt, was Harry. "I can have the lads hump yon heavy bits up the stairs. They're a fair bit steep and awkward for a wee lass such as yourself. If ye don't mind me saying, that is."

I managed a smile, one I hoped was encouraging and full of competence. The fact that he referred to me as a 'wee lass' was such a generosity of spirit that I could hardly bear to disappoint him.

"Thank you, as long as it's no trouble. I really don't need half of this stuff," I waved a hand feebly at the piles of boxes. "It's just my mum imagines I'm living on the far reaches of civilization..."

Harry gave a good-natured, tobacco-stained grin. He, like the rest of his lads, was the sort of person who smiled often.

"Aye, well. That's mothers for you, in't it? It were right hard on me own missus when our first one left the nest. If she'd known the youngest would hang about as long as he has, she mightn't have made such a fuss, aye?"

"Oh, this isn't my first time away from home," I began, mortified and wanting to explain that I was far more worldly than was immediately obvious, not to mention the fact that I was bearing quickly down on forty. But then I remembered I really wasn't all that worldly and so let the thought trickle away. I didn't feel up to the inevitable questions and comments when I explained how I ended up here.

"Isn't it? Sorry lass, it's just you look barely old enough to be out of school and I thought what with your mam being so particular an' that and she were quite definite in how we were to go on when she phoned, I can tell ye."

I flushed, embarrassed for his mistake; a mistake I supposed I should be delighted he'd made, and also on behalf of my mother. I'm often embarrassed on other people's behalf — it saves them the trouble. As to looking younger than I am, it's a blessing and a curse, a combination of genes (allegedly magical) and a mother who was fanatical about sunscreen and broad brimmed hats.

"She can't help herself," I said, compelled to apologize on my mother's behalf, "My mum, I mean. Of course, she means well," I added, not wanting to sound ungrateful or leave Mum standing in a bad light. "But she forgets I've been living in London for the last seventeen years."

Please don't ask me why I'm here, I added in my head. I realized it was the next obvious question and I internally kicked myself for opening up the opportunity. I was reaching such a level of overstimulation I couldn't trust myself not to blurt out the entirety of my tragic backstory.

Fortunately, Harry wasn't of the nosy persuasion, preferring to talk about himself.

"Ah, big city girl, are you? Won't it be a bit quiet out here? Being used to all the bright lights and the goings-on? Can't abide the city, meself. A trip into Newcastle a few times a year to watch the football is as much as I can manage. Far too many folk milling about for my liking. Are ye a supporter?"

I stifled a whimper. Conversations with strangers are a tremendous strain. I'm happiest when they're willing to uphold both ends themselves. I find that some people, given even the tiniest bit of encouragement, are quite content to chat away without requiring much more input than an occasional nod or murmur of interest. Harry was one of those people so I didn't bother to answer his question. He continued on.

"You see a fair few more lasses at St.James' than ever you used to in my old man's day. Families, an' all. I think it's grand, meself, but I'm not sure how the old boy would've liked it. Mind you, it were different times back then. A bit more rough, y' see? Not really a place for lasses."

"Oh, no. I mean, yes. Of course," I said, blushing again. The danger of letting people carry on their own conversations was drifting out of focus from time to time. My mind had a great propensity for wandering. At that moment, it was wandering in the direction of a cup of tea. I flicked my glance, somewhat involuntarily, behind me into the kitchen.

Harry caught the look and peered around me.

"Something amiss, lass?" he asked, "Ye've gone a bit peaky, like."

"No, no," I said, summoning the will to act like a normal, socially capable person. "It's been a long day, I think I'm just a bit done in."

I tried to mentally calculate how much longer they were going to be versus how desperate I was for a cup of tea versus what was expected in the circumstances. Summoning my last reserves, I smiled brightly and said, "I'm just about to put the kettle on. Would you and the...lads, like a cup of tea before you go? I'm sure there's mugs around here somewhere."

"Eeeh! That'd be grand, lass. Ta very much. I don't know about that lot, but I'm fair gasping. I'd say we'd stop in at the pub for a pint, but we've got another job on after this and we can't be turning up all pie-eyed, now can we? And no mind about the mugs, we always bring our own."

I cleared myself a place on my Nan's balding tartan sofa and sank into the sagging cushions with an audible sigh. In a painful act of desperation, I'd asked one of the moving men, a froggy looking fellow named Warren, to carry in a box of logs from the wood store so that, despite the state of upheaval in which I found myself, I could at least have a fire burning merrily in the grate. I gazed into the flickering light, my hands wrapped around a steaming mug of soup. Edie had stopped by just after Harry and the Lads - as I'd started calling them in my head - had departed for their next engagement, bearing a welcome basket of provisions.

"Just to keep you going 'til you can get into the village for some shopping," she'd said. "I've taken the liberty of letting the milkman know you're here - oh, aye, we've still got the milkman. Young Craig — you won't know him, he and his mum, that's old Mr. Talbot's sister, moved here after you...well, you know. Anyway, he took over from his uncle last year. He's all modern, mind, drives a funny little van, but he still keeps up the deliveries. You'll have to let him know what exactly you want. But here's a bottle to get you started and a lump of my apple-walnut cake."

She'd also tucked in a loaf of bread (baked fresh this morning), a pot of blackberry jam (last year's but still lovely) and a flask of leek broth (Alfie has leeks all winter long, none of them insipid shop-bought ones in here).

I could've wept with relief. I hadn't had the forethought to bring much more than tea bags and some sugar, imagining I would've had plenty of time to get to the village shop before it closed. Of course, that was based on my foolish assumption that the village grocer kept the same hours as the corner shop I'd frequented near the London flat. It was Harry who'd laughed and told me that "I imagine nowt much happens 'round here after four o'clock. Folk want to be getting home for their tea."

The only other sustenance I had with me was a packet of Hob Nobs and I'd given them to Harry and the Lads to go with their cups of tea. I'd resigned myself to dining on the squashed bar of chocolate I'd found at the bottom of my handbag, when Edie had knocked on the door.

I sipped slowly at the mug of the fragrant leek broth enjoying the feeling of spreading warmth. I was utterly and profoundly exhausted - mentally and emotionally. There had been a few moments in the course of the day that I'd let the doubt creep in. I could hear my mother's voice, shrill with worry and fear, trying to convince my dad, at the last minute, that I shouldn't be allowed to move into Nan's cottage, that it would be easier to hire a firm to take care of the place.

It had been an argument that lasted for weeks. No sooner was Nan's funeral over than mum was trying to make sure I wasn't intending of moving up here. She tried anything and everything but in an uncharacteristic act of sustained defiance, I held my ground. There was no reason for me to go back to London - the last thing I wanted was to remind myself of the humiliation and I'd no intention of staying at home with them, despite having been deeply grateful for the respite it had offered. Dad was on my side, reasoning that the cottage ought to be occupied in case a wandering vagrant moved in and insisted, that at thirty-nine years of age, I was fully capable of knowing my own mind.

He'd kindly left out the 'after all she's been through' qualifier that we were all thinking but wouldn't dare say out loud. Still, I admit that the chance of wandering vagrants was a bit worrying, but I shoved that possibility deep within my collection of things that didn't bear thinking about. Getting myself a dog, preferably a large and intimidating one, was at the top of my to-do list.

An ember popped, sending a kaleidoscope of sparks up the chimney. Outside, the light was fading and there was a faint whistle from one of the crooked windows as the wind wound itself around the cottage. I stared around the sitting room, taking in the uneven plaster of the walls and the old botanical illustrations and country scenes, hung in crooked, cobbled-together frames. There were two long strips of horse brasses, dull and tarnished for want of a polish, on worn leather straps, hanging on the wall on each side of the back door. When I was a child, Nan had made me memorize what each of them meant, what they were designed to guard against or encourage. In the old days, she'd tell me as I sat, enthralled, smoothing a small hand over the gleaming metal, horse brasses weren't just ornamental. They were wards and protection against faery mischief. She'd also shown me how to weave rowan twigs and strands of sheep's wool into charms and countless other little things that just seemed funny little activities meant to entertain a child.

Looking back now, I see they were so much more than that. They were her way of helping me cope with a world that always seemed too loud and too fast. The little charms and rituals, the stories and songs, all helped me raise a feeling of protection around myself, as if I had an invisible armour shielding me from the worst of the taunts and exclusions that invariably come to the quiet and the odd. Nan fostered my childish beliefs in unseen companions who were my protectors and my champions when I was forced out into a world that wasn't always very kind to people like me.

When things at school were most dire, which was most of the time, I'd retreat to books - to the worlds that comforted and consoled me. Because of that, every wardrobe held the potential to lead to Narnia, every large tree might lead to Moon-face and Silkie. One of my most fervently-replayed daydreams was of finding my very own abandoned cottage or walled garden with a mysteriously locked door. I would happily retreat into the safety of that cottage with a satchel full of books and jam sandwiches where I would find a stray cat or a pet crow to be my companion whilst I tended my garden and wrote stories. I suppose that's why I ended up writing books. They were a way to keep my escapist fantasies alive. Though, even that had somehow gone in the wrong direction. I shoved that thought down too. There was time enough to address it later. Much later. I dragged myself back to the present and tried to take it all in.

Being here was a dream come true, like every one of my favourite stories come to life. So why wasn't the nagging dread gone? Why did I feel exactly the same?

A log shifted in the grate making me startle. I got up off the sofa and used the poker to readjust the burning wood. Nan had taught me to be very respectful of fire, both in its tending and its gift. She was that way with everything, really. It showed in the care she took of the cottage — everything neat and tidy, yet always with the feeling of it being lived in and welcoming. She struck a balance that was often missing in my childhood home where mum had created a showplace rather than somewhere you could lie on the floor to read or crayon. Nan never minded me draping myself over the arms of chairs or putting my feet on coffee tables (providing I'd taken off my shoes, of course). My time at Rookery Cottage always felt like a deep exhale; it was where I could take off the armour I wore to walk through the world and be entirely myself.

I stayed kneeling down on the hearth rug, gazing at the flickering, snapping flames, feeling the warmth on my face. The tension in my shoulders was beginning to ease ever so slightly as I let myself imagine what it could be to truly live the life I'd always hoped for myself. What if I really could make it work here? What if I could really walk away from everything that London was and had done to me, from the misguided detour in my writing career and the great disaster of my failed marriage to Teddy. A simple, quiet, solitary life. Was it even possible? I hoped so, with all of my tired heart.

I got to my feet and went back to the sofa, noting the film of dust on the mantle as I stood up. Nan hadn't lived in the cottage for a while before she died and the absence of her tending hand showed in the dust and cobwebby corners. The thought came to me, unbidden, that there was more to be done here than me trying to salvage the wreckage of my life. I shook off the thought, avoiding the depths that it would require of me when all I felt able for was the barest skimming of surfaces. A gust of wind rattled the kitchen door and swept down the chimney, skittering the flames into a brief frenzy.

"No," I said, my voice sounding uncomfortably loud in the relative silence. "I'm just not ready for more than this, do you hear me?"

The cottage was quiet, the wind tapping playfully at the windows and the clock on the mantel ticked in companionable time to my heartbeat. I stood for a moment more, waiting, but nothing happened. I sighed and took myself back to the sofa and my mug of broth.

I woke up to a dwindling fire and a creeping chill. I don't know how long I had slept but it was full dark and I couldn't see the clock. I thought about getting up and turning on a lamp but I was comfortable and didn't want to move. I'd been dreaming of one of the summers I'd spent here as a child, though the details escaped me and only a sensation of warmth and happiness remained, a sensation I wanted to hold onto.

I'd asked my dad once, when I was much younger, why he'd taken the name of Price. Nan's surname was McCorrigan, and so was his grandmother's. There was a habitual lack of male presence in the McCorrigan family, which was another mystery that didn't invite discussion, especially not around my mum. He'd smiled and winked, and told me that in the realms of magic, which were never far away when he was growing up, it was said that all good things must come at a price. The world demands a balance, he'd said. So when you take, you must give something back. He'd given himself the name Price so that he'd always remember how much he'd taken and how much he needed to give back to keep the balance of the worlds. He'd spent most of his adult life giving back, from what I could see.

I don't think I truly understood his answer until I first walked across the threshold of the cottage that morning. It was still quiet, with only the cackle of rooks and the hum of a distant tractor to break the silence; the boisterous, booted, moving men had yet to arrive. Even though it isn't a large cottage, it felt cavernous without Nan's presence. It all seemed so desolate and without its usual welcoming warmth. There was no smell of baking or drying herbs; no sound of the kettle whistling on the hob. To make a home, here, in the little cottage at the edge of the moor, had been my most precious secret wish since the first summer I'd come to stay when I was six years old. Now it was mine, but the world had exacted its price.

"Oh, Nan," I whispered, curling up into a tight ball in the corner of the sofa. "I really, really miss you."

Chapter Two

I awoke to the sound of whistling.

Blinking and slightly disoriented, I sat up. I'd fallen asleep on the sofa, or, more accurately, I'd sniffled myself to sleep on the sofa. The fire had gone out and the sitting room was as bleak as it had been the night before; cold and heartless, the stacks of boxes and general disarray doing nothing to dispel my feelings of loss and overwhelm. I pulled my cardigan more tightly around me, trying not to think about what a rumpled sight I must be, and got up to locate the source of the cheery whistling. The clink of glass on the stone step solved the mystery before I got to the door. I pulled back the bolt and lifted the latch, opening the door in time to see the retreating figure of who could only be Young Craig, the milkman.

"Hello," I said, feeling that I probably ought to make an effort, despite the overwhelming urge to just quietly pick up the milk and slide back inside, unnoticed. Besides, I wasn't likely to go through two bottles of milk in one day so thought I should mention it, before I accumulated an excess.

He turned around at the sound of my voice, his face going from intense concentration to a beaming grin; he started back down the path towards me. I tried not to back away, mortifyingly aware as I was by my freshly-awakened-from-a-night-of-sniveling state. This was one of the rare times where I hoped my McCorrigan genes would serve me well. I willed myself cheerful.

Young Craig looked to be in his early fifties. He wore stereotypical farmer attire; brown corduroy trousers and a shapeless woollen jumper with tiny bits of straw sticking, atmospherically, from the cuffs and visible front. The spotless white coat of the formal milkman variety seemed out of place, more an afterthought in service of looking the part. A pair of sturdy black wellingtons and a peaked tweed cap completed the outfit. He looked as if he'd walked off a page of Country Living magazine, albeit without a pair of matching labradors or a poised-for-action border collie as accessories.

"You must be Hazel," said Craig, holding out a big hand.

I took it, watching my own small one disappear into his giant paw. He didn't seem to notice me wince as he pumped it vigorously.

Is everyone around here so boisterous? I wondered.

"Yes, and you must be Craig. Edie told me you'd probably come by. I just wanted to tell you that I'll only need the one bottle, if that's alright. I don't go through much milk, you see, and Edie already gave me a bottle. I suppose if I'm going to be doing any baking I can just let you know ahead of time but normally, I think just the one would be sufficient. I'd hate to have it go to waste."

I knew I was over-explaining. It was one of the things that drove my mum mad but I can't help myself. It's all part of my burning desire to not be a bother.

"Right! No problem at all," he boomed, his voice warm and jovial. "Shall I take one back, then? Oh, and do you need eggs? Only as my old mum keeps a few hens and we've always got extra. Mind you, that's only on offer to a few folk, so I wouldn't mention it at the post office, if you know what I mean. Mrs. McCorrigan, your Nan that is, always had a couple of dozen. She did a fair bit of baking, as you probably know."

He smiled sadly, no doubt wondering if such a specimen as myself could even hope to fill the shoes of a wonderful woman as my Nan. He wasn't alone in that thought.

"I was right sorry to hear of her passing," he continued, "She was a lovely person. When my uncle took ill, she walked across the moor to the farm every Tuesday to sit with him while my mum got away to do the shopping in town. And it were her that told me I should take up the milk run, so that he wouldn't worry about it and could concentrate on getting better. I didn't much think I'd fancy it at first, but it's the sort of thing that grows on you after a bit. Now I quite enjoy getting up before the rest of the world and getting on with the deliveries before I have to see to the beasts and the rest of it. We've a lad that comes to do the milking, like. The cows wouldn't stand waiting 'til the deliveries were done and to be honest, I'm not really one for the livestock. I'm more of a fruit and veg bloke meself, but me old uncle can't fathom not having the cattle and sheep. Of course, his Lordship is mad about his pedigreed stock an' all so we'll never be shot o' them. Which is alright, really. Rather them than sheds full of engineered sods. Eeeh! I'm sorry! I never thought, I must've woken you up, did I? I can't help but whistle, it just comes over me sometimes, d'ye know what I mean? The early mornings are the finest bit of the day if you ask me."

I couldn't, in all fairness, say that I did know what it was like to be overcome with the need to whistle. Even in my moments of greatest bliss, whistling wasn't my likely expression. But I smiled, in a hopefully comradely way, and murmured something about knowing exactly how he felt. Because, other than the whistling, I did know how he felt; though my love of early mornings was more aligned with the silence of them. Young Craig's barrage of chatter was a benign assault on my nervous system. Nevertheless, I kept smiling.

"It's no bother, I was just awake. I fell asleep on the sofa."

I shrugged feebly and flapped a hand, attempting to dismiss the whole thing as utterly inconsequential. He seemed happy to let it go. There was a brief, slightly awkward silence as he looked at me, questioningly.

"Oh! The eggs! Yes, please. Only not two dozen, perhaps just a dozen to start? I haven't done any baking recently but I hope to start doing more along those lines."

I thought happily of my newly-acquired collection of Mary Berry cookbooks and nostalgically of the old Be-Ro booklet that Nan had given me when I was nine. Being a person-who-baked was part of my vision for my fresh start in the cottage.

Craig nodded approvingly.

"Good lass. It's a relief to think of you carrying on with your Nan's ways. I don't mind telling you, things haven't been quite right with yon cottage standing empty. It does the whole village a good turn, after all. Mind you, not many of the new folk have any use for the old ways, but we like to carry on with things nonetheless. Nowt's gone amiss in a long, long, time and we like to keep it that way, aye?"

I nodded sagely, despite not really knowing what he was on about. I knotted my fingers in my cardigan so as not to succumb to the temptation to reach up and feel just how frightening my hair must be after my night on the sofa.

"Well, I'm not quite sure I can do *everything* my Nan used to do. I mean, I've got my writing and well...I haven't spent much time here since...well, for a while," I finished, a bit feebly, not wanting to go into the sordid details with a complete stranger.

He waved a beefy hand.

"Nowt to worry about, lass. I'm sure it'll come, natural-like. You're one of them McCorrigans, that's fair obvious, what with your colouring and you being small and a bit skittish. Me mam has always said you could spot the faery blood and let me tell you, there's more as have it than not in these parts. Though, none as clear as the McCorrigans, mind."

He wagged a finger and then tapped the peak of his cap.

"Right, I'd best be off. I've still got a few deliveries and I'm sure you've got plenty to keep you busy what with getting unpacked an' all that an' I've talked yer ear off long enough. Are ye fixed for eggs then, until I get back 'round this way?"

I didn't have a single egg, but rather than create an awkward feeling of obligation, I nodded.

"I'm fine, thank you. I don't expect I'll get much baking done in the next day or so anyway. I've loads to do with tidying and unpacking."

Craig grinned and turned to go

"Oh, Craig?"

He turned back.

"Is it alright for me to go walking on the moor? I wouldn't be trespassing or anything or disturbing the livestock? I like to go for walks, you see, but I wouldn't want to upset anyone."

Craig gave me a quizzical look and then burst into a rumbling chuckle.

"You really are a city lass, aren't you?"

I blushed, really not wanting to be identified with cities at all and yet painfully aware it must have rubbed off on me..

He reached out and patted my arm in a consoling gesture.

"Never mind, pet. We'll get you sorted. Nowt to worry about out there but stepping in a rabbit hole and turning an ankle. All that's out there is sheep and they won't take any bother, as long as you haven't got a dog chasing them."

He peered around me into the house, his face creasing into a frown.

"You haven't got a dog, have you?"

"No," I said, deciding not to mention I thought I'd get one. "Am I not allowed to have one?"

He laughed again

"You can do whatever you like, lass. Only I asked as it's often the city dogs that don't know about sheep that cause bother. As long as they're raised around them, and they're kept an eye on, they're usually alright."

I heaved an internal sigh of relief. A dog really was very much a part of my vision. I mentally adjusted that vision to accommodate a puppy that could be raised around the sheep.

Craig started off down the path, waving an arm as he went.

"The only place you probably oughtn't go is over by the edge of the grounds of the Big House," he called back as he climbed into his little van. "They're a funny lot over there, if they don't know ye. At least, the estate manager is. Odd body, that one. Gets very testy about the ramblers straying off the footpaths and disturbing nests and whatnot. So's just as well to steer clear. You don't want to get off wrong-footed 'til everyone knows who ye are."

With that he pulled away, tooting the horn as he disappeared up the lane. I stared out after him, suddenly exhausted by the verbal onslaught and the sudden, creeping sense of having bit off more than I could ever possibly chew.

I made my way to the kitchen, weaving in and out of the piles of boxes. I really didn't need half of what Mum had sent, but of course she wouldn't have listened so I hadn't bothered trying to explain it. She'd taken it upon herself to demand half of the things from the London flat and I daresay even Teddy didn't have the nerve to refuse her. The fact I wanted none of it didn't really come into consideration. I had a very specific idea of how I wanted things to be here and none of either hers or Teddy's decorative influence was going to fit. If I was truly going to claim my place here, it had to be firmly on my terms. Matching towels with ridiculously high thread counts didn't really factor in as all that important.

The kitchen was tiled with old slate flags so it was uncomfortably cold on my feet, even through my woollen socks and slippers. The whole *cottage* was uncomfortably cold. Damp, really. Nothing a good airing wouldn't fix, I thought, making a mental note to bring more wood in from the shed. A few days with the fire going should chase the damp away.

The window had a deep sill and was placed perfectly above the sink so I could gaze at the view of the garden as I filled the kettle. It had changed so much over the years, and yet somehow looked exactly the same as my first memory of it. Smaller, perhaps, but that was always the way with childhood memories. The apple trees at the bottom of the garden had grown, gnarled and bent, leaning slightly towards one another. The plum and peach trees which Nan and I had planted as bare-rooted saplings the last time I'd come to visit, exhausted and wrung-out right after finishing uni, were still slender and young-looking in comparison, though that was almost twenty years ago now. I wondered if she'd had any fruit from them. She had joked as we planted them, that it would be a miracle if she got to taste the fruits of her labours that day. The memory stung and I felt the well of tears rising in my throat. I shook my head, attempting to jostle myself out of my morose mood, and set the kettle on the hob. I leaned over the sink and unlatched the window, pushing it out a fraction to let in the morning air. It was cold, but the freshness was welcome. Nan had always believed in moving the air around. A light breeze wafted in, smelling of damp earth and the distant sea. A tinkling melody of wind chimes sang alongside the birds.

While I waited for the tea to steep, I pulled out a chair and sat at the scrubbed oak table with a pen and notepad. I was determined to bring life and warmth back to the cottage so decided to make myself a list of what needed doing. I thought it most sensible to give the place a good cleaning before I bothered to unpack too much. That way, I'd only unpack what I needed. There was very little that I wanted to add, preferring to keep everything just the way Nan had it. I've always thought that certain things hold memories – even inanimate objects -- and everything of Nan's meant something to me. Leaving it all as it was meant I could just carry on where she left off. So all I really had to unpack were my clothes and books and a few bits of pottery - favourite mugs and a bowl and plate. I briefly entertained the idea of carting all of the unwanted stuff straight to a charity shop but reconsidered. There were a couple of old storage sheds at the bottom of the garden, I would just shove the boxes in there. One thing I *was* grateful for, was the highly efficient way mum had labeled the boxes - which is why I was so easily able to find the "tea things" yesterday. The box of "cleaning" sat next to the refrigerator, right beside "cookbooks" and "candles". I had the vague suspicion that she'd packed everything alphabetically. Still, I was in no position to complain. She'd taken control of the situation when I wasn't in any shape to be doing so and had saved me a world of further heartbreak.

As I sipped my tea and nibbled some of Edie's apple-walnut cake (the breakfast of champions), I outlined a plan of attack. I would start at the top and work my way down. I didn't relish another night on the sofa, so wanted my bedroom to be a priority. I remembered, with a delicious thrill, the fresh new linen sheets and duvet cover that I'd bought for the bed. I'd already washed and ironed them, and tucked them into their box with sprigs of lavender between the folds. Just because the cottage hadn't felt instantly like home, didn't mean it wouldn't with a little care and attention and what better way to start showing it that than making the space bright and clean again. I could let myself dwell on the uneasy feelings that kept creeping into my awareness, but that wouldn't help. Action was what was required. With that bold thought to arm me, I picked up "cleaning" and headed for the stairs.

I worked steadily for about two hours. I scrubbed and swept and polished, removing the dust and neglect of the months since Nan died. I took down the curtains to be washed and threw open the windows. Soon, the scent of beeswax and lemon replaced the musty dampness. I got down on my hands and knees and scoured the uneven floorboards. They were oak planks, worn and pitted from the years of people walking across them. I allowed my imagination to drift into the realms of what those boards had borne over the years, which prompted an idea for a story about a woodsman and an ancient oak tree. Naturally, I had to pause in my scrubbing to scribble it down on the notebook I kept in my pocket for just such an occasion. I pushed away the intrusive thought that I'd be better served by a story about a chambermaid and the bachelor of a country estate and went back to daydreams of forest sprites and a grasping lumber merchant. There was time enough to face the reality of my writing career.

The bedroom finished, I moved on to the little bathroom, polishing the taps on the old clawfoot tub and shining the cracked and speckled mirror above the sink. The toilet was of a dubious vintage, with an old-fashioned cistern and chain, but it flushed efficiently and appeared sturdy so didn't need replacing. That, in itself, was an act of rebellion as the voice of my mother was a running narrative in my head, tallying up what would Need Doing in order to turn the cottage into somewhere anybody In Their Right Mind would want to live. Happily, I wasn't In My Right Mind and had the paperwork to prove it. I felt a sense of freedom and lightness that had been missing for a long time as I imagined Teddy's reaction to the cobwebs and mouse droppings I swept out of the corners. His preoccupation with Appearances had morphed over time into a cruel obsession with belittling everything that wasn't up to the impossible standards he set. In all of the many disappointments that life had served to him, he liked to point out that I was the biggest. My therapist had suggested I was simply the closest target, and it was more about how he was unable to take responsibility for his own actions than anything I'd done. In my reasonable mind I knew that she was probably right, though in my wobblier moments I sometimes wondered how much of his criticisms possessed a grain of truth, given that I'd fallen short of so many people's expectations so often. "Unrealized potential" was a common theme running through my life. Even Rhonda, my literary agent, was forever haranguing me to write more and write faster because of the great demand for my type of books. The fact I didn't really view them as *my* type at all was the sticking point. A sticking point that I was determined to unstick. Just as soon as I'd summoned the courage, that is. So even when I was being successful, I was falling short.

The largest bedroom had been Nan's and that was the one I decided to claim for my own. The smaller one, the room where I used to stay when I visited, wasn't much more than a box room - small and narrow, with just enough room for a single bed and a small chest of drawers. I contemplated having the furniture taken out and using it for storage, but then decided against it. Not that I expected any house-guests, but it just seemed right to leave it. I decided I would set it up as a writing room, with the convenience of the bed for "thinking naps", which were an integral part of my process.

I finished tucking in my crisp new sheets and smoothed my hand satisfactorily over the surface of the duvet. The pattern of blue flowers against the white background was fresh and clean and had the effect of brightening up the room. The bed was positioned with the headboard under the window because Nan liked to feel the night air on her face. She said it helped her to sleep. I paused for a minute, considering. As a child, I'd had a vivid phobia about being the victim of a changeling switch, after reading one of the many books of faery stories that Nan left scattered around the cottage. I'd made her arrange my own little bed in the box room so that I was facing the window when I was lying down, arguing that if I could see them coming, I could raise the alarm and thus prevent my being whisked off to the Otherworld. Even though it was my most treasured and secret childhood hope to be able to visit the Otherworld, in my imagination I went there voluntarily and so was able to return just as soon as I wanted to. I'd never, since, placed my bed under a window. Whether it was habit or some residue of my childhood fear, I was never quite sure. Maybe it was a bit of both. Well, that ended now, I decided firmly. It was all silliness. Who ever heard of a grown woman being whisked away to the Otherworld? The idea of a grown-up changeling being left in my place made me giggle and so I left the room, just as it was. I paused in the doorway and looked back, feeling very happy with myself.

The sound of the telephone ringing jolted me out of my self-congratulation. Roger! I was supposed to phone him when I arrived. I clattered down the stairs to reach it, grabbing it with a breathless, "Hello?" Before it rang off.

"You said you'd phone, you lying minx," accused the laughing voice of my best friend, "I had visions of you attacked by a band of marauding badgers or something. Or do you have to wind up the phone by hand before you use it and you were too tired?"

"Very funny, Roger," I said, suddenly overcome by a wave of emotion at the sound of his voice. I did my best to swallow down the unwelcome tears. "Everyone knows badgers don't travel in packs."

Roger chuckled on the other end, before becoming quiet. I was still working to get control of myself.

"Haze?"

"Mmhm?"

"You alright, love?"

That was almost my undoing. When you're a hair's breadth away from breaking down, having someone ask if you're okay is bound to set you off. I was determined to hold it together. I *needed* to hold it together.

"Fine, sure. Just a bit tired, that's all," I replied, probably not very convincingly. Roger knew me best of anyone. He'd been the first one to point out to me how horribly Teddy was treating me and the effect it was having.

"Liar. I know it must be hard being in your Nan's house. Are you sure you don't want me to come up and help? I could get a few days off."

"No really, Roger. I'm okay. And you're far too busy to be leaving the shop right now. I'll be okay," I paused, taking a shaky breath. "I need to do this."

Another silence.

"I know, love. I know. Have you had a good cry yet?"

"No, nothing yet. Nothing more than a bit of a snivel and whimper, anyway. I can't break the habit of a lifetime in a few short days you know."

It's true, you can't. I used to cry – a lot – but somewhere along the way I'd trained myself out of it. My years with Teddy certainly hadn't encouraged displays of weakness so I was in a perpetual state of emotional constipation. Roger was always telling me I'd feel better if I could cry but the best I could manage, even after Nan died, was a bit of gentle weeping. I think perhaps you can forget how.

"I know, Haze, I know. I just wish...oh, never mind. Listen, promise you'll phone me if you need me to come? You know I love roughing it in the countryside."

His laughter rang down the telephone line, easing the tension I didn't even know was there.

Chapter Three

I was just sitting down to a bit of lunch — a cheese and salad sandwich (gleanings from the garden by way of a hardy, volunteer lettuce and straggly spring onion from under the not-shredded end of a small polytunnel) and cup of tea — when there was a knock on the door. I swallowed my mouthful and a brief surge of irritation, followed closely by a lurch of dread. I hadn't been here twenty-four hours and already I'd entertained more visitors than I could wish for in a whole month. I prayed it wasn't someone planning on staying because I was determined to take myself out for a walk over the moor after my lunch and having to entertain someone would set my whole day out of schedule. I scolded myself for my inhospitality and went to open the door.

It was Edie, bearing yet another basket over her arm. She smiled widely, her little blue eyes crinkling merrily. Edie has always reminded me of a faery-woman, or at least, my idea of what a faery woman might look like. Small and nut-brown from being outdoors, with a bun stuffed full of white hair, she's forever flitting about baking or gardening or otherwise being industrious. She has a vast collection of flowery aprons that she always wore over her neatly ironed blouses and tweed skirts. I was immediately ashamed of myself. She was kindness itself and I'd be in real danger of becoming a hermit if someone didn't knock on the door once in a while. Not that I was ruling out the hermit option.

"Edie," I said, with a genuine smile, "Gosh, but it's lovely to see you again. Will you come in? I've just boiled the kettle."

"No, lass. Ta very much, though. I'm just on my way to the Big House to do my bit cleaning and thought I'd pop in with a few more bits of things for you. I made a big pan of soup for our Alfie's supper and there's no way we'll get through it all. It's barley and mixed veg, this time. And some fresh buns to go with it. Are you getting on alright?"

She peered past me at the pile of boxes that hadn't really changed all that much from the day before.

"Brilliantly, actually," I said, beaming. "I've just stopped for some lunch. I've been giving the upstairs a good clean."

She nodded approvingly.

"Excellent," she said. "I used to come and do a turn for your Nan in the last while, before she went into the hospital. She couldn't manage like she used to and she enjoyed a bit of a natter as well."

She tilted her head, questioningly.

I wasn't sure what I was supposed to say. I had a feeling I was supposed to admit to enjoying having a bit of a natter myself, but I couldn't bring myself to say it. I was hopeless at the sort of nattering that other women seemed to come to naturally. It wasn't that I didn't *want* to chat with people, it just didn't seem to be something I was good at. I was invariably left feeling awkward and slightly stupid.

I cleared my throat.

"Are you sure you wouldn't like a cup of tea?" I asked, reaching for the one thing I did feel comfortable with.

"No, no. I really must get on. Old Dummy doesn't like it if I'm late. It makes him anxious. His father was a military fellow, as you might remember. Very decorated or some such and fair browbeat his Lordship over punctuality. Gave him a bit of the terrors, I shouldn't wonder, poor auld soul. That's all the influence the old tyrant had on him, mind you. Thanks be and all that."

She thrust the basket into my hands and turned to go. I noticed there was a bicycle leaning against the wooden fence at the end of the path.

"Isn't it far?" I asked, "The Big House, I mean. Only I noticed you were on your bicycle."

I remembered Malmont Manor as being a vast distance from Rookery Cottage, although everything was bigger and further when you were small. I'd only ever been to the house once or twice and only when I was very young and with my Nan. The previous Lord Dummell was a cantankerous old fellow and didn't have much tolerance for children, even well-behaved ones. I wondered briefly what his successor was like. I think he was in his thirties or so when I was visiting regularly and not around much.

"It's about two miles over the moor," she said, "There's a good sheep track to go on so it's faster going that way as long as it's not too wet for the bicycle. It's twice as far around by the road. Two cattle grids and as many gates to faff about with."

"Are they nice people?" I asked, "Young Craig said I should steer clear of their grounds when I go walking. He said they were strange folk."

Edie laughed.

"Aye, he would. Him and Lord Dummell had a bit of a set-to a while back – over money, of course – the farm isn't paying its way but old Dummy won't hear of modernizing things. Since then, things have been a bit strained, that's all. Rookery Farm is tied to Malmont, you see, and Young Craig's never really taken to farming like his uncle hoped he might. Poor mite wasn't born to it; he was sort of dropped into it when all the Talbot children took off for other places. None of them wanted it either. I think he felt beholden a bit, his aunt and uncle having taken him and his mum in after his dad scarpered. Then once his auntie died, the old man would've fallen to bits without Craig and his mum. But never you mind with all that. Old Dummy's not a bad lot. A bit eccentric mebbe. All them titled folk are, though, if you ask me. Still stuck back in the olden days half the time. There's a young lad about your age that works as estate manager - Toby his name is - but you'd know him, he's the one you used to chum around with when you were little. He came back from Scotland a few years ago now to help old Dummy."

She looked at her watch.

"Eeeeh! Look at the time. Here's me nattering on."

She opened the gate, hiked up her skirt and swung her leg over her bicycle with a limberness that belied her age and pushed off down the lane.

"What about your basket?" I called after her, still trying to digest everything she'd said, including the dropping of the casual bomb that was Toby MacDierran. I realized I also still had the jar from yesterday's soup and said as much.

She waved an arm.

"Drop it into the house, later," she shouted back. "Alfie's fair dying to see you. About five-ish…."

Her last words faded as she disappeared around the bend in the lane.

Oh dear, I thought. Now I had a social engagement. Technically, yes, it was a 'drop in' but I felt as if it were an obligation, nonetheless.

Sighing, I closed the door and carried the basket into the kitchen.

After Edie's visit, and the feelings that it had stirred, I felt too scattered to carry on with my orderly list of cleaning chores. I couldn't face tackling the stacks of boxes in the living room, either, and could feel the old, familiar dread of overwhelm rising.

I decided, after washing up my lunch things and unpacking the food basket (soup, bread, a jar of homemade marmalade and a small bunch of muddy spring onions that were far more robust than the ones I'd pulled from the garden), that I really needed a walk to help clear my head. I had planned on doing that anyway, but had hoped to be a bit further on with my organizing before I allowed myself a break.

It was typically ridiculous of me, I thought, as I pulled on my wellingtons and buttoned up my coat, to have something as innocuous as a casual invitation send me into a low-grade panic. I knew when I took on the cottage, that I'd be expected to mix in somewhat with village life. After all, if I was to keep things going, just as Nan had, I could expect knocks on my door and invitations to join in the various goings-on. Just because Rookery Cottage was at the very edge of the village, didn't mean I was so isolated as to not be part of the community. Nan had been the life and soul of the village, even when she didn't leave her house. But the fact remained that my main reason

for coming here was to retreat into a peaceful and quiet life. If I'd
wanted to be relentlessly gallivanting about, wearing myself down to
a nub, I'd have gone back to London.

Mixing has never come easy for me; in fact, it's my worst nightmare.
I've spent my whole life feeling as if I was the odd one out, never
quite fitting in, even in places where I ought to have. I've joined book
clubs and volunteered at the library; done art classes and been on
bird-watching outings — all things I desperately enjoy doing and yet,
as soon as it involves a group of any kind, suddenly everyone else seems
to be doing so much better than I. Even those first, early, confidants,
the other people who look as shy and awkward as I feel and with
whom I would exchange nervous chatter on the first day of something,
suddenly they seemed to blossom and expand as soon as activities
were underway, leaving me still standing awkwardly on the fringes. I
grew up believing that there was something deeply flawed about my
character that made me this way, something that my own mother, in
her strange but well-meaning way, managed to confirm by constantly
wondering out loud what was the matter with me and despairing that
I never brought any friends home. Her ultimate solution to that was
to find friends *for* me, hence my being thrust into the London social
scene and my subsequent marriage to Teddy, which resulted in almost
a decade of reminders of how hopeless I am at normal life.

Edward Finchley-Bottomsdowne III ("Bottoms up, Teddy! As his
cronies were fond of shouting) has a desperate case of Peter Pan syndrome and a narcissistic streak that meant I was in a state of perpetual
apology for simply being myself throughout our entire relationship.
At least that's what the ten weeks at Serenity Meadows following
our break-up taught me. The benefit of hindsight shows me that we
were doomed from the onset, despite my having tried really hard to
be the sort of person who could keep up with him and his friends.

Time and again I put on an act of enjoying the endless parties and country weekends, pretending to be delighted by the binge drinking and bed-hopping scandals that seemed to follow that crowd around. I mean, you'd expect that of twenty-somethings, but as I said, Peter Pan syndrome meant Teddy and his chums behaved that way well into their thirties and beyond. The end result was always me feeling like a damp squib amid the sparkling personalities of the who's-who of the idle rich, suffering the pitying glances and passive-aggressive comments. It was like boarding school all over again, only it didn't end when we got home because Teddy delighted in telling me the various and assorted ways in which I was ridiculous, an embarrassment and hardly worth the effort.

As is usually the way with these things, and not before time, it all ended in tears. All mine, of course, when I realized he'd been having an affair with a woman I'd invited to stay with us after her own relationship had gone sour. That was right in the middle of Nan having to go into hospital and then her subsequent death. It speaks volumes of what kind of man he is that he opted for a weekend house party in Scotland over coming to her funeral. Funerals are too upsetting, he'd said and besides, he'd had enough of my tears to last him a lifetime. I can see it all now, but it took ten weeks at Serenity Meadows to enlighten me. I suspect it'll take longer than that to undo the damage.

So it's not that I don't *want* to mingle with people, only that socializing has come to signify something so fraught with emotional trauma and humiliation that I tend to anticipate disaster before it even occurs. For instance, the idea of just 'dropping in' at the Fisher's cottage, terrified me, despite the fact they're old and dear friends; they're essentially my second grandparents, for heaven's sake. Already I was imagining my arriving just as they're sitting down to their tea, or that I would go and no-one would be there, leaving me standing on the doorstep looking foolish; or that only Alfie, lovely, taciturn Alfie, would be there and we'd have nothing at all to talk about without Edie oiling the conversational machine with her comforting domestic chatter.

Normal people don't have these problems, of that I'm fairly certain. On the odd occasion I'd confided these neuroses of mine to other people, they'd simply stared, bewildered and quite unable to take in the enormity of my idiocy. Even Roger, my best friend and anchor in the emotional maelstrom of the past year, who quickly forgave me all of my weirdnesses and idiosyncrasies and who took me in when everything blew up, gets exasperated with my grim prophecies of what could potentially go wrong every time I'm victimized by invitations to dinner parties or other social gatherings. But the lovely thing about staying with Roger was that I could opt for a quiet evening by myself while he went and painted the town with his cheerful and unfailingly kind group of friends. It was the first time I'd caught a glimpse of what it might be like to live my life the way *I* wanted to, rather than to satisfy someone else's story of who I ought to be. Once I'd had a taste of that, there was no dissuading me.

Never mind, I told myself firmly, there'd be plenty of time to sort it all out. It was technically an open-ended invitation, after all. 'Later' could mean later in the week. And I *did* have the excuse of needing to finish my cleaning and unpacking. *And* I was quite confident that after the initial excitement, such as it was, of my arrival, the novelty of me would soon wear off and people would leave me mostly alone. I just had to soldier through these first few weeks. Surely that was worth the infinite stretch of peace and quiet that would come afterwards?

I stood in the small hallway by the front door, taking deep breaths and convincing myself to settle down. I caught a glimpse of my reflection in the old hall-stand mirror. I looked pale and anxious, the bright, lime green of my corduroy coat standing in sharp, slightly sickly, contrast to my dark hair and peaky expression. There were dark smudges under my eyes and the smile-lines were deepening into full-fledged wrinkles. Whatever people said about faery blood, there was no escaping the signs of strain on my face. Sighing, I wound my favourite striped scarf – of Doctor Who proportions – around my neck, it was still only February, after all, walked back through the kitchen and unlatched the door.

My original plan had been to walk into the village, to visit the greengrocer's to pick up a few things and the post office to buy some stamps, but since Edie had ensured I wouldn't starve, and with the uneasy turmoil of what other social expectations might be lurking in the village, I decided I'd go for a ramble down the lane and out towards the moor. I stood for a moment, under the cover of the porch just outside the back door. A pair of Nan's clogs were still tucked under the little wooden bench and a cracked flowerpot held a slightly rusted trowel and several crumpled paper seed packets. The air smelled of woodsmoke and wet grass. The kitchen garden, which lay just to the left of the path was a tangled snarl of pea scaffolding and the remains of last year's lettuce that had been left to bolt. I sighed. Nan would hate to see it like that. I told myself I had better get that sorted as soon as the inside was seen to. It was a delicious sort of feeling, really, to know that I had so much to occupy myself. It was the yawning void of idleness that was my great undoing; it provided too many opportunities to think.

I made my way down the stone path towards the gate, noting the incursion of various weeds, almost relishing the thought of getting down on my hands and knees and coaxing it all back into tidiness. A clump of merry snowdrops were pushing valiantly through in the herbaceous border to the right of the path and just the sight of them began to turn back the gloomy tide of my mood. If they could look so jolly amongst the still-cold soil and detritus of last season, then why couldn't I shake off the silly niggling doubts that were creeping into the back of my mind? I was so busy admiring them and reflecting on that uplifting metaphor for life, that I bumped hard into the little man that was emerging from the stone shed, sending us both staggering backwards.

Chapter Four

I'm not certain which of us was more surprised. I was certainly taken aback to find a heavily whiskered man at the bottom of my garden, but the intruder seemed to come down more on the side of irritation than guilt or shame, which is more what you'd expect of someone caught trespassing in another person's garden shed. We stood regarding each other for a moment or two. My mind was a sudden blank, followed quickly by a staccato stream of panicked thoughts, ranging from mild amusement to outright terror.

What a funny little man! Are those whiskers real? Is he dangerous? Should I phone the police? Is he trying to steal something? Oh god, is he living in there?

Those were my thoughts in no particular order. I took in his abundant beard and halo of thistledown hair that stuck out in all directions from under his hat. He wore a much-mended, many-pocketed coat over a knitted argyle vest and pair of tan coloured trousers with distinctly muddy knees. I fished around inside my empty head for something appropriate to say.

Fortunately for my addled brain, the trespasser spoke first.

"What are you staring at me like that for?" he asked, his voice a rumbling sort of growl. He narrowed his bright green eyes, looking me up and down before leaning towards me. He was barely five feet tall and had to peer up at my face. Being taller than people isn't one of my usual accomplishments and it was a tiny bit disconcerting. I took a step back. He took a step forward. I shifted uncomfortably to one side. He smelled faintly of liquorice.

"Are you mad, or what?" he said, reaching out a knobby finger and poking me hard in my middle.

I gasped and uttered a loud "Oh!", putting my hand over myself where he'd jabbed me. It hadn't hurt, but it had surprised me.

"What did you do that for?" I squeaked, breathless. "You don't just poke people!"

I'm not sure where I'd garnered this social truism but it was all that was available to me at the time.

"Nor do you just blunder into people," he retorted, turning his head to spit dramatically into a small bag that seemed to appear from the folds of his patched overcoat.

"What?" he snapped, obviously noting the horror on my face. "Aniseed balls. I don't like 'em once they've been sucked. Me old pegs don't like the crunching part."

I nodded, because what else would you do?

"Well?" he prompted, tucking his spit-bag back into his pocket. A rustle of paper from another pocket resulted in a fresh black sweet being popped into his mouth. I don't know how he could find it amongst the tangle of beard.

"Well, what?" I said, fascinated in the way one is fascinated by things mildly revolting.

"Are you mad?"

"Mad? No, of course I'm not mad!" I replied, although, to be truthful, despite professional assurances, part of me sometimes wondered just a bit.

He burst into sudden, loud and wheezing laughter, causing me to flinch and move even further away.

He nodded, his too-small pork-pie hat wobbling with the vigorous movement.

"Aye, you'd do well to wonder an' all," he chuckled, in genuine delight at himself. "It's the ones that don't wonder that you have to worry about, my lass!"

And with that he hoisted a large leather satchel over his shoulder and across his chest and walked past me to the garden gate. Still chuckling, he unlatched the gate and ambled through, not bothering to close it behind him. He turned right and set off down the lane, presumably towards the village.

It was some time before I was able to digest exactly what had just happened. It was just as well that I was on my own, as a passerby might wonder at the small woman left standing by the open gate, her mouth open and a look of utter bewilderment on her face.

Once I'd got over the initial incredulity of the interaction, I immediately started tidying it up into manageable explanations. Obviously, he was just a harmless vagabond of some kind who had known that the cottage was unoccupied and so had taken to sheltering in the shed at night. Of course, now that he knew I was living there, he'd move on to some other location and I'd never have to trouble myself with the thought of him again. Any thoughts I had surrounding his odd, not-quite-human appearance and his apparent ability to read my mind were carefully swept into the room I keep in my mind for inexplicable things. To entertain the alternative would mean admitting that my life at Rookery Cottage was going to be far less than the quiet, solitary one I had envisioned and I simply couldn't go there. I quickly locked the mind-room door behind those thoughts and proceeded through the gate, carefully avoiding looking at the open door of the lopsided stone hut that I had once believed served as one of my Nan's garden sheds.

Rookery Cottage is situated at the end of a long, leafy lane, bordered on each side by a wildly overgrown hedgerow. I'd spent many a childhood day in late August with an old seaside pail in my hand, filling it to the brim with fat, juicy blackberries, while Nan collected basket after basket to make into her much-prized blackberry jam. We would pick our way down one side, as far as the gap to the moor and back up the other, our fingers and lips stained purple for we sampled as much as we collected. Just to make sure they were good and sweet, we'd tell ourselves, laughing at our mischief. In February, though, the hedge was much more sparse. The first signs of leaves - elder and hawthorn could be seen, unfurling from tight buds, and even a creamy-white sprinkling of blackthorn blossom. Despite the northern climate, the natural world always woke up early in Winkle. If you asked a science-minded person they might bang on about microclimates, but Nan would wink tell you it had more to do with Certain Arrangements. Either way, spring comes earlier here than other places of the same latitude. Birds, robins and a few chaffinches, flitted in and out at intervals, perhaps scouting good places for nests.

The hedge along the lane is part of the much larger one, one of the Ancients, my Nan used to say, that stretched around the edge of the moor, dividing the village and surrounding forest from the wide open spaces. While the larger, infinitely older hedge was a venerable thing of mature oak and hazel, beech and elm, the lane way hedge was its scruffier cousin, made up mostly of bramble, elder, blackthorn and hawthorn. A hostile stretch of shrubbery, it was full of vicious thorns that snagged at hair and clothing and bare skin, but that was what Nan had loved about it. It was the perfect illustration of how we should view nature, she'd say, full of life and generous with its gifts but demanding care and respect. In late spring, it's a froth of blossom and birdsong, it hums with life, then all the way through summer and autumn, providing food and shelter and safe passage for the birds and small creatures and countless butterflies and insects.

A flutter of white caught my eye and I paused briefly to extricate a piece of paper that was run-through by a sharp prong of blackthorn. I glanced at it – something to do with hedge preservation – and stifled a grimace at the irony of it littering up the hedge. I stuffed it into the pocket of my coat, refusing to allow someone's carelessness to spoil the delights of being in one of my favourite places in the world.

Walking down the lane, the earth soft and springy with recent rain, all sound seemed muffled and distant. Only the occasional call of a bird and the far-off tinkle of wind chimes from the garden, *my* garden, I thought with a sudden thrill, could be heard. It felt soothing, like a cocoon of safety, and despite the unsettling events of my morning, I could feel the tension leaving my neck and shoulders and the anxious tightness in my stomach easing away. My worries about the cottage, my writing, my up-ended life all seemed distant and vague, hardly worth bothering with.

The air was cool and damp, but not unpleasant, and I lengthened my stride, enjoying the feeling of expansiveness that was settling over me. I reached the edge of the lane and squeezed through the gap in the hedge to stand on the edge of the moor. The laneway hedge continued to the right, joining up with the larger one but, to the left, it petered out to blend in with the edge of a small hazel coppice. The coppice itself was part of a larger stand of woodland that edged the village before it, too, thinned out altogether and stopped at the main road. A system of smaller hedges and free-standing trees, more recently cultivated, lined the road before gradually vanishing the closer you got to the motorway.

The moor spread out in undulating hills. Clumps of reddish-brown bracken and an occasional scrub of hawthorn and outcrop of mossy stone offered the only contrast in a sea of green. I spotted the sheep track that Edie had mentioned and decided to make my way up there and follow it for a while. My other option was to take one of the bridle-paths through the larger forest, along the right-hand side of the ancient hedge. I very much wanted to go walking in the forest; I've always found trees to be of great comfort in times of strife, but there's always a chance of coming across a dog-walker or rambler on a bridle-path and I didn't think I could cope with the inevitable interaction. Instead, I trudged up the slight incline and set off on the sheep track, in the general direction of the Malmont Manor Estate, or, as Edie calls it, the Big House.

I had been walking for a good twenty minutes or so, blissfully lost in my own thoughts, when, coming over a rise, I spotted slate-grey rooftops which could only belong to Malmont Estate. The manor house itself was barely visible behind a rampart of evergreens; it stood atop a small hill, the outbuildings scattered around and below like the drape of a skirt. A low stone wall was also vaguely noticeable in the distance so I stopped, thinking to turn around and go home. Despite Edie's assurances, I didn't fancy getting too close to the boundaries of the estate. The last thing I wanted, now that my happy mood was restored, was any kind of human interaction. There was time enough to pay my obligatory respects.

I had just set off back in the direction I'd come when I heard the sharp rumble of an engine. I glanced around, a motor vehicle being the last thing I'd expect out on the moor but couldn't see anything. I looked up at the sky, imagining perhaps it was an aeroplane but the expanse of grey was unmarred. At the sound of shouts, I spun around in time to see a blurred brown shape hurtling toward me, followed by one of those quad bike things that farmers use to carry feed out to their sheep.

What happened next was one of those 'it happened so fast' scenarios and I'm still not entirely sure how it came about. One minute I was standing, staring, marvelling at the speed with which a sheep could travel, the next I was lying flat on my back in the damp grass, buried under a foul-smelling pile of fur.

My first instinct was to panic. I'd obviously just been attacked by a mad sheep. There was a cacophony of shouts and yelps, coming, I assumed, from the farmer and his sheep dog, attempting to get the rogue beast under control. It felt like an eternity, but I imagine it was mere seconds before I realized that the shrieks and yelps were coming from the creature lying on top of me. I flailed and scrambled, no doubt doing my own share of shrieking and yelping, and somehow managed to divest myself of the quivering mass that was trying to bury itself in the pocket of my coat. I staggered to my feet, only to come face to face with the wrong end of a shotgun, which actually turned out to be a shepherd's crook. The beast pressed itself, quivering, against my legs, almost sending me sprawling again. I stood, gasping, trying to form the necessary words of righteous indignation that I felt at having a gun-that-wasn't-a-gun pointed at me. Upon later reflection, it seems like blood-curdling terror would've been a more appropriate response, had it actually been a gun, but the rush of adrenaline in the moment had clearly made me super-human. In that same moment of reflection, I was grateful that I hadn't acted in the manner of blood-curdling terror as it would have been completely out of place in the presence of a wooden staff. The creature, I eventually realized, wasn't actually a mad sheep, but a very dirty and smelly dog.

"That your dog?" demanded the bearer of the not-gun, who had, thankfully, lowered it, allowing me to recognize it for what it was. He was a tall, broad-shouldered man, dressed in a waxed jacket, tan corduroys and olive-green wellingtons. His head was bare, showing a tangle of slightly-too-long dark brown, almost black, hair, silvering slightly at the temples. Piercing green eyes stared out from under heavy black brows, which were lowered in a menacing scowl. He looked a bit Kilwillie-meets-Mr.Rochester. Strange and slightly off-putting. Toby, I thought, with a frisson of something I didn't care to identify. Toby

MacDierran. A far cry from the seventeen year old version that I'd last seen.

"Are you planning on hitting me with that?" I said, still breathless and in a small bit of shock. The man positively oozed hostility and I had no intention of handing over the terrified creature who was practically rattling in fear. I wondered if he recognized me.

"Not you. Might thrash the bloody dog, though. Shouldn't be running out on the moor. Be worrying the sheep. As it was, sniffing around the pheasant pens. It's a good way to get shot around here. Most farmers would shoot first and ask questions later."

He spoke in a strange, staccato way. His voice was guttural and harsh, as if from lack of use, the Highland accent giving a rolling burr to his words. He hadn't lost it, then, I thought, even after all these years. I realized that he hadn't recognized me, probably because he was looking at the dog and not my face. Small mercies. Not that it mattered, he seemed very far removed from the Toby I'd known twenty-odd years ago. That Toby wouldn't be chasing a poor, defenceless dog across the moor and threatening to thrash it. The intervening years had clearly changed him, and not for the better. Still, best not get on his bad side.

"I take full responsibility for the dog," I said, pushing back my shoulders and trying to appear haughty. I felt a sharp twinge under my left shoulder blade; haughty wasn't a stance my musculature was familiar with. "I apologize for any emotional trauma his sniffing might have caused your birds. I assure you it won't happen again."

He stared at me for a moment. The ghost of recognition fleeting across his face. The barest hint of a smile may have tugged at one corner of his sullen mouth. He opened it, as if to speak, then closed it again, a scowl clouding his face.

Instead, he nodded, slung the staff over his shoulder and turned to climb onto his quad bike.

"You're back then," he said, stowing away his weapon. Moved into Rookery Cottage, have you?"

I contemplated fibbing, my thoughts suddenly going wild with the possible consequences of claiming a pheasant-worrying dog and the ensuing complications to my hermit aspirations.

I nodded, deciding not to speak at all.

He narrowed his eyes with a speculating stare.

I forced myself to glare back. His green eyes were that astonishing shade that makes it hard to look away. I found myself thinking it was a shame he'd turned into such a hateful person. He hadn't always been.

"Washing-up liquid," he said, firing up his little machine, gesturing toward the cringing heap of dog at my feet.

By reflex, I looked down, then back up at him, somewhat bewildered.

"For the stink!" he shouted, as he roared away, clumps of sod flying up from the wheels of the vehicle.

I wrinkled my nose and sniffed tentatively at the sleeve of my coat. Sure enough, the foul, musky odour had transferred from the dog to my clothes.

"Well, then," I said, to the sad little bundle. He looked to be some sort of terrier mix, or perhaps a lurcher, it was difficult to tell with him curled up on himself as he was. He was thin and filthy and still terrified. "It looks like I'm in charge of you now. How on earth am I going to get you home? If I were an organized and properly countrified person I'd have a spare leash or lead rope in my pocket." Nestled right next to a clump of soggy dog biscuits and a handful of pony-nuts, I added for my own amusement.

As it was, I needn't have worried about not having a handy bit of rope in my pocket, because as soon as I started walking, the dog followed. He stuck to my side like a cocklebur, at times making it difficult to walk without stepping on his paws or tripping over him. I kept up a running chatter, talking soothingly of nonsensical things and gradually he stopped vibrating and relaxed enough to allow me to walk unfettered.

"There's a good boy," I said, reassuringly. "It's all over now. Nothing to worry about. Well, unless you're afraid of having a bath!"

I looked down at the shivering creature, watching the way his eyes constantly shifted from side to side and then up at me. I'm sure he was just as frightened as he was when Toby had been chasing him, after all, I was as much a stranger to him. But perhaps he saw it as a lesser of evils; perhaps I was the least threatening option and when the world is just that terrifying, it becomes a matter of terror-by-degree. I could appreciate his thought process.

"Never mind, pet," I said, echoing an oft-uttered phrase of my Nan's. "It'll all turn out in the end."

We made our way through the gap in the hedge and when I opened the gate at the bottom of the garden, my new friend shot through as if afraid he'd get left on the wrong side of it.

I smiled to myself, shutting away all of my worries in favour of offering solace to this poor, unhappy creature, who was even more challenged than I, a feat I hadn't ever thought possible.

Chapter Five

I t turned out that the dog was neither afraid of the bath, nor a boy. After several rounds of shampoo – I had to use my own shampoo in the end after using up most of my washing up liquid – and a thorough comb and de-tangle, it was revealed that my new friend was, indeed, a girl. Which better suited the hints of rose-petal and ylang-ylang that were wafting up from her fur, all of which was worlds better than the stink of fox poo.

After rinsing away the filth and stench, and rubbing her vigorously dry (with my good towels), she was revealed to be a beautiful russet-brown in colour. Her coat had that faintly wiry appearance typical to lurchers, but was surprisingly soft to the touch, although that may have been in part due to the half-bottle of expensive salon shampoo I'd used. I looked at her, appraising her soft brown eyes. She had enjoyed the bath but now sat, trembling, on the pile of wet towels. Her long tail was clamped between her hind legs and she still had an expression of pained concern on her whiskery face.

"Bracken!" I said, suddenly inspired by the colour of her coat. It also seemed fitting considering where we'd first made each other's acquaintance.

The tip of her tail wiggled and she shifted her eyes from left to right. I flattered myself to think she was pleased with my choice.

"Right, Bracken," I said, moving her off the heap of wet towels. I tried not to think of the hours I'd spent scrubbing the bath and carefully laundering my brand new linens. "Let's see about getting you a bit of something to eat, shall we?"

Of course, having still not ventured into the village for provisions, we were both at the mercy of that which Edie had brought me. I poured the new batch of soup into a saucepan and set it to heat on the stove, and rummaged in the bread bin for the remains of yesterday's loaf, tearing it into small pieces in a bowl. I contemplated giving her the last bit of apple-walnut cake but decided it might prove digestively inappropriate. Besides, facing, as I was, a supper of marmalade sandwiches, it only seemed fair that I save myself a bit of cake.

As I waited for the soup to heat, I pondered the particulars of the situation. It was entirely possible that Bracken belonged to someone, despite her terrible state and her not wearing a collar. She could have been lost while her owners were out walking, or perhaps stolen from someone's garden and left on the moor to fend for herself. She was obviously used to being in a house as she'd already gone to the door to ask to use the garden facilities and was familiar with taking a bath. My instincts were terribly uncharitable, though. Already she'd managed to squirm her way into my heart and I felt that whoever may have owned her surely didn't deserve such a nice dog to allow her to be lost or stolen!

Growing up, I'd always wanted a cat but was never allowed to have one. Mum claimed to be highly allergic although I think her aversion had more to do with hair on the carpet and sharp claws in her design-er furniture. Having Bracken hurtle into my life in such a dramatic way was a typical storybook dream-come-true. I took a moment and imagined myself the long-suffering heroine, finally rewarded for her steadfastness by the arrival of a faithful companion. Granted she was a slightly different version to my original wish for a clever, slightly otherworldly, feline familiar, but I suddenly didn't mind that she was a dog and not a cat. I'm nothing if not flexible.

I poured the soup into the bowl, letting it soak in around the pieces of bread. While it cooled, I made myself half a marmalade sandwich and set it on the table. Bracken sat quietly, her eyes following me around the kitchen. At least she'd stopped trembling.

"Well, lovely girl," I said, as I put the bowl of cooled soup on the floor, "It looks as if I'm going to have to go into the village, after all. As much as I don't want to, I really ought to let it be known I've found you."

She tiptoed over to the bowl, her nails clicking on the flagstones, and sniffed it appreciatively before beginning a vigorous lapping and slurping of the contents. After she was finished, she chased the bowl around the floor, licking it clean.

I laughed.

"Steady on," I said, bending down to retrieve it. "The pattern doesn't come off!"

She wagged her tail, it having emerged from between her legs. It was disproportionately long and windmilled around as she expressed her approval of Edie's cooking.

"We'd best not let on that I gave Edie's good soup to a dog," I said, putting the bowl in the sink. "She might take offence."

Bracken wagged further and then took a wander around the kitchen, snuffling around the floor. Clearly my offering her a meal was proof of my good intentions. I ate my marmalade sandwich, then started rooting through the kitchen drawers in search of something that might do for a collar and lead. I had a feeling that she would follow me, but I didn't want to take the risk of her getting frightened and possibly running into the street when we got to the village. I found a roll of cooking twine and twisted it into a loop for a collar but had to settle for the belt off my mackintosh to do for a lead.

"Never mind," I assured her as I looped the belt through the twine collar. "When I go into town, I'll get you a nice new collar and lead from the pet shop. And we'll have to get you a proper bed, we can't have you lying on the hard floor, can we?"

I kept up my ridiculous nattering as I put my coat and wellies back on and let us out the door. Bracken was reluctant to go outside at first; perhaps she was worried I was going to take her back to the moor, but I made a big fuss and praised her general goodness and she soon fell into step beside me. We turned right outside the gate and followed the lane out to the main road.

The Fisher's cottage was the first — or the last, depending on how you looked at it — at the village boundary. It was similar to Rookery Cottage in that it was a two storey, stone affair, with a low brow of roof that was probably thatched at some point in history. It was roofed in grey slate now and had bright blue shutters at each window. The front door was the same shade of blue and the presence of window boxes and several planters lining the path promised a colourful garden come spring and summer. A low stone wall, similar to the one that edged parts of the moor, ran along the roadside boundary and continued to the house next door, which, by virtue of the generously wide front gardens wasn't too close beside. There were no houses on the opposite side of the road, it was left to woodland, so the atmosphere was one of quiet seclusion, while still being a part of the community.

The road was a cul-de-sac as the paving ended just past the Fisher's cottage. The lane which led to my house was more gravel and dirt than tarmac and anyone who didn't know it was there was unlikely to find it. Which, of course, suited me right down to the ground. I stepped out onto the paved road, mustered my social courage and pushed Alfie and Edie's garden gate open.

I didn't get as far as the door before it opened and a familiar, much-beloved face appeared. He grinned wide and waved.

"Young Hazel!" he said, slapping his hand against his corduroy-clad leg. He was wearing a pair of brown tartan slippers that Nan used to call Tetley slippers, after an old advert from television involving tea-swilling chimpanzees. Corduroy, it seemed, was the unofficial uniform of Winkle. I had a sudden flash of belonging, clad as I was in my corduroy coat, despite it being a vivid green and not regulation earth-tone.

"Hello, Alfie," I said, presenting myself awkwardly for a kiss on the cheek. His face was stubbly and he smelled of grass clippings and pipe smoke. I hadn't seen him since Nan's funeral and it felt so good to smell those familiar, comfortable, smells. He had been like a granddad to me, all the summers I'd spent with Nan. He and Edie would come and collect me for a day out to the seaside when they'd taken their own grandchildren, treating me to ice cream and packets of hot chips, wrapped in newspaper, deliciously drowning in salt and malt vinegar. It was ridiculous of me to feel so awkward. Of course I was welcome.

"Eeeeh, lass! Don't you look a picture! Come in, come in. Our Edie's just in the kitchen getting tea made."

Inwardly, I groaned. One of my 'drop-in' fears realized. I shuffled my wellies on the front step.

"Sorry, Alfie. I didn't mean to interrupt your tea. It's just that I've found this dog out on the moor...."

I stepped aside to reveal Bracken, who had resorted to her default position of cringing heap when Alfie had come to the door. She was trying to insinuate herself into my right Wellington.

Alfie peered around me, no doubt having trouble seeing through Bracken's disguise of muddy boot.

"She's a bit terrified," I said, "She was being chased across the moor by a quad thing, having a shotgun waved at her. Apparently she'd committed a crime of sniffing." I absolutely own the fact I was exaggerating; I felt it was necessary to communicate the degree of trauma the poor dog had experienced. Call it poetic license.

Alfie blinked, confused for a moment, before shaking his head and chuckling.

"You do have a way with words, lass. No wonder you ended up writing them books. And it's not hard to see you've grown into a proper McCorrigan woman, picking up the waifs and strays. Now then," he moved aside from the doorway, "Get yourself in there. No, no, never mind your muddy boots, lass. That can't be helped this time of year. Maybe your wee dog won't be so scared if I'm not standing right in the way."

I had to half-carry, half-drag poor Bracken across the threshold into the little hall. The smell of bacon frying wafted down the passageway. That served to soften her reserve a little. It was becoming obvious that the way to her heart was through her belly because she suddenly began showing an interest in walking further into the cottage. I held onto her collar, not wanting to disgrace ourselves with bad manners.

"Will you have a cuppa, lass?" asked Alfie. "You can tell us all about your new friend here and then you can tell me what you've got planned for yon cottage. The missus tells me you're mad keen to have a go at the garden?"

It was so tempting. Now that the initial social hurdle was navigated, there was nothing I'd have liked more than to let myself be absorbed into the warmth and comfort of the Fisher's cottage. The familiar smells and sights - the carved, walnut hall stand and umbrella rack, the gallery of family photographs, black and white and sepia portraits of the long-dead, mixed in with the bright colours of children and grandchildren, the scent of beeswax and lemon polish that I'd tried to replicate for myself since ever I had furniture of my own to wax and polish. It was as much of a sense of home as Nan's cottage had always been. But I couldn't. It was getting on for closing time in the village and I had several stops to make, not the least of which was the grocer for some food for both Bracken and myself.

"Oh, Alfie! There's nothing I'd like more, to be honest. But I've really got to get into the village to pick up a few things and put a notice in the post office about the dog. Can I ask a tremendous favour?"

Alfie grinned, his impossibly straight, white teeth a testament to modern denturists.

"Aye, leave the wee beast here, lass. I'm sure the missus'll find a bit of something to win her over. Hurry along to the shops now, and us'll have our tea then we'll have our natter on your way back through."

"That'll be lovely! Thanks ever so much. She won't be any bother, I'm sure. She seems to be very used to houses so won't mess on the carpet or anything."

I frowned, suddenly seized with the worry that perhaps she might, that she'd prove herself a menace and run riot through the beautifully clean and ordered home.

Alfie must've sensed my hesitation.

"Go on with you! You'll not catch the post office if you don't get going. Mrs. Trout doesn't stay open a minute past 5pm, wouldn't matter if the King hisself wanted a stamp. Take the missus' bicycle, you'll get on a fair sight faster. It's just in the shed out the side. It isn't locked. I do that last thing of an evening."

He gave me a good-natured thump on the shoulder and took Bracken's leash out of my hand. She seemed to have forgotten me already, nosing down the passage in the direction of the kitchen. Obviously the promise of a rasher of bacon had divided her loyalties.

I laughed.

"Alright, I'm going. I'll be as quick as I can!"

I turned right as I stepped back out the front door, following one of the many little stone paths that Alfie had laid around his various garden beds. In true Victory fashion, there was no grass to be seen. All of the available space had been turned over to beds of various purposes. He'd always been a frequent winner in all categories at the village festivals - whether it was flowers or vegetables, he seemed to have a talent for coaxing the best and brightest from his garden. I imagined it was much the same now. I followed the path around to the side of the cottage. A small, corrugated metal-clad shed stood next to the low stone wall that bordered the garden. It was trellised on the side closest to the wall with what was probably a rambling rose, so even though it wasn't the prettiest of buildings, Alfie had made it so. True to form, it was neat and tidy inside. A place to park Edie's bicycle and the wheelie bins for the rubbish. A broom and rake and a few other gardening implements hung neatly on nails hammered into the wooden studs of the shed and a collection of clay plant pots was stacked neatly on the floor. I remembered that Alfie had a much larger shed at the bottom of the garden where he kept most of his tools, but this one had just enough supplies to allow a bit of tidying should the need suddenly take a person. I thought wistfully of the falling down ruin of Nan's sheds. Oh, to be so tidy and organized! At least I had something to work towards.

I wheeled the bike out and shut the shed door behind me. I pushed it out of the garden gate and set about trying to tuck my dress in, lest it billow immodestly as I cycled. Not that I'd any preoccupation with observing old-fashioned standards, indeed I've been known to shamelessly flaunt my ankles (and well-turned they are, if I may say so myself) but flashing my undergarments to the poor innocents of Winkle probably wasn't the best way to reintroduce myself. I always wondered how women of days gone by managed to do so much in skirts and dresses. Or maybe they just rode their bikes more slowly. Somehow I managed to secure it and set off down the road.

It'd been ages since I'd ridden a bike and although the old adage is true about not forgetting how, doing so with skill and confidence was obviously something that needed refreshing. I wobbled and lunged a fair bit before I found a rhythm and was soon gliding happily down the quiet road into the village.

The main part of the village is typical in its arrangement. There's a large, central green, complete with oak and willow trees and a small duck pond, fed by a tributary of Winkle Beck. Wooden benches are placed at strategic locations, depending upon whether you want to feed the ducks or sit in the shade. One side of the green is devoted to a sort of high street - a row of shops in an assortment of buildings, some of which date back to the 1600's. The result is a delightful mash-mash of ancient and slightly-less ancient that makes you feel as if you've stepped back in time. Across the green is the village pub, The Forge, which used to be, not surprisingly, the old blacksmith's shop. Next to it, in an amusing juxtaposition, are the church grounds and cemetery as well as the old church. St.Barnabas is a lovely old church, built of local stone. The original portion which now serves as the vestry, has a date stamped into one of the old stones of 1287. It was added onto over the centuries, the newest addition dating at 1878. It's uncomfortably cold in winter and smells faintly of damp in all seasons, but it has centuries of life soaked into its stones which gives it an incredible weight of awe and silence. Despite not being a church-going sort, my Nan would often take me in there, just to soak up the atmosphere, she'd say, as she went to leave bunches of flowers for the flower ladies, or a jar of something for the vicar's wife.

I followed the circle of the green around to the row of shops. The street was fairly quiet. There were some cars parked over at the pub, and a few along the frontage of the shops, but clearly Harry had been right, most people were at home getting their tea at this hour. I thought I'd better get to the post office first, not wanting to run afoul of Mrs. Trout's punctuality. I leaned the bicycle up against the bright red pillar box and went inside.

The tinkling of a bell announced my arrival. The post office also doubles as the drop-off and pick-up of the dry-cleaner's so a rack of plastic-clad shirts and trousers with claim-slips hanging off them stood to the right of the service desk, slightly spoiling the pleasing postal atmosphere. A wall of post boxes took up the right side and a glassed-in display of collector stamps and coins hung next to a large bulletin board, titled Village Happenings and Announcements. That was what I was hoping for. I walked up to the desk and waited.

I assumed that because of the door-bell, someone would know that I was there. I glanced at the clock on the wall, breathing a sigh of relief that it was only 4:35pm. Hopefully, I could get to the grocer's before 5pm - although Edie had assured me it was the only shop that stayed open late — until 7pm — to accommodate the people who drove to and from the city for work. I just didn't want to leave Bracken for too long, in case she outstayed her welcome. I also didn't want to be sitting too late with Edie and Alfie in case I outstayed *my* welcome. A few minutes passed and still no-one came. The faint sound of a radio or television came from somewhere in the back. I wondered if Mrs. Trout lived in the back of the shop.

I was just contemplating tapping the little bell that stood on the desk when there came the sound of a door crashing and heavy foot-steps on the wooden floor. A tall, thin woman with a helmet of tightly curled hair appeared from one of the back rooms. She wore over-sized, round-lensed glasses that magnified her eyes to an alarming size. They were grey-green, fringed by almost invisible lashes and glared from under high-arched, penciled-in eyebrows that gave her a look of perpetual surprise. A sharp, narrow nose ended above thin lips that pursed in what could only be severe disapproval. Impulsively, I looked again at the clock. Only 4:40pm. She had no obvious reason for such constrained outrage.

"Yes?" she said, "May I help you?"

Her tone was such that I was quite sure she wasn't particularly pleased to see me. Perhaps I'd interrupted her tea. I quailed briefly, her implied hostility triggering waves of low-grade panic through me. Under other circumstances, I might have just apologized and run out in a fit of deep humiliation. Bracken, I told myself, it's not for you, it's for Bracken.

I did my best to smile.

"Yes, thank you. I was just wondering if it would be alright to place a notice on your board?"

I gestured a shaky hand toward the notice board.

She peered at me, frowning. The effect through those glasses was most upsetting.

"I'm sorry, only village residents are permitted to use the notice board. You'll observe," she gestured with a long finger, "that it specifically says Village. It isn't there for advertisements or solicitations of any kind. That's what the newspaper is for."

The emphasis she put on the word 'solicitations' made it sound as if I wanted to advertise my brothel. My face grew warm with a combination of nerves and indignation.

"Actually," I said, in a voice more firm than I expected to come out of my mouth, "I *am* a resident of the village. My name is Hazel Price. I just moved into my grandmother's house – Rookery Cottage – I'm sure you know it."

I smiled, winningly and with a great confidence that I didn't at all feel. People like Mrs. Trout never cease to unsettle me. They're like every stern headmistress and disapproving aunt all rolled into one and it required every ounce of courage I possessed to stand there. Such were the depths to which the state of my nerves had plunged me.

Her surprised eyebrows rose even higher and she leaned forward, as if to look at me more closely. She must be quite blind without her glasses.

"Ah," she said, her lips twisting in something that may have been distaste, "I see. There's something of a resemblance, yes."

There was a brief silence. I fought the urge to apologize for having moved to the village and for looking like my Nan. I briefly wondered if she was going to ask me to show her a proof of residence. She cleared her throat.

"I'm very sorry for your loss," she said, "Your grandmother was well-liked here in the village. Most people found her funny ways to be charming. Not everyone, mind you. But that's neither here nor there now, is it?"

I had the distinct impression that she wasn't one of the people in the charmed camp.

"Yes, er, no," I stammered, "thank you."

My face grew redder and I began to feel too hot in my coat and scarf.

"Hmmm. Yes, I see."

She managed a semblance of a smile, but it was rather more predatory than amiable. People like her have a knack for smelling weakness and she clearly caught a mighty whiff of mine. But I had to press on.

"The notice?" I asked, avoiding her eye contact by looking back at the board. "I'd like to place a notice for a lost dog."

She scowled.

"You've lost your dog already? That's terribly irresponsible of you, don't you think?"

She folded her arms over her non-existent bosom.

My smile was more of a grimace.

"No, as a matter of fact, I've found one. Running loose on the moor..."

"Running loose on the moor?" she echoed, her face a vision of scandalous shock. "That's quite unacceptable around here. There are sheep out on the moor. Some them are Lord Dummell's sheep. They're of a pedigreed variety and quite valuable. A loose dog can cause all manner of damage. Farmers are well within their rights to shoot such an animal."

"Yes, I realize that. That's why I made sure to catch hold of her. As it is, she was already in trouble with the people over at the manor. Bit of an hysterical lot, aren't they?"

I was aiming for light-hearted and comradely; peasants versus the gentry, as it were.

Her shock turned into prim disapproval again.

"If by 'people' you mean Lord Dummell, then you'd do well to have a bit of respect, young lady. We don't go around criticizing the gentry in this village, no matter what you young upstarts get into in the cities. Here we're quite happy to carry on in the old ways. Lord Dummell is an important part of this village — plenty of families, good, hard-working families, mind you, pay rent to him and he takes good care of us all."

There comes a point where, if pushed by situation and circumstance, I somehow manage to transcend my social awkwardness, painful shyness and paralyzing fear of making a terrible blunder. It usually involves the defence of other people, or, more often, if I'm to be honest, animals. I suddenly forget that I'm terrified and my tongue unties itself and my words come easily, without stammer or stutter or flaming cheeks. It's a rare and terrifying thing.

"For your information, Mrs.Trout," I emphasized the fact she was named after a fish, pouring every bit of the outrage I was feeling into what I hoped was a commentary on such a misfortune, "the person you are so valiantly defending, was not, in fact, the lord of the manor, though he apparently authorizes the chasing of a poor, innocent creature across the moor on a motorized vehicle. Not only that, his employee was brandishing a gu...weapon, with what seemed to be every intention of attacking the dog in cold-blood. In addition, he was rude and extremely off-putting. Now, I have no feelings either way on the gentry, they are as good or bad as the next person, but this man seems quite undeserving of your accolades."

It was her turn to go red in the face.

"Now," I continued, while I still had some momentum, "May I please put a notice on the board or shall I go across to St.Barnabas and ask the vicar if I may place my query there? I'll let him know that I only have to ask because you wouldn't allow it in the post office."

I was gambling on the fact she was a regular in the congregation. No-one that self-righteous would miss an opportunity to gather ammunition in the form of scripture to hurl at the lesser mortals around her.

I must have struck a nerve because she took a deep breath and reached under the counter for one of the regulation 4x6 cards upon which the Announcements and Happenings were written.

"What would you like the notice to say?" she asked, her lips barely moving as she spoke.

"Oh, I can write it myself," I said, reaching into my pocket for the pen that was always there.

She took another deep breath and closed her eyes briefly, as if gathering strength. When she spoke, it was in calm, measured tones, as if she were explaining something to a simpleton.

"It is the policy of the post office to have all notices written in a uniform hand."

She peered at me, pasting a smile on her face. It was a horrifying sight.

"So as to keep things legible, you understand. Not everyone has neat handwriting."

I felt a familiar queasy feeling as my wave of indignant courage ebbed away. The down side of these righteous uprisings is that they leave me feeling weak and wobbly, probably the rush of adrenaline. I no longer had the strength to argue and knew that she had, ultimately, emerged victorious. I ought to have known better.

I nodded and told her what I wanted it to say.

Chapter Six

I couldn't get out of the post office fast enough. The post-outrage wobbles were making me feel quite ill. I found myself flooded with shame and remorse. It was an old dance and I knew the steps by heart. Why did I have to be so over-reactive? Why did I have to take such ridiculous stands? Why did I act like such a spoiled child? I need to grow up and stop living in a fantasy world where everyone is wonderfully pleasant and kind to animals and small children. I took a deep, quavering breath and closed my eyes, trying to steady my thundering heart. That was Teddy's voice; of course it was Teddy's voice, Teddy's words, Teddy's accusations echoing around my head. A litany of criticism, heavily laced with sarcasm and ridicule, blaming me for everything that had gone wrong in his life, even though it wasn't me who had consistently behaved horribly and made bad choices. Knowing it and doing something about it were two different things, however, and so I stood, shaking stupidly for several minutes, as the waves of panic rolled over me. I could never go back in there. Never.

I was on the verge of tears as I parked Edie's bicycle outside the grocer's. Every cell in my body was screaming at me to go straight back to the cottage. I could leave Bracken with Alfie and Edie; they'd be able to find her people, they had better connections in the area anyway. I'd be better off going back to the cottage and shutting myself in there until I felt better. No matter how long that took. I wanted a quiet life, that's why I'd moved here. I *needed* a quiet life, I needed to look after myself for once and that meant being on my own.

But I couldn't stop thinking of how frightened Bracken had been when she'd run into me on the moor. I understood that kind of primal fear, the kind of panic that takes over and won't let you see what's actually happening around you. But I also understand that there's always something to hold onto, if only you look, something to restore your faith in the world, in people; I wanted to be that something for Bracken and I couldn't keep feeding her soup. So I smoothed my hands down the front of my coat, then calmed their shaking by readjusting my scarf. I took several deep, fortifying breaths and tried to remember the things my therapist had taught me. I glanced around me, taking an inventory of my surroundings, noting sights, smells and sounds. My breathing slowed, as did my heart rate and I began to feel a little more steady. I was here, in Winkle, not in a London flat with an unreasonably irate husband shouting at me.

I looked through the window of the grocer's and gave silent thanks that it seemed quiet. With any luck, I could just slide in and slide out without attracting any unwanted attention. My mind flitted anxiously over the possibility that Mrs.Trout had already called ahead and warned them about me but I slapped the thought down quickly, before it grew legs. I pulled my shopping bag from the wicker basket on the front of the bike and pulled open the door.

At first glance, I could see that there literally wasn't anyone in the grocer; only a bored-looking teenage girl with blue hair, sitting on a high stool at the one-lane check-out. She barely looked up when I walked in and I kept my head down and headed for the dog food aisle. I'd forgotten to write a list, being too preoccupied with Bracken and thoughts of the many complications that finding her could produce. I picked up a few tins and a small bag of biscuits then, perusing the other aisles, grabbed myself a couple of tins of beans and more chocolate biscuits. I added the makings of a salad, a couple of apples and a box of porridge oats. On impulse, I picked up a lovely ceramic bowl with the shoots of what the sign promised would eventually be narcissi poking through the soil.

I waited patiently while the girl at the checkout – Astrid, according to the name tag pinned to her red smock – finished the article in the magazine she was reading. She eventually looked up, her large brown eyes, outlined in a disconcerting amount of black eyeliner, gave me an appraising stare. I tried to hold eye contact but failed miserably after about half a second. Under the edge of my eyelids, I saw her taking in my bright green coat, madly striped scarf and the blue flowered print of my dress, which, in my current state of extreme self-criticism seemed like the worst kind of middle-aged woman desperately trying to be cool vibe, rather than simply my general preference for bright colours, thrifted clothes and hand-knits. I felt the familiar heart-hammering shame for my existence rising and tried to shove it back down into the pit of despair from whence it came. Her fingernails, also black, drummed impatiently on the counter. She crooked a heavy black eyebrow down at my basket.

"Oh! Sorry!" I said, lifting up my basket. "I was miles away."

She grunted and began to lift my items out and scan them. She shoved them, none too gently, to the end of the conveyor belt and

I started repacking them into my bag. I looked around the shop, wondering suddenly if they had a notice board, too. At the same time, I wasn't sure I was up to another confrontation. I agonized for a moment then reminded myself it was for Bracken.

"Um, do you have a notice board here?" I asked, trying to sound as if I didn't care either way.

"Wha?" she said, jolted from the rhythm of scanning my items. She paused, a cucumber poised in mid-air.

"A notice board," I repeated, the first frisson of alarm creeping up my spine. Why does this have to be so difficult? Stop being ridiculous. "You know, for putting announcements on. It's just, I found a stray dog…"

Her expression changed immediately. She transformed from a sullen teenager into an excited child.

"A dog?" she said, a beautiful smile widened on her face. "Oh, what sort of dog? I love dogs, me, but mum and dad won't ever let me have one."

"Oh, she's a bit of this and that, I think. Mostly lurcher, I think, but smallish. I found her running on the moor."

I decided to leave the bit out about her being terrorized. For some reason, this girl's innocent enthusiasm over the mention of a dog made me want to shield her from the atrocities of her neighbours.

"Oh no! Do you think someone actually lost her? Or did she get dumped, I wonder."

"Dumped?" I asked, confused.

"Oh yeah," she said, waving her black-nailed hand. I noticed a tiny tattoo on the underside of her left wrist. "It happens all the time. You get these posh gits come in from the city and drop their dogs off, figuring some farmer has all the room to take them in. It's criminal, it is."

She gave me a firm nod, resuming her scanning of my vegetables.

"It was right good of you to pick her up then," she said. "Most people just call the dog-catcher and that never ends well, as you can imagine. No-one ever claims the poor things. I tell you what, I'd love to take some of them people and drop them off in the middle of the moor. Rotten bastards, the lot of them."

I inwardly congratulated myself for not mentioning Toby and his ride of terror. The last thing I wanted was to stir up any more fuss.

She gave me the total and I handed over my money. She tilted her head to one side and narrowed her eyes.

"Are you the one that's moved into Rookery Cottage, then?"

I nodded and forced that so-glad-to-meet-you smile. Not that I wasn't glad to meet her, she seemed a lovely girl. Her heart was definitely in the right place. But I was starting to experience the hollowed out, raw-edged feeling of too much social interaction, combined with the hangover of a mildly traumatic event.

"Yes, it was my Nan's."

"Ah, you're Elsie's granddaughter, then. She told us all about you."

I must have looked confused.

"A bunch of us used to go up to hers of a weekend and help her in the garden. There'd been, um, a bit of bother with littering on the moor and such like,"

She flushed under her light brown skin.

"So she'd invited us in for some tea and biscuits after the clean-up and it sort of got to be a regular thing. Until she got really poorly and had to go into hospital, that is."

She swallowed hard and blinked down at her hands where they rested on the conveyor. With a swift gesture, she ran them over the front of her smock and looked up, her eyes shining.

"She was a lovely person," she said, and then picked up her magazine and sat back down on the stool.

Feeling as if I'd been dismissed, I picked up my bag and started for the door.

"Over by the vending machine," she called. "There's some bits of scrap paper you can use but don't dare ask me for a pen. I'm fair sick of not getting them back."

Feeling ragged, I tucked my bag of shopping into the basket of Edie's bike and then realized, with a pang of idiocy, that there was no conceivable way that the bowl of bulbs was going to fit into the basket as well. I really wish I could have burst into tears; great, heaving snotty ones. At the same time, I was overcome with irritation at my immediate thought of how this only went to prove how right Teddy was about a lot of things, followed by even further irritation that I was still *having* such thoughts. So much work to do there. So much utterly exhausting work.

"Not ower bright, are you?" came a growly voice from behind me.

I made a concerted effort not to leap into the air at the sound of it. As it was, I was only just able to keep a grip on an almost audible shriek. I didn't need to turn around to know that it was my old nemesis from the bottom of the garden. The smell of aniseed was pervading. I sighed and then turned around anyway.

"Not ower nice, are you?" I retorted, mocking his dialect, suddenly incapable of even trying to get along with people.

The little man grinned widely from the depths of his bushy whiskers, showing teeth rimmed with black. An unfortunate side effect of the aniseed balls, I supposed.

"Eeeh! Mebbe you're not as gormless as you seem, after all," he said, lapsing into his wheezing chuckle. "And anyone who can't pass by a bit of the green can't be all bad, I reckon. There's hope for you yet, my lass. I'll have my coin on you afore it's all said and done. You might just be alright after all."

I frowned, not sure whether to be flattered or aggravated by his assessment of me.

He shifted his satchel and set off down the street, walking with a jaunty, rolling gait. He stopped at the entrance to a narrow alleyway that I hadn't noticed before. Maybe he was looking for somewhere else to doss down. He turned to wave and disappeared between the gap in the buildings. Quite involuntarily I lifted my arm and waved back.

I managed to get back to the Fisher's cottage without further incident, assuming one doesn't count several near-collisions with walls as I strove to balance the bowl of bulbs on top of the shopping in the basket. At one point I tried riding one-handed, cradling the porcelain bowl in the crook of my elbow, but that nearly proved disastrous when I had to swerve out of the way of an oncoming lorry. The driver glared and honked his horn. I pretended not to notice.

"Halloooo!" I called, opening the front door and stepping into the hall. I felt a sudden pang of nostalgia for the days of my childhood summers when I'd come to visit on an errand from Nan, usually with a jar of something or the copy of a recipe for Edie. Looking back, I wonder if it wasn't just a ruse to have me visit them. I must've been a tiresome child for my Nan to have to look after. Endless questions and endless curiosity. Nan and the Fisher's were the only ones who made me feel safe enough to be myself so they got the full force of me, questions, curiosity and all. I'd learned early on that Mum didn't appreciate my constant chatter and inclination towards the fantastical and so I'd learned to stay silent; that silence, over the years, had become a habit. My years at school only served to reinforce this default to staying quiet, but not when I was in Winkle. For those too-brief weeks every summer, I could be myself.

"Back here, lovey!" came Edie's voice from the kitchen.

I set the shopping and the bulbs on the floor and took off my coat and boots, hanging my scarf over one of the wooden pegs, carved into the shape of a fox's head. I followed the warmth and pleasant smells to the large kitchen at the back of the cottage.

Edie and Alfie's kitchen really was the heart of their home. It was twice as large as most; they'd had a piece of wall knocked down between the original kitchen and the unused dining room, enlarging it enough to include a couple of comfortable chairs by the Aga. The kitchen was separated from the sitting room by a half-wall, which was enough to keep the rooms apart, but not feel closed off from one another. The open-concept design was very avant-garde for a cottage style that favoured tiny rooms but, as Edie always said, open rooms were the way things were done back in the very olden days but at least they weren't sleeping in there with their chickens. Rookery Cottage was set up much the same and I always thought it was more cosy that everyone could still be together, even if they were in different rooms.

The rough plaster walls were a bright white which contrasted happily with the exposed beams. In the sitting room portion of the room, there was a lovely cast iron log-burner in the hearth, with two chairs set on either side and a small sofa facing it. Bracken had made herself comfortable on the clippy mat that lay in front of the hearth. She wiggled the tip of her tail and crept toward me, pressing up against my legs, quivering with what I hoped was delight.

"She's a lovely little thing, isn't she?" said Edie, handing me a steaming mug of tea which I accepted with deep gratitude. My hands were freezing. "She's had a terrible scare, poor wee mite, but I'm sure she'll come around. She's been good as gold the whole time you've been gone. Come and warm yourself by the fire, lass. The evenings still turn chilly this time of year."

She patted the back of the green wingback chair.

"Have you had anything to eat, pet? We've just finished ours. Alfie's out the back closing up the shed. Knowing him, he'll find something that needs pottering with while he's out there."

"I had a sandwich before we left the house," I said. "So I'm fine."

I knew if I'd admitted to being starving, Edie would put her pinny back on and start cooking me a meal. I couldn't bear it if she did.

"A sandwich? Good heavens, child. You can't get by on a sandwich. Here, there's a bit of supper left in the pan. Bacon, egg, and tomatoes, do you?"

She didn't wait for an answer but went back to the stove and started scooping a large helping onto a plate.

"Oh, and there's even a spoon of mushrooms."

She put the plate on a wooden tray and brought it to me while I sat warming my toes by the fire. My rumbling stomach betrayed me.

Edie chuckled.

"There, get that down you," she said, tucking a doorstep of bread under the edge of my plate. "You want feeding up a bit, you're far too thin, and peaky with it. When Alfie gets in, you can tell us all about how you got on in the village."

I hadn't eaten such a marvellous meal in what felt like years. I almost started getting teary, which was ridiculous of me. Who gets weepy over a plate of dinner? I decided just to let myself enjoy it; the flood of memories and the warmth and safety that were Edie and Alfie and this house. It had welcomed and sheltered a shy, anxious child and was doing much the same for her rather more grown counterpart.

Just as I was mopping up my plate with the last piece of bread, Alfie bustled in through the back door. Bracken got up to welcome him, in her slithering way, as if he'd been gone for months. Even she, after all the upset of her day, felt safe here with them.

"Ah, I knew you were back!" he said, "Manage the bicycle alright, did you? I keep it in good nick, you know. Have you got a bike? You'll need one if you want to get around at any speed. Still not driving a car, I take it?"

I managed a smile.

"No, Alfie. I just don't fancy it. Great hurtling lumps of metal, that they are. Terrible for the environment."

Alfie laughed his wheezing laugh. Nan had also had a great distrust of cars. She'd take the bus into the town every other Saturday, but wanted nothing to do with driving. I must've inherited her dislike, although I at least didn't mind being a passenger. Besides, no road examiner in their right mind would ever grant me a license.

"But no, I haven't got a bike. I suppose I should have one, like you say, it's much faster than walking. I'd be very grateful if you keep an eye out for one going spare. It needn't be anything fancy. Then again, if I've got Bracken..."

I stopped then, suddenly mindful of the fact that I'd just spent a torturous hour ensuring that I *wouldn't* have Bracken. Why did I have to be so stupidly responsible? I ought to have gone with my initial perilous thought that suggested whoever she might belong to didn't deserve her.

I looked down where she lay on the mat, curled in a tight ball, her nose tucked into her paws . Every once in a while, a tremble would ripple through her thin frame and she'd lift her head, as if to check that we were all still here. I could feel my own heart reach out to hers. I knew just how she must feel.

Edie stood up.

"More tea, anyone?"

"Aye, ma," said Alfie, handing up his mug. "I'll have a top up. Hazel?"

"Oh, yes, please. If there's enough."

I wanted to sit there by the fire with them and drink tea all night. A clog of tears burned at the back of my throat at the thought of going back to Nan's cold and empty cottage. How could I ever make it into the home that she'd created? Perhaps this had all been a giant mistake after all. I swallowed hard.

Edie's hand on my shoulder brought me back to myself. She squeezed it gently as she handed me back my mug. I looked up and she smiled. I had every reason to believe that she knew just what I was thinking.

"You know, lass. You're always welcome here. It's no use hiding yourself away up there, thinking you have to do it all on your own. Our door's always open."

She patted my arm.

"Now I'll say no more of it, I don't want you getting upset, because when you get upset, our Alfie gets upset and I've no mind to listen to him fretting all night long!"

She grinned and handed Alfie his mug. Alfie made an attempt to look fierce which provided the necessary comic relief.

"So," said Edie, settling into the chair opposite. "How did you get on in the village? How was that old harpy in the post office?"

I told them about my altercation with Mrs. Trout. Alfie slapped his thigh in delight when he heard what I'd said to her.

"Eeeh! The old harridan probably didn't know where to put herself when you lipped back at her. Would be a fine thing if more folk give her a taste of her own medicine. She's always queening it over the rest of us. Thinks she's a cut above, you see. Just because her old man works for the government. Something to do with the Ministry of Agriculture or some such. And him never so much as dug up a tatie in all his life. I don't warrant he'd know one end of a sheep from the other but there he is, one of the higher ups. Mark my words, the country'll get itself into a right bother with toffs like him in charge of the land instead of folk that were raised with it."

"Steady on, Alfie," said Edie, chuckling. She turned to me, tilting her head toward the red-faced Alfie, "he's fair got a bee in his bonnet over this, as you can see. He probably wouldn't go on so, but old Fish-face gets on everyone's wick. "My husband this' and "my husband that'. She can't help it, poor thing. Must be a sorry life you lead to feel like you have to put everyone else down just to feel important. And she's got a captive audience half the time, everyone needs a stamp or to send a parcel at some point."

"It's a bit of a relief to know she's always like that," I said, feeling genuinely happier. "I was afraid it was just me and I'd rubbed her the wrong way."

Alfie snorted.

"I doubt very much that she has a right way, so I wouldn't lose too much sleep over it."

"I won't," I said, with a smile, knowing full well that I'd do just that. Confrontation of any kind had a way of haunting me and that one, with its after-effect of self-recrimination would linger for a while.

"I did meet an interesting sort of young girl in Halverson's. She seemed to take an interest in Bracken."

"Ah, that'd be the Patel girl, would it? The one with the blue hair and black eyes?"

I grinned.

"Yes, Astrid, her name-tag said."

"Yes, that's the one. Her father's an optometrist and her mum's something to do with the high school over in Westham. A psychologist, I think. Nice family. I think it's hard on the young people, living here. There's not much going on and she's an only child, poor thing."

"Aye," said Alfie. "That's when they get theirselves into trouble."

"She did mention something about littering," I said, "She knew Nan."

Edie nodded.

"There was a bit of bother a year or so back. The young ones took to drinking beer and driving motorbikes and having fires out on the moor. Made a terrible racket and tore up the heath something awful. Course it sent the sheep off their heads and there was all sorts of rubbish left strewn about."

"Nothing a bit of hard work wouldn't fix," said Alfie. "In my day...."

Edie patted him on the knee.

"Think of your blood pressure, love. No need to get yourself aeriated."

"Anyway," she said, returning to the explanation. "There was a right hullaballoo about it, talk of charges and youth detention centres but your Nan stepped in and convinced everyone to let the little blighters have a chance at making it right. I don't know what she said to the young ones, mind you, they were a horrible stroppy lot. Still, they tidied up and made their apologies. Most of them were from over Westham way and never came back but young Astrid and one of the others stuck in with your Nan and were a great help. She was never really one of them yobs, I don't think. Just a bit lost really. Probably lonely. I expect she thought it was a bit of an adventure, gadding about with the older ones from the big town. The other one, Sidney, seemed as adrift as our Astrid. Anyroad, seems a decent sort. Bit earnest, you know, one of them bookish types," she winked and gave Alfie a knowing look. He smiled at me, indulgent. "Anyway, the two of them chum around together now and have been right good for one another so it all ended well enough. They do the theatre group and pub quizzes. Very civilized."

I thought back to my own lonely days and how I wanted so badly to fit in. I didn't much care who, at that point, I would've been happy with any group that would have me. Unfortunately, that's how I ended up where I did, though on a more catastrophically adult scale. I could appreciate how Astrid must've felt when she got in with the dubious crowd.

"She seemed nice," I repeated. "And she let me write out my own notice."

We sat in silence for a while. The only sounds were the ticking of the kitchen clock and the snap and tumble of a log in the fire. I was overcome by the soporific effect of a good meal and much beloved company. I let my mind drift to my other encounter of the day.

"I met another fellow, today," I started, cautious because I didn't want to create a fuss. The little man looked like a vagrant but it never paid to make assumptions. Still, I wanted to be sure I didn't have a transient squatting in my shed. Or if I did, how I might best encourage him to move along.

"Oh?" said Alfie, muffling a contented belch. "Who was that then?"

I blushed.

"Well, to be honest, I didn't actually get his name, but he seemed to know who I was."

I paused, rubbing my finger around the rim of my mug. I felt a pang of regret for bringing it up. I could feel the rise of worry prickling the back of my neck, as if talking about this was going to irreversibly alter things. I shook my head, telling myself to stop being so melodramatic.

"Funnily, I first met him coming out of the stone shed at the bottom of the garden..."

The sound of a spoon clattering to the hearth sent Bracken scrabbling for her life. She pushed her way between my feet, making my knees bump my elbows and sloshing tea onto my lap.

"Good heavens!" exclaimed Edie, leaping up from her chair. She bustled to the kitchen for a tea towel and made a big fuss over mopping the tea from my dress.

"I'm ever so sorry," she said. "Clumsy that was and now the poor wee dog is all in a frizzle again."

She glanced over at Alfie, giving him one of those meaningful stares that seem to be a sort of secret married-people skill of communicating vast amounts of information without ever opening their mouth. My mum had a complete repertoire of those looks with which she could control my dad.

Alfie cleared his throat and shifted in his chair.

"Coming out of the shed, you say?" he said, adopting an air of mild surprise. He wasn't a very good actor. My feeling of regret deepened. It was another one of those times when I wish I had the power to slightly rewind time. I usually wished for that particular super-power in awkward social exchanges when I'd said or done something idiotic but I desperately wanted it now.

I nodded, then shrugged, affecting utter nonchalance.

"Yes, and then I bumped into him again in the village. He was going down an alleyway." Ha, I thought, reaching for a perfect change of subject. "It's funny, I don't remember that alleyway before. What's down there?" I asked. "More shops?"

There was another exchange of looks between them.

"Oh, nothing much lass," said Edie, smiling and patting my arm. "It's mostly closed-up shops and empty premises. More tea?"

I really ought to have made my excuses and left just then, but I wanted a few minutes more by the fire, surrounded by the warmth and familiarity. Their odd reaction to my visitor made me even more uneasy about what I'd seen and heard that day. I could feel my peaceful and uncomplicated existence slipping slowly between my fingers. But no, I wouldn't think that way. I was making too much of nothing.

I smiled with a forced brightness. "Yes, please, Edie. Just a drop more and then we really must be going."

Edie bustled back into the kitchen, humming a tune that I recognized from the ceilidhs we used to go to when I was in my early teens. There was one every August at the village hall and it was one of the highlights of the Winkle social calendar, even though it always meant the end of my summer and a return to the horrors of school. My thoughts drifted to Toby but I reeled them quickly back.

Alfie leaning over towards me pulled me from my memories.

"Don't you go fretting over things, lass," he said, putting a gnarled hand on my arm and squeezing gently. "Me and Edie are going to help you with all this, we promised your Nan, aye? And never you mind our Edie, she's a worrier by nature and she looks on you as one of our own. She's every confidence in you, pet, but worrying is just her way.

I'll leave a word with them lot across the border and tell them to ease up a bit for now, give you time to get settled before they call again, right?"

He winked knowingly and eased back into his chair as Edie returned with the pot of tea. I held out my mug, more confused than ever. I felt as if I'd walked into a room in the middle of a conversation and missed all of the important bits. It was only exhaustion that stopped me from asking for further details. I thanked Edie for the tea and leaned back in my chair, gazing stupidly into the fire. I could feel Bracken shivering under my seat. I let my hand dangle over the arm and she nosed it, snuffling quietly before giving my fingers a brief lick.

"Eeh well!" exclaimed Edie, after a spell. "This won't get the pots washed!"

"Oh, let me help," I said, rushing to stand. "It's the least I can do." I glanced at the clock. "Then I really must be getting home. I've stayed too long as it is."

"No such thing, lass," said Alfie with a wink. "But I wouldn't say no to you doing the drying so's I can sit here and warm me old bones for a while longer. I've some good company here, with your wee dog, it fair pains me to think of getting up."

On impulse, I leaned down and kissed him on his whiskery cheek. He smelled of earth and laundry soap.

"I wouldn't dream of disturbing either one of you," I said, and followed Edie over to the sink.

Chapter Seven

I t was dark by the time Bracken and I made our way back to the cottage. On Edie's insistence, I'd left the bowl of bulbs behind. She would give them to Craig to leave with the milk, rather than have me try to manage the bowl, my shopping and Bracken's leash. For the hundredth time, I bemoaned my foolishness. Now I'd created a bother for everyone over a stupid impulse. It would've been far more sensible to buy a bunch of tulips instead. I sighed.

"Oh, Bracken," I said, fumbling with the latch on the gate. "Did you know you'd saddled yourself with such an oafish creature?"

I took her lack of response to be a matter of politeness.

The cottage was dark and cold, as I knew it would be. The contrast between the warmth and welcoming feeling of the Fisher's home was almost a physical shock.

It was difficult knowing the cottage in this way. It was a side of the place I'd never seen, and I'd been so caught up in my memories of how it was when I was here with Nan. I so badly wanted it to feel like it always had, but the reality was that it felt distant and stand-offish and I'd even had moments when I didn't feel quite wanted. Thanks to my Nan's influence, I've always believed that dwellings can have a life of their own - a distinct character - some more so than others. With Rookery Cottage it goes far beyond a whimsical notion, it was a reality; the cottage really did have a spirit of its own, which I'd always assumed was one of warmth and welcome. It had never occurred to me that part of that character was infused by the people who lived there, that the cottage was responding to its occupant. What did I have to offer this little cottage that had known such brightness and delight during all the years my Nan lived there? Of course it wasn't going to respond to me the way it had to her, especially given all the emotional baggage I was carting around with me. Knowing that on an intellectual level didn't really help how desolate the reality felt.

I bustled around, turning on lights and closing the windows. No wonder it was so cold, I'd left them open when I'd gone out and the evening air was distinctly damp. I pulled the wood basket closer to the hearth and set about building a fire. This was another one of those things I should've done before I left, so as to just have to set a match to it when I got home. Bracken sat, pressed against me, shivering.

"I know, I know," I said. "I'm an utter failure. Dragging you away from cosiness and companionship, not to mention bacon drippings, to shiver here in the cold and dark."

My voice caught as I said the words, a clog of tears building in my throat. I will not cry, I told myself in fierce tones, I will not cry. But the battle was lost and the tears began to trickle down my cheeks. Bracken burrowed her head under my arm and, this time, I just let them fall.

Waking up burrowed under the covers of my lavender-scented bed was a much better way to start the day than cold and cramped on the sagging sofa. The sound of a robin filtered through the slightly-open window and the first fingers of daylight were creeping over the horizon. I'd left the window uncovered, having not got around to washing the curtains, and I thought I might leave it that way. To be able to look out at the stars, or the sunrise, seemed far preferable to observing the niceties of decor. Besides, it wasn't as if I was overlooked by another house. I briefly considered getting up but after putting an experimental arm out of the covers and feeling the chilly air, I retreated back to the warmth of the bed.

At some point during the night, Bracken had made her way up off the floor and was lying, quite comfortably, stretched out beside me, under the duvet. I'd thought perhaps I ought not to allow her on the bed so had gathered a pile of old blankets for her to lie on, but when she'd climbed up and settled down, I found the weight and warmth of her against me to be a tremendous comfort. In fact, it wasn't until she'd curled up beside me that I found myself able to sink into a deep and restful sleep.

I felt her stirring and reached a hand out to her wiry head. She sighed and wriggled, quite content, it seemed, to lounge about for a while longer. I cast my thoughts back to the upset of the night before. I never did manage to get the fire started and all I'd wanted was to come to bed. I'd made myself wash the few dishes and put away the shopping first, to avoid more untidiness when I got up. Then I rummaged in an old blanket box and found the best of the moth-eaten, musty smelling blankets for Bracken and come straight upstairs. Curled up in the dark, I wanted nothing more than to let myself sob. Not the quietly suppressed weeping from the discovery of Teddy's affair, or Nan's death through to the funeral, nor the random escapee tears that had welled up since, but proper, body-wracking sobs. For Nan, most of all, and the years lost to us because of doing what other people wanted. But also for the arguments and the fighting it took to get myself here, for the uprooting of my life, and for all of the stress and anxiousness I'd felt since I'd arrived.

Then there was Bracken. Foolishly, and quite knowingly, I'd let her steal my heart. I clung to the hope, though, that Astrid had been right and that it was highly unlikely I'd hear anything from my adverts. Besides, who ever came through the village but people who lived here? It wasn't a convenient side-trip from the motorway and not exactly a tourist hot spot at this time of year. No, I reasoned, it wasn't likely I'd hear anything at all and this way, my conscience was eased. I'd give it a few weeks then take the notices down.

I sighed, relishing the warmth of the bed. Through the window, a weak sun was battling for supremacy in the overcast sky. It was so quiet here. There was none of the sounds of a city waking up - the clang of dustbins, the honking of cars and symphony of sirens and engines. There wasn't the sound of Mrs.Dimitri shouting at her husband to get up, nor the frantic yapping of Mr. Wallace's dachshunds as they hurtled down the passage toward their morning walk. I'd loved our flat in the city - it had been a boarding school for boys during the Victorian era and I always fancied I could hear the sounds of children's booted feet and (more fantastically) someone singing their morning hymns. But I certainly didn't miss the way the noise and crowds left me feeling ragged, or the way I wasn't ever able to find the sort of peace and calm that simply existed here without effort. I decided then and there that I needed to stop feeling sorry for myself and appreciate everything I did have. Sure, it wasn't the same as I'd remembered, but then I couldn't expect it to be, could I? I'd only just arrived and the cottage had been empty for months. It was rude and selfish of me to expect it to welcome me when it had stood so long in neglect. I wondered if it was grieving Nan's loss as much as I was. I suspect it was. Not to mention, I hadn't spent an appreciable amount of time here since I was in my early teens. We were strangers to each other. It would take time for us to reacquaint ourselves.

I gave Bracken a gentle prod and pushed back the covers, immediately regretting it by the blast of cold air hitting my legs. I must get some warmer nightclothes, I thought, mentally adding it to the list of what I needed to buy when Mum and Dad came to take me shopping. I was simultaneously dreading and looking forward to their visit. Mum had wanted to stay with me for the first week, the source of one of the many arguments we had over my moving here, but happily Dad had sided with me and they settled for waiting a week. We had an appointment with the solicitor anyway, to get the full details of Nan's will, so it was a combined trip. Their looming visit was all the more reason to shake off my doldrums and get to work putting things in order.

"Come on, lazy bones," I said, as Bracken yawned and stretched, showing no signs of budging. "All we've got time for is a quick breakfast then we must get cracking and get this place in order. No more distractions. We've got to convince the house that we're worthy of living here. Not to mention only a handful of days until Mum descends and starts looking for reasons I ought not to be here at all."

Bracken thumped her tail and jumped off the bed. She clattered down the stairs in front of me and we started the day.

I spent the next three days gloriously alone, other than Bracken, of course. Edie phoned every evening to check in with me, but otherwise, I didn't see nor hear from another soul, including, thankfully, my little vagrant friend. Craig made his milk and egg delivery in relative silence and I grew happily accustomed to waking with the sunrise and birdsong. It was precisely what I needed to soothe my ragged nerves. I allowed myself to believe that, despite the bumpy beginning, I really was going to find my peaceful, quiet life here.

I scrubbed and polished and tidied to my heart's content. I washed the curtains in Nan's old poss-tub and hung them on the line to dry. Everything smelled of wind and sunshine. In no time, the cottage began to lose its air of neglect. Open windows and posies of snow-drops, hellebore and violets, gathered from under the hedge in the lane, along with my merry bowl of narcissus, helped to dispel the stale, musty smell and bring some light back to the shadowed rooms. I had become instantly expert at laying the fire and Bracken and I enjoyed our evenings, curled up under one of Nan's many crocheted blankets, with a mug of cocoa and a book by the crackling flames.

I'd managed to wiggle the door of the big shed at the bottom of the garden - the lock had long since rotted off but the wood was so warped as to not sit flush in the frame. It was mostly empty inside –Nan's wheelbarrow was propped up against the outside – but other than a few garden implements, there was only dust, cobwebs and evidence of rodent occupancy. I hoped very much said rodents were only mice. Bracken seemed quite disinterested after her initial sniff-around, so I'd hoped that meant the squatters had moved on. Speaking of squatters, I made a point of not looking at the tilting stone structure opposite.

After giving the shed a good sweeping, I carried box after box of things I didn't want and stacked them in the shed. Much of what Mum had insisted I bring, ended up there. I found that, once I'd cleaned and tidied, all I really wanted was my books and my few bits of kitchen things. I certainly didn't want anything that reminded me of my life with Teddy. I added a clock to the living room so I didn't have to turn my head to look at the one in the kitchen and my few potted plants but that was all. I'd found an old bookshelf in the spare room which had polished up beautifully to a dark, walnut stain and so I carried that downstairs to hold my books. The white laminate bookcase I'd brought with me seemed terribly out of place in the simple, rustic room and so into the shed it went. Freeing the living room of the clutter and chaos of endless boxes went a long way to easing the unsettled feeling I had when I was sitting in there. It was as if the cottage approved of my decisions, too, as the general feeling of the place seemed less, well, prickly.

It was when I was in the middle of sorting the stacking of those boxes when I had a visitor. I heard the sound of the gate opening and someone called a tentative "Hallooo!"

Bracken immediately glued herself to my leg.

"Fine guard dog you'd be," I muttered. "Aren't you supposed to rush out, barking and slavering?"

She whined helpfully.

I popped my head around the shed door; a pair of black-and-white striped legs came into view under the tangle of holly bushes just inside the gate.

Astrid.

"Hello, Astrid," I called, wiping my hands on the canvas apron I was wearing for my tidying.

She started and turned around, peering around the shrubbery. Her eyes were a dark smudge and her hair seemed more vividly blue than the last time I'd seen her.

"Oh, hullo," she said, "Sorry to barge in on you, I don't mean to intrude."

She glanced around at the garden. The beds were a tangle of dead vegetation, although bits of green could be seen poking through the black soil. Daffodils. Nan always had a great drift of them down by the shed.

"It's a bit of a mess, isn't it?" I said, pushing a rather unclean hand through my bird's nest of hair. Not unlike myself, I thought. "I heard you helped my Nan with the gardening this last while."

She nodded.

"I didn't know that much about it when we started. We only have a useless bit of a garden at home and no-one's got much interest.," she frowned, scuffing the toe of her boot into the gravel path. "Your Nan taught me lots about growing things. And looking after it, like. I liked being here. It's a peaceful sort of place."

I had a feeling for what I ought to say at this point. A normal person would've sensed what needed to be said, and I suppose the fact that I did actually know what I ought to have said gives me some merit. But the fact that I didn't say it, rather erased any points I may have earned. I just wasn't ready. I was still finding my way and wanted desperately to defend my solitude. Of course, every single one of those arguments sounded horribly selfish in my head and so duty outweighed personal feeling at that point.

"Well," I said, after far too long of a pause. "The garden is in a bit of a state. If I want to get it sorted in time to plant things, I might need a bit of help."

Astrid avoided looking at me. Instead, she made a point of fussing over Bracken who was leaning against her striped legs in an attempt to absorb herself into the fabric.

It struck me, suddenly, that perhaps the appeal of the garden had been more about Nan rather than the digging in the muck bit. I scrambled to salvage the mutually embarrassing situation.

"I'm sure you're very busy with school, though. And I'm not really the best company. Nothing like my Nan, anyway. She always had such an easy way with people. I'll see if Mr. Fisher can recommend someone if I need help."

Astrid looked up sharply, her eyes narrowing.

"I never said I didn't want to do it," she said, although her tone seemed grudging at best.

I'm terrible at understanding the subtleties of teenage moods. I have a hard enough time navigating my own, never mind those of an angst-ridden misfit like Astrid. Considering I'd been one of those angst-ridden misfits most of my life, it didn't say much about my interpersonal skills.

I stood, fiddling with the edge of the pocket on my apron while Astrid paid particular attention to the area behind Bracken's left ear.

"Well, let's just leave it open, shall we? I won't be starting on the garden until at least next week. My parents are coming for a visit at the weekend and I've an awful lot of tidying to finish."

I hoped this would be taken for the hint that it was. I had been having such a marvellous time, puttering away on my own, though I wouldn't have minded some less prickly company, I'm sure. It was almost time for my tea break and I agonized over inviting Astrid for a cup. Happily, she rescued me from my inner wrangling.

"Sure, whatever. Anyway, I only came to give you this."

She dug into her coat pocket - an army surplus affair with a collection of tiny, unreadable badges pinned to it - and pulled out a crumpled bit of paper. Handing it to me, she gave Bracken one last scratch and turned for the gate.

"I thought you might be interested," she said, pausing with her hand on the latch. Her fingernails were bitten to the quick and the black polish was worn and chipping. "We need all the support we can get and since you like dogs, I figured you'd be a good target."

I smoothed out the paper and caught the words "hedge defence alliance'. It looked vaguely familiar and then I remembered the bit of paper I'd plucked from the hedge a few days earlier. It was for a village meeting concerning the possible sale of land for use as a wind farm. Meetings and local politics - two of the exact things I wanted to avoid. I opened my mouth to say something noncommittal when she pushed through the gate.

"Your Nan would've been there like a shot," she said,"As a matter of fact, it was her who gave me the idea in the first place."

Well, I thought, staring down at the paper, that doesn't leave me much choice then, does it?

Friday morning dawned bright but cool. My parents were due in at mid-morning. Dad had an early meeting in town then they were to drive up to meet me at the cottage. We had an appointment with Mr.Reed, the solicitor, then dinner at the inn where my parents were staying. After three days of relative solitude, I finally admitted that I was looking forward to catching up with humanity. At least, as much as my parents represented humanity.

My father is what they call a self-made man. He left Winkle at seventeen with only a village school education. He worked every odd job he could find before getting an apprenticeship with a carpenter.

He'd always been good with his hands, Nan had told me. She would wink and say it was his faery heritage. The Good Folk were master craftsmen, she'd tell me, it was only natural he'd taken after his faery kin. I'd never known whether to believe her or not, but with our small, dark, features, it wasn't a great leap for an imaginative child and it was desperately thrilling to think I might be descended from faeries. As I got older, it became one of those family jokes that always created a bit of an atmosphere so was best not discussed, especially around my mum.

From labouring for other builders, Dad went on to start his own firm, specializing in preserving heritage houses and buildings. He also custom built beautiful homes for people who'd rather their home blended with the landscape rather than stood apart from it. He was enormously successful and in high demand, both in England and other parts of Europe, which meant I had an embarrassingly generous living allowance that meant I didn't have to do much of anything if I didn't want to. It was a source of quiet shame and so I had set it up so that most of it was donated to various charities. Incidentally, that was one of the sore points between Teddy and I, due mostly to how quickly money had flowed through Teddy's fingers.

I managed to further assuage my guilt over the allowance by working for Dad's charitable foundation that, among other things, helps non-profit groups find suitable premises for their organizations as well as funding restoration projects all over the world. I put my otherwise pointless university degree to use by functioning mostly as a grant writer and processor of application forms. It was surprisingly gratifying work and between that, helping Roger in the flower shop and writing my books, I managed to keep myself busy enough to not notice how my life was falling apart.

In addition to financial success, and much to the never-ending delight of my mum, Dad also had an OBE and was in the running for a knighthood for his service to preserving English heritage. It was a bit bewildering to think of, really, and I never could quite get used to my gruff, down-to-earth Dad as being someone with all of those accolades. My idea of wealthy people looked nothing like Dad who still wore the old canvas coat that my Nan had saved for and bought him when he first left home. Mum was another thing altogether. She'd embraced their good fortune to the highest degree. I was sometimes embarrassed by her airs and hints of snobbery and had brought it up with my dad, once, asking him to tell her to stop.

"Nah, lass," he'd said. "She doesn't mean any harm by it. You have to remember, times were hard when she was growing up. Her folk didn't have much of anything, same as me and your Nan, and it left a mark on her. And it wasn't a whole lot better when we were first married, either. But she stuck with me, through the thin times, and that says a lot about a person. No, you let her have her ways, pet. She's the same person underneath. A good heart and a generous soul. She'd give you the world, and you know it."

I *did* know it, but it didn't make it any easier to withstand her persistent efforts to have me be something I wasn't. I was never meant to be the millionaire's daughter. I was never meant to be upwardly mobile and the darling of the London social scene. Endless charity balls, serving on the board of this, that and the other thing, had slowly worn me to a nub. I said yes to all of it and had genuinely tried, not just because that's what was expected of me, because that's what people like Teddy and his friends did, but because I assumed it would make me a good person. Of course it could never work and I was constantly left feeling like a disappointment, in more than just my failed marriage.

The years I spent in London left me in a state of nervous exhaustion, then when Nan got ill amid things going catastrophically wrong with Teddy, it pushed me right to the brink. Still, I kept pushing onwards, determined to not fulfill anyone's — mostly Teddy's — vicious prophecies. After the funeral, I'd gone back to London, fully planning to stay with Roger and keep working. Then I ran into a pack of women from Teddy's social set and their false sympathy and empty platitudes couldn't hide the mockery in their eyes. I went back to Roger's flat, climbed into bed and wouldn't, *couldn't*, get out of it. That's how I ended up at Serenity Meadows.

Mum could never admit that I'd had a breakdown. She insisted it was a lingering 'flu, and told everyone I was at a health spa. I left there in time for Christmas, normally my favourite holiday of the year, but without Nan and with my future uncertain, it all fell a bit flat, despite everyone's best efforts. I knew I couldn't go back to London, it was the very last place I needed to be, so I stayed on with my parents through the new year. Soon enough, it became very obvious I couldn't stay there indefinitely. I was still too fragile and my mum's well-meaning attempts to live my life for me were suddenly intolerable. Then we had an inquiry from Mr. Reed about the occupancy of Rookery Cottage and things seemed so much clearer all of a sudden. The idea of the cottage gave me permission to admit just how much I loathed living in the city, and I'd been there for no reason other than that's what Mum thought young people of privilege were supposed to do. I think the only reason I hadn't fought it harder at the time was because I also thought it was what all aspiring authors were supposed to do.

I knew I'd have a fight on my hands, Mum had never liked me staying in Winkle, and she would be devastated to think I'd consider leaving my life in London. She would think of it as me admitting I'd been the one who had done something wrong, that I'd lose face, but for once, I didn't much care and was willing to face the onslaught of her disapproval.

And now, here I was, sitting at Nan's kitchen table, sipping an old pot mug full of steaming tea. It was everything and nothing like I'd imagined. But at least the place was clean and tidy, and bore the semblance of being lived in. I'd lit the fire, to warm the place through, knowing that would be Mum's first objection – it was too cold and damp. I knew that the visit to the solicitor was just a formality, to sign the papers and whatever else was involved in property transfers, but I still had a gnawing feeling of apprehension deep in my belly. I wouldn't be able to properly relax until it was all official. Only then would I be safe from the influence of familial disharmony and my burning compulsion to keep the peace at all costs. I was also clinging to the idea that having proof of my right to be here would somehow chase away the quiet, niggling feeling that was plaguing me; that, despite a desperate desire, perhaps I didn't belong here after all.

Chapter Eight

I had arranged to meet my parents at the inn for the very simple reason that I planned to drop Bracken off to stay with Alfie, thereby avoiding confrontation on that particular subject. The last thing I needed was Mum banging on about rabies or fleas or muddy paw prints on the furniture. All I wanted was for the weekend to go smoothly and without undue incident. I wanted a swift resolution on the paperwork front, a trip into town to pick up a few things and a few nice meals with my doting parents. Surely that wasn't too much to ask?

I tied my makeshift lead to Bracken's makeshift collar,

"That's the first thing on my shopping list, girl. A nice new collar and lead. We can't have you looking like a stray any longer!" and set off down the lane towards the Fisher cottage.

The sun was glorious. It seemed that spring was really making a concerted effort to properly arrive. I spied more tiny clumps of snowdrops and primrose under the hedge and an assortment of birds were flitting and darting in and out of newly-blossoming blackthorn branches. Now and then, there would be a flurry of wings and out-burst of chirping as one bird would scold another for encroaching upon established territory.

I smiled.

"Now, now," I said to the squabbling birds. "There's plenty of room for everyone. It's a big hedge, you know!"

I felt almost light-hearted as I knocked on the door of the Fisher's cottage. The walk down the lane, surrounded by the sights and sounds of spring had done wonders for dispelling the pervasive anxieties over the day's meeting.

"I oughtn't be too late," I told Alfie as I handed over Bracken's lead. She didn't hesitate in the slightest in sidling past him and through the door, no doubt in search of more bacon drippings. "We have to see Mr.Reed at eleven and then we're going to have a meal at the inn."

"Don't you worry, lass. Take all the time you need, she won't come to no harm here. Bit of company for me, anyway. She can help me do a few jobs in the garden. The missus has had to go off to the Big House. There's trouble stirring over there and she's gone to put a few fires out, as it were."

"Oh?" I said, remembering Astrid's leaflet. "Is it something to do with Lord Whatsit, then?"

"Aye, isn't it always?" he replied with a shrug. "Poor old sod is forever having some crisis or other. This time it's something to do with his account at the feed store. I think he has to sell off bits of the silver tea service to pay the heating bills, never mind all that fancy food he feeds yon sheep. Trouble is, them titled folk never did learn properly how to make a living, you see? He has all of these grand ideas but not a great hand with the business side of things I don't think. Still, that doesn't mean he's going to roll over on this land situation, though. They think he's so hard up he'll sell the land with nary a second thought. They're in for a shock on that score. He's not so green as he's cabbage-looking and I think yon wind-farm folk have misjudged him."

"But what has any of that to do with Edie?" I asked.

"Oh, whenever the old codger gets himself in a state she's allus the first one he phones. She goes and does a bit of faffing and makes him tea and a meal and settles him down. She's a dab hand with the accounts and housekeeping budget and can usually sort it all out. She used to work there full-time, aye? That were part of her job. But he couldn't keep up with the wages so she just does the odd morning now. More for love than owt else, really. Her family was in service there all the years when it was still a grand house. Times have changed, that's for certain."

I shook my head. It sounded to me like the just desserts of a family who had probably lived off the backs of peasants for centuries. Then again, I tended automatically to take up the side of the underdog. Or maybe it was my recently developed prejudice for the idle rich.

"Well, as long as you're alright with having her on your own?" I said, worrying suddenly if it would be too much for him.

"Don't be silly, pet. We're going to do a bit of pottering in the garden then bring ourselves back in by the fire to have a spot of lunch ourselves. Cheese and pickle sandwich do you, girl?"

Bracken answered the question with a tail-tip wiggle.

"I think that means she's ecstatic," I said, grinning.

The village inn, known presumptuously as The Hostelry was tucked, almost apologetically, in behind The Forge. It had, in days long gone, been a place for weary travellers to lay their heads, or sleep off the drink, while their horses were being shod or rested in preparation for the next leg of their journeys. It had originally just been a few rooms above a stable, but with the perilous designation of a listed building, had been renovated into a boutique sort of inn, complete with a starred chef. It was difficult to fathom how it ever paid for itself, Winkle not exactly being a tourist hotspot, but Mum had assured me that it was a Destination – a place where one went specifically for a bistro meal and charming period accommodation. Considering she spent a great deal of time investigating and designating Places of Interest, I took her word for it. If it met her high expectations, then it must be of a standard. I know Dad was curious about the way they'd done over the inn, his company having consulted on the design and materials.

I followed the meandering footpath from the main road, down a small flight of stone steps to the front of the Forge. It was a low, whitewashed building with a heavy thatch and leaded windows. The door was clearly authentic as it looked as if anyone much over five and a half feet tall would have to duck under the broad timber frame or else risk a concussion. A sweet-scented spray of winter blooming jasmine sprawled across a trellis on one side of the door and a climbing rose, still bereft of foliage, scrambled wildly on the other side, disappearing around the corner of the building. Window boxes stuffed full of smiling pansies completed the vision of English country heritage. It wouldn't have surprised me to know that the frontage of the pub was featured in a wall calendar.

Despite its charming floral disguise, though, it was still a pub and I still had to open the door and go in alone. I would've much rather met my parents at the inn. There's no greater sense of apprehension than opening a door to the great social unknown. I was comforted by the fact that it was still early and unlikely to be full of loud, pint-swilling workmen on their lunch break from roadworks, building sites or other boisterous occupations. I thought, briefly, of Harry and The Lads and allowed that I wouldn't mind if *they* were in there, because at least I sort of knew them.

I took a steadying breath and pushed open the door, ducking my head slightly. I really didn't need to, but it gave me a rare opportunity to blend in with the rest of the world. A narrow foyer complete with coat racks offered a brief buffer to the main room of the pub which was open concept with a huge stone hearth as the focal point. I had no doubt it would be the merriest of places in the depth of winter, with a roaring fire and the murmur of conversation. Despite the low ceilings and small windows, it didn't seem dark or oppressive as many of the old pubs can often feel. The white-painted walls and unfussy wooden tables and chairs gave a feeling of space and brightness. Mirrors behind the bar reflected the light from the windows and small jam jars filled with snowdrops and daffodils lent the place a cheery, spring-like feeling.

I scanned the room, it wasn't that big, but could see no sign of my parents. I checked my watch. I tend toward a pathological brand of punctuality with a preference for being early, rather than late, but one distinctly unpleasant disadvantage of this is the risk of being the first person on the scene. Therein lies the discomfort of having to sit or stand alone, without feeling or looking awkward, as you await your party. It's easier to do that when there's at least a few people in the room. There didn't appear to be a single soul, not even a barman. I tried to decide on whether to sit at a central table near the fire, or tuck myself into one of the booths against the wall. Instinct pointed me to the relative comfort and security of the booths, so I slid onto the polished trestle, making sure to stay at the outer edge so I could see the door. I took my notebook and a pen out of my bag, more to give the illusion of being occupied than for any practical reason. I decided to go over my list of the things I needed in town while I waited.

I didn't have to wait long. I heard my mum before I saw her, she was exclaiming loudly and enthusiastically about the jasmine, my dad's deep rumble murmuring in the background. The door flung open and she walked in, ahead of my dad, chattering as she came. I stood to greet them, suddenly overcome with relief at their familiar and beloved faces.

"Hazel!" my mum exclaimed, hurrying over to me, her eyes narrowed as if to scrutinize me for signs of undue strain or suffering. I made a point of projecting calm confidence, stuffing my sudden urge to burst into tears well below the surface. I accepted her hand-grasp and cheek-peck with practiced London-scene grace and then let myself be enveloped in my dad's squeezing bear-hug. I could've stayed like that for days, breathing in his scent of old leather and pipe smoke, but I could hear mum tutting over the public display and making loud inquiries about whether there was anyone working behind the bar. Dad gave me one last squeeze and pulled away, keeping hold of my hand and guiding me back into the booth. I slid along to sit beside the wall and he slid in beside me. Mum sat opposite, placing her handbag beside her on the bench. I noticed, with slight resignation, the way we'd naturally gravitated into this seating arrangement. Me and Dad, opposite Mum and thought, not for the first time, how that summed up this entire situation. At least I had him on my side.

"I don't suppose they have anyone serving tea or coffee at this hour," said Mum, more as an observation than a question. She was dressed smartly, as always, in a pale pink skirt suit with a cream blouse. Dad used to jokingly ask her if she was wearing the old Queen's hand-me-downs but she hadn't seen the humour in that. She always wore gloves, and matched her handbag to her shoes, dedicating the time and energy to her outfit the way some people performed complex neurosurgery (she was very passionate about making an impression). My preference for thrifted Liberty print dresses and Doc Martens was a constant source of contention between us. When, in a fit of quiet rebellion, I started knitting my own cardigans she vowed to never be seen in public with me again. I'm only slightly ashamed to admit that I was quite happy with that arrangement. At least she'd given up making suggestions, or comments about my clothing. Out loud, anyway.

"I can't imagine they'd bother unlocking the door unless they had something to sell people," said my dad, winking at me. "Maybe the server had to use the toilet."

"Rowan!"

My mother is always scandalized at the mention of toilets. She goes to great pains to create the illusion of never having to go herself. I'm sure it isn't good for her.

Just then, a small, rotund man in a pin-striped apron advanced upon the table, a waiterly-looking notebook in one hand, a pencil in the other.

"Hello!" he said, beaming as if he couldn't believe his great good fortune to see us. "My name's Ernie. What can I get you this fine morning?" He spoke with a melodic, faintly Welsh accent, that practically insisted you were the very reason he came into work that day.

I could see my mother wince. Overt enthusiasm is another of her pet peeves. I truly think she was born in the wrong era. She would've been far happier with the repressed reserves of Victorian times.

"Just a pot of tea, please," she murmured, her deliberately quiet voice meant as an admonishment to the little man's joviality.

"Coffee for me," said my dad, grinning at my mum who merely raised an eyebrow.

"I'll just have some of the tea," I said, avoiding everyone's eye.

"Alright then!" said Ernie, clearly delighted. "Anything to go with it? Got some lovely bacon in yesterday from Rookery Farm, it'd be just the thing in a sarnie. Bit of toast and jam, to go with all that?"

"Oh, a bacon sandwich *would* be just the thing! Hazel, will you have one?"

"No thanks, Dad. I'm not very hungry."

"Mebbe the young lass would like a pastry of some sort? I can see what Cookie left in the larder?"

I couldn't help but smile at the little man. He'd cocked his head on one side, giving me his full attention and I could see that it was utterly genuine. I felt like I ought to agree to a pastry. He was making such an effort to think of something I might like.

"Alright," I said, "But not a pastry. Just some toast and jam, please."

"Blackberry suit?" he asked. "Local, they are, the blackberries what's in the jam. Picked from the hedge just up the road."

He beamed again.

I smiled back, happy that I could make him happy.

"That would be lovely, thank you."

"Right! Won't be just a minute."

He tucked his pencil behind his ear and headed through a swinging door beside the bar. He walked with an ambling sort of gait that was so full of energy as to be almost jaunty. A bowler hat and a twirling cane wouldn't have been out of place.

"Cookie?" said mum with a disapproving pursing of her lips. "I hardly imagine a four-star chef would appreciate being referred to as Cookie. I read somewhere that King Charles himself provides the vegetables for the kitchen here. From Home Farm directly!"

She looked over her shoulder, then around at the large room.

"Do you think he might be making a delivery today, then?" asked dad, pretending to study the salt cellar in the middle of the table.

I suppressed a smile.

"Delivery?" asked Mum, walking right into it.

Dad looked up, blue eyes twinkling, his face a picture of innocence.

"Charles," he said. "Do you think it's his day to drop off the veg? Only I thought I might have a word with him."

My mother just sighed.

"Rowan," she said, carefully smoothing the surface of the wooden table. "Why do you persist in mocking a serious situation? As you well know, I didn't mean HRH himself, only that if it's known that the Royals have business dealings in the village, that will surely be an attractive selling feature. We want to attract the right sort of person, after all."

A sudden chill ran up my spine, prickling my scalp. I felt my face flush and my mouth went horribly dry.

"What do you mean, selling feature?" I croaked, knowing full well her answer.

She tilted her head and smiled at me. It was her real smile, the one I remembered from when I was a child. She reached out her perfectly manicured hand and rubbed the side of my upper arm, expertly controlling her grimace as she touched the wool of my hand-knit cardigan. My own hands were clenched in my lap, my fingers knotting the fabric of my dress.

"You knew that was the idea, all along, darling," she said, her voice pitched low. She had a desperate fear of Scenes and recent experience had taught her that this was a potentially Scene-inducing subject.

"Your father and I have discussed it thoroughly..."

"You mean you talked and he just went along with it," I interrupted, shooting my dad an accusing look. He frowned and went back to studying the salt cellar. I love my dad with all my heart, he's my undisputed hero, but he's also a peace-maker, just like Nan. He gave into my mum far too easily. All for the easy life, he'd say. And no, the irony of my indignation was not lost on me.

"No," corrected Mum, "it was a proper discussion. Your father still isn't pleased with me, if that will make you feel any better. But he couldn't argue with the facts."

"Oh?" I said. "And what facts are those?"

I was on the edge of tears. This just wasn't fair! I had fought and argued and thought I'd won.

"The fact that you living here in this out-of-the-way little village is simply not good for a person of your...tendencies."

She had the courtesy, at least, of not looking at me when she said this. If she had, she would've seen the betrayal on my face.

"You need to be among people, Hazel. It's not good for you to shut yourself away like a hermit. You're far too young to become a recluse. And what about dear Roger? He'll be missing you terribly."

I swallowed a lump of tears.

"Roger," I said, biting out the word, seething with resentment that she'd use him against me, "Is quite fully aware of how I feel. He knows that London living isn't good for me. Anyway, he can manage on his own perfectly well. I was only ever helping him for my sake, not his. Not only that, he's completely supportive; not only supportive but enthusiastically encouraging. Which is what I'd expect from someone with my best interests at heart."

My voice wobbled at the last. I swallowed hard and forced myself to look up at my parents, the tears shining in my eyes.

"Please don't do this to me. You promised not to fight me on this. I can't bear anymore arguing..."

My voice broke and I stifled a hiccuping sob. This was just too much. It was bad enough that I was struggling to feel settled, but now it seemed I was on the brink of losing it before I'd even had a proper chance to make it my own.

My dad reached into his waistcoat pocket and handed me a hanky. It was a crumpled, soft linen, embroidered with a border of hawthorn leaves. My Nan's handiwork. That was the last straw. I accepted the hanky, sniffing loudly.

"I know this is upsetting, Hazel darling," said Mum, without a genuine clue of how upsetting it was. She had never understood the power of the cottage the way Dad and I did. She resented it sometimes, I think, because it was something she would never be a part of. "But it's for the best and, after all, it's ultimately your father's decision because the cottage belongs to him now."

"Don't be putting this at my feet, Patricia," warned Dad, "This is all you."

Then why don't you do something about it? I raged in my head. I didn't have the strength to voice the words, nor would I have been able to, betrayed as I was by my emotions.

"I won't go back to London," I said, finally summoning the composure to speak. "I won't. And I can't live with you, so would you have me homeless?"

"We can discuss that another time," said Mum, scenting victory. "Besides, darling, you needn't be so upset just now. After all, the cottage will undoubtedly need some tidying and fixing up before we put it on the market and as a matter of compromise, I agreed with your dad that you should spend the next few months here, getting it all in order, putting the garden to rights and such, and then we'll put in on the market in June. I think that would be the best time to show it off to its greatest advantage, don't you? All the flowers will be in bloom, it'll look picture-perfect!"

I think she truly thought she was doing the right thing. As much as she always seemed to miss the mark by a mile, I never doubted that she wanted only the very best for me; that what she did and said, she did and said out of love. I'm not sure if that made it easier or worse. What I did know, in that exact moment, is that I wasn't going to let her have her way with this one. I was going to stay and I was going to make my life here, on my terms.

"I imagine that will have to do for now," I said, fumbling with Dad's handkerchief. I dried my tears and cleared my throat, just as Ernie returned with a tray.

"There we are now!" he exclaimed, putting the various pots and mugs on the table. Our tea was in a lopsided teapot that looked as if it had been made in a beginner's pottery class. It was delightfully cartoonish, with large blue spots painted against the white background. I must've smiled because Ernie let out a chuckle.

"Isn't that a funny little thing?" he said, patting it affectionately. "Cookie likes to support the local trade and this was on offer at the Christmas craft fair last year. He likes to have what he calls an eclectic motif."

He shrugged, full of good nature.

"I don't quite get it meself," he said. "I always thought the pots and things were supposed to match. Not a pair of anything in the place since Cookie took over. Then again, nothing's quite the same, come to think of it. But," he rubbed his plump little hands together, "a body has to move with the times if it wants to keep up, eh?"

Then he did the unthinkable. He clamped a hand on Mum's shoulder and gave it a companionable squeeze. The look on her face was enough to make me forget my misery for a moment. Dad and I exchanged a glance and smothered our giggles.

"Bacon sarnie is on the way," he said, evidently unaware of his catastrophic breach of etiquette. "Cookie doesn't mind me frying up the bacon, as long as I don't use his good pans. And for you, *cariad*, a nice bit of toast and jam."

He bustled back toward the kitchen and took the air of gloom with him.

Chapter Nine

Mr. Reed was an old friend of Nan's. Dad told me that they'd courted once, about a hundred or so years ago, but that she'd broken it off, telling him it was for the best. She was a wild thing, apparently, which wasn't looked upon very fondly in those days and she didn't want to bring down his respectability. The McCorrigan women had been viewed with a bit of suspicion back then - part awe, part fear, I think. I suspect at one point in history, the women might have found themselves tied to a ducking stool. Nan didn't talk much about the in-between years – from when she was about fifteen to when my dad was a young boy. It was family tradition, she said, for the girls to go away for a spell. To study, she'd say, with a wink that I never quite understood. She would shrug at my questions and say that my mother didn't want her filling my head with unsavoury stories and that she would respect that. The price for not respecting it would be cutting off my visits, though I only found that out later.

Sitting across from him, in front of a massive old desk that looked like it might have been modern in the Middle Ages, I could see why

Nan might have been sweet on him. He had bright, merry green eyes that crinkled in the corners when he smiled, which was often, and a head of thick hair, a faded ginger, that had been Bryl-creamed into submission. He wore what I was learning was the standard country gentleman's uniform of corduroys – dark grey in this case – and a tweed blazer. Underneath that, a green checked shirt and grey woollen pullover. I couldn't see his feet, but I wouldn't have been surprised to know he was wearing wellies. He'd been out in his garden when we arrived, sorting out his pea trellis, he explained, only slightly apologetic for his dirty hands and tardiness.

He'd ushered us into his office, which was, he told us with pride, the parlour in bygone days, before disappearing to wash up and put the kettle on. I appreciated the fact that no business ever seemed to get done in Winkle without a comforting cup of tea. Mum had tutted impatiently but said nothing, after a warning glance from Dad. It was hard for her, she was so used to everything being done at a city-pace. Already, I much preferred Mr.Reed's office to that of the city solicitors who dealt with the odious terms of my living allowance and the other discomfiting details of my family's wealth. The slight smell of damp dog and pipe smoke felt real, and comforting. The source of the damp dog odour soon revealed itself in a rather aged spaniel who blinked sleepily from a basket by the fire where it thumped a plumed tail in greeting.

"Don't mind old Kip," said Mr.Reed, when he'd shown us into the room. "He's quite deaf, mostly blind and I'm not sure he knows where he is most days," He smiled affectionately at the old dog. "But he's happy enough in himself and never argues with me. That makes him grand company. Right, I'll just go and get washed and see if Mrs.Potts can rustle us up some tea."

"We're a bit short on time," said my mum, to his retreating back. "No need to bother with the tea…"

But he'd already gone and either didn't hear her, or chose to ignore her. I could see that Mr. Reed and I were going to get on famously.

"I beg your pardon?" said Mum, her mouth agape, "That can't be right."

She looked at Dad, who avoided her gaze. I could see he was trying not to smile.

My own silence was of the stunned variety.

"I don't know," said my dad, "That sounds right enough to me. My mother always told me that the cottage was passed down through the female line. I suppose if I'd been a girl, it would've come to me. I often wondered if I wasn't a small disappointment in that regard."

He smiled and winked at Mr. Reed who smiled in return. Neither one of them believed that, knowing how proud my Nan had been of her only son.

"But what on earth is Hazel supposed to do with it?" exclaimed Mum. "You know she can't possibly manage…"

Mr. Reed held up a hand.

"The stipulation is quite clear, Mrs. Price. The deed transfers to Hazel after she has lived in the cottage for exactly one year and one day. Under no circumstances is the cottage to be otherwise dealt with until such time has passed. Any alternate decisions are to be made only at Hazel's behest."

He paused, I think he might have been enjoying the look of righteous indignation on my mum's face, before adding,

"Remember now, in order to have the deed transfer, Hazel must live there. Herself. Alone."

"Alone?" exclaimed Mum, incredulous. "You can't possibly think that's a good idea! Rowan? Please, tell this man that our delicately healthed daughter cannot possibly be expected to live in that run-down hovel. On her own!"

Delicately healthed? Is that even a thing?

Not bothering to actually wait for my dad's input, she directed herself to Mr.Reed.

"Mr. Reed, you must understand that there are extenuating circumstances, things I'm sure my husband's mother neglected to take into account when she devised this ridiculous scheme."

I could feel her eyes on me. I was sitting, hardly daring to breathe, eyes downcast, torn between delight and confusion. She reached out a hand and patted my knee, then leaned forward in her chair.

"Hazel has had some...difficulties," she said, lowering her voice. "As a result, she finds it challenging to cope with certain everyday things and, having recently suffered a bit of a setback, she's even more delicate..."

"That's enough, Patricia," said Dad, standing up. He placed a gentle hand on my shoulder. "Hazel, love, can you give us a minute?"

I nodded, only too happy to leave the little office. I had a feeling of bitter resignation that there was probably some tiny loophole in the will that would yank it all cruelly away, my mother being the one who would do the yanking.

Closing the door quietly behind me, I made my way out into the garden. There was a little wooden bench near what might soon become a leek trench, so I sat myself down to reflect on what just transpired.

My first thought was that my dad obviously must have known this was going to happen. That had to be why he hadn't put a stop to my mother's big plans, knowing they'd all be for naught once the legalities had been made clear. My second thought was for my Nan, and that nearly reduced me to unsightly sobbing. She knew, all along, how I felt; how the promise of my visits with her were all that kept me going most days during the school year. I could never have articulated such a thing — I was too young and too unaware to understand how much my daily ability to cope with school, friends, my parents, depended upon knowing I could leave it all behind just as soon as the school term ended. When Mum had put a stop to my summer long visits when I was fifteen, ostensibly so that I could work for Dad's heritage foundation, it almost destroyed me. But I'd kept on going, getting on with life as best I could, because that's what you do, isn't it? All the while, I'd be dreaming of the day when I would make my way back to Winkle. We spoke on the phone every week and we regularly exchanged letters, there were day-visits — all of us — when we'd take her out for a drive and a pub lunch. But I was never allowed to stay with her again, though no-one would tell me why. Not the real reason, anyway. Mum insisted it was because I needed to focus on my studies and that I was old enough to do some volunteer work. Even Dad agreed that I should keep up my work for his foundation in the summers, to learn the value of having to earn a living. It was a devastating time for me, it felt like something very important had been cruelly excised from my world. Then, once I was an adult, life took over and hurtled me along at speeds that didn't leave much time for extended holidays in Winkle.

Something nudged my ankle. I looked down with a start to see a raggedy ginger cat rubbing himself against me. I reached down a hand to absently stroke his head. He had a large piece missing out of his left ear and a drooping eyelid. It made him look a bit like a pirate. His tail was slightly too short and had a kink at the very end.

"You're a bit of a wreck, aren't you?" I asked, chucking him under the chin. He purred loudly, a rasping sort of sound.

"Never mind, lovely boy, I'm sure you're..."

The cat's purr stopped abruptly and he flew across the leek trench in a single bound, dashing across the garden to clamber up the fence where he sat, crouched, his tail flicking back and forth.

"Aye, go on with you, you filthy beast," said a good-natured voice behind me. I turned to see Mr.Reed, his hands tucked neatly into his waistcoat.

"He knows he'll have my slipper 'round his arse if I catch him hanging about near the vegetable beds," he said, gesturing to the seat. I nodded and he sat down beside me.

He winked at my look of alarm.

"Don't worry, lass, it's never an attempt to actually harm the little sod. More of a futile response to his exasperating habits, and well he knows it. He takes no offense, I promise you, because he also knows I always have Mrs.Potts leave a saucer of cream and a bit of cooked fish for him at the back door."

I smiled, feeling immediately at home with him. He had such a grandfatherly air about him. I wondered if he'd ever married after he and my Nan parted ways.

"You know, I never found a lass I wanted to marry more than I wanted to marry your Nan," he said, as if having read my mind. "She was such a beauty, but not in the usual way and that made folk suspicious. Folk like to know things through and through, but nothing about that family, the McCorrigans, was typical and that didn't sit well. Such a good heart, she had. And a wild spirit."

He glanced at me, giving me a studied look.

"You favour her quite a bit."

I blushed, taking it as a great compliment.

"Anyway, I knew she wasn't for me, even from the start. I could never have hoped to be the one to tie her down to a regular life. Still, we had a grand time of it and we parted friends. But she spoiled me for the other lasses. None of them seemed to have the depth she had, that way she had about her, the way she saw the world. I would've walked over hot coals for Elsie McCorrigan, and even though she knew that, she never took advantage. Not like some might. So, in the end, I went off to study the law then came back here so I could at least be breathing the same air as her."

He chuckled.

"Eeeh, but that's just poetic foolishness, isn't it?"

"No," I said, my voice quiet. I looked over at the cat who remained on the fence, assuming an air of nonchalance. "That's just how I remember her."

I wanted to ask him why she wasn't for him. No-one ever mentioned my grandfather, my father's father. I'd assumed it was one of those situations that was considered the height of scandal back in those days, especially in a small village and I'd always been too keenly aware of causing embarrassment and upset to bring it up.

We sat quietly for a moment.

"I left your parents on their own to argue," he said, finally, giving me another wink. "At least, that's what I told them. But what I really wanted,"

He paused, rummaging in the pocket of his tweed jacket and withdrawing an ivory coloured envelope.

"What I really wanted was the opportunity to see you on your own. I know your mum means well, but I didn't want her to know I'd given you this."

He held out the envelope.

I saw on the front my Nan's familiar looping handwriting. My breath caught as I reached out and took it from him.

"What is it?" I asked, my voice wobbling.

He smiled.

"I can't rightly say, lass," he said. "Elsie wrote it her own self and gave it to me for safe-keeping. I was to give it to you once her will had been read. I think she had an inkling it might not go over well with your mother."

I smiled a watery smile.

"That's the understatement of the year," I said, folding up the envelope and putting it in my coat pocket. I would save it until I was home again.

Home.

I had to ask, despite being terrified of the answer.

"Did my mum..."

Mr. Reed leaned into me, tilting his head inwards.

"Even your old mum won't be able to wiggle out of it," he whispered. "Your Nan made me promise it would be iron-clad. I might be just a country solicitor, but I've got friends in high places. They looked it over and assured me it would hold."

I blinked away the tears, the accumulated tension of the day rushing through me. I gulped back another sob, this time of immense relief.

Mr. Reed squeezed my hand.

"It's all yours, pet. And never was there a more deserving soul. Do your Nan proud, aye?"

I nodded, speechless, wiping the sleeve of my coat across my face.

Mr.Reed stood up, sketched a courtly bow and held out his arm with a grin.

"Shall we return to the fray, my lady?"

"Penny for your thoughts," said Dad, glancing over at me. I sat, staring out of the passenger side window. It had just begun to rain, the wipers squeaked rhythmically across the windshield.

I shrugged, then turned to offer a him a quick smile.

"Not a good investment, I'm afraid," I replied.

He chuckled.

"I'm sure I'd be getting great value."

We drove on in silence for a few minutes more. Dad was giving me a lift back to the Fisher cottage so I could pick up Bracken.

"Am I a great disappointment?" I asked. "To you and Mum, I mean. I didn't manage very well in London and obviously the thing with Teddy and my....breakdown and now all this upset over the cottage...well, I just feel like I'm constantly letting you both down. I'm almost forty, for heaven's sake. Shouldn't I have my life together by now?"

Dad shot me a look, frowning, before setting his eyes back on the road. He took a deep breath.

"You could never, ever, be a disappointment to me, Hazel. Not ever."

He punctuated each word with emphatic feeling.

"But what about Mum? She seems to think I can't cope with the smallest things."

"Living out here on your own isn't really a small thing, Hazel. It isn't a small thing for anyone, much less a person like yourself."

"What kind of person would that be, then?" I said, turning in my seat to face my father, though to hear, from his own lips, that he considered me incompetent would have crushed me .

He rubbed a hand over his face.

"Sorry, love. That didn't come out very well,"

He glanced over at me again. In a fit of uncharacteristic challenge, I held his gaze until he shifted it back to the road. I closed my hand on the envelope in my pocket, drawing strength from it.

"Well," he said. "You can't deny that you're extraordinarily...sensitive. And you can be quite shy," he added. "Neither of which is bad, of course. It just makes things a bit more difficult for you. And those years with that rat-bastard Teddy...well, they've left some scars, haven't they? I suppose I just want to be sure you're feeling up to it, that's all."

I sighed and turned to face the front of the car.

"You're starting to sound like Mum," I said, deflated.

Dad put on the indicator and steered into the turn off for the Fisher's road. The car wound slowly down the narrow street, leafy fingers of the bordering hedge reaching out to brush against it as we drove.

"Why do you suppose Nan left me the cottage, with the stipulations being as they are? Other than to aggravate Mum, that is."

"I think," said Dad, speaking slowly and carefully, as he brought the car to a stop and turned off the engine. "That your Nan knew you better than any of us, and that she knew that not only could you cope just fine, but that you belong in Rookery Cottage."

I inhaled sharply.

"Do you think she's right?"

My dad nodded.

"And so does your mum. Which is why it terrifies her so much."

I declined Dad's offer for a lift back to Rookery Cottage. He'd come in, at their enthusiastic insistence, to visit with Alfie and Edie. After a restorative cup of tea and a ginger biscuit, I'd collected Bracken and started off for home. The rain had eased and, besides, I didn't mind getting wet. The gloom suited my pensive mood. Dad was to pick me up again in a few hours. The meeting with Mr. Reed had gone on longer than expected, thanks to the startling revelation and Mum's subsequent hysteria, so our lunch arrangements became dinner ones. I wanted nothing more than to close myself up into the cottage, *my* cottage, and not come out for at least a week.

Bracken had been delighted to see me, which made me feel a bit less rubbish. Dad had given me a knowing smile when I'd explained the situation surrounding her vagrancy, echoing everyone's thoughts that someone claiming her would be highly unlikely. I wished I could be so sure. I think there was still a part of me holding back from loving her entirely, to save myself from the heartache should she be taken away. If enough time passed, then I'd be less worried, I told myself.

We ambled off down the road toward the lane. Bracken was quite happy to trot along beside me, not showing much interest in doing the usual sniffy things that most dogs seem to do. Perhaps she sensed I wanted her close by. It was a great comfort, I found, to not be entirely alone with my turbulent thoughts.

The initial elation I felt at having been told that the cottage was mine, was subdued by the obvious trouble that the announcement was causing. Causing trouble is something I've avoided my entire life. I've always gone along to get along. Overall, it's made for a less upsetting, if slightly less satisfactory, way to live, especially when it comes to my mother. She's a person of firm opinions and I couldn't be more the opposite. Although, no, that's not entirely true, I suppose. I actually *do* have very definite ideas about things, but I'm never quite able to bring myself to be in opposition to people. Mum's obvious displeasure made it difficult to take complete joy in my newly revealed circumstances. Still, I thought, it was a measure of progress that I'd held my ground. Granted, it was a bit feeble and I'd had no real idea how I was going to work around her, but my convictions held up. I was cheered by this thought and it put me in a much lighter frame of mind by the time we reached the garden gate.

I was torn between reading Nan's letter right away and leaving it until I finished my social obligations for the day. If the contents were upsetting in any way, I wouldn't be able to hide it and Mum would be all over me, adding my emotional instability to her list of reasons why I wouldn't be able to cope living here on my own.

I stoked the fire and put the kettle on to boil. I'd had enough tea to float the Titanic already but the ritual of making it always soothes me and I felt in dire need of soothing. I propped the letter against the fruit bowl while I pottered about the kitchen, spooning tea into the pot and setting myself a mug on a tray.

I'd got into the habit of making myself a tea tray when I lived in London, much to the amusement of my friends. Well, I say *friends,* but they were only ever acquaintances, second-degree friends of Teddy's. I know they found me strange and awkward but as I came attached to Teddy they were obligated to include me. Looking back, I think I'd have preferred it if they hadn't. Anyway, making up a tea tray was an attempt to shield myself, it always brought a sense of home and comfort to an otherwise hostile and alien atmosphere.

I managed to find a tiny sliver of not-quite-stale apple-walnut loaf in the cake tin and put it on a plate, even though I wasn't hungry. Bracken followed my movements, already convinced she'd be getting the bit of cake, which she very likely was.

Once the kettle was boiled and the water poured into the pot, I carried the tray into the sitting room and put it on the low coffee table. I was just about to sit, when I decided to retrieve the envelope. I placed it on top of the stack of books which had made their way to the side of the sofa and then sat down. Bracken immediately jumped up beside me. I'd contemplated shooing her off, intending to train her to be mannerly and not a sofa-dweller. Then I remembered how well that worked on the subject of sleeping on the bed and simply shifted over so she'd have more room. I poured myself a mug of tea and leaned back into the yielding softness of the sofa cushions.

I was exhausted. Mentally and emotionally. I'd been running on fumes for the last few months — never really having had the opportunity to just stand back, gather my thoughts in peace and pull myself together. I blamed the chronic containment of my emotional outbursts on this ragged state. I'd been warned about that at Serenity Meadows. Apparently, over a lifetime of micro-traumas, I'd learned to tamp down my emotions rather than experience and process them properly. This confused me because I always felt – and was accused of being – very emotional. It seems that having them and allowing them are two different things.

I knew that if I could just have a break — time to settle in properly without any further agitation — then I'd stop acting like the ineffectual flake that I was becoming. I needed some time to digest things, sort out my feelings, to *allow* my feelings, instead of being hurtled from one thing to the next with barely a chance to get my bearings. But that wasn't likely to happen, not until my parents had gone home again at least. The upset of today aside, I was really glad they'd come to visit, though. I think I needed that connection to home and familiar things to anchor myself here, to reorient myself from the fast-paced and superficial world of my life in London, to this new way of being. Staying with Mum and Dad after I left Serenity Meadows felt liminal, transitory, and I never really settled in there either; I felt like I'd been in a strange emotional limbo since everything fell apart and I was craving certainty and steadiness. I decided then and there that I wasn't going to open Nan's letter until my parents had gone home. I wanted to enjoy every minute of time that I had with them.

I felt much better having made that decision. I got up and put the envelope behind the carved-coal pit pony, a souvenir from a school trip to Beamish that I'd given to Nan one Christmas, that lived on the mantle. There it would stay until at least Monday. Then I curled back up on the sofa. Bracken nestled into the crook of my knees and I pulled the tartan rug around us, telling myself I'd just rest my eyes for a half hour before I got up and put myself together for dinner. The tea would go cold, but it had already served its purpose.

Chapter Ten

T he rest of the weekend passed without undue incident, just as I'd hoped. Mum only came into the cottage very briefly, long enough to wrinkle her nose at some perceived unpleasant odour, frown down at Bracken and advise me on what sort of curtains would look best in the kitchen window. Considering I'd thought to leave the window without curtains, so as not to block the lovely view of the garden, I took the recommendation without comment. Although the atmosphere was somewhat frosty at first, once we drove into town and began our shopping, she returned to her former self. Nothing made Mum happier than shopping and she even made helpful suggestions about having someone come and check the roof and gutters before winter rolled around again. I was cautiously optimistic that meant she'd come to terms with my staying there. At least for the year and day required by the will. I was under no illusions that she'd given up the fight, but I was happy to settle into unspoken disagreement if only to avoid further argument and upset.

I was eventually able to relax and we spent a few companionable hours poking around in little shops and boutiques. I bought Bracken a lovely hand-tooled leather collar and matching lead and some gourmet biscuits. Mum refrained from pointing out that it was entirely possible I wouldn't be keeping her but her pained expression spoke volumes. I considered that great progress, although allowed that Dad must have had a word with her. Mum had the uncommon ability to target my deepest fears and drag them to the light, usually with a sensible outlook attached. Always well-meant, but never very helpful. Who likes to have the painful and obvious pointed out? So the relief at their departure on Sunday evening was bittersweet. I was looking forward to getting back to my settling in, but would miss the comfort of their familiarity. Not to mention the lovely pub lunches.

"Right," said Dad, from the other side of the garden gate. They'd dropped by on their way out with some bags of shopping. Just to keep me going, according to Mum, who was convinced I lived solely on tea and toast. She wasn't far wrong. "You'll give us a ring if you need anything?"

I nodded, my hand on Bracken's head. She stood, wagging her tail expectantly. Dad had been very free with the gourmet biscuits. I think she felt quite smart in her new collar as she had developed a bit of a swing to her wagging since I'd buckled it around her neck. Having moved on from a frightened tail-tip spasm to proper full-on bum-wiggling tail-wave, she seemed quite recovered from the trauma of her run across the moor.

"I'll be fine, really," I said, actually believing it. "You needn't worry about a thing."

He smiled and leaned across the gate to kiss me on the cheek.

"I know, love. I know. But your mum..."

He didn't bother to finish the sentence. We both shrugged at exactly the same time and then giggled.

"I know. I'll phone anyway, just so she feels needed."

He grinned.

"That's a good lass. Now, I'm going to be in France next week and then I'm off to Berlin but don't hesitate to leave a message with Mrs.Foxworth, she'll get it to me wherever I am."

I nodded again. Mrs.Foxworth was Dad's secretary. She was a formidable force of efficiency and organization. Even Mum was afraid of her.

"I'll be fine," I repeated. "I've got Edie and Alfie in the village and a magnificent guard dog to keep me safe from marauding sheep."

Bracken whined and pressed herself against me.

We laughed again and he turned to go back to the car. Mum waved and blew a kiss from the passenger seat and then they were off.

I walked back up the garden path in the early evening light. I fancied there was a tiny hint of warmth in the air that hadn't been there last week and the buds on the hawthorn were getting more and more full. The hazel catkins in the hedge looked like faery chandeliers. I'd actually thought that's what they were when I was small, no doubt Nan told me so. Naturally, I'd believed her. Who wouldn't want to believe that the Wee Folk threw great parties in the hedge at night, strewing catkins and cobwebs like streamers and lights, gilding it all with crystal dew drops?

I sighed and hugged my arms around myself.

"Alone at last, eh girl?" I said to Bracken who wriggled amiably. "What shall we do first, a nice hot bath or a cup of tea and slice of toast? Or, I think I saw a packet of Hob Nobs in one of the shopping bags?"

Her whiskery face smiled up at me in benign agreeableness; she would be happy with any and all of the options. Laughing, I made an executive decision and went upstairs to run myself a bath.

Feeling clean and cozy in my new favourite pair of Cath Kidston flannel pajamas and my old favourite blue cardigan, I tucked myself and Bracken under the blanket on the sofa. The fire crackled happily and with only one lamp lit, the atmosphere in the sitting room was the warmest and most inviting as I'd felt it to be so far.

"Maybe we're starting to make it feel lived in again," I said to Bracken, noting with a twinge of alarm that chatting out loud to the dog was becoming something of a habit.

I had a mug of tea cupped in my hands, following on from a light supper of baked beans on toast with a plate of Hob Nobs sitting on the coffee table to finish. Nan's letter lay, unopened, underneath it.

I nibbled at a deliciously oaty, chocolate-topped biscuit and contemplated the letter. The sensible thing would have been to open it up and read it, but having put it off for so long, it had taken on a menace of its own.

Maybe it was a warning to me, telling me about the many problems I'd likely face in the cottage – leaking roof and a temperamental boiler. Maybe the villagers would be hostile – if Mrs. Trout was anything to go by it was an entirely rational worry. Or perhaps it was about a roving band of vandals – I was thinking of Astrid and her fellow miscreants – who would chuck empty beer cans into the garden and rampage through the vegetables. Then there was the mild terror of the stone shed being a haven for vagrants. My worst fear, though, was that she would encourage me to leave after the year and day was up. She'd always had a penchant for the old tales, where the heroine would be set an impossible task which was to last a year and a day, in which much would be learned, trials would be faced and adversity overcome, only to release the imperilled person at the end, to go on with normal life. Albeit stronger, wiser and more enlightened. I was afraid that this was Nan's idea of a test; hat I would face the challenges of living here alone only to be expected to set off into the real world again, healed of my wounds and character flaws and ready to behave like a normal person.

Except I didn't want to be a normal person. I saw nothing wrong with wanting to live a quiet life in a tiny cottage in a remote corner of the country. I could think of no better company than the birds and flowers and, apparently, a scruffy little dog who was possibly just as much a misfit as I was. I could never understand, nor relate in any useful way, to the idea that everyone should be busy and striving and accomplishing great things. In my mind, I could accomplish quite enough in my own quiet way.

I had it all planned out: there was no reason I couldn't carry on my work for Dad's foundation from the cottage. I was really just a paper-pusher anyway and I could just as easily write the letters and go through the various applications from the comfort and sanctuary of the tartan sofa. Obviously, I could write my books from anywhere. In the meanwhile, there was the garden to tend and I thought about having a little chicken coop built. I would plant a cut-flower patch and perhaps think about bee hives. The possibilities were of endless delight.

Sighing, I reached over and picked up the envelope.

"Might as well get it over with, eh?"

Bracken squirmed her agreement, her eyebrows waggling hopefully at the last Hob Nob.

"Chocolate isn't good for dogs," I warned her, breaking a tiny corner off the biscuit. "Here, just a crumb. Don't blame me if it upsets your digestion."

I tore open the envelope. The paper was that delicate, almost transparent kind that used to be called airmail paper. But instead of airmail blue, it was a soft bone colour, with a tiny gold edge trim. There was a faint watermark that might have been a thistle. It smelled a tiny bit musty, but with a strong overtone of lemon. Everything of Nan's seemed to smell like a combination of wood smoke and lemons. I felt the breath catch in my throat as I looked at her familiar looping handwriting. Even well into her eighties, she never had that cramped and shaky old-lady handwriting; it was as free and smooth as it had ever been. It was dated over a year ago, in the January before her health started failing.

My dearest Hazel,

If you're reading this then I'm no longer of this world, quite happily ensconced in the next. The doctor has just left and has told your Da to make arrangements to move me into the nursing home in Westham. I take that to mean the prognosis isn't good. I always thought I would stay here in Rookery Cottage until my last breath, but, if I'm honest, I'll be glad to go into the home when the time comes. It's getting far too hard to take care of the things that need taking care of and I'll welcome the respite from all that beckons by staying here. Because indeed, what's involved in living at Rookery Cottage is far more than a person might imagine, and definitely more than most people know. Your Da knows, since he grew up here, and I suspect, from the way she acts around me and how she made sure to stop your stays here, so does your Mam. I don't blame her, though.

She's only doing what any loving mother would do. She wants to protect he r child.

Do you remember the stories I used to tell you when you were just a wee thing? The stories about houses that were alive, that cared for the folk who lived in them? Sometimes those houses were trees and sometimes they were charcoal burner's huts in the Wildwood. I remember you loved them. I remember you carried your tatty old copy of The Secret Garden with you everywhere and how you asked me when you were 7 years old if you "might have a bit of earth".

I smiled at the memory of this. I still had that old copy tucked on my bookshelf. I re-read it at least once a year until I moved to London. I love Mary Lennox. I understand how she felt at the beginning of the book – lost and disoriented, not to mention petulant and bad-tempered. I was always cheering her on. I had wished with all my heart to have a best friend named Dickon; a wild boy who would show me badger setts and tell me the names of birds. I used to stand at the bottom of the garden path, right near the gate, looking hopefully down the lane in case such a person might stroll past. Much to my delight, someone eventually did. I glanced at Bracken and reached out a hand to smooth her wiry fur. It was unfortunate that someone hadn't held onto his Dickon-ness.

Shaking off the thought, I remembered the stories she was referring to. My favourite had been the one where the house was built into the trunk of an immense beech tree. The little woman who lived there was charged with stopping the woodsman from chopping it down and in return, the tree would shelter her and, by magic of course, make sure that her pantry was never empty.

You'll know, of course, that your Da and I never spoke much of your grandad, of your father's father. I suppose you were far too polite to ask, that's always been your way. Too polite for your own good, sometimes, I fear. So much so that you've let folk run roughshod over you. Anyway, he wasn't spoken of because of the usual scandalous reasons, but I suppose, even nowadays, it might still be thought of as outrageous just the same. Most folk, if they knew, would consider it an elaborate tale, meant to cover up the more common sort of scandal that was far easier to believe. That's why it wasn't something we spoke of - not because of our own shame, but because of things being the way they are and there not being anything to be gained from trying to turn people's minds on certain subjects. Anyway, it's been this way for generations of McCorrigan women and gradually folk just stopped questioning it. Never mind the details though, they stopped being important the moment I knew I was carrying your Da. What is important, though, the only thing that will really matter for the purpose of this letter, is that your Da being born a boy marked the end of a generations-long agreement between our family and the Otherworld.

I almost choked on my mouthful of tea. Coughing and spluttering, I had to put my mug down before it spilled everywhere. The sudden movement made Bracken leap off the sofa with a yelp and she ran to hide under the kitchen table. A log spat and crackled in the fireplace, adding to her trauma.

Suddenly, I felt a pang of regret, of something like disappointment. My heart sank and I could feel the tears prickling behind my eyes. The letter was just rambling nonsense. I thought it was going to be instructions of some sort, or maybe her recipe for blackcurrant jam. Nan must have been losing her wits when she wrote it. I remember one of my visits where she seemed to be drifting in and out of reality. It had been difficult to see her like that, and at the same time she seemed content, peaceful. Wherever she'd gone to in her mind, it was a happy place with good memories.

"Come back here you silly goose," I said to Bracken, patting the sofa beside me. "I promise not to spray tea on you. I just had a bit of a shock."

She wiggled the tip of her tail but remained under the table.

"Suit yourself," I said, pretending not to care. I took a deep breath and went back to the letter.

Now I know what you're thinking, that the silly old bat has lost her marbles! And well you may be right. As soon as I leave the boundaries of Rookery Cottage, I'll begin to deteriorate more quickly. I know this, but I'm at peace with it. I'm tired and it's time to pass on the tenancy to the next in line. So I'm asking you to consider all I'm saying here with an open mind and an open heart. I'm counting on the fact you still carry the ability to believe the impossible, that the world hasn't stolen it from y ou.

Your mam stopped your visits here so that I wouldn't tell you any of this, to prevent you from following in the McCorrigan footsteps. As it was, she made me promise not to fill your head with "foolish notions", as she called them, when you were little. I had to respect her wishes, even though I didn't agree, because you must never get between a mother and her only child. Still, I tried to get around that promise with my little stories. I wanted to plant the seeds of magic in your heart.

You see, my darling girl, Rookery Cottage is more than just a house. It's a living, breathing part of the landscape. These are ancient lands under your feet. It's also home to races as old as the earth Herself, folk who have been here since long before the first human settlers. Many, many, many generations ago, the McCorrigan women made a pledge of caretaking to this bit of earth, in return for the shelter and gifts of abundance that the Old Ones could offer. There were times in every McCorrigan woman's life when she needed sanctuary – and so that's where we all went, in our turn – to spend some time in the Otherworld, learning what we needed to know to take care of this land and all who dwell here. Most of the time, we came back with the greatest gift of all.

Your Da made that journey too, when he was a young lad. He learned his talent of building from them. He learned to work in harmony with wood and stone, to coax the natural strengths of the materials rather than just hammering and chiseling it into place. When he left there, to make his way in the world, the door to the Otherworld closed behind him. What happened is between him and the Old Ones. I didn't ask and he didn't offer. But it was bound to end, because, as my son, he would never have been expected to live here — the Caretakers have always been women. That was the way. That is the way.

I worry, my dear, that the march of time will be unkind to this place. To leave it unprotected fills me with dread. Folk aren't so dependent upon the land like they used to be, or at least, they believe they aren't. The motivation to keep it safe is much less. If a person isn't at the mercy of nature to provide, they tend to treat her with less respect. Which is foolishness of course, and wrong thinking. Even the city-dwellers are dependent upon nature. But because they don't live it, they don't believe it

Which brings me to the reason for this letter. You will know, by now, the contents of my will. Hamish Reed has been a good friend to me all these years, and he'll make sure to uphold my wishes, even against those who would have it another way. (of course you know I'm talking about your mother!). Believe me when I tell you, my brave, brave, Hazel, that I know without a doubt that you are more than capable of becoming a Caretaker. All that's needed is a good heart and a belief in the magic of ordinary things. These two, you have in great quantity. You may think that life has drummed the magic out of you, but the spark of it never truly dies. It may fade to a tiny glimmer, but in you, I know it's strong.

I had to pause to fish my handkerchief out of my cardigan pocket. Tears streamed unchecked down my cheeks and an unseemly amount of them ran out of my nose. Bracken whined from under the table and slithered out to crawl up onto the sofa. She shoved her muzzle under my elbow and rested her chin on my knee. Her eyebrows trembled and a shiver ran through her thin body. I pulled the blanket out from underneath her and tucked it in around us both.

It was just too much.

Nan's words had unleashed a flood of memory; remembrances of a childhood spent living in other worlds, worlds from books and my imagination. I remembered the little plates of bread and honey we'd leave out on the back step, the posies of wildflowers, and sometimes, on special days, a thimble full of whiskey from the old, dusty bottle from the cupboard under the sink.

How had I forgotten? When did I stop believing that it was real? I can't think of a particular incident. Perhaps it was growing up, seeing and hearing the things that people around me said, the way my class-mates dismissed it as something only "babies" believed in. I learned, as I so often did, to take my cues from other people. I didn't ever want to appear to be foolish, to become more of a target, so, somewhere along the way I think I made the decision to pack the magic away, like mementos from another time. I thought it was something you grew out of, and the rest of the world seemed to support that theory.

I blew my nose.

Your Da was the last of the McCorrigan line. He wasn't a girl – obviously! – so the original pact was dissolved. But as far as I can see, the only thing that changes is that now, the role of Caretaker is one of choice, not of obligation. Which means that no-one — human or otherwise — has any claim to you. No creature can compel you to take this on. Remember that, whatever happens!

It's not something to be entered into lightly, Hazel, my love. I say that because I know you'll want to leap at the chance and at the same time doubt that you're able. I know your heart and I know the world is, by and large, unkind to a person such as yourself. It has difficulty understanding quiet hearts and the desire for solitude, because so much of it is run on loud voices and fast movements. To be able to hide away here will be very tempting. What you'll find, though, is that you won't be able to hide. Not really. That is why I asked that you stay only for a year and a day. That will be ample time for you to make your choice. There are arrangements in place to support you — but the choice remains yours. At the end of the year and day, you can decide what happens next.

Now don't fret if it comes to you that it's not what you want! I realize my asking this of you seems an obligation of its own variety, but that's not my intent. The land will persevere, no matter what. It will be altered, perhaps irreversibly, but it will endure. So don't let it weigh too heavily on your conscience. To have you in a place of Caretaking, though, will ensure that it thrives. It's no exaggeration to say that much depends upon i t.

I'll leave you now, to ponder all I've told you. I only wish I had the chance to explain it to you in person, to answer all the questions I'm sure you have, but your mother was insistent. There are so many other things I wish I could tell you, but time and experience will have to be the one to do that. If I'd been a braver soul, I would have defied your Mam, but for the sake of peace, I let it be. Perhaps that was a mistake. Perhaps that will cost this piece of earth its stewardship. I didn't ever pretend to have all of the answers, I just did the best I could at any given moment. I held fast to the knowledge that the thread of magic was woven tightly into your bright soul and so I have to trust that the spirits of this place will forgive me my human frailties.

Be well, my darling, darling girl. And know that your Nan has always loved you – every bit of you — with all of her heart and soul. You were the light of my days as only your dear Da was before you. I won't ever be far away, so do not grieve my absence.

All of my love, Nan xx

ps. If Hamish's ginger cat comes to call, let him in.

pps. I'm sure you already know this, but you have good friends and allies in Edie, Alfie and Hamish. They Know. xx

I sat for a quiet moment, the letter trembling in my shaking hands. The fire hissed and Bracken flinched, burrowing deeper under the blanket. Absently, I put a hand out and rested it on her back.

Suddenly, I had a sudden twinge of paranoia. My strange friend from the bottom of the garden crept back into my conscious mind. The trouble was, Nan hadn't really left me any clear directions on how I was supposed to go about this caretaking business. Was I just supposed to keep the cottage and the garden in good order? That seemed to cover my own definition of caretaking. Were there particular duties I had to uphold – things I was supposed to plant, things I wasn't supposed to plant? Was a chicken coop out of the question? What would happen if I didn't uphold these duties, not because I didn't want to, but because I just didn't know about them? That made me a bit panicky. I wasn't very good when I didn't know what was expected of me, particularly when there *was* something expected of me. I preferred to have everything laid out in a neat, orderly, way. Like a checklist I could tick off every day. How could Nan have ever reasonably thought I'd be fit for this job? It was no wonder the cottage had felt so cold and distant, it must have instantly recognized me for a clueless git.

"Oh, Bracken," I groaned, setting the letter on the table. "Why do I do this to myself?"

Thanks to my panic-mongering brain, in a span of five minutes pondering, all that had felt like a dream come true, started to feel like a complete nightmare. One way or another, my vision of a peaceful, quiet life breathed its last.

I glanced at the clock on the mantelpiece. It was after eight o'clock. I couldn't possibly phone over to Edie and Alfie. Nor could I bother Hamish. I had so many questions!

Suddenly, a crash from the vicinity of the kitchen sent both Bracken and I hurtling off the sofa. Bracken immediately tried to wedge herself under the armchair opposite. I found myself standing with my back to the chair, reaching down for the poker that was propped against the hearth. There came another sound, like scratching against the window. My heart was now lodged firmly in my mouth. Surely, there was some foul denizen of the Otherworld trying to gain access to the cottage. Perhaps word had already got out about my raging incompetence – the little man! I knew it! He'd passed on word that I was a witless numpty. I wracked my brain for any magical, otherworldly lore I could remember from Nan's stories. Oh! Surely there was some rule about crossing thresholds! That was it! It couldn't come in unless invited. Or was that just vampires?

Bracken whined, quite unhelpfully.

"If you were a dog of any use whatsoever," I whispered balefully, "you would be barking and slavering and making all manner of terrifying fuss."

Her response was merely to tremble violently.

"Excellent," I muttered. "Good to know I can depend upon your assistance."

Gripping the poker tightly in my hand, noting happily that it was more than likely made of iron, I advanced towards the darkened kitchen. I cursed my penchant for mood lighting, wishing I'd left a light on.

"Hello?" I called, trying to sound bold and confident. "Is anyone there?"

An increase in the scrabbling noise came as an answer.

"I shan't let you in until I know of your intentions," I said, feeling I should allow for the possibility of it being a benign visitor. I wouldn't want to get off on the wrong foot.

I lunged quickly for the safety of the wall and began to shuffle along it, keeping my back pressed against it like I'd seen police personnel do on television. I inched my way closer, holding the poker horizontally, ready to stab or swing as the need arose. I slid my other hand up the wall until I felt the light switch. In one dramatic gesture, I flipped the switch and leapt into position, my feet spread wide and the poker held up like a great sword.

The light in the kitchen flickered on in an unsatisfactory way. It was hardly the blast of illumination and surprise I'd been hoping for. I glanced quickly around the kitchen but saw nothing amiss. Movement at the window caught my eye and I had to strongly resist the urge to run back to the relative safety of the sofa. An orangey sort of blur seemed to be moving around on the outside sill. I remembered the stack of empty clay plant pots that had been sitting there. That would explain the crash. What was it? A ball of malevolent energy? Some sort of spell-cloud?

I slowly advanced to take a closer look. I would have felt much braver if Bracken had been beside me but she was still vibrating violently under the armchair. I took a moment to consider the value of getting an additional dog, one that was more suited to interactions with potentially hostile magical beings. I conceded that it might be difficult to find such a creature.

Ever so carefully, I crossed over the flagstones towards the sink. The window was right above it, set into a deep sill where Nan had kept pots of kitchen herbs and jars of flowers. The orange smudge appeared to be weaving itself back and forth along the outside sill, pausing every rotation or so to scrabble against the window.

"Oh for heaven's sake!" I said, lowering the poker. I leaned over the sink and unlatched the window.

A loud meow, full of reproach, came through the open window, followed closely behind by a raggedy orange cat.

Chapter Eleven

I spent the next few days putting the finishing touches to my tidying and sorting in the cottage. As I hadn't really added too many of my own things, other than books and some dishes and linens, there wasn't much left for me to do. Besides, every time I had tried to replace a picture with one of my own or add a knick-knack, something would go awry. The pictures would never seem to sit straight on the wall, no matter how much I fiddled with them and my few oddments had the strange habit of falling off the edge of things and breaking.

After the last decorative vase came crashing to the floor I gave up.

"Fine!" I said, to the air. "I get it. You don't like my things. It doesn't matter anyway, come to think of it. I never much liked that stuff either."

It was true. Given the choice, I wouldn't have had anything different to what was already in the cottage. Simple, rustic and everything had a purpose. Even the botanical illustrations were instructive. The only picture that seemed out of place was the painting that hung over the mantle. It was of a herd of black horses, galloping out of the foaming surf. They had a sort of menace to them, with their flashing eyes and bared teeth, not quite the benign ponies of my own experience. I'd always been slightly terrified of that painting. I was convinced, as a child, that the horses would come alive and leap out of the painting to devour me. I would avoid looking at it or lingering by the hearth. No matter how chilled I might have been from playing out in the garden or walking on the moor with Nan, I would refuse to sit and warm myself too closely to the fire. It still made me a bit uneasy but I wouldn't dare take it down and so simply avoided looking at it after dark.

As I settled into the rhythm of my days, Hamish's orange cat made himself quite at home, much to Bracken's disappointment. He claimed the hearth rug with nothing more than a venomous glare to which Bracken meekly submitted. He had a disconcerting habit of popping up, seemingly out of nowhere, demanding saucers of milk or the crusts of my toast. That last was a point of contention with Bracken, who had previously been the recipient of such bounty. The cat seemed to prefer blackberry jam to marmalade – which was Bracken's favourite – so I made sure to alternate my breakfasts.

"Aren't you ever going home?" I asked him, as, without warning, he jumped up onto the bench beside the sink, making me drop a soapy dish onto the draining board with an alarming clatter. His answer was his strange yodelling meow. He really was a very unattractive creature and given how he upset Bracken, I wasn't entirely happy that he'd decided to stay. But, Nan had said I was to let him in, so in he came. Each time that I let him out, I hoped he wouldn't come back. But like the cat in the song, he always did.

After the first couple of weeks, where every day seemed like an exercise in organized chaos, things had finally settled into a comfortable rhythm. I woke early, usually to the sound of birdsong and worked steadily and quietly, content in my own company and Bracken's with very few interruptions. I was starting to think that, despite my initial misgivings, that life could be peaceful and quiet after all. Even the prospect of being Caretaker seemed a reasonable option, given that no-one actually seemed to be demanding anything of me. I chalked my previous worries and mild hysteria up to overtiredness and emotional strain.

I met two more of Winkle's occupants – the postman (Colin) and a delightfully odd character (Wendell) who was advertising his services as chimney sweep and taxi driver. This last service was more of a driver-for-hire situation rather than an actual taxi service as there wasn't a lot of call for it, or so he said. He specialized in lifts to and from the train station and jaunts into Westham "for the bigger variety of shopping". The bus service had been reduced to only twice weekly, much to the dismay of the residents of Winkle, though at least the train was still running. Albeit not as often. I had all of this information relayed to me in a rambling flow of dialogue, punctuated by eye-opening expletives and pauses to spit tobacco juice into a cracked china teacup. I was mesmerized the entire time he was speaking. He looked like a cross between Del-boy and one of the fellows from Last of the Summer Wine. Marvellous stuff. I immediately went indoors and jotted down some notes to use as a possible character outline.

I spoke to Edie and Roger most days, checking in by telephone so as to assure them both I was still in possession of my sanity (and had plenty to eat) and had my daily visits from Young Craig with the milk and Colin with the post, so I wasn't entirely cut off from civilization.

But the relative solitude was doing me a world of good and I felt myself unwinding a little more each day.

One morning, after seeing Colin through the kitchen window, I wandered out to collect the post from him directly, rather than hiding until he'd put it through the letterbox. (Sometimes, you just can't face having a conversation). He was a lovely man, unusually taciturn for a Winkle resident, so I knew I wouldn't get trapped in a lengthy exchange. Plus, I had a birthday card to send to Mrs. Foxworth and wanted to avoid having to go into the village.

"Lovely morning, Colin," I said, handing him the card, "Could you drop this in the box for me, please?"

He smiled shyly and nodded, tucking it into his satchel. He handed over a large brown envelope and a couple of smaller ones. I winced as I saw the return address on the larger envelope.

"Nothing amiss, I hope," said Colin, no doubt seeing the grimace on my face. "'Tis too grand a day to be weighed down with worries."

"No, nothing too terrible," I said, "just some paperwork I've been avoiding, that's all."

Colin nodded.

"Aye, well then. Best not put it off any longer, eh? These things have a way of following you around."

He gave another sage nod and ambled back off down the path, pausing to smooth holly leaf through his fingers before opening the gate and heading down the lane.

The wisdom of posties.

He was right, though. I wasn't going to get any peace from it so I may as well face it head on.

I settled myself at the kitchen table with a fresh mug of tea and one of Edie's rock buns, the wheels of executive function best greased with tasty refreshments.

After a few sips and several bites of crumbly bun, I slit open the envelope. Inside was a thick stack of paper and a smaller folded sheet. I set the stack aside, and opened up the single paper.

Rhonda's handwriting was barely legible — long, looping strokes with words that ran together and she always chose a particular shade of green ink that looked as if her pen were perpetually on the brink of running out. After much squinting and puzzling, I got the gist of the message. It wasn't something I didn't already know; she was enclosing a publisher's proposal that she wanted me to read, sign and return to her as quickly as possible. The sooner I indicated my interest, the proper contracts could be drawn up. I glanced briefly at the papers and got up from the table to go and stand at the kitchen window, my thoughts racing.

It was exactly what I was expecting and everything that I was dreading: a five book deal with a very generous advance and full marketing and publicity support. It was an absolute dream, really. Unless, of course, it wasn't.

I started writing novels quite by accident. Roger had done the flowers for a photo shoot for a popular bridal magazine and he'd brought several copies of it into the shop to put on display. Over our tea break, we were flipping through and marvelling at the sheer excess of it all when he noticed an advert for a writing contest. It being a bridal magazine, they were looking for proposal stories –The Most Romantic Proposal Ever. As a joke, Roger suggested that, seeing as I was a great fan of Jane Austen, I should whip up something from the Regency era. Without really thinking about it, I did. Quite unexpectedly, not only did I win the contest (£250 and a spa weekend, neither of which I really wanted) but I caught the attention of Rhonda, who became my literary agent. Next thing I knew, I was writing books. And they were selling. Quite well.

Now I'm never going to disparage any story with a roguishly handsome, lace-at-his-throat Byronic hero and a repressed-but-fiery and scandalously independent heroine, but I can only take so many heaving bosoms and mud-spattered breeches before I get a bit bored. The stories were great fun to write, until they weren't, and the idea of committing to five more along the same lines filled me with dread. And also shame and guilt, because wasn't I just being handed every author's dream?

If someone were to ask me, and if I were to answer them honestly, I'd tell them I wanted to write children's books. I would write fantasy and faery tales and stories with plucky girls and their faithful companions, both two and four-legged. But it seems that's not what people wanted from me and the idea of walking away from guaranteed success into very possible failure wasn't something I felt up to, given the recent upheavals in my life. Unfortunately, I didn't feel like facing another five bodice rippers, either.

I groaned and poured the dregs of my tea down the sink. Bracken, hearing me stirring, got up from her spot on the sofa and padded over, eyebrows waggling in a hopeful way.

"A walk? Yes, I think that's just what we need. Nothing clears the head like a brisk walk. After all, I opened the envelope which is a start. I'm sure even Colin would agree that these things ought not to be rushed. He strikes me as the long-thinking type."

The next morning, after a leisurely breakfast of tea and toast (marmalade, to make up to Bracken for the cat), I looked around the kitchen and living room and declared myself finally content with the state of things indoors. It was a bright spring-ish sort of morning so after I'd washed up, I bundled myself into coat and wellies and made my way outside to take an inventory of what needed doing in the garden. Bracken trotted after me in the slightly skulking sort of movement that she'd adopted since the cat had started his visits. In addition to jumping out at me, he liked to do the same to Bracken, usually delivering a swat on her nose for good measure.

"You really are the most cowardly of creatures, Bracken," I said, fondling her ears. "You're three times his size. I'm sure that if you just gave him what for, he'd never bother you again."

She whined and pressed herself closer.

"Oh for heaven's sake, relax. He's not even here. Maybe he's gone back to bother Mr. Reed by now."

The mid-morning sun was warm on my face as I stood surveying the garden. I wore Nan's old blue denim coat that she always wore when she gardened, over my flowered apron and a thick green woollen jumper. It was one I'd knitted several years ago, whilst trying to cope with the stress of London life and it was sturdy enough to keep off the chill. With my hair tied back under a hunting print scarf and my black wellingtons on, I was the epitome of country fashion. At least, if you accepted the image portrayed of Queen Elizabeth at Balmoral, circa the 1970's. Nevertheless, I was comfortable and it made me feel equipped to tackle the trials ahead.

And trials indeed they would be. Nothing much had been done to put the gardens to bed last autumn and the tired remains of last summer's peas still hung limply on their sagging bamboo teepees. The currant bushes were wildly out of control and I couldn't remember whether it was better to prune them in spring or autumn. The rhubarb bed was a mass of dead vegetation and an incursion of mint, which seemed to have burst loose from the confines of the old stone sink that Nan had sunk into the soil. The more I looked around, the more certain I was that the garden hadn't had proper, vigorous attention for the past few years. I knew Alfie had done a bit of work on occasion and, apparently, so had Astrid and her fellow hoodlums, but the truth of it was, Nan didn't really like other people in her garden. Similarly to how some people consider their kitchen as off-limits to interlopers, that's how Nan viewed her garden. You were welcome to come and visit it, and to reap the bounty of it, but I think she preferred to do the actual tending of it herself. The exception, I think, was me. She'd given me my 'bit of earth' when I'd asked for it, and encouraged me to do things on my own, even when I was obviously making a mess it. A metaphor for life, I suppose. I remember trying to grow a tree from seeds I'd saved from a Christmas clementine. She never once tried to tell me I hadn't a chance with it, but commiserated with cups of tea and slices of lemon drizzle cake when it became clear to me it wasn't going to work. I realized, later on, that she'd given me the gift of making my own mistakes which wasn't something I was allowed to do at home. Far better to make a small mistake early, than a bigger one, later on.

I could feel myself drifting into a place of not necessarily helpful memories, so I gave myself a shake and decided to go and take inventory of the garden tools. In the face of such an immense task, it seemed like a reasonable place to start.

As I've said, there are two sheds at the bottom of the garden. The larger one, where I'd stashed all of my excess boxes is the sturdier of the two. The smaller one, the one which I'd been avoiding looking at, for Obvious Reasons, had been built at the same time as the cottage and was made of local stone. The mortar had crumbled in places, eased from between the stones by fingers of ivy or some other clinging vine, which had long been cut away, and so had the air of being slightly off-centre, leaning ever so gently to the left. It had been that way for as long as I could remember. Nan always warned me against going in there, lest it suddenly decide to give up it's war on gravity and collapse. I'd certainly never questioned it, because that was the sort of child I was, and so always gave it a wide berth, convinced it was going to come crashing down if I dared even disturb the air around it. Looking back, knowing what I know now, she was clearly warning me off it for quite different reasons. I still made a concerted effort to not look at it as I cast my eye over the other shed, realizing that if I wanted a chicken coop, it would have to be built separately as I had no other options for storing my boxes of unwanted things. Well, other than disposing of them, I suppose. One trip to the charity shop would take care of it, but I wasn't sure I was quite mentally or emotionally there yet.

I rummaged about in the larger shed, unearthing a few more plant pots, a spade, a fork and a collection of trowels. The spade and fork seemed to be in very good repair - they each had a stamp on the base of the handle, that looked to have been burned into the wood. I peered closely at it, but it was worn from years of use. It must have been the manufacturer's mark. Considering the weight of them, and Nan's penchant for keeping things forever, they'd probably been made in the village forge - which is to say, when it was an actual forge and not The Forge. Satisfied that I had at least enough to get started, I wandered back out into the garden.

Looking at it from that vantage point, the sheer enormity of what lay ahead made me wobble again, ever so slightly. What had I been thinking? Never mind, I told myself, sternly, you can always ask Alfie to find someone to give you a hand with the heavy bits. Surely there'd be some sturdy fellow in the village that would be happy with a few hours of work. Desperate for a distraction, I turned my attention back to the little stone shed. In a fit of utter madness, I was seized by the sudden impulse to look inside. After all, if I was going to take on this Caretaking lark, surely I needed to know what lurked in the wonky old building.

I fought my way through a snarl of rogue brambles, which seemed to have infiltrated through from the hedge on the other side of the wall. I'd have to have them trimmed back, I thought, as I pulled my skirt free from the clutches of a particularly intrusive spray of thorns. The little door had been painted a bright blue at some point, although now it was faded and peeling. It was set, crookedly, in the frame and seemed to be held in place by nothing but the generosity of the sagging lintel. I couldn't see any hinges or even a latch. It was as if it were just propped into the opening. I wasn't sure if that was a good thing or not. I tried to remember if the little man had closed it behind him but couldn't conjure the image. If it was wedged in, I'd definitely need help getting it open. I put my hand on the flaking wood, to test its sturdiness.

"I wouldn't go in there, if I were you. Which I'm not, but there you have it."

I almost, quite literally, leapt into the air at the sound of the voice. I spun around, my heart hammering and my nerves jangling.

There wasn't anyone there.

Bracken sat, shivering, some distance away, whining softly. Her eyebrows trembled as she shifted her gaze between me and the path that led back up to the cottage. I could tell she was at war with herself, fighting the battle between fleeing and staying put. I hadn't thought it possible that there was a creature more flighty than myself.

Sighing with exasperation, I called out.

"Hello?"

I was sure it was Astrid, no doubt lurking about to pester me about the village meeting.

No answer.

Maybe I'd been hearing things.

I turned my attention back to the door.

"You're really not ready to go in there."

The voice was a low rumble, lazy and indolent, like the speaker had to really force themselves to be bothered speaking at all. Who would be so rude?

I struggled back through the brambles, stomping them underfoot as I came and walked around the side of the shed from where it seemed the voice had originated.

Hamish's cat sat on the wall, idly running a paw over his tattered ears. That would explain Bracken's terror, I supposed. I looked around the garden, but still couldn't see the source of the voice. I was convinced then that I was, indeed, hearing things. Probably spending too much time alone.

"No," said the voice, "You're not hearing things and I've always found myself to be my own best company."

A slow prickle of alarm ran up from the base of my spine to my scalp and I felt a flush of panic rising. I stared at the cat who returned my gaze, unblinking.

It couldn't be.

"Whyever not?" said the voice, a hint of amusement in the dry tone. "Stranger things have happened, surely."

My voice came out in a wavering whisper.

"Is that you?" I asked the cat, hardly believing it possible, but knowing, somewhere deep down that it was more than so.

"Who else?" said the cat, standing up and stretching to the tips of his toes. "Any chance of a saucer of something?"

He leapt nimbly down off the wall and started up the path, his crooked tail held aloft like a flagpole, barely glancing at Bracken who threw herself sideways into the tangle of currant bushes to avoid him.

I saw no other option but to follow.

Chapter Twelve

The village hall was teeming with people. The meeting was supposed to start at seven o'clock and I'd been torn between getting
there very early and avoiding having to walk into a busy room and
getting there later and sliding in the back without attracting notice.
As it was, I decided, upon urging by Edie, to have a late tea with her
and then walk over together. I'd taken Bracken with me and we left
her curled up on a blanket beside the log burner. After licking clean
her own plate, piled high with shepherd's pie, she was in a happy,
full-tummy sleep and I don't think she even noticed we were leaving.

"I'm right glad you decided to come to the meeting, lass," Edie had
said, beaming. "It'll do you a bit of good to get out among folk and
knowing what goes on in the village is very important."

I didn't think it worth mentioning that I'd been practically bullied
into attending by both Astrid tucking notices into the garden gate (I
didn't actually see her do it but who else would it have been?), daily
phone calls from either Alfie or Edie (they alternated) and then, finally,

the imperious suggestion by Hamish's cat that "if I knew what was good for me" I should attend.

Edie added a knowing wink and while I knew it must be some reference to the goings-on of being a Caretaker, I didn't feel up to exploring the topic. I hadn't spoken about it to anyone after reading Nan's letter, but I'm fairly certain they were aware that I'd been enlightened. To that end, I was quite unprepared as to the relevance of my presence at the meeting, despite having spent the previous afternoon discussing it in detail with the cat.

Murk, as he announced he preferred to be called, was infuriatingly obtuse. First, he refused to divulge any further details on his warning about the little stone shed and then proceeded to launch into a lecture on why I needed to attend the meeting about the wind farm. With the rather obvious exception of having the power of speech, he was cat-like in every other way, particularly in his single-minded persistence. I hadn't dared bring *that* up with Edie, either, not being quite sure whether his special ability was common-knowledge. Broaching the subject of talking cats was one of those precarious situations where someone might get the wrong idea.

"Yes, well I thought that it might be something Nan would like me to do," I said, chickening out at the last minute, abandoning my plan to casually mention to her that I'd been convinced to come by a talking cat. "And if it's going to impact the village, then it'll impact me, won't it?"

I also didn't add that it would give me a perverse pleasure to see a faceless corporation beaten down in its attempts at financial gain by the irate peasant populace. Or, at least, that was the angle which Astrid had been selling. I was of mixed feelings, really. Surely, the more green energy the better?

"Come on, pet," said Alfie, with a firm grip on my elbow. He'd met us outside the hall, having been away on some mysterious errand prior that meant he hadn't joined us for shepherd's pie. "Edie'll get us a seat. You come with me and I'll introduce you to young Toby. He's not a bad lad and he knows these parts like the back of his hand. He's the one to tell you the best places for walking."

"Alfred Fisher, you've got a memory like a sieve. Don't you remember our Hazel already knows Toby? They were bairns together all them years ago? Still, it won't hurt to go and get reacquainted. I'll keep the seats, you two go on."

I didn't have time to protest. There was nothing I would've liked less than being shown around and introduced. I was here strictly on a fact-finding mission, albeit one assigned by a cat. Nevertheless, I would've hated for Alfie to think me ungrateful, so I plastered a benevolent expression on my face and allowed myself to be led into the milling crowd.

The hall was almost as old as the village itself. It had apparently been a fleece exchange at some point in history and the fact that it was once an agricultural building was obvious in the bare stone and beam structure. The walls had been insulated and plastered up to about eight or ten feet and then the rest had been left to the original stone, soaring up to an impressive system of rafters. The windows were large, obviously added much later in its history, although still quite old as was evidenced by the uneven panes of glass. Somewhere, a wood-burner was attempting to chase the chill out of the air, although I surmised that in an hour or so the sheer volume of body heat would make the hall unbearably stuffy. Several trestle tables had been set up down the sides of the seating area. They held large urns, presumably full of tea, and covered plates and dishes. I smiled to myself, remembering Nan telling me that most people only showed up for regular meetings on the promise of a good feed afterwards. The local chapter of the Women's Institute was responsible for the refreshments, as evidenced by the little sign and pile of pamphlets inviting "all comers" to their once-monthly, Thursday meetings. Apparently, a Mrs. Beauchamp was to be sharing slides from her visit to the Ivory Coast at the next gathering. Without thinking too much about it, I picked up a pamphlet and folded it into my coat pocket.

"Ah, there you are, laddie. Come here, pet,"

Alfie led me toward a pair of men in deep conversation, one of whom had his back to us. He was tall and broad-shouldered and his tangle of black hair looked uneasily familiar.

A strange feeling roiled in my stomach. I wasn't entirely sure if it was a good or bad one.

"Toby," said Alfie, clapping a hand on the man's woollen-clad shoulder.

Toby turned around, a wide smile creasing his weather burnt face.

"Alfie!" he said, reaching out to take Alfie's hand in a friendly grip. "Good to see you, how's that poultice I gave you? Giving you any relief? Oh, hello, again."

His smile faded instantly. His blue eyes narrowing as he looked from Alfie to me. I stood there, as much an idiot as ever, quite unable to speak for a combination of embarrassment and confusion. What does one say in such a situation?

Alfie frowned, as confused as I was.

"I thought you two knew each other," he said, giving me an elbow, "Why've you got a face on like that, our Hazel?"

"We ran into one another already," I muttered, not looking at Toby, "Out on the moor the other day."

"You what?" asked Alfie, looking at me. "You never said...oh!"

He broke off into a peal of wheezing laughter.

"Eeeeh! Never! Is this the devil who was chasing your wee dog?"

I nodded, raising my chin and glaring defiantly at Toby.

"Aye, and rightly so," he said with a scowl. "Bloody nuisance, dogs roaming the moor, having a go at the sheep. It's lambing season, we cannae have it. I was doing the beast a favour. Anyone else would've shot it."

"She wasn't *roaming* the moor," I retorted with a matching scowl, while noting with an unwelcome pang how his speech lapsed into his native burr when he was agitated. I used to tease him on purpose just to hear it. But that was neither here nor there. "And there wasn't a sheep in sight. Aren't they all in pens if it's lambing season?"

I dug deep into the recesses of my memory for my scant supply of sheep husbandry knowledge.

"Besides, from what you said when you were waving your big stick in my face, she was only guilty of sniffing around your pheasants."

"Oh aye, well we all know what comes from sniffing, don't we? Hungry dog and a nice plump bird? Next thing there's blood and feathers..."

"Hardly!" I snapped. "If you had any animal sense whatsoever you'd have seen she was frightened out of her wits. I don't think she'd have the inclination to eat one of your bloody birds if it was sitting right in front of her nose."

That one was way off the mark. Toby had more animal sense in his little finger than most people had in their whole person. At least, that's the Toby I remembered.

"Now, now!" said Alfie, with a chuckle. "I can see you two got yourselves off on the wrong foot. That's no way to renew your acquaintance, is it now? So settle yourselves down, the meeting hasn't even started yet and already there's blood in the water!"

He patted my arm and gave Toby a good-natured thump on the shoulder.

"Let's start again, why don't we? No harm done, after all. The wee dog is safe and sound and so are Dummy's pheasants."

He smiled questioningly between us. I felt myself deflating into shakiness. Once again, a temporary burst of courage had left me wanting to curl up in a corner and be quietly sick. I returned Alfie's expectant gaze with a small smile.

"Of course, you're right," I said, with an effort to seem conciliatory. I'd be polite for Alfie's sake but had no desire to spend one more minute in Toby's company. There was too much conflicting emotion rattling around inside my head and that's never a good place from which to make small talk.

"Go on and have a catch up, I'll see you back at the seats, Hazel pet. I've just seen someone I need a word with."

Alfie grinned, looking between us, then pushed his way through the crowd. My face burned hotly and I shoved my hands deeper into my coat pockets.

Toby shifted awkwardly and cleared his throat, looking down at the leaflet he held in his hands, apparently engrossed in what it said.

I took a quick opportunity to study him from behind my over-hanging fringe. His woollen sweater was as many darns as it was origi-nal stitching and his grey corduroys were patched at the knees. Add to that, his disheveled mop of hair and at least three days of stubble, he looked more like a vagabond than the manager of an estate. I tried to see any remnant of the boy I'd known – the playful, mischievous boy who had shown me how to take a deep breath for the first time in my anxious little life.

"Dog alright, then?"

Toby's voice startled me. Naturally, I blushed in the most ridiculous way possible.

"Um, yes, actually. She is. Thank you for asking."

Good lord, really?

"Got the smell out?"

"The smell? Oh, yes. Eventually. I had to use almost a whole bottle of shampoo. She smells much better than she did..."

Someone just put me out of my misery now.

Alfie returned, a rescuing angel, and interrupted my humiliation.

"Friends again?"

Alfie's beaming magnanimity suggested there was no other reasonable option.

I smiled a feeble smile.

"Now Hazel, our Toby's Lord Dummell's estate manager, don't ye know? A man of great importance in Winkle. Old Dummy had to drag him back from across the wall, didn't he, laddie? Shocking defection that was. Anyroad, there's not a man hereabouts more knowledgeable when it comes to the land. I'm just glad he's on our side."

He winked at Toby who, flushing, had merely grunted.

I stood awkwardly, looking everywhere but at Toby. I wished, not for the first time, that I was at home on the sofa, curled up with Bracken and a mug of tea. There were no tatty orange cats in my daydream, either.

Salvation came in the unlikely form of Mrs. Trout.

"May I have your attention, please?" she trumpeted from the front of the hall where a lectern had been shoved across the floor into position. There was a microphone attached to it but she clearly didn't require one.

"If we could all please find our seats, the meeting will commence."

Ah, I thought, the royal we. Why did that not surprise me? I thought back to what Alfie had said. Mrs.Trout would give my mum a run for her money in the putting on airs race. I immediately scolded myself for that thought; my mum was nothing like horrid Mrs.Trout. Well, except in the putting on airs department.

There was a general shuffling and scraping of chairs as everyone found a place. Edie beckoned from our seats and I fled gratefully without bothering to say goodbye to Toby. I'm quite certain he neither noticed or cared.

Edie smiled and patted the chair beside her, handing me a folded pamphlet and passing one across me to Alfie. It was an outline of the speakers and the subject. The one that Toby had been studying so earnestly. I saw that Toby, himself, had the floor from 7:20 until 7:35pm. It certainly was highly organized. The only other name I recognized was Abernathy Trout, who I assumed was none other than the unfortunate spouse of Mrs. With a name like Abernathy, one had to wonder if his ascension to greatness within the ranks of middle government was an attempt to compensate for such a handicap. It would explain why Mrs.Trout went to such great pains to itemize his accomplishments. I scolded myself again for such uncharitable thoughts.

Alfie leaned in to stage whisper to Edie.

"Our Hazel and Toby have already been reacquainted. Can you imagine it was him who was chasing poor wee Bracken across the moor?"

"Never!" she exclaimed, looking at me for confirmation.

I pursed my lips and nodded, not wanting to go into it again.

"He's always been a bit of a hot head, our Toby," she said, shaking her head, "When he ran off like he did...well, never mind that now. It's all water under the bridge."

"Aye," said Alfie. "No doubt comes from his people being from the wrong side of the wall."

He winked as Edie reached across and slapped his arm playfully.

"What do you mean, the wrong side of the wall?" I asked, confused.

"Hadrian's!" said Alfie with a wicked chuckle, ignoring the first part of the question. "He's from island stock, aye? Tough lot, them. And hot-tempered. A bit like you, come to think of it," He gave me an elbow. "He's the Viking to your Pict, isn't he then? Still, plenty of faery blood in there. That's what makes him so good with the beasts. Well, except when he's chasing them ower the moor!"

"Alfie!" hissed Edie, "Quiet down and stop your teasing."

She leaned in towards me.

"He was at The Forge for his meeting," she explained. "He can't hold his lager like he used to."

Whatever I might have thought about any of it was soon rendered unimportant as the first speaker stepped up to the lectern. The customary microphone tapping and shrieking occurred, followed by the furtive scuffling of someone off-stage as they tried different wiring combinations. A few cheeky suggestions were called out from the audience followed by loud shushing as the microphone scratched into life.

The first speaker was a Mr. Hobart Guthrie, official senior representative of BMZ Corporation; according to the speaker schedule, there was also a junior representative by the name of Glenn Collins. I assumed that was the younger, mini-me version standing behind him. As a unit, they were the ones in charge of smoothing the way for the sale of the land in question.

I have to confess to not paying very close attention. He was a very uninteresting speaker who kept referencing a large stack of papers and quoting studies and statistics about affordable energy and the appeal of rural living for Today's Professionals. Evidently, if the sale went through, the concession to the village for its inconvenience was a new enclave of Elite Housing, the likes of which were famous for Bringing In Money to the area. He was a tall, imposing man who might have been considered handsome if not for something about the way he carried himself that was profoundly off-putting. He sort of loomed over the lectern. I had a suspicious notion that he was doing it on purpose, trying to make himself seem larger and more menacing, to intimidate or bully the audience into taking in his information. I fancied he had a larger than usual shadow casting behind him, too. His greying hair was slightly too long for a man of his age, which was probably about sixty or so, and profession. You'd expect such a high profile business person to be all clipped and shorn but he was vaguely out of fashion in a way that I couldn't quite put my finger on. His complexion was almost a sickly pale and his heavy black brows frowned down over deep-set eyes. He was too far away for me to tell their colour, but they looked like black holes against the paleness of his skin. If you'd told me he was playing a funeral director in a low budget horror film I wouldn't have been surprised.

From what little I gathered, he and his company were wanting to annex a parcel of land from the estate of Lord Dummell to use for a wind farm. According to Mr. Guthrie, the land wasn't in active agricultural production and going sadly to waste. In addition, a modest housing enclave made up of executive dwellings would be shoved in at the edge of the village. As a quiet aside, he mentioned that the enterprise would involve removing a substantial section of the hedge that bordered the moor as well as the large tract of woodland adjacent to allow for assembly and maintenance of the turbines. I wasn't exactly clear on what constituted an executive dwelling but I assumed it to have something to do with Today's Professionals. Great, I thought, gobbling up the green space to provide designer homes for people looking for a symbol of their material wealth. I was momentarily surprised by my vehemence in that thought, seeing as how it could easily be pointed out that my own father had built a career and fortune on doing the exact same thing. No, not really, though. My dad rarely took on new building projects and when he did, he took extreme care with the planning and building so as to make sure it blended cohesively and as harmlessly as possible in with the landscape. Although I suppose that was splitting hairs when it came right down to it.

I shook the thoughts off and tried not to look at the time. Everyone got fifteen minutes to plead their case. According to the clock on the wall, he'd only been talking for five of those fifteen. That seemed odd, because it certainly felt like so much longer than that. People were starting to fidget in their seats and I wasn't the only one sneaking a look up at the clock.

I heard Edie mutter beside me

"He's one of them, sure as I'm sitting here."

I leaned over.

"One of who?" I whispered.

She started and smiled, almost guiltily, and shook her head, putting her finger to her lips and tilting her head toward Mr.Guthrie.

I sighed, allowing myself to drift back into a daydream in which I was sharing a plate of Hob Nobs with Bracken. Again, the cat was notably absent.

I was jolted out of that pleasantness by a smattering of applause. Mr.Guthrie had finally finished. More than a few people were frowning down at their wrist-watches and Mrs.Trout approached the lectern with a vague expression on her pinchy face.

"Thank you, Mr.Guthrie," she said, gathering her composure. "Next, we have Mr.Abernathy Trout..." she smiled indulgently, smoothing her long-fingered hands down the sides of her neatly pressed tweed skirt. "...from the Ministry of Agriculture, Land Use Department. He plans to share with us the results of the feasibility study and environmental impact assessment that was carried out on the land in question, on behalf of Mr.Guthrie and BMZ.

That promised to be riveting. I groaned inwardly, looking across at the refreshment table where the tea urns sat, steaming invitingly. Two more speakers before we'd be released to the mercies of the WI. Alfie elbowed me again, grinning, no doubt sharing my thoughts.

Mr.Trout, in tones reminiscent of those designed to bore the poor, unsuspecting pupils of public school classrooms to death, listed the results of the studies which, according to him, made it seem contrary to the laws of nature to *not* hand the parcel of land over to be pillaged and built upon. Indeed, the fact that legions of people hadn't succumbed to torturous and horrifyingly slow deaths by the various hazards incumbent in that particular bit of earth was nothing shy of miraculous, to hear him tell it. I had no idea that a hedge could pose such a terrible threat to public safety.

Alfie snorted more than once during Mr.Trout's litany of woe and Edie hushed him several times when he started to speak up. He wasn't the only one, though. I could see Young Craig sitting near the front with an older gentleman that I took to be Old Craig, his uncle. I wondered how the sale of that land would affect Rookery Farm.

According to the handy map that had been taped to a panel of blackboard, as well as being helpfully projected onto a screen behind the podium, the proposed land sale would require the acquisition of several large fields belonging to the farm. Young Craig had made more than one derisive noise during Mr.Trout's diatribe of despair. Thankfully, though, his speech seemed to conform to the normal time parameters and soon he was being politely clapped away from the lectern. Mrs. Trout beamed horrifyingly as she rose from her seat.

"Thank you, Mr. Trout, for those enlightening words. I'm sure I speak for the entire village when I say how dearly we appreciate the way that our government has taken our best interests to heart when assessing the wisdom of this acquisition."

A few folk continued to clap, but mostly there was a stony silence. A low rumble of chatter erupted as people turned to their neighbours, exchanging muttered words and shaking heads.

"I've never heard such codswallop in all me life," grumbled Alfie, rubbing his hands in agitation over the thighs of his trousers. "I don't know how they can get away with it, telling outright lies like that."

"Surely they can't be making it all up," I said. "It's a government department, they're supposed to tell the truth."

Two pairs of elderly eyes stared at me, blinking.

"Okay, okay," I said. "That was a silly thing to say, but surely when it comes to something as important as this..."

I trailed off as they continued to look at me in the way one might look at a toddler attempting to write their name.

"But why?" I said. "The only person who could possibly benefit financially is Lord Dummell. Why would the government go to such nefarious measures to make sure he's able to charge them a fortune for his land?"

I didn't get an answer as the microphone squawked as Mrs. Trout announced the next speaker.

"Next on our agenda is the representative for Lord Dummell and Malmont Estate. Will you all welcome Mr. Tobias MacDierran to the floor? Mr. MacDierran will state the position of the Estate."

There was a low, murmuring rumble from the crowd. Clearly, Toby was a respected person among the local people, but at the same time, he represented a possible opposition to development and good fortune. I didn't know how many of the residents were in favour of the wind farm but I could see how things could quickly get complicated. People would struggle with loyalty in times like these.

"Thank you, Mrs. Trout," said Toby, smiling stiffly. He looked quite uncomfortable standing up in front of everyone. I felt a brief stab of empathy for his situation, but squashed it quickly by remembering the state of Bracken when I'd found her. "I won't take up much of your time, there's not much more that needs to be said."

"Aye, there is!" came a shout from near the front. I guessed it to be Young Craig. "What about the Hedge, eh? You of all people should know what's being chanced with this. Don't let them gloss over it, lad."

A few people called out in agreement. There was a sea of nodding heads and people turning to their neighbours and exchanging whispered comments.

I leaned into Edie.

"What does he mean about the hedge?" I asked. I knew it was obviously a case for the wildlife and for the village heritage but I was starting to get the feeling there was more to this than met the eye. My mind flickered involuntarily back to my vagrant friend. I shook my head. For a person I'd met only twice, and briefly at that, he was certainly on my mind a great deal more than felt reasonable. I looked quickly around the room, scanning faces but could see no sign of him.

Mrs. Trout strode to the front to stand beside Toby, as if her authoritative presence might quell the burgeoning outbursts. She held up a skeletal hand, her lips set in a thin line.

"Please," she boomed. "Please observe the protocols of our village gatherings. The speaker has a right to do so, unmolested. There will be time enough for questions and discussion at the follow-up."

She patted Toby on the arm and went back to her seat. His expression was one of barely-disguised annoyance although I wasn't sure who he was annoyed with – Mrs. Trout or the cat-calls from the crowd.

"I would've got to the Hedge if you'd let me," he said, scowling over at Young Craig. "And aye, I know very well what's being chanced. But I also know that if Lord Dummell can't keep the estate afloat, then there's far more at risk than the Hedge. And you, Craig Talbot, know that better'n most. This isn't as straightforward as it looks and we have to make sure we get it right." He paused, giving the crowd a piercing look.

A scrape of boots and muffled cough from the front row was the only response.

"None of you, well, most of you anyway, are new here so you know how we go on in Winkle,"

I felt a rush of outrage rise up my neck and flush my cheeks a burning red. Was that a dig directed at me? Edie and Alfie both reached over and squeezed my hands. I straightened my back and stared firmly at the speaker.

"The most important thing to Lord Dummell is taking care of what's been the responsibility of his family for hundreds of years. There's plenty of you who've known the benefit of that dedication and I think we can all agree that he's always done right by the village and all who live here,"

More nodding of heads and murmurs of agreement.

"Well now it's Lord Dummell's turn to ask for your help. To exercise your right to vote on the subject of this land sale — and as you know, by right and custom, it *must* be a vote," he paused then, to scan the crowd, fixing his eyes, it seemed, on every person in turn. I immediately looked down at my hands.

"To take a vote in this," he repeated, "is to take a vote for the future of this village and *all* who call it home."

He placed emphasis on the word "all", staring around again at the crowd, as if trying to say something without actually saying it. I felt like I was the only person who was missing an important piece of information.

"Malmont Estate has been at the centre of this village since the Domesday book. In actual fact, Winkle grew *around* the estate and the Hedge has always been an important part of our way of life. So it goes without saying, that despite the potential for enormous financial gain, Lord Dummell and Malmont Estate will be opposing this development"

The room erupted in cheers and the stamping of feet. Mrs. Trout flushed angrily and marched back to the lectern; just as she opened her mouth to speak, Toby held up a hand. The noise faded away into quiet mutterings. I grinned with ungenerous delight at the look on Mrs. Trout's face. Quite unexpectedly, I caught Toby's eye and saw the corner of his mouth twitch. I smoothed out my smile and looked down at the itinerary. Toby continued speaking.

"In days past, it would be the responsibility of the Manor to take up challenges like these from its own coffers and it has, many, many times. But times have changed and money, as you know, is tight. So, on the advice of Hamish Reed, we're setting up a legal defence fund and anyone who is able, is encouraged to contribute. We won't surrender this fight and we hope to have your support. Thank you for your time."

With that abrupt ending, Toby left the lectern, and Mrs. Trout floundering to provide a smooth segue into the next speaker who was Glenn Collins, the minion of Mr. Guthrie.

"Our lad did well," whispered Alfie, leaning into me and across to Edie. "Short and to the point, none of this flowery nonsense that makes noise and doesn't say owt."

He was, of course, referencing Mr. Collins (assigned as our community liaison representative), who was now waxing poetically on the natural beauty of Winkle and the desirability of preserving it by making sure there was viable industry and something about sustainable economies. The irony of his argument about preserving natural beauty by destroying a large chunk of it wasn't lost on anyone. But still he went on. And on.

Suddenly there was a loud crash and the unlikely sound of a tambourine.

Heads swivelled wildly as people looked to see where sound was coming from. I craned my neck along with everyone else. There was a brief disturbance near the back and then, all of a sudden, a group of brightly-garbed young people came cartwheeling and back-flipping down the main aisle. I spotted Astrid, striding behind them, her boots echoing strangely in the sudden hush of the hall.

Mr. Collins paused in his effusion, his eyes narrowing at the disturbance. His fingers briefly clenched the sides of the lectern, before relaxing. A tolerant smile beamed from his face and he tilted his head to one side in a gesture of mild curiosity.

I turned back to look at the collection of youngsters who had grouped themselves around Astrid. I could see that they were dressed in various representations of birds and small animals. There was a blackbird and a wren, a dormouse and a hedgehog. One very tall, gangly individual sported a slightly sinister fox mask. It was all very theatrical. A slow murmur rustled through the captivated audience, but otherwise there was silence. Even Mrs. Trout seemed at a loss for words.

The silence was broken by a hare shaking a tambourine. The willowy young woman raised her arms and leapt daintily around Astrid who appeared to be dressed as a hawthorn tree.

"We are here to claim the right to life and liberty of the creatures of this land," she began, her voice carrying through the hall. "What is proposed here is no less than ecological genocide!"

Another sharp rattle of the tambourine and suddenly the players moved into formation and began miming what could only be described as some sort of extinction scene. Birds flailed around a person with windmilling arms, suggesting the perils of a wind turbine and the dormouse darted around as if looking for somewhere to hide. It sounds a bit affected, but it really was quite moving. The audience was mesmerized, whether by emotional investment or sheer incredulity, it would be hard to say.

After a few fraught minutes, and an especially earnest rattle of the tambourine, the young thespians all collapsed, en masse, onto the floor, twitching slightly before lying still. The tambourine spun tragically on its edge before tipping over. Astrid, in her blue-haired sylvan glory remained standing. I felt like I should start clapping but since no-one else was, I kept my fingers wrapped tightly in the fabric of my dress.

"We challenge you, denizens of destruction, to face the consequences of capitalistic greed and the rape and pillage of this land." Here, she made a dramatic gesture at the limp bodies of her woodland brethren.

There were about five heartbeats of silence before Mr. Collins removed his hands from the lectern and started a slow, rhythmic clap.

"Excellent," he said, his voice like warm honey, "What a fabulously talented group of young people. It's so encouraging to see you occupied in such admirable artistic pursuits," he paused, running a long-fingered hand down the front of his immaculately pressed shirt. He must have been aiming for man-of-the-people in his wardrobe choice as his shirt was a linen weave of greens and browns and ochres, countrified and yet strangely foreign at the same time. "Alas, the passion of youth and your creative licence has strayed far, far from the facts of the situation,"

I could see Astrid's shoulders stiffen. Several of the corpses on the floor began to stir. Mr. Collins narrowed his eyes and leaned over the lectern and continued, a hard edge creeping into his expression and his voice.

"So how about you tidy yourselves up and go back to your little clubhouse and let the grown-ups discuss their important business in peace, aye? You've no business interfering in the things that don't concern you."

Well, that was that.

The hall erupted in a volley of shouts and scraping chairs. Astrid stood her ground, her face twisted in fury, her fists clenched, as the woodland contingent scrambled up off the floor and started chanting something unintelligible above the rest of the commotion. The tambourine rattled in violent accompaniment. Mrs. Trout waved her hands ineffectually and tried to restore order as Mr. Collins looked on, an unreadable expression on his face.

Eventually, Mrs. Trout's calls to order settled down the hubbub. I watched as Toby walked over to Astrid and her friends where they clustered around him, gesturing wildly. After a few moments, Astrid nodded her head and motioned to her merry band and they grouped together with their backs to the podium, sketching elaborate bows to the audience before exiting down the centre aisle in the same elegant flurry of cartwheels and handstands with which they had entered.

"Well!" breathed Edie, once the door had closed behind the protesters. "What do you think of that?"

I didn't get a chance to offer an opinion as Mrs. Trout had regained control of the podium. She boomed loudly over the residual bustle and chatter that rippled through after the dramatic exit of the young people.

"Ladies and gentlemen! Please may I have quiet?"

The noise lowered rapidly and after a brief spell of shuffling chairs and shushing, the room was silent again. Everyone stared, expectant. No doubt wondering what the next bit of delicious outrage would be.

"I'm sure I need not remind *most* of you," she paused to glare malevolently in the general direction of the closed door, "That we like to observe a civilized approach to our village meetings and so allow me to reiterate that should certain persons show themselves unable to maintain an air of civility and decorum they will not be made welcome."

She folded her hands in front of her and pressed her lips firmly, looking around at the entire audience, making sure with her glare that everyone had heard. I saw people dropping their eyes as her gaze swept over them. She reminded me of the nasty headmistress from the Roald Dahl novel, Mathilda. Miss Trunchbowl, I think. I made a mental note to look it up when I got home. Toby was standing up at the front of the room, his own arms folded and his face clouded with his own fierce scowl.

"Do you have anything further to add Mr. Collins?"

She asked this with a voice that dripped sweetness.

He curled a lip and narrowed his eyes, causing her smile to falter slightly.

At least he wasn't fooled by her, I thought, grudgingly giving him a point of favour.

"No, that will be fine," he said, easing back towards the microphone in a movement that forced Mrs. Trout aside. "Thank you. It's both mine and BMZ Corporation's hope that folk can see past their own private agendas to the advancement of the community as a whole. The unfortunate truth is that there's no benefit that comes without a price, I'm sure you all know that, living here as long as you have."

He looked right at me, his green eyes bright and intense, then added,

"Most of you, anyway. The important thing is to not let nostalgia stand in the way of progress, because to always be looking back at yesterday, is to miss the opportunities of tomorrow."

He gave a small, almost imperceptible bow and stepped away from the lectern, walking along the back of the refreshment tables and then disappearing out of sight.

Mrs. Trout seemed momentarily off-stride but quickly recovered and announced that it seemed like an appropriate time to end and would we all like to help ourselves to the refreshments courtesy of the Women's Institute.

"Well," breathed Edie again, amid the general upheaval of people getting up and moving in drifts towards a welcome cup of tea.

"What do you think of *that*?"

Chapter Thirteen

I had a pounding headache by the time Bracken and I made our way back to the cottage. I'd refused another cup of tea with Alfie and Edie once we'd got to their house, knowing that the nagging ache in my neck and shoulders would bloom into a full-on thumper before too long. All I wanted was to lie down on the sofa with a cool cloth over my eyes.

We stayed after the meeting for the tea and a bit of cake, which was enjoyable in and of itself – there was a lovely Victoria sponge and I had two rock buns wrapped in a paper napkin in my pocket for later – but I could well have done without all of the chatter. Of course, the disruption caused by Astrid and her friends was the height of scandalous delight and there were more than a few theories as to what that group of "ne'er do wells" or "inspiring young people", depending on who was talking, would get up to next. I wanted to point out that speaking out in support of their community and natural surroundings was hardly on par with defacing graveyards or spray-painting public buildings as you might have guessed was their crime from the attitude of the more agitated villagers, but in the end I just didn't have the strength to argue my point. I was utterly exhausted. The combined strain of having to be sociable and the buzzing energy of so many people in a state of heightened emotion had my nerves in a frazzle. It would take me a week to get over this outing. Suddenly, the thought of quiet conversations with Murk didn't seem such a terrible alternative after all.

I asked Edie why there hadn't been more speakers on the 'against' side of the argument — why, other than Toby, it was only the pro side that was represented and she'd chuckled and told me that was because everyone was against the proposal by default. The meeting had been designed to sway the people who might be less convinced, and there were only a relative handful of those. The village had to decide whether to pass the vote to the county council, which would set the official wheels in motion. It was an old tradition and possibly not legally binding but was observed anyway, just like it had been for centuries. The county council had the authority to recommend a compulsory purchase order if BMZ could produce a convincing argument. There was another site up for review but for some reason, BMZ was determined to secure the land around Winkle.

"And other than eejits like the Trouts," continued Edie, "it's only folk who aren't really from around here that are likely to think it's a good idea. New people, you see, ones that've bought houses here but don't really *live* here."

"What, you mean holiday places?" I asked, trying to think of what could attract the average city dweller to Winkle as a holiday destination.

"No, no," said Alfie, who'd just arrived with plates of Victoria sponge. "Some folk buy houses here, but never really settle in, like.

They've come from the town, they still work there and so they still do all of their shopping and things there."

"Well, doesn't that make sense if they're already there at work?" I asked, thinking of the dearth of shopping possibilities in Winkle. "Don't most people from here go into the town to do some shopping?"

"Oh, aye, from time to time. But it's not their first *thought*, you see. The folk who don't really *live* here, still behave like they've never left the town."

That explanation seemed to have satisfied everyone but me as the topic was shifted to how Mrs.Evans got her sponge so wonderfully light and fluffy.

At some point Glenn Collins re-materialized and introduced himself to me. He was making the rounds, pressing the flesh, as it were, like a campaigning politician. He seemed friendly enough, quite earnest in that enthusiastic-hand-shake sort of way that you associate with people who convince other people of things for a living. He appeared to be trying his best to not be public enemy number one, anyway. He and Alfie had an animated discussion about the best sort of seed potatoes, Mr.Collins coming down in favour of some newly-engineered variety that would resist the apocalypse itself. I noticed that he kept shooting sideways glances at me as he chatted – or was it me shooting sideways glances at him?— either way, I couldn't shake the feeling that he was trying to keep my attention. For what reason, I couldn't fathom, nor did I intend to expend too much effort trying, my head being fully occupied with attempting to understand the various layers of mystery surrounding this seemingly innocuous sale of land.

By the time we left the village hall, I was still none the wiser. I couldn't get my head around why, if so many people were against the sale of the land – an overwhelming majority, according to Alfie and

Edie – it was even an issue. Surely a vote could be cast immediately and the whole thing tidied away. The proposal should end before it even got to the county council and Lord Dummell could resort to selling off the family silver to pay his heating bill. The people of Winkle, including me, could continue on as they always had. In a fit of inspiration that was both funny and terrifying, I resolved to ask Murk for further details when I got home.

It was fully dark by the time I got to the end of the lane and opened my garden gate. The hedge was silent of birdsong, only the occasional rustle and scurry of some night creature broke the silence. A train whistled from far across the other side of the motorway and the sharp bark of a fox caused Bracken to startle and press herself against my leg.

"Silly dog" I said, unlatching the gate. She scurried through, as if coming to the other side of the fence offered her protection from the evils lurking in the twilight shadows. "I really ought to find myself a dog who would be of some service, should a rogue faery come strolling through."

"Yes, you really ought to do that," murmured a voice, from just above my head.

"Murk!" I said, once I'd tucked my heart back where it belonged. "Do *not* sneak up on me like that!"

He was sitting on top of the little stone shed, his crooked tail wrapped neatly around his paws and his large yellow eyes blinking slowly. He stood up, stretched, and hopped neatly down onto the garden path. Bracken leapt sideways, her tail clamped between her legs, whining softly.

"I wasn't sneaking," he replied, moving purposely toward Bracken until she skittered away. "I was sitting."

"Don't tease her like that," I said, walking toward the cringing dog and petting her comfortingly. You know she's scared of you, you don't need to be so obnoxious about it."

If cats could shrug, I'm sure he would have. He proceeded up the path in front of us, his tail held straight in the air like a banner. Well, as straight as his tail could be.

"Fancy a nibble of something?" he said, looking back over his sho ulder."You can tell me how you got on while you're opening up a tin of salmon."

"But what I don't understand," I said, flaking the salmon with a fork, "Is why on earth it's even an issue at all. If, according to what I understand of the thing, that it can't go forward to the council without the approval of the village, then why don't they just cast the vote and be done with it?"

I placed the saucer on the draining board where Murk had sat, a pained expression on his features, as I went through my rituals of fire-lighting and kettle-filling before rummaging for the salmon and a tin-opener. Clearly I'd been expected to attend to him first.

He neglected to answer and tucked into the plate of salmon, smacking his slips in a very undignified fashion. Bracken took advantage of his preoccupation to come into the kitchen, grubbing on the floor for crumbs, as if that was all that was on offer.

"Oh for heaven's sake, you silly dog!" I exclaimed, as she performed elaborate gymnastics in an attempt to reach a morsel lodged in the tiny gap between the bottom of the cupboards and the floor. "I've got a whole plate of Hob Nobs to share as soon as the kettle's boiled. Can't you hang on?"

She wriggled her bottom in reply but refused to be dissuaded from her quest. If only she were so steadfast in her duties as guardian of the threshold I need never fear a hostile incursion.

"It can't help it," mumbled Murk, as he licked up the last remaining bits of salmon, casting about under the saucer for anything he may have missed. "Once you've gone hungry, you don't soon forget."

He commenced his post-prandial ablutions.

"It's been hungry a lot" he added, swiping a paw over his tattered ear.

"How would you know?" I asked, incredulous. "And she's a she. Stop referring to her like an object."

Murk ignored me.

"It told me."

He jumped down off the bench, startling Bracken so that she scrabbled suddenly backwards, banging her head off the open drawer where I'd been rummaging for a fresh tea towel.

"Oh, Bracken!" I said, swooping down to comfort her. "Silly old girl. Don't let him get to you like that."

I turned to Murk, who was settling himself on the hearth rug.

"You're a terrible bully, you know that? And that's nothing to be proud of, let me tell you. I don't care who or what you are, I won't allow you to continue to torment her like that so you'd better decide, this minute, how you plan to go on. If you can't behave, well I'm sorry but you're no longer welcome here and I'll ask you to leave right now."

I surprised myself with that outburst; I hadn't planned on telling him to go away, despite having secretly wished, several times a day, that he'd stop coming. I had mixed feelings about him, actually. On the one hand, I despised his arrogance and his superior, cryptic attitude - not to mention the way he upset poor Bracken - but on the other hand, it felt like he was someone (something? somecat?) I could depend upon to be utterly truthful about everything that was going on around me. I had a million questions swirling around in my head since reading Nan's letter, added to now since the village meeting, and I really didn't feel as if there were anyone else I could ask. I was too hyper-aware of not wanting to hurt people's feelings or disappoint their faith in me or my abilities as a potential Caretaker, to risk asking any of the humans in my life. Murk seemed like my best bet for honesty and it was with immense relief that I found that I didn't even care if he liked me or not.

The kettle whistled and I busied myself pouring the water into the pot. I kept my back to the living room and the hearth rug, not wanting to see if he'd stayed or gone. Bracken crept out from underneath the kitchen table where she'd retreated after bumping her head and sat down on my slippered feet. This was one of her endearing habits, as if to say that as long as she was on my feet, I couldn't go anywhere without her knowledge. I reached down to stroke her head. Her tail thumped happily on the floor.

"They can vote all they want," said Murk, strolling casually past us, giving Bracken a withering glare but not, at least, swatting at her as he went by, "But it's entirely ceremonial at this point. The mortal world stopped valuing tradition a long time ago," Leaping up onto the bench, he wound his way through the plant pots to the window, left slightly ajar to enable his comings and goings. Halfway through, he turned back and added, with an insolent flick of his tail.

"You may wish to visit the shop down the side street. There's someone there who might be of assistance. And I'm not referring to explaining that pointless meeting, either."

With that last cryptic message, he was gone.

I wondered if that meant he was gone for good because he had no intention of being pleasant to Bracken, or gone because he was in a huff and would eventually be back, or gone because he was intending to leave anyway and hadn't listened to a word I'd said. It's impossible to tell with a cat.

"Cats!" I said, frustrated beyond measure once again. I carried the tea tray over to the sofa, a much-relieved Bracken in my wake. "Why do I even bother?"

Bracken whined, either in commiseration or to remind me of my promise of Hob Nobs.

"Ack," I exclaimed, getting up and going back into the kitchen to retrieve them. "He's a menace and a distraction even when he's not here."

I was just about to sit down again, having given Bracken her (non-chocolate) biscuit, broken into several pieces, a strategy I inexplicably felt diffused the ill-effects of feeding her people-biscuits in the first place, when the phone rang.

I glanced at the clock. It was nearly half-past nine, far beyond a socially-acceptable time for telephoning anyone. Even Mum respected that unspoken rule. Come to think of it, it was probably her rule. It rang twice more, shrill in the otherwise silent room. I wavered. Perhaps I ought to answer it, it might be Edie or Alfie. What if one of them had taken ill?

I went back to the kitchen and picked up the receiver. It crackled briefly.

"Hello?"

"Hello, is that Hazel?"

Who else would it be, I wondered before answering in the affirmative. It was a male voice that I didn't recognize.

"Oh, hello again," came the voice, brimming with bonhomie. "Sorry to bother you this late, but we're off early in the morning and I didn't want to miss you."

"Erm, yes. Who is this?"

A shout of laughter startled me and I held the phone away from my ear, the light suddenly dawning.

"Sorry about that! It's Glenn, Glenn Collins? We met at the meeting earlier tonight. I'm the community liaison...."

"...representative, yes," I said, inwardly groaning. "The one with the robot potatoes," I added, before I could engage my filter.

There was a brief silence on the other end before another shout of laughter made me wince.

"Yes, yes, of course. Robot potatoes. Very clever. I was just wondering if perhaps you might agree to have lunch with me next week? We're off to London for a few days but then we're back in the Westham office for the duration. I was hoping I could bend your ear on a few things."

I blinked, remaining silent for probably too long. Lunch with a stranger was quite possibly the last thing I wanted to partake in. Why would he want to bend my ear? I felt that familiar deflating feeling.

"Hello? Are you still there?"

"Yes, yes, sorry. Erm. Sorry, yes, alright. That would be lovely," I said, only because saying anything else was anathema to my entire way of being.

"Brilliant!" he practically bellowed. "I'll be in touch when we're back, shall I? To sort out the details?"

He didn't wait for me to answer but promptly rang off. I stared at the receiver for a minute before slowly hanging it up. What on earth had I just agreed to?

I didn't have time to ponder that any further as there was a sudden loud rapping on the door. Oddly, Bracken merely lifted her head, yawned and then put it back down again, settling her chin more firmly on the rug.

"Oh for crying out loud," I muttered, "What now?"

I strode over to the door and pulled it open, worn well past patience and prepared to even be rude if absolutely necessary.

"'Allo again, lass," said a familiar growly voice. "Care to ask me in?"

Chapter Fourteen

There was a time, when I lived in London, that every weekend and at least another two weeknights were devoted to visiting and being visited. Teddy had a vast network of friends, stemming from boarding school, university, work, rowing club, darts league; you name it, he was involved in it, and they were, to a person, wildly outgoing and perennially in search of the Next Exciting Thing. For a while, I almost enjoyed myself. Most of them were decent people; they seemed to be kind and good-hearted, if a bit shallow, and I allowed myself to be whirled along in their social wake, delighted with the novelty of being included. It was theatre nights here, lunch parties there, weekends with so-and-so in the Cotswolds; a last minute booking on the overnight to Edinburgh or throwing together a pop-up dinner party with a 1980's theme. I can't say for certain when it all began to change, when I started feeling pangs of dread when the telephone rang or when I started avoiding certain places because I knew someone would be there, just waiting to pounce on me with an invitation. Maybe it was when I realized that beneath the veneer of fun-loving exuberance, often lurked cruelty, mean-spiritedness and a lack of tolerance for those they considered lower on the social ladder. Perhaps it was the steady, unrelenting criticism from Teddy, or the way certain people stopped talking when I walked in the room, or the sideways, pitying glances and veiled insults. To this day, Mum insists my breakdown was brought on by too many late nights and a vitamin B12 deficiency – but I'm fairly certain it was more to do with the fact that I was trying to live someone else's life, one based on someone else's idea of what it meant to live well and be a good person.

My life, the one I *know* I'm meant to be living , the one I wanted, with every fibre of my being, to create in my Nan's cottage – consists of nights in on the sofa with a book or my knitting and afternoons tramping across the moor. At it's very wildest, I might stop in at Alfie and Edie's without ringing first. It's a life of quietness and simple pleasures, of kindness and relative solitude. It feels like a manageable kind of life and I'm at the point where 'manageable' needs to be the defining feature.

It seemed entirely within reach, until the sight, on my doorstep, of an uncommonly small man who I just knew, deep down in my bones, was going to put an end to all of that. Not that it hadn't already started unraveling, in fact it was doing so at an alarming speed, but the fact that he'd knocked on my door and requested an invitation over my threshold somehow seemed to chime the death bell of my peaceful, solitary existence. For one brief moment, I considered slamming the door in his face. It was a lovely moment and I'll treasure the memory of it for always.

"Well?" he barked, scowling up at me.

I sighed, letting my shoulders droop and stood back, waving him in.

He didn't budge, but stood there with his arms crossed over his ample middle, glaring at me as if I were simple.

"Oh," I said, remembering myself. "Sorry, yes."

I cleared my throat and tried to remember the phrase from Nan's stories on the subject of inviting otherworldly creatures into your home, because I'd finally admitted to myself that that's exactly what he was.

"Please," I said, resisting the urge to bow, "Won't you come and share my fire?"

The little man snorted and pushed past me, unbuttoning his overcoat as he came.

"Nice touch," he said, "But a simple 'come in' would've sufficed. Still, it's an encouragement to see you've had a bit of education, like."

My face burned with embarrassment. Trust me to do something stupid. At the same time, the implied criticism of Nan rankled.

"I've always thought it best to observe good manners," I said, following him into the living room where he was making himself comfortable in the chair by the fire. "Even in the company of those who may not deserve it." I added, with a touch of mad rebellion. "Especially, I think, in the company of those undeserving."

My sarcasm was lost on him, however as he had got as far as unlacing his heavy, hobnailed boots and was struggling to remove them. I folded my arms and watched him, raising a questioning eyebrow.

"Bunions," he puffed, red-faced with the effort. "I bin on my feet for hours and they're fair smarting."

I nodded, because the situation was increasingly awkward and what else could I do? Bracken, I noted, appeared unconcerned by the presence of my visitor and was actually wagging her tail tip at him. Again, I questioned the point of such an inadequate guardian.

At last, the war of the boots was over and the second one thumped solidly to the floor. My guest breathed a gusty sigh and stretched out his legs towards the fire, wiggling his toes which were encased in thick woollen socks.

For moment, I thought he was going to doze off. In a mild panic, I made a point of clattering my tea mug and plate on the table.

He opened one eye and regarded me for a minute or two, the duration of which seemed an eternity as I fully rearranged my tea things then sat, perched on the edge of the sofa.

"Speaking of manners," he said, with a sly grin. "I'm fair parched and wouldn't say no to a drop of something."

I blushed, realizing he'd taken my jibe after all.

"Would you like some tea?" I asked, determined not to speak a word more of apology to this exasperating little person.

"Got anything stronger than that?" he asked, peering over my shoulder towards the kitchen. His eyes rested on the cupboard where Nan always kept the special bottle of whiskey. Of course, I realized with a sinking feeling, this wasn't his first visit to the cottage.

"Just tea, I'm afraid," I replied, brightly, getting up to go and fetch him a mug. There was absolutely no way that I was going to let him sit there and get sozzled. My day had already gone on far too long. A quick cup of tea to refresh him and then he was to be on his way.

He squinted at me, his merry eyes disappearing in the folds of his nut-brown skin. He reached up a gnarled finger and smoothed his whiskers.

"Aye, I reckon you're right," he said with a wink, "We've lots to talk about and we can't have me nodding off in the middle, can we?"

"I suppose not," I replied, suppressing a groan. I'd had as much conversation as I felt I could be reasonably expected to weather for one day.

"Don't you worry about that, my lass," he said, leaning over to take the mug from me. "All you need do is sit yerself down and listen."

And listen is what I did. I stole a glance at the clock at the point at which my friend — Aberfoyle Goodship by name – began his dissertation on exactly What I Ought To Be Doing and it was just past ten o'clock. When he made his closing comments, it was just gone half-past eleven. Bearing in mind my preference for having my bedside light out by ten at the very latest, I believe I could be excused the series of yawns which accompanied his speech.

The gist of it was that as Current Resident of Rookery Cottage, albeit known that I had yet to live out the trial term and be deemed worthy of role as Caretaker (and there I was thinking it was entirely up to me when I was allegedly on trial) it was my duty to make it certain that the sale of land to BMZ would not go through. Furthermore, I was honour-bound to uphold the Rights of Trespass wherein Mr.Goodship and any of his contemporaries, exceptions to be noted forthwith, be allowed free passage through the Common Portal.

The Common Portal, I was given to learn, was the stone shed at the bottom of the garden.

"Are you telling me that the stone shed is some sort of magic gateway?" I asked, jolted from my stupor by this little addendum to my lengthy list of duties.

Mr.Goodship closed his eyes briefly. I got the distinct impression, both by his choice of words and the slow, measured cadence of his speech that he was quite convinced that I was a simpleton.

"The term," he said, steepling his fingers and placing them momentarily against his whiskered lips. "Is *Portal*. It is neither a gateway nor is it especially magical, although there are those who would argue those points."

"Oh. So then if it's not magic, then anyone could go through it?"

"Absolutely not!"

"Well, why not? If it's not magic, then conceivably anyone should be able to pass through."

"And how, my dear girl, do you come to this conclusion?"

"Well," I said, suddenly faltering in my argument. It seemed obvious when I said it but his response made me think I may have missed something. "Well if it's *not* magic, then one wouldn't need to *have* magic at one's command to be able to use it. Ergo, anyone can use it...shouldn't they?"

I avoided looking at him. I felt like I did a hundred times before, standing before a teacher's desk, burning with shame over some display of idiocy or other.

He was silent for a moment, no doubt, I thought, wondering if it were possible he could find someone else to take over these duties.

"You are so very cruel to yourself," he said, his voice soft. "Would you ever speak that way to another soul, the way you do to your own self?"

I didn't know how to respond. First of all, it was becoming apparent that he could somehow read my thoughts – a distressing and slightly embarrassing notion. Secondly, he'd called me out on my non-existent self-esteem which felt far too raw to be discussed with a bossy little man I'd only just met.

I stood up, abrupt and with the intention of ending the conversation.

"I don't appreciate your rummaging around in my thoughts, if that's what you're doing," I said, my voice wobbling slightly. I was tired – physically, emotionally, mentally – I wanted a hot-water bottle and bed. I glanced over at Bracken, she hadn't stirred at all during Mr.Goodship's speech but now she lifted her head and whined.

"Your wee dog knows," he said, "She understands cruelty and she's wondering why you'd want to do that to yourself."

"Stop it!" I practically shouted at him, feeling my stomach coiling and my whole body vibrating with panic, "Stop it this minute! You don't know me, you can't possibly know me so you have no right to march in here, telling me what I should and shouldn't do. Never mind the unsolicited self-help advice."

I busied myself tidying up the tea things, reaching over and grabbing the empty mug from his hands. If I let myself, I'd collapse into a weeping heap. I bustled into the kitchen, snapping on the light with a violent flick and turned on the tap, filling the sink to wash the mugs when normally I would've just left them for the morning. Anything to occupy myself, anything to stop him from continuing along that line of discussion.

With a series of loud gulps, I swallowed the rising clog of tears in my throat. I was just overtired, I told myself, feeling particularly sensitive and extremely overwhelmed by the day's events. A good night's sleep is what I needed, and tomorrow, a day spent in the garden. Alone.

"Aye, lass," said a voice behind me. I stiffened but then turned, leaving my hands in the sudsy water, making sure he knew I'd no intention of yielding further to him.

"Oh?" I said, trying to make my voice as flat and unemotional as possible. I avoided looking into his eyes. Those eyes that saw far too much.

"A day in the garden," he continued, pulling on his overcoat. I saw that he'd put his boots back on, although they remained untied. "It'll do you a power of good."

He walked to the door then stopped, his hand on the latch. I let the soap suds run down my hands and drip onto the floor as I turned to follow his progress. Some part of me wanted him to say something else. What, I don't know, but I felt it all the same.

"I'm sorry, lass," he said, pitching his voice low again, turning the growl into a pleasant, soothing sort of rumble. "It were wrong of me to upset you, I can see that. The missus is allus going on about my tone. She says it puts folk off when they don't know me. It fair pains me to see you take on so. There's a world of folk that need you, pet – really and truly need you – and it won't do any of us any good if you're to be always at yourself with the whips and lashes."

He paused a moment, looking back towards the flames, flickering and snapping in the hearth. Frowning, as if in some inner argument with himself, he jiggled the latch of the door and then spoke again.

"If you've a mind to, and only if you truly want," he said, raising a finger to wag at me and fixing me with his fierce green gaze. "I can take you to see what needs seeing. I think it'll help settle it all in your mind, aye?"

I blinked, unsure still and not trusting my voice.

He blinked back at me, holding my gaze for an uncomfortable minute.

I cleared my throat and nodded.

"Yes, thank you. If you think it would help then I would like that," I said.

He nodded as well and slipped quietly out of the door.

It was some minutes before I realized that I'd actually meant it that time.

Chapter Fifteen

T he next day dawned clear and sunny. There was a slight breeze and it carried with it the glorious scent of blossom. I had discovered that a pair of robins and another pair of blackbirds had taken up residence in the garden – one each on either side of the vegetable patch -- and they were full of song and industry as I stood at the sink, waiting for the kettle to boil.

I'd slept like the dead. I had half-expected to be awake all night fretting over the events of the previous day, there was so much swirling around in my head, between the village meeting, the revelations of Mr.Goodship and everything else in between. Not to mention the fact I'd agreed to lunch with a complete stranger. Still, as soon as my head had hit the pillow I was out and I didn't wake until well past sunrise.

Gazing out of the window, watching my feathered neighbours flitting about their business, I came to a sudden decision. It was no use trying to avoid the things that were clearly unavoidable at this point. Granted, it was going to make for a great deal of discomfort and possible overwhelm in the short-term, but the sooner the matter of the land sale was laid to rest – one way or another – the sooner I could get back to building my fortress of solitude. I would simply need to call on the reserve that I knew I had, having dipped into it on so many occasions when I was living in London, and get myself through the next couple of weeks.

"There's just no way around it, Bracken," I said, smiling down at her as she snuffled around the floor on a crumb safari. She wagged her tail without looking up. Such an agreeable companion! "If I have lunch with that fellow from BMZ then no-one can fault my attempts to intervene. Surely that will satisfy them. And, I'll go with Mr.Goodship, to see whatever it is he needs me to see and then I can happily retire, knowing I did my bit and let the village get on with voting and the proper legal channels."

"Do you really suppose it's that simple?" remarked Murk, blinking lazily in at me through the window.

I sighed, turning my back on him to pull the whistling kettle off the hob.

"You're back," I said, not bothering to hide my disappointment. I poured the hot water into the tea pot and made a point of stirring the tea leaves around and around. If I ignored him long enough perhaps he'd take the hint.

Unfortunately I heard the sound of him jumping down off the window sill onto the draining board. A spoon clattered to the floor as he picked his way around the bench to sit expectantly in the spot where I usually served his meals. I glanced over and he looked pointedly at the can opener where it was resting next to his clean saucer and a tin of salmon.

"Indeed I am," he said, yawning widely, showing an alarming set of teeth. "You didn't think your little huff would put me off, did you?"

He extended a paw and gently batted the can opener. I assume that was his attempt at playful charm.

I wondered how long I could hold off ignoring his hints.

I spooned sugar into my mug and slowly walked across to the fridge to retrieve the milk. I took out the bottle, but not the smaller one of cream that I'd taken to asking Young Craig to deliver with the milk. Slowly, I stirred the tea leaves again before pouring the stewed tea into my mug. I carefully dribbled the milk in, stirring as it went, attempting to get it just the right colour. I could feel Murk staring daggers at my back. Bracken whined.

I went back to the fridge and put the milk away, turning to face the scruffy orange cat as I closed the door.

"Oh!" I said, feigning surprise, "You're still here."

If looks could kill, his withering glare would have dropped me like a stone. I congratulated myself on this small, albeit petty, victory. I just needed him to know that he wasn't entirely in charge.

"I suppose you want a bit of breakfast, then?" I said, wiping down the bench where I'd spilled a drop of milk. I dried my hands thoroughly and crossed into the living room to retrieve the tea cosy which I'd left there the night before.

"If it's not too much trouble, thank you," he said, through gritted teeth. The crooked end of his tail flicked back and forth in sharp, twitchy movements. I suppressed a grin.

"Salmon alright?" I said, picking up the tin.

"Marvellous," he grunted.

Once I'd served up a forkful of salmon, and a dribble of the special-ly-ordered cream, I took my tea out into the garden, leaving Murk to mutter and grumble. I'd found an old wooden chair in the shed, minus a few of the spindles from its back but quite serviceable as a garden chair and settled myself just outside the back door. I sat, sipping my tea, soaking in the warmth of the early morning sun. I envisioned a proper little set of table and chairs out there, perfect for sitting with a book and a mug of something. I thought about getting a string of twinkle lights to suspend from the eaves, they could wind around the post of the proposed umbrella table and would add a lovely ambience. I even went so far as to imagine inviting a couple of friends over for an evening — some dandelion wine (made by my own hand, of course) and nibbly bits of things. It was a wonder that I could imagine a time when I would feel like doing that, when I wasn't so incredibly exhaust-ed and overwhelmed that the idea of inviting friends over didn't seem like a nightmarish way to spend an evening. Perhaps the cottage was beginning to soak into my pores. If I stopped fretting long enough, I could feel the peace trickling in. Sighing gustily, I closed my eyes and listened to the birds. I heard the sound of Bracken rummaging about in the basket by the door, no doubt looking for remnants of bird seed that I may have dropped when I went out to fill the feeder.

I was in the middle of mentally designing my future henhouse when I heard the jangle of the telephone. I grimaced. Who could possibly be phoning this early in the morning? Of course I knew the answer. I also knew it wasn't worth my while to ignore it, hoping the caller would give up.

I poured out the dregs of my tea into what was once a potted rosemary plant (now sadly deceased) and went back inside. Murk had finished his salmon and was performing his ritual ablutions while sitting in the middle of the kitchen table. I didn't bother trying to hide my annoyance.

"Hello?" I said, picking up the receiver, bracing myself.

"Hazel!" exclaimed my mum, her voice full of accusation. "Don't tell me you were still in bed at this hour? What took you so long to answer the phone?"

Mum came from the school of early-to-bed-early-to-rise. I imagine she'd already done a yoga class and a pilates session by now and was halfway to having the rest of her day organized.

"Hello, Mum. I'm fine, thank you. I was in the garden."

"The garden? Surely not in this weather. Hazel, the damp is apocryphal in that dreadful place, you really should try and stay indoors until at least midday. Think of your health."

"I thought you said the inside of the cottage was damp," I replied, seized by a fit of rebellion, "Where am I supposed to go?"

Out of the corner of my eye, I saw Murk pause in his cleaning. At my glance, he resumed with an air of indifference that was so very much a part of his persona.

"Listen, dear, I heard from Mavis Riley that you were having lunch with Glenn Collins, is that right?"

I took a brief moment to reflect upon the fact that she either wasn't listening to me at all or was choosing to ignore everything I said. I then reflected on the fact that it seemed as if there was no escape from my mother's social telegraph network. How in the world did Mavis Riley know about my lunch plans? Fortunately, I didn't get left wondering for too long.

"Glenn Collins' sister-in-law has the same housekeeping service as Mavis Riley's daughter. Jessica, you remember Jessica. Lovely girl, you went to her twenty-first I believe. Anyway, I'm thrilled that you're seeing Glenn, he's a very important figure at BMZ and altogether a charming fellow. Where are you going for lunch? Have you got any-thing to wear? Please darling, do *not* dare wear any of those dreadful tatty cardigans..."

"I'm not *seeing* Glenn Collins," I said, choosing to ignore her ref-erence to my cardigans and instead mentally noting I needed to order myself some wool to start another one. "He merely asked me to lunch to discuss a land sale that's affecting the village. Apparently as the resident of Rookery Cottage I have some sort of vested interest in these matters."

I don't know why I tried to make it sound like I was actually involved. Perhaps it was to rub in the fact that I was dead serious about staying in Winkle. If my mum knew I was getting involved with village affairs, she might see it as me being less inclined toward becoming a hermit and set her mind at ease, thus eliminating her nagging and scheming.

Unfortunately it had quite the opposite effect.

"Absolutely not!" she exclaimed, using her I-will-brook-no-argu-ment tone. "You are *not* telling me that you're getting involved in village politics! Hazel Elspeth Price that is *not* why you're there and surely you must know that entangling yourself in the petty squabbling is entirely inappropriate. Besides which, BMZ is an extremely pow-erful and influential company. The situation is none of your concern, certainly not something in which a person of your delicate sensibilities wants to become embroiled."

There was a brief moment when I wanted to absolutely agree with her. It would be the perfect excuse to just let it all pass me by; it would be far simpler, after all, to travel that familiar, well-worn path of least resistance. I let the ease of that decision wash over me for a brief and glorious moment.

"Actually, mother," I said, as casually as possible. "I'm already quite involved with the situation, as you call it. I'm meeting both with Mr. Collins and also with a party from the opposing side, a Mr.Goodship. I feel as if I need to see both sides of the argument before I decide my loyalties."

The line buzzed quietly. I could imagine the look on her face. Murk, I noticed, had inched slightly closer. I ignored him, turning my back slightly. I'm almost certain he snorted.

"Hazel," my mother's voice was soft, she was changing tactics, "Hazel, you must know I only want what's best for you, in all things, which is why it's absolutely imperative that you listen..."

Just then, Bracken started barking. It was that slightly frantic, slightly excited bark she used when someone she knew was approaching. It was the closest she'd come to acting even remotely guard-like.

"Sorry, Mum," I said, "There's just someone at the door. I'll have to ring off now. Love to you and give my love to dad, will you? I'll phone later in the week. Bye!"

I put the receiver down before she could get a word in. I only felt a tiny bit wobbly and went out to see who had arrived.

"There might be hope for you yet," said Murk as I walked past him.

"Oh sod off, you aggravating cat!"

A curious mixture of yowl and purr emanated from deep within his chest. It was, I realized, the sound of the raggedy old cat laughing.

My saviour had come in the form of Astrid. Bracken had waylaid her, halfway down the garden path, by rolling onto her back and demanding a belly-rub. That's where I found them, Bracken's legs waving in the air and Astrid telling her what a beautiful and clever dog she was. She spoke in a soft, sing-song voice that was quite a contrast to her usual clipped tones and surly teenaged demeanour.

"Hello, Astrid," I said, genuinely happy to see her. Anyone who could see the beauty and intelligence in a dog such as Bracken was someone with whom I could relate wholeheartedly. I also suspected that she felt far less sure of herself than she might portray and that was *definitely* a point on which I could relate. "I see you've been attacked by my guard dog."

Astrid looked up and smiled. Her eyes were ringed in her regulation black eyeliner and her blue hair was scraped up into an untidy arrangement that managed to incorporate several bobby pins, a spotted bandana and a series of thin plaits. Nevertheless, pulled back from her face, it was quite a flattering look.

"Isn't she a love?" she asked, giving Bracken one last tummy-rub before straightening up. Bracken wriggled back onto her feet and stood, leaning heavily against Astrid's legs. She wore a pair of batik-patched jeans today, and scuffed purple Converse. "I can't believe someone would just throw her away like a bit of rubbish."

"No, nor me," I said, looking fondly down at the scruffy little dog. She'd moved away from Astrid, momentarily attracted by a whiff of something among the raspberry canes. "She's so much more settled now, she hardly shakes at all." I paused, remembering Murk, "Well, only when the cat agitates her,"

Astrid's face brightened into another smile.

"Oh? You've got a cat as well?" she asked, peering past me, hopefully, as if it might stroll down the path. "I love cats, they're just so Other, don't you think? Barely domesticated, if you ask me."

"Hmmm," I replied. "Well you could certainly say that about this one. But no, he's not mine, he belongs to Mr. Reed, the solicitor."

"Ah," she said, knowingly. "*That* cat. I can understand why he might upset Bracken, then. He upsets just about everyone, I think."

"You know him, then?" I asked, wondering exactly how well she knew Murk. His propensity for conversation, for instance.

Astrid shrugged.

"Sure, he gets around the village, upsetting milk bottles and digging up seedlings, that sort of thing. He's had more slippers thrown at him than hot dinners. I don't know why people get that upset, he's only doing what cats do. Can't blame him for following his nature."

Inwardly, I questioned the upsetting of milk bottles and unearthing seedlings as being innately feline behaviour but chose not to mention it. It seemed, though, that he hadn't revealed his knack for speech to her.

"Would you like a cup of tea?" I asked, feeling expansive. The beauty of the morning and my mini-victory with Mum was filling me with all manner of confidence. "I was about to make a fresh one. The phone rang just as I was having my first and I don't feel quite ready to start the day yet."

"No, thanks," she said, swinging a small patchwork bag from where it was slung across her front. She plunged a hand into it, rummaged about for a moment then pulled out a large clipboard with a sheaf of papers attached.

I frowned, looking between the bag and the clipboard, visions of the TARDIS and Hermione's beaded handbag swimming into view. She must have noticed my expression because she grinned and winked.

"Brilliant, isn't it?" she said, smoothing a fingerless-gloved hand over the brightly coloured patches. "I got it in the village, at the shop down the side street. It doesn't fair get me some looks!"

I smiled back, mentally adding "the shop on the side street" to my list of things I didn't know about but clearly needed to investigate. That list was growing to an alarming size.

"Super!" I said, pretending as if I had a clue. "I bet it comes in handy for...well, for just about anything, I suppose."

She looked at me with great pity. In my dotage, I had obviously only a faint working grasp of the true appeal of such a fantastic item to a young person such as herself.

"What's on the clipboard?" I asked, in an attempt to wrest the focus from my idiocy.

"It's a petition," she said, handing it over to me. There was a blue biro tied to the metal clip with a bit of dirty string. "My friends and I are collecting signatures to take to the council office in protest over the land sale. It's a good idea to be proactive in these situations."

"Yes, very much. It's an excellent idea," I said, fishing for the pen. Unfortunately, the string was short and tied with a bias to the right-handed person. I struggled for a moment, pulling it from across and then from below in an attempt to arrange it so that I could use it. As it happened, I ended up with not much leeway and my signature and then printed name looked as if a three year-old had written them.

"Sorry about that," I said, awkwardly, handing back the clipboard. I'm sure she tried to hide her disappointment in the legibility of my signature but it didn't quite show on her face. "It's hard being left-handed in a right-handed world," I added, as an attempt at mild, situation-salvaging humour. It passed by unnoticed.

"That's okay," she said, still frowning down at the page, no doubt contemplating how best to remove the blight of my signature. "I'm sure it won't matter."

She took one last look and then stuffed the clipboard back into the bag, a feat of dimensional manipulation that both delighted and disturbed.

"How many signatures do you think you'll manage to collect?" I asked, keen to show my support.

"Pretty much the whole village," she said, with a shrug. "It's not like we have to convince anyone – well, most people anyway – that this is a bad idea. But BMZ is your typical capitalistic beast in that they've got half the county council in their pockets. If the council decides to, they can force the land sale by compulsory purchase whether we want it or not. And we just can't let that happen."

Her eyes flashed and she looked at me with such vehemence that I felt as if it were me who was forcing the sale of the land.

"But surely, if everyone is against the sale, they can't force it through! Whatever happened to the democratic process?"

Astrid looked at me with something akin to sympathy; with a healthy overtone of mild contempt.

"Have you never heard of the Enclosures Act?" she asked, slowly and enunciating carefully so that I might keep up. "Nothing much has changed. It's always been the rich trampling over the common people, only now it's big corporations doing it while trying to pretend they're doing us a favour."

I scrambled frantically in my brain for the remnants of my history lessons of years ago. Wasn't the Enclosures Act something to do with taking away common lands from the peasants? I wondered if that was even still valid. Wasn't it very 12th century, or thereabouts? I wasn't prepared to risk further humiliation so just nodded, with an air of great sadness.

"And there's no recourse for the village?" I asked, wincing slightly in advance.

"Oh, there's recourse, alright," she said, menacingly, "Don't you worry about that. This is far from over, I can tell you. We'll start out politely enough, but they'd best not push it. This land isn't anyone's to sell, not even Lord Dummell. Not that he'll sell voluntarily, mind you."

She paused to push her bag back over her hip.

"We're not going to let this happen," she repeated, again, as if I were the one suggesting they would.

She turned abruptly, ending the conversation, and stalked off down the path, leaving a trail of uneasy hostility behind her. I was getting the feeling that Astrid and her friends wouldn't hesitate to defend their patch by any means necessary, the idea of which was daunting.

Bracken noticed that her friend was leaving and trotted over for one last round of affection. Astrid stopped in her tracks and bent to fondle Bracken's ears, murmuring softly that started the dog's tail waving. She stood up and turned, raising a hand in a wave, the militant energy having dissipated as quickly as it had arisen.

"Thanks for your signature," she said, "It's good to know we can depend on you for your support!"

"Well," I said to Bracken who had returned to my side. I blew out a breath I hadn't realized I was holding. "That was strange and slightly off-putting. I think I really could use that cup of tea now."

I spent the rest of the morning toiling in the garden. Sorting out the chaos there was a convenient metaphor for sorting out the chaos in my brain. At least, that's what I was aiming for. I cleared the worst of the tangle away from the raspberry canes, pruning them hard, even though I wasn't sure if I ought to be doing so. I never could remember whether to do it in spring or autumn or if it even mattered. Or maybe it was different depending on whether it was raspberries or blackberries, or even what kind of raspberries. It really didn't matter, I rationalized as I stood with the pruners in my gloved hands, gazing at the snarl of cane. I simply had to get it all under control and if it meant sacrificing this year's crop then so be it. There was always next year.

After the raspberries, I tackled the vegetable patch. I 'chopped and dropped' the remains of last year's vegetation and cleared away the area around the burgeoning rhubarb which was already putting on a valiant effort to overcome the choking layer of detritus. I wheeled several barrows of compost from what looked like the oldest pile and layered it over the tidied beds. In a few short hours it had lost that despairing look and was transformed from neglected into expectant.

At half-past noon I put down my shovel and stretched my aching back. Between the sun and the exertion I had long since shed my coat and was working just in my cardigan. Bracken had found herself a sunny spot on what could generously be referred to as lawn and had been of great support throughout my travails. She approved of every decision I made and always opted on the side of more compost instead of the exertion and disruption of digging. I was just admiring my handiwork, finally feeling as if I was making progress when the sound of the gate latch caught my ear. The tip of Bracken's tail twitched briefly but she was otherwise unperturbed.

"Ah, 'tis grand to see you at toil in the earth, lass," came Mr.Good ship's growly voice. "That's what heals the heart best, I allus say. Nowt like a bit of communion with the dirt to settle an addled soul."

I turned to greet him, mustering as much enthusiasm as I could, although in truth, my heart had sunk when I heard his voice. I was only just beginning to forget all of the unpleasantness of the day before.

"Peace offering," he said, holding out a large brown paper sack.

I took it from him, wary. Wasn't there something about accepting gifts from faery folk?

"Bulbs," he said, with a grin. "No strings attached, I swear on me old mum's grave. In fact, they're dug from that very same place."

"Oh!" I said, peering into the bag, not certain whether I ought to feel flattered or creeped out. "Should you have dug up your mum's flowers?"

Mr.Goodship laughed his wheezing laugh.

"No need to worry, lass. She's not in it yet!"

It turned out that the stash of bulbs had come only from the proposed *site* of the elder Mrs.Goodship's grave. Apparently that was a thing you did to show your friendship to a person — it showed that they were deemed worthy of an offering from the land fit to hold the remains of a dearly departed. I was very touched and told him so. It seemed that we were starting afresh and I was very happy about that.

"What are your plans then, lass?" asked Mr.Goodship, from where he sat on the edge of the leek trench. He had a large mug of tea in one hand and a rock bun in the other. Mrs.Goodship (the Younger), his wife, had also sent along a gift. Award-winning rock buns, apparently. I had made us fried egg sandwiches for lunch and the tea and rock buns were serving as our afters.

"Do I have to decide now?" I asked, suddenly gripped with panic. Surely I wasn't expected to know my future plans already. "Aren't I allowed a year and a day to decide?"

Mr.Goodship chuckled, shaking his shaggy head.

"Not your grand plan, you numpty! I meant what are you going to plant in the garden? You know, in the way of veg and flowers, like."

Relief flooded over me in a rush, together with mild embarrassment.

"Oh! That!" I said, giggling in a slightly hysterical fashion. Even that as a question was over-facing to me. "I don't know, to be honest. I'm late getting started, especially since things weren't looked after last autumn. I haven't got any seedlings started and I don't even know what might pop up. With the exception of some salad greens, carrots and onions, some tomatoes in the poly-tunnel, oh and potatoes of course, I was mostly going to have a wait-and-see year. You know, see what comes up."

The little man nodded approvingly. He took a bite of rock bun and then a swig of tea. Several currants from the bun remained lodged in his whiskers. It was a bit distracting.

"Sounds like you're planning on staying, then," he said, avoiding my eyes and instead breaking off a crumb of bun and handing it to Bracken who sat, eternally hopeful, at his feet.

"I *am* staying," I said, with utter conviction, "This place is my dream come true, there's absolutely nothing that will budge me."

"Not even your mum?" he asked, still not looking at me.

"Especially not my mum," I answered, albeit with slightly less conviction.

He nodded. The currants shifted slightly but remained trapped. I tried not to stare.

"Right!" he said, standing abruptly, brushing the crumbs from his lap. Bracken leapt upon them with the air of a starving creature. "That settles it. Are you ready?"

"Ready?" I said, blinking in surprise, my mind immediately racing in search of whatever it was that I'd forgotten.

"Aye, lass. Come on, we haven't got all day. We need to be there and back before sundown."

"Sorry, where are we going?"

"To see what needs seeing," he said, waving a hand in the general direction of the moor. "Get your coat and bring the hound, do 'er good to have a bit of a jaunt."

I'd forgotten all about our little field trip. Wordless, I collected the mugs and plates and left them in the sink. I took my coat from the back of the chair and closed the door behind me, unsure if it was anxiety, excitement or the greasy egg sandwich that was causing the sudden churning in my stomach.

Mr.Goodship stood halfway down the garden path, hands clasped behind his back, booted foot tapping. He grinned when he saw me and waved me on, heading for the bottom of the garden. I trotted obediently behind, Bracken wagging in my wake.

He stopped at the bottom of the garden, between the two sheds.

"This way," he said, sweeping a courtly bow and beckoning towards the crooked open door of the stone shed. I peered in from where I stood, it was dim and shadowed inside.

"In there?" I said, doubtful. I had a brief vision of being shoved in and the door locked behind me.

"Aye, go on! Don't worry, I'm not going to lock you in!"

There he went again with the mind-reading. I turned back and scowled. He had the decency to look sheepish.

"Sorry, sorry," he said, his hands spread in a gesture of apology. "Can't be helped, lass. You fair scream it out of yourself."

That gave me pause. Was I that transparent?

"Here," he said, pushing past me through the open door. "I was trying to be gentleman-like but obviously that sort of thing is wasted on you modern lasses. I'll go first, shall I?"

Without waiting to hear me protest that gentlemanly behaviour never went out of style, he disappeared into the gloom of the shed.

"Well, Bracken," I said, glancing down at her. She seemed keen enough, no trace of a tremble or quiver. "In for a penny, eh?"

I walked through the door.

The inside of the shed was dark and smelled the damp smell of old stone. I blinked several times, trying to adjust to the lack of light. I felt Bracken press herself beside me but she didn't seem afraid. Either she'd become brave all of a sudden or there really wasn't anything to be scared of. I couldn't see Mr.Goodship anywhere. Suddenly, my fear of being locked in reared up again. I spun around but the door was still open, leading out into my garden.

"Oi!" came a voice, echoing as if from a distance. "Over here!"

"Where?" I said, wondering how the voice could possibly be coming from a distance when the shed was, at the most, five feet square.

"Here!" A light flickered and came on, bathing the inside of the shed in warm yellow glow. Mr.Goodship stood about ten feet distant, waving his hand at me to follow. I hesitated, realizing the external dimensions of the shed weren't balancing with these internal ones. I glanced back again, the door was still open, still leading out into my garden. I was overcome with the notion that I was standing on more than just the threshold of a peculiar stone shed in my Nan's garden.

"Coming!" I called, and walked towards him.

Chapter Sixteen

W e walked for what seemed like hours. Mr.Goodship went on ahead, holding aloft a light, although, looking back, I don't recall him having a lantern. The path felt like packed earth underfoot and wound up and down and around. I wondered aloud if we were underground.

"Not as such," came the reply from in front of me,"More alongside."

I didn't quite understand what he meant by that but decided not to pursue it. The fact that I was walking for ages inside a five foot square shed was enough suspension of disbelief for one afternoon. Bracken padded beside me, occasionally lifting her head to nose my hand. It was a comfort to know that she was there.

Eventually the path started to incline and our surroundings seemed to be getting brighter.

"Almost there," huffed Mr.Goodship as we climbed steadily upwards. He grinned back at me. "One too many of the missus' cakes, I think."

I smiled back at him, feeling much easier in his company the longer we walked. Which I suppose was a good thing, I thought, as I was quite at his mercy in the dark tunnel. I decided not to dwell on that too heavily.

The air began to change as we walked. It lost it's old-stone and damp earth smell and now smelled of apple blossom and warmth. We rounded a bend and then suddenly, the tunnel widened into an opening, revealing an expanse of green, sun-dappled meadow.

"Oh!" I said. "Are we here?"

Mr.Goodship chuckled.

"Inasmuch as we're anywhere," he replied, annoyingly cryptic. "Look behind you."

I turned around and felt a rush of dizziness, of the kind you get when you stand up too quickly.

Behind us, not three feet distant, the door to the shed stood open, leading out into my garden.

I swallowed hard.

"How...." I trailed off, feeling quite unable to continue.

The little man chuckled again and shrugged.

"It doesn't pay to think too hard about some things in this world," he said, gesturing towards my garden. "Needing to have explanations about everything all the time is what got you lot in trouble in the first place. Some things aren't meant to be known, only believed."

He paused, giving me an appraising look.

"But you've an inclination for that, haven't you lass?"

"Do I?" I asked, surprised. I would love to think I was the sort of person that could accept the wonder of the world without question. I know I used to be that way. But I was afraid that everyday life drummed that out of me long ago.

He didn't answer but reached out and patted my arm.

"Come on and meet the missus, will ye?"

Mr. and Mrs. Goodship lived in a low, thatched cottage on the outskirts of the bustling village of Nether Winkle. It was a market town, I came to learn, and Mrs. Goodship had a bakery stall on Wednesdays and Saturdays. As this was a Thursday, she was busy in their tiny kitchen baking goods for the Saturday market, which, I also learned, was the busier of the two as people from the Outside would often visit.

"The Outside?" I asked, accepting a glass of raspberry lemonade. I was assured most heartily that I was in no danger of becoming trapped in Faery by drinking it. That, I was told, was a terrible misunderstanding stemming from a long-forgotten custom among the less savoury elements of the Otherworld. The myth, I was promised, was only perpetuated as a means of conjuring an air of mystery and menace to a place that was, by and large, quite ordinary.

"Ordinary?" I spluttered, hastily dabbing my chin with an exquisitely embroidered napkin that appeared, most conveniently, on the table beside me. "What about this place is ordinary?"

On our way to his home, Mr. Goodship had pointed out no less than ten marvels – anywhere from trees which produced chocolate-covered nuts to a squirrel-type creature that collected the cottony flowers of a nearby shrub and used them to build their elaborate nests. In the autumn, once the nests had been vacated, the soft fibres could be untangled and then woven into a shimmering cloth that had the ability to protect the wearer from faery-induced harm. Apparently, the process of nest-building and young-rearing infused the cloth with protective powers. Without this interim step, the fibres were abrasive and rash-inducing. I spent most of the journey in open-mouthed disbelief.

Mrs.Goodship grinned and waved a floury hand. She was a tiny woman, smaller than her husband by almost a foot, with a mass of brown hair piled in an intricate bun on the top of her head. A brightly coloured head-scarf kept the whole thing in check and gave her the appearance of wearing a crown. When she smiled, her twinkly brown eyes disappeared into the folds of her wrinkled cheeks.

"Ah, 'tis nobbut a bit of fancy," she said, wiping her hands on her tartan apron. "More lemonade, lovey? A bit of cake? Try this one, it's a new recipe I'm trying out. Macaroon and toffee with an elderberry glaze. Himself says the glaze is too much but then he's always been one for avoiding fruit on a cake. Says it's oil and water."

"I really shouldn't," I said, thinking of the three previous slices of 'testers' that I'd eaten. Bracken was at full attention. She'd been doing plenty of testing on her own. I counted myself among the worst of dog custodians, letting her eat like that.

"Ah, go on, lassie!" trilled Mrs.G, "You're just a wee strip of a thing. Could do with a bit of fattening up. Himself tells me you have toast for your supper more often than not. What sort of a way is that to go on? If it weren't for our Edie I dare say you'd have expired of the malnutrients by now!"

"You know Edie?" I asked, surprised into accepting another slice of cake.

"Of course, lassie," said Mrs.G, topping up my lemonade from a blue and white striped jug, "We go way back, Edie and me. That lemon drizzle you had two helpings ago is from her recipe. And she herself got it from a lassie up Glencarragh way who is a friend of another fellow we know from the old days. It's a family sort of feeling that we have."

"Aye, that it is," said Mr.Goodship from where he sat by the hearth. He'd had several helpings of cake as well and was now filling up his pipe from a pouch of tobacco that hung from a large iron hook set into the stone of the fireplace. "Which is precisely why you need to stop playing at wanting to be the hermit and get stuck into things around the place."

I bristled slightly.

"I'm not playing at anything," I retorted, somewhat less vehemently than I would've liked for having a mouthful of macaroon and toffee cake. "And I'm not a hermit. I just want to be left alone to live a...."

"...peaceful and quiet life," he finished. "Aye, I know." He paused to strike a match. He set it to the bowl of his pipe and puffed vigorously until it caught. A wreath of sweet smelling smoke wound around his head. "But did it ever occur to you that it takes a bit of effort to have that sort of life. That mebbe it comes at a price?"

I frowned, feeling myself getting defensive.

"Did you just bring me here to lecture me?" I asked, setting down my plate, but not before brushing a few crumbs onto the floor for Bracken. She'd already enjoyed a plateful of sausage and fried potato that Mrs.Goodship just happened to have on hand. Her ribs would disappear in no time at the rate she was eating.

Mrs.Goodship tutted loudly.

"He most certainly did not," she said, flapping a tea towel in her husband's direction. "Stop aggravating the lass, Mister. You know as well as I do that getting folks' backs up is no way to ask them for help. You've upset her enough already."

"Ask *me* for help?" I said, looking between them. Mrs.Goodship was giving Mr.Goodship one of those married people stares that defied him to say one more word. "What could I possibly help you with?"

"Oh, nowt much," said Mr.Goodship, airily, avoiding looking at his wife who tutted again. "Only protecting our livelihoods, saving our village and otherwise stopping everything we know and love from being wrenched from our hands."

The view from the Goodship's garden was a vast expanse of rolling green on one side — I had no idea my north from south — and a well-worn path to the other which led into the main part of the village, just visible on the near horizon. A large and wild hedge ran alongside the path and into the village itself. It looked suspiciously similar to the hedge at home. Although who could tell one hedge from another, I rationalized.

I'd come into the garden when my gentle hosts had started bickering at the top of their lungs. It had gone from glares to stares to shrill berating. And that was just on Mrs.Goodship's end. Mr. Goodship sat in stony silence for a while before being moved to start arguing back. The raised voices had upset both Bracken and myself and so we quietly slid out the back door.

There was a small wooden bench just outside the door and that's where I sat, leaning against the warm stone of the cottage wall, and marvelling at how very similar the surroundings were to Rookery Cottage. If you could forget the strange and magnificent flora and fauna, the two places were almost identical, although it seemed as if spring had arrived here a good while ago. I closed my eyes and breathed deeply the scent of blossom and green things.

"Just like home, isn't it?" said a voice from beside me.

I started, opening my eyes and then saw that it was Mrs.Goodship and relaxed again. There was something infinitely soothing about that little woman and I could feel all of my tensions melting away in her presence.

"I was just thinking that," I replied, shuffling along the bench so that she could sit down. "Spring is earlier here, though, isn't it?"

She nodded.

"The seasons run a bit different," she said. "Time doesn't pass quite the same and we tend to be a might warmer altogether, but for the most part, we're just the same, aye. What happens on yon end, happens here and vicey versey."

"So if they sell that land on my side and pull down the hedge...then what? Does your hedge disappear?"

"Not exactly," she said, glancing sideways at me. "Did Himself not tell you how things stand between us?"

"Between 'us' meaning you and him, or 'us' between our worlds?" I smiled at her, enjoying the twinkle in her eyes.

She chuckled.

"Ach! Don't take any notice of us squabbling like that. It always sounds more fierce than it is. He's a soft-hearted old lump, that one."

I must have looked surprised because she laughed louder, flapping a hand at me.

"Oh, don't let all that grumbling and growling fool you," she said, patting my knee. "He's a proper clart, he is. Puts on a bit of a show for folk, being all surly-like and acting the bad-tempered auld..."

"Yes," I said, smiling again at the memory of our first meeting, the waves of irritation that rolled off him when I caught him coming out of my shed. I told Mrs.G how I thought he was a vagrant living in the empty building. Her laugh turned into a roar at the thought of it.

She shook her head, the mass of brown curls bobbing precariously under the head-scarf. She wiped a hand across her face, then took the edge of her apron to mop away the tears that she'd found there.

"Aye, well, that sounds about right. But he was right sorry that the two of you got off on the wrong foot like that. He hadn't wanted to meet you like that, but he got held up running an errand for Mr.Trott down the shop and he do get all flustered..." she paused, frowning. "Eh, but never mind all that. Point is, lass, we were all hoping to meet Elsie's girl under better circumstances. Truth of it is, once she was gone from Rookery Cottage, things started to get muddled and then, without someone taking care of the place, well, that made things a bit difficult for us lot."

She broke off and smiled up at me, a smile of impossibly white teeth in her nut-brown face. For a brief moment, I could close my eyes and feel like I was in Nan's presence, so similar was their gentle warmth and the feeling of being unconditionally safe and held. I was overcome by the strong impulse to want to preserve that feeling, no matter what it took.

"How do you mean, difficult?" I asked.

And so she told me.

The trip back to the shed took far less time than the trip to Nether-Winkle. Or at least that was my impression. Mr.G just smiled and shrugged when I commented on that fact. We walked in silence for most of the journey. Bracken trotted at my side, tail held aloft, waving happily . She had every reason to be happy, having been the eager recipient of numerous snacks and tidbits from Mrs.G's kitchen. I had a large wicker basket over one arm, packed with jars of soup and stew, a ham and egg pie, pots of marmalade and jam and several large wedges of assorted cakes wrapped in cloth; added to that were half a dozen of last autumn's apples and two each of bottled raspberries and plums. It came with firm instructions to return the empty jars and pots, in the basket, to Mr.G who would bring them back to her for regular refills. I had no fear of starvation in my near future. Well, as long as I could find a way to keep the portal open.

It seemed that the caretaker of Rookery Cottage was actually in care of more than just the house and garden. According to Mrs.G, safe passage to and from their world and ours depended very much upon the preservation of the land, particularly the Hedge, surrounding. By virtue of a very old (much farther back than anyone could be expected to remember, apparently) agreement between the McCorrigan family (namely, the women) and the people of the Otherworld, the Caretaker of Rookery Cottage would vouchsafe the passage of folk to and from for the purposes of commerce and mutual benefit (the details of those mutual benefits seemed vague and Mrs.G wouldn't elaborate; she had, in fact, become a bit shifty when pressed so I didn't pursue it) of folk on both sides of the Hedge. The Hedge, it seems, is more than a long stand of vegetation; it serves as a boundary between the two worlds, thereby earning the capital H. The shed at the bottom of my garden was built of both faery-mined stone and mundane-world timber and so created a bond between the villages. It was also, apparently, built on one of the few remaining 'thin' spots on the border between the two places. Because of the potentially harmful nature of interchange between the worlds – here she alluded to 'that lot with the dodgy food' – it was deemed necessary to monitor and protect the portal. Without a Caretaker, the portal was considered unstable and so travel was discouraged. Given enough time without a Caretaker — more than a year and a day — then the portal would have to, by mutual agreement of the long-ago document, be closed for the safety of all parties. Furthermore, any major damage to the Hedge weakened the boundary, which, if it persisted, also warranted closure of the portal for safety's sake.

Additionally, and this is where things started to get complicated, there were factions in a place she referred to as Deep Faery, who believed all interchange between humans and the fae-folk should be prohibited and, as such, were campaigning to have all of the portals closed on a permanent, irreversible basis. There were vague references to 'meddling' and 'interference' towards that end but she wouldn't provide any details. I had my suspicions, though, remembering passing comments made by Edie at the village meeting. Building a wind farm that necessitated the pulling down of sections of the Hedge seemed like a good, even noble, way to achieve that less-than-noble purpose.

I mused over this information as we walked. The entire trip – through the shed and back again – had asked a lot of me. Or at least, that's what the Hazel of several days ago would have said. The Hazel of the moment, however, seemed perfectly at ease with the idea of a portal to the Otherworld at the bottom of her garden and a magical Hedge that separated the land of Faery from the everyday world. That sudden shift made me briefly wonder if I wasn't under some sort of enchantment, uncharitable thought though it was; I never once believed the Goodships would either wish, or do me, harm.

Looking back on it, though, it wasn't really that much of a change in outlook; the world that held magical hedges and wardrobes to Narnia was the world I had inhabited for a good part of my life. It was only in the years since I'd stopped visiting my Nan, culminating in my move to London and immersing myself in an entirely different life that my sense of wonder had faded away, trodden under by the bright lights of expectation and striving to fit in. It was as if my childhood visits to Winkle had laid the foundation of belief and coming back had slowly started to reawaken it. The years in between had definitely eroded my sense of the magical, but it hadn't truly gone. I realized with a start, and an easy well of tears, that that's what Nan had meant in her letter when she'd said the threads of magic were woven into my soul. Perhaps I was more suited to the role of Caretaker than I had given myself credit for.

I swallowed hard and reached down my hand to touch Bracken's wiry head. She lifted her nose to bump my hand, whining softly.

"Silly dog," I whispered, "We're quite a pair, aren't we?"

She responded with a soft whuffling sound as we started the climb towards the door to the garden.

Chapter Seventeen

"**I**'ll leave you here, lass," said Mr.Goodship as we emerged into the cramped space of the shed.

I stood, feeling awkward. What do you say to someone after they've shown you that your shed is a TARDIS and led you to an enchanted world that exists right beside your own?

"Okay, then," I said, feeling I had to say something. The light was dim but I could see the outline of his face. He smiled gently, seeing me looking.

"Go on, pet," he said. "Get yourself inside and have a good think on things, aye? Sleep on it all. There's no call to be turning yourself inside out, as I rightly know you will!"

I laughed softly. Already he knew me well.

"When will I see you again?" I asked, because now it was important that I did. If I were completely honest, I was afraid that the whole adventure had been a strange dream and that I'd wake up and none of it would be real. I realized with a pang that I couldn't bear for it to not be real.

Mr.Goodship shrugged.

"When you need me, lass, that's when you'll see me and probably before besides."

I turned at the sound of the gate latch clicking. Bracken whined, pressing herself against me. I could feel a tremble run through her body.

"Who..."

I looked back to Mr.Goodship but Bracken and I were alone in the shed.

Feeling a bit silly, I walked out, blinking in the sudden brightness of the warm sunlight only to run sharply into the back of a tall man.

"Umph!" I said, staggering slightly back.

Toby turned around, a look of amusement flickering across his face. I noticed that he was more pleasant to look at when his face wasn't creased into its perpetual scowl. I also noticed that he was leaning a bicycle up against the toolshed. It looked familiar; I recognized the faded purple paint and the tattered remains of streamers coming from the handlebars. I swallowed hard and gripped handfuls of cardigan.

He looked past me towards the shed, his eyes narrowing. Quickly enough, the scowl was back in place.

"Were you in there?" he asked, without the usual courtesy of salutation.

I felt myself stiffen, not wanting to give too much away. If the portal was a secret, the last person on earth I wanted to know about it was him. I have no idea why I had that thought. Probably something to do with the load of emotional baggage I was carting around with me.

"Yes," I replied, my tone clipped, "I've been thinking of converting it into a hen house and I just wanted to see how roomy it was."

He raised a dark eyebrow.

"A hen house, is it?"

"Yes, a hen house."

I squared my shoulders, refusing to be withered underneath his bold gaze. His eyes had a way of boring into your face, something I found very unsettling in a person. I had a difficult time not glancing away, especially as his features had softened in bemusement. Maybe Alfie was right, maybe he was part faery. He had a discomfiting way of holding your gaze and making you feel, well, looked at. For someone who tried to be mostly invisible, this was a disconcerting feeling. I decided that if he was part faery, then he had to be one of the less savoury variety that Mrs.G went on about. Thankfully, the sensation of Bracken burrowing up against me served as a reasonable excuse to look down. When I realized she was shaking in a way she hadn't done for a long time, my temper flared, all potential enchantments broken.

"Can I help you with something?" I asked, moving to stand more firmly between the shivering dog and the imposing figure of a man. "Only, my dog is terrified of you and quite rightfully so, if you remember. It might be best if you could state your business and then be moving on."

His lips quirked into a smile, not altogether unpleasant but unsettling all the same. He looked down at Bracken who just whined and pressed closer. He sank down on his haunches.

"Ah, whisht now, little lassie," he crooned, his voice taking on a lilting, sing-song element. "Come by ye now, come by," I frowned, all of a sudden remembering a young Toby capturing a blackbird that had been caught in a strand of fishing line that some idiot had draped in a tree. I blinked, pushing the memory out of my head. He'd obviously changed since then.

Bracken had stopped trembling. She stood, uncertainly, beside me but was no longer trying to blend into my legs. Her tail unclenched and she waved the tip, cautious but curious. A regrettable part of me almost wished she was still frightened.

"That's it, lovely girl. That's it, my one."

I could hardly believe what I was seeing. Or hearing, for that matter. His voice was like molten honey, all softness and sweet; cajoling and reassuring all at the same time. This from a man who, so far, had barely uttered a complete sentence in my company.

Bracken took a step towards him. He lowered himself gently onto his knees, reaching out a work-roughened hand. Bracken extended a tentative nose to sniff, then took another step towards him, allowing him to gently scratch under her whiskery chin.

Traitorous beast, I thought. If I didn't have her terror to arm myself against this deeply unsettling man, then how could I continue to despise him? I liked it better when I could despise him. He was one less thing to think about.

He rose slowly, taking care not to startle her. She yawned and shook herself, breaking the spell, then wandered past him and set about sniffing around the path, no doubt checking there hadn't been any rabbit incursions during our absence. She was completely relaxed and unbothered by the presence of him, despite being a cringing heap only moments before.

"Well," I said, unsure of what just happened, but not willing to concede the point, "I suppose there's a lesson there on the powers of forgiveness. Dogs are definitely a more enlightened species, aren't they?"

He shrugged and glanced away. If I wasn't determined to disbelieve any evidence of conviviality in this man I would say that he blushed.

He cleared his throat and replied, gruff once more,

"Aye, well. It would be a sad thing for the human race if we weren't able to learn something from the four-footed ones, wouldn't it? I believe the wee dog and I have made our peace. I'm not above apologizing when I know I'm in the wrong."

The last bit hung like a lead weight in the air around us. A thousand thoughts and feelings raced and swirled in me, leaving me feeling somewhere between enraged and devastated. In a fit of defiance, I looked straight at him, waiting for the next logical apology.

"I brought you a bike," he said, obliterating the opportunity by ignoring it completely. "Your bike, actually. From when…" He paused, shifting his weight and looking everywhere but at me. "Anyroad, our Alfie asked me to bring it over. It was in the tractor shed at the Manor. I've cleaned it up and oiled the chain. It should be alright."

As he spoke he kept his eyes on the bicycle, refusing to meet my glare. When I didn't say anything, he looked up. There was something in his expression that I couldn't read. If he thought bringing me my old bicycle was a substitute for a proper apology, he was sorely mistaken. Suddenly, I just wanted him gone. I had too much thinking to do and wanted to be alone to get on with it.

I smiled a tight smile.

"I appreciate you bringing over the bicycle, thank you," I said, with as much frostiness as I could summon. The effort of it was exhausting. I'm not good at grudges and I really thought I'd put it all behind me. Seeing him again, though, had stirred up some unwelcome feelings. My therapist said I had a lifetime of repressed emotions to confront, a lifetime of squashing myself down so as to avoid conflict and other messy interchanges; a lifetime of contorting myself into the shapes other people required. It turns out, once you open that door, it's hard to close it again. It was taking every scrap of resolve I had not to smooth this whole thing over and make it easy for him.

"Anyway," he said, bringing us back to the matter at hand. "I really only came by to ask if you'd stop by the Manor tomorrow. For lunch."

Lunch at the manor. Now things were spiralling far beyond comfort. I had absolutely zero desire to hobnob in those kinds of social circles again. I'd had my fill of rich aristocrats. I wanted no part of it.

"Oh, I don't think so," I said, nevertheless chafing uncomfortably over having to refuse. "I'm not really interested in socializing with the gentry. Sorry and all that. Give Lord Dummell my apologies but I'm really very busy and don't have time to be going for lunch and things."

Lunch and things?

Why couldn't I just leave it at 'no thank you'.

I smiled, probably quite fiendishly and gave a little nod of goodbye and turned sharply up the path towards the house. It took every ounce of self-control to not break into a run.

"Wait!" he called, "Hazel, wait!"

Hearing him use my name stopped me cold. It was something in the way he said it — he added in a certain lilt, extending the first syllable and shortening the second— that seemed oddly familiar and forgotten at the same time. Whatever had happened to us that we were such strangers now? How do you go from being the best of childhood friends to barely capable of civility? Crushing betrayal and disappointment, that's how.

I turned to look at him. He stood with his cap in his hands, looking smaller and almost vulnerable. Something in me reached out to him, just for a moment, before snapping sharply back. I tucked it firmly away in the place I put the things I didn't want to consider.

"Please will you come?" he said, his voice soft, "It's not just for Lord Dummell that I'm asking."

I turned that over in my brain for a moment. If not for Lord Dummell, then who? My scalp prickled and a sudden warmth flooded my face when I realized that it was he, Toby, who was asking me to lunch. I was disappointed in myself for how pleased that made me feel.

"There's a few of us working on something to stop the land sale," he went on, "The Fisher's and a couple of the young ones from the village. We thought you might want to see what we've come up with,"

I stood, blinking stupidly. A tidal wave of inner humiliation swept away the previous feelings of secret delight. I hoped I just looked like I was still considering.

"Oh, and your one from the shed." He actually had the nerve to wink, "He'll be there as well. So will you come?"

I nodded, not trusting myself to speak, and turned back towards home and comfort and freedom from social blunder.

I heard the gate click behind me. I fought the urge to look back at him although every traitorous part of me wanted to.

"Come by around noon," he called. "Edie's putting on a grand spread."

I raised my hand to show I'd heard but didn't turn around. I kept walking, a bit stiffly, up the path.

"My oh, my," purred a familiar and so very unwelcome voice.

"Aren't we all in a fluster?"

"For the hundredth time, you wretched, wretched cat, Just. Shut. Up!"

I first met Toby the summer when I was seven years old and he was nine. I'd come to stay with Nan as usual and had been playing in the lane, just outside the back gate when I heard a frantic thrashing coming from inside the hedge. I followed the noise to where I found a blackbird, its head bent back at an odd angle and one of its wings pinned close to its body. It was flailing and flapping its one free wing but was in great danger of hurting itself dreadfully. I froze for a moment, unsure of what to do but knowing I needed to help it. I tried talking soothingly and reached out towards it, only to have it begin thrashing ever more wildly. Close to tears, I started to panic as I picked up on the bird's terror and my own helplessness. I was just about to run back to the cottage to get Nan when I heard the humming.

I turned to look and there was a boy standing behind me. His black hair was in a wild tangle around his head and he had a smudge of dirt on one cheek. He gave me a shy smile.

"If you let me get a hold of her, I can keep her still while you get the line off. It's fishing line. Someone's been careless, or cruel, though I'd rather think it was the first. She's made it worse with the thrashing. It's a two person job, this. Will you do it?"

I nodded, spellbound by his lilting voice and gentle eyes. He seemed completely unlike any other boy I'd ever met. Those tended to be loud and boisterous and fond of hair-pulling; the kind who would probably find it funny to see the trapped bird.

He started humming again, a strange tuneless tune and soon the blackbird stopped flapping about. He reached into the hedge and gently pulled her out, cupping her in his grubby hands and nodding to me to get to work. I stared at him, barely able to contain my delight at being so close to a wild bird. He nodded again and I quickly went work untangling the line. It took quite a while, it had been wound tightly around the one wing and then hooked cruelly in her beak, I suppose as she'd tried to pluck it away from her body. My hands were shaky at first, but the boy's wandering humming calmed me as much as it did the bird, who sat quietly in his hands.

Eventually, I eased the last of the line away and stepped back. The boy slowed down the cadence of the hum and finally stopped. The bird sat still for a moment or so then burst from his hands and away into the sky. We stood watching her for a moment as she became just a black speck in the distance.

I turned to look at the boy, thrilled beyond measure. We had rescued the bird!

He grinned at me, blue eyes dancing.

"I know where the badgers have a sett," he said, "D'ye want to see?"

"Yes, please!"

And that was the start of it all.

I learned later, from Nan, that Toby had been 'taken in', as the saying vaguely goes, by the current Lord Dummell's father. Toby had been living with an elderly uncle on some remote Scottish island who'd become unable to take care of him any longer. What was the connection to Malmont, I never did know and didn't ask. All I cared about was that I'd made a friend. I finally had someone who didn't make fun of me or question my quietness. He was as content to sit in thoughtful silence as I was and despite the fact we spent every waking moment together for the rest of that summer, I never felt exhausted in his company. Quite the opposite. We roamed the woods and the moor, watching the birds and animals, creating adventures for ourselves. Sometimes we'd play with Edie and Alfie's grandchildren but they quickly grew bored of our kind of games and would go off to do something more exciting. That suited us just fine, content as we were in our own company. I can say, without a doubt, that those were the happiest days of my childhood. Summers with Nan were the beacon I was ever walking towards during the trials of the school year and once I'd met Toby, that only made the light shine brighter.

I suppose it was inevitable that our childhood friendship blossomed into something more as we got older. We were best friends and romance seemed the next obvious development. It was blissful and sweet and I was as starry-eyed as any teenager in love for the first time could be. Even as life away from Winkle became more and more complicated, I felt I could handle anything knowing that Toby loved me and I loved him.

He was seventeen to my fifteen when things went wrong. The previous Lord Dummell was a difficult man, very set in his ways and of the old school where young men did their duty and didn't question the authority of the patriarch. His son, Cornelius (known to us then as Corny) who is now the current Lord Dummell, had been sent away to manage some business interests in Scotland and that left Toby to the full attention of his guardian. Corny had always been a buffer between them and had helped Toby with the often difficult transition from living on a remote island, to village life. I think he'd been more of a father figure than a foster brother, and Toby was gutted when he left. Once that buffer was gone, the senior Lord Dummell decided that Toby should be working towards some kind of higher education, rather than roaming about the moors or grubbing about in the farmyard. Both of those things taken together made for a very miserable Toby.

At the same time, my mum was making noises about me spending my holidays with Nan and my association with 'undesirables'. At the time, I assumed she meant Toby but knowing what I know now, I wonder if there was more to it. I suspect there was. There were whispered arguments and angry phone calls. Mum and Dad were at odds and the tension in the air was unbearable. I was told that it was to be my last summer with Nan and thereafter I would only see her when the whole family was together. I was devastated, convinced my world was coming crashing down. Not only would I lose my time with Nan at Rookery Cottage, my place of peace and safety, I would lose Toby.

That last summer we spent countless hours plotting and planning. We couldn't let the adults in our lives take away everything that mattered to us! Of course, being teenagers, we were very dramatic with it all, fancying ourselves a modern day Romeo and Juliet. Still, it felt very real and very urgent at the time."

When neither side seemed to be budging, we decided our only option was to run away. Yes, a horrible cliché but what else were we to do? We were going to track down Corny and have him take us in. We had it all planned: we were to ride our bikes to the train station in Westham (leaving from Winkle would be too obvious) then take the train north to Edinburgh. From there, I think we were relying on a miracle. Not that it mattered because all of the planning was for nothing.

On the morning we were set to leave, I crept out of the cottage just before dawn, a backpack stuffed with my worldly treasures — a few books, my fountain pen and writing notebook, a box of teabags and a spare cardigan (which speaks volumes about my idea of what running away would entail), and rode my bike to the edge of the Malmont Estate where we'd arranged to meet.

I waited for two hours before walking back to Rookery Cottage, alone. I couldn't even tell Nan why I was so upset because if she thought I had planned to run away she may have felt she had to tell my parents and they'd surely have dragged me back home early. So I had to suffer in silence, though I think she knew what had happened. I got a postcard two weeks later from Toby saying he didn't think it was right for him to take me away from my family and that I should just forget about him.

It took almost a year, much of which I spent scribbling tear-sodden letters that I never sent (I couldn't, I didn't know exactly where he was), but I did manage to forget him, or at least file him away under "things I'd rather not remember".

And then he chased my dog across the moor.

Chapter Eighteen

I spent the morning before The Lunch weeding the garden path. I wanted something mindless yet productive while I sifted through the myriad information and emotion of the day before. I could have used at least three more days to process all of it rather than attend the lunch meeting — because a meeting is precisely what it was, nothing more, despite my lapse of sanity on the previous day. A lapse which I was chalking up to weakness and general addlement caused by my trip to a parallel world. I dug and gouged and ripped my thoughts and feelings into a semblance of order. Murk, whose presence I was finding increasingly vexing, perched on the wall of the leek trench, blissfully silent, while Bracken had found herself a patch of sunshine and was stretched out in a contented slumber. If not for the looming social awkwardness, it would have been a perfect way to spend my morning. The looming awkwardness, however, was foremost in my mind.

My brain turned events over and over; the health of the Hedge, the threat to the village and villagers, the world that ran so close to ours that was interdependent and just as threatened, perhaps even more so.

It was all so huge and complex and frighteningly close. I was equal parts distressed and excited. Why must *I* be such a seemingly integral part of the whole thing? But wasn't it wonderful to think I could be a part of such a magical, storybook existence? Surely they'd do better to get on without me. Don't I have a lot to offer, though? The nagging worry was that I was hardly a force of energy and accomplishment at that particular point in my life. I was certain that everyone who'd met me to this point couldn't help but notice my propensity for bumbling, awkwardness and a pervading aura of feebleness. I wasn't exactly the poster child for effective social activism.

My mind drifted back to the winter when I was fourteen; I'd tried to circulate a petition to ban the use of rabbits in cosmetics testing. In an effort to Join In, I'd been part of a school club of animal lovers who'd got wind of a larger organization working towards that goal and we'd taken it upon ourselves to contribute to their efforts. My mum had put a quick end to my endeavours. I'd asked if I could circulate the petition at one of her lunch parties. She'd regularly gather groups of friends to eat tiny sandwiches and drink white wine in the garden and since all of those ladies were of the well-turned-out variety, I thought they'd be pleased to take part in ensuring that their cosmetics were cruelty-free. Anyway, Mum took one look at the flyer I'd made up — nothing too drastic, just a full-colour photo of a rabbit with a horribly ulcerated eye — and she'd told me, in no uncertain terms, how futile my efforts would be, how big cosmetic companies were far too rich and important to take notice of a list of signatures — because couldn't anyone just write down a list of false names and pretend they were real? — and absolutely I would not upset her guests with such gore and violence.

If she'd shouted it might've been easier to talk back to her, to tell her that the gore and violence was a real and terrifying truth and that yes, the cosmetic companies would have to listen, especially if her well-heeled friends decided to stop buying their products. Those were the things that I wanted to say. But she spoke to me kindly and gently and pointed out how easily upset I became; she reminded me of how my pathological degree of sensitivity made me prone to over-reacting and that high emotion would never win the day. She suggested I go and make myself a nice cup of tea and perhaps I could write a firm, well-worded letter — I was so good at writing, surely I could conjure something moving and powerful — and leave the shouting and placard-waving to people more suited to such things.

That wasn't the first thing to make me doubt myself, and it certainly wasn't the last, but it was definitely one of the most memorable.

I sighed, viciously stabbing at a clump of resolute grass that was convinced it needed to live between the flagstones.

"You know," said Murk, lazily switching his tail back and forth. "They wouldn't have asked you along if they didn't think you had something to contribute. You're not as useless as you suppose yourself to be."

"Is that meant to sound encouraging?" I asked, leaning back on my heels. My back was aching but I really wanted to get the first part of the path done. "Because I wouldn't hire myself out as a motivational speaker if I were you."

He chuckled his murmuring, yowling laugh. He stood up, arching to the tips of his toes in a stretch then sat down and started washing his face. He ran a paw over his tattered ears.

"The trouble with you," he said, after paying close attention to the spaces between his toes. "is that you're always playing a part in someone else's story, instead of living your own."

"Is that so?" I said, resenting his implications, "And I suppose you have the solution to this perpetual mis-casting of mine?"

"No," he said, jumping down off the wall and started off down the garden path. "Because then that would mean you were living in *my* story, wouldn't it?"

He really was the most exasperating creature. The fact that he seemed to have uncannily accurate powers of observation, particularly when it came to pointing out my numerous flaws, did nothing to endear him to me.

"Murk?" I said, returning my attention to the stubborn lump of grass.

"Hm?" He stopped and turned, his tatty ear swivelled towards me.

"Do you have any particular reason for hanging about here? I mean, other than the fact you seem to imagine I've an endless supply of sardines and salmon? Surely Hamish must miss your charming company."

I glanced up from under my fringe, curious to see what effect, if any, the question had on him. I was beginning to think he was utterly without conscience.

The tip of his crooked tail switched once or twice then he turned and carried on walking up the path, holding it aloft which, had he fingers instead of a tail, would have been an unmistakable gesture. Knowing him as I did, I got the message.

I smiled to myself; point scored.

My intention had been for Bracken and I to set off for Malmont Manor with plenty of time to spare. I wanted to walk there, using the moor path, to give myself ample time to mentally prepare for the occasion. I also couldn't face getting on that bike again, especially as it would be making the same trip as the last time I'd ridden it. As it happened, I stayed in the garden for longer than I ought to have, leaving myself not very much time to get cleaned up and changed. Then I stood for twenty agonizing minutes looking in my wardrobe, having given absolutely no prior thought to what I was going to wear and despairing of the fact I hadn't taken my mum up on her offer to buy me some new clothes when we'd gone into the city. I then spent an additional fifteen minutes mentally berating myself for spending that first twenty minutes agonizing over something I would never do, which is to say, allow my mum to buy me new clothes. Anyway, when had I really cared what I wore, particularly in the context of pleasing anyone but myself? My outward appearance had always been my one constant act of rebellion during all of my years of otherwise doing what I was told. So why now, all of a sudden, did my thrift shop dresses and collection of hand-knit cardigans seem lacking? I refused to acknowledge the answer to that question, as it raised up an entirely new and unwieldy set of thoughts and emotions that I absolutely wanted no part of.

Bracken watched with her usual benign detachment. She was quite content to snooze on the bed while I chose and rejected several combinations before finally settling on a deep purple crushed velvet dress and a pair of black and white striped tights. I'd always found that wearing stripy tights made me feel rather more confident and sure of myself and heaven knew I could well use more of that. I added a much-beloved cardigan in my favourite shade of shocking apple green. I'd embroidered a vine of honeysuckle flowers around the cuffs one desperate evening when Teddy and I had been quarrelling and I liked to think they were the equivalent of Wonder Woman cuffs. I mentally used them to deflect unwelcome attacks of attention.

"This is ridiculous," I muttered to Bracken as I gathered my hair into a fat plait. The dampness of the morning had turned it into a frizzy mess and it wasn't safe to run a brush through it in that state. I'd normally wrangle it into submission with two plaits but I thought that the combination of those and the striped tights wouldn't serve me well in the being taken seriously department. Teddy had said he liked my two plaits; he said I reminded him of his older sister reading Heidi when he was a child. That was Teddy all over, a compliment wrapped in mockery.

I really didn't enjoy that I'd thought of Teddy twice in only half an hour. It spoke volumes about my confidence level.

"It's only lunch, for heaven's sake," I continued. Bracken remained unmoved. "And there are going to be all sorts of people there and why would I even give a rat's backside what anyone thinks of me anyway? They only want me there because they think I've got special dispensation to block the sale because of being Nan's heir. Imagine their surprise when they find out I'm about as useful in conflict, and about as filled with magic, as that wardrobe."

My stomach sank and I felt my shoulders slumping. That was the crux of things. That's what was filling me with such utter dread — the realization that sooner or later I'd be discovered to be a fraud.

"Oh, I wouldn't discount the magical potential of wardrobes," said Murk, slinking through the half-open door. "I hear they were a popular..."

"Why are you back?" I snapped, "I thought you'd gone off in a huff."

"I don't care enough to be huffed," said Murk, jumping onto the bed. Bracken yelped and flung herself to the floor, sending piles of wool and linen slithering to the floor.

"Stop it!" I said, picking up the pile and stuffing it back into the wardrobe. I held it all in and shut the door. "You're a menace. A rude, inconsiderate menace." I placed a protective hand on Bracken's quivering head.

"And *she* is a complete charlatan," spat Murk, glaring at Bracken who whined and waggled her eyebrows. "She's no more afraid of me than she is of that black-haired Pict."

I flinched at the reference to Toby.

"Ah, I see," he purred. "Charmed by the halfling, are we? Well, not to be surprised at that, I suppose. Like calls to like and all that. Never mind, are you ready?"

I stared, unbelieving, at his insolent face. Cats are impossible to read at the best of times and he was a master of illusion. Or was that delusion? I decided to leave it be, not wanting to bring up Toby and my feelings or not-feelings about him. I had been for more content when I was despising him.

"Yes, as a matter of fact, I am ready," I said, my voice prim. "Come along, Bracken, we don't want to be late."

"Oh but you are late. You spent far too much time tarting yourself up for Heathcliff," said Murk, jumping down, dashing ahead and slipping through the door in front of us in that aggravating fashion that cats have of almost tripping you up.

"You'll have to take your bike. But don't worry," he called, already at the bottom of the stairs. "The hound can run alongside and I don't mind riding in the basket!"

In his usual aggravating way, Murk was right. I checked the clock in the kitchen and there was no way we could get there on time by walking. Which is why I came to be making my unsteady way along the bumpy sheep path on my old bike. It's true what they say, you don't forget.

Bracken trotted merrily beside me, staying just close enough for me to worry about running her over every time I had a wobble. Which, considering my rusty cycling skills, especially obvious on the uneven ground, and my uneasy relationship with my old steed, was fairly often. Murk perched in the basket like a malevolent ship's masthead, shouting out points of interest (rare orchid and an Iron Age barrow) and warning me of rabbit holes. Twice I had to stop to tuck the skirt of my dress up into the waistband of my tights. I giggled inwardly at what mum would say if she could see me but the hem kept getting caught in the chain and I was afraid of both tears and grease stains. Besides, I thought, who's going to see me out here anyway?

The thought had only just drifted across my conscious mind when I heard the sound of a quad bike behind us. Surely not. Above the noise, I could've sworn I heard the sound of Murk's rumbling laughter. Bracken shot forwards, instinctively running from the sound of the machine. I tried to call to her but at the same moment felt the front wheel drop sharply, yanking the handlebars to the left. I braked but that only served to send the back end of the bicycle, together with Murk and I, swinging into a jackknife and sprawling in an untidy heap.

"Serves you right," I muttered, scrambling to my feet. The heather was soft and springy so I was quite unhurt. Well, other than my pride, of course.

Toby pulled up beside us, just as I was trying to yank my dress out from my tights. I don't even want to think what I must've looked like. My face burned, whether with embarrassment or irritation or a combination of both hardly seemed important. Murk had landed with typical feline grace on his feet. Apparently even being jettisoned from a bicycle basket wasn't enough to ruffle his impassivity.

Toby made no comment on my appearance but I did notice that he avoided making eye contact. He turned off the engine.

"You're on your way, then?' he asked, his voice gruff. Gone was the honey-dripping charm of the day before. The Toby that I remembered from our first meeting seemed to have returned. Our first re-meeting, anyway.

"Clearly," I replied, stiff and unsure, "I imagine we might've arrived already if not for you giving poor Bracken a flashback and sending us all into a rabbit hole."

I realized after I said it how waspish I sounded. I regretted it only a little, though, because it *was* his fault for breaking my concentration.

"Sorry," was all he said, "I'm just out looking for a couple of stray sheep. We've had a bit of a bother with...well, never mind. I don't suppose you saw any on your way over?"

"No, sorry, we didn't."

That effectively ended the conversation.

I picked up my bike and pointed it towards Malmont. I stared pointedly at Murk who merely sat with a noncommittal look on his face. Bracken had sat herself down at a safe distance from the machine. She may have forgiven Toby but she was still wary of his steed.

"That Hamish's cat?" asked Toby, nodding towards the orange scourge.

"Yes," I said, not sure how to explain why I was carrying a cat in my bicycle basket across the moor on my way to a luncheon.

Apparently it didn't need explaining because Toby just nodded and glanced skyward. "Might rain, " he grunted, "You'd best be on your way."

"That was my intention," I said, motioning to Murk to get in the basket. I was absolutely not going to lift him in. He could walk before I'd do that. He merely sat, blinking pointedly.

I followed his gaze to the front wheel of my bike. It hadn't fared well in its tussle with the rabbit hole. It was bent at an odd angle. Great. Now we'd all have to walk the rest of the way. Not only was I going to be late, I would have to explain why.

"Oh!" said Toby, glancing down at my wheel. "You've got a bent wheel."

Amazing powers of observation. I gritted my teeth and endeavoured to squash my irritation.

"So it would seem," I replied, striving for lightheartedness. "I suppose that's what happens when one runs afoul of a rabbit hole."

"I suppose one should've watched where one was going then, shouldn't one?"

I glanced up sharply but Toby's dark face was as impassive as Murk's. I thought I saw the hint of a smile quirking the corner of his mouth but if it had been there, it was soon gone.

I shrugged, lying the bike down.

"Well, no sense wheeling it all the way to the Manor," I said. "I'll just carry on by foot and pick it up on my way home."

Part of me was hoping he'd offer me a lift. I didn't much fancy being late and surely he was going that way anyway. The thought of sitting behind him on the quad bike, however, made the more sensible part of me want to just hurry away before he could suggest it. I listened to the sensible part of me. I straightened my coat and gave Toby a quick wave, calling Bracken to me as I set off. I couldn't have cared less what Murk did.

"Hang on!" called Toby. I felt a tingle of something creep up the back of my neck. My hands clenched and unclenched. I turned, stepping back towards him with an expectant look on my face. So much for being sensible.

"I'll put your bicycle on the back here and drop it off at yours. That way you needn't worry about wheeling it all the way back."

I flushed hotly, and hoped desperately he couldn't see from where he was standing. I smiled, my lips pressed firmly together so surely it was more of a grimace.

"Super. Thank you, that's very kind." I said and turned back towards Malmont, cursing my stupidity for the thousandth time. "Come on, Bracken," I called, forcing my voice to be light and jolly when really all I wanted to do was weep with frustration and embarrassment. "We don't want to be late."

I marched off, willing myself to seem casual and carefree. I heard the roar of the bike firing up.

"Hang on!"

Toby pulled up alongside me, sending Bracken skittering again. I kept on walking, keeping my eyes firmly on the distant manor.

"Don't you want a lift?" he shouted over the engine, "I meant that I'd take the bike back *after* I'd dropped you off."

I stopped walking and turned to look right into his laughing eyes. His face transformed when he smiled and he was my Dickon again. I winced at the treacherous thought. My humiliation knew no bounds.

He patted the seat behind him and shifted forwards to make more room. The seat was almost long enough to seat two, but it meant being in uncomfortably close proximity to the person you were sharing with. Ah well, I thought, I've already made a complete arse of myself, I might as well finish the job. I glanced at him to see if he was watching but he stared straight ahead, his mouth twitching infuriatingly. I shrugged inwardly and hitched up my dress again, climbing in distinctly unladylike fashion onto the back of the smelly, puttering machine. There was a soft thud behind me as Murk leapt on board as well. He clawed his way up the back of my coat and settled into my hood, purring almost as loudly as the quad bike rumbled.

"Your breath stinks of sardines," I muttered to my passenger.

"My breath, what?" said Toby, turning to look at me in surprise and confusion.

Dear lord, could I make things any worse?

I shook my head vigorously.

"Not you. I was talking to the cat," I explained, digging myself even deeper.

"Oh, alright then," he sounded doubtful, "Hold on, then. It's a bit of a bumpy ride."

With that, the bike shot forwards. I lurched backwards, a victim of inertia and only just stopped myself falling off the back by grabbing hold of Toby's coat. There was no way I was putting my arms around his waist so I clung, terrified, fistfuls of waxed jacket all the way to the big house.

Malmont Manor wasn't at all what I was expecting. I imagined, probably from touring too many National Trust properties, that it would be well-preserved, but dated, and filled with 18th century charm. It was, speaking generously, a crumbling ruin.

Alfie met me in the yard – a lovely, atmospheric place, all cobblestones and old stable blocks. I chose not to dwell on the doors that hung off and the faint whiff of old, damp straw.

Toby paused the quad bike long enough for me to scramble off and then tore away again without so much as a backward glance. It took me several moments to get my land-legs again, and longer still to twist my dress back into shape. Murk, having curled himself up in a ball in my hood, appeared to be in no hurry to get out. Bracken, her tongue lolling happily after her run across the moor, *beside* the bike rather than in front of it, greeted Alfie like a long-lost friend, despite having just seen him the day before.

"Don't ask," I said, waving away Alfie's question, "Let's just say that whatever points he might have gained by charming Bracken, he's just lost in triplicate."

Alfie just grinned.

"Am I terribly late?" I asked, following him through a door leading off the yard. It led into a dim, damp sort of mudroom area where I was instructed to remove my boots and put on a pair of worn sheepskin slippers. I found that a tiny bit off-putting. I have an aversion to wearing other people's footwear. Something to do with the panic-mongering surrounding verruca warts and swimming baths when I was little.

"It's a strangeness of his Lordship," said Alfie, when he saw the look on my face. He pointed down at his own feet, clad in a splendid pair of tartan slippers, complete with mock sporran fluffy bits at the toes. "Trying to keep the wear off his good floors, I suppose." He finished, chuckling.

I saw the irony of his comment as we made our way through into the kitchen. The floors had obviously once been of fine hardwood but were now worn and scuffed. There were several buckets placed at intervals into which water dripped. It wasn't raining so I couldn't imagine where the water was coming from. Worn clippy mats and threadbare Turkish rugs were thrown haphazardly over the floor, no doubt disguising the worst of the damage. The whole place had an air of benign neglect. It seemed clean enough, the floor that was visible was without dirt or dust, but it just seemed so very...well, tired, I suppose.

The kitchen, on the other hand, was a different thing altogether. A vast room which probably hadn't changed much for centuries, it held a long scrubbed wooden table in the centre, around which ranged several people, plates and glasses in hand, deep in lively conversation. Walking into other people's fun is another one of my most hated things to do. I tried to hide behind Alfie.

"Hazel's here!" announced Alfie, pushing me forwards. I could've killed him. Surely I could have just slid into the group quietly.

Conversation stopped abruptly and four faces turned to stare at me. Astrid, I knew, and one of her theatre contingent stood beside her, a tall , androgynous person with round Harry Potter glasses and wearing an old army jacket. Mr.Goodship sat on a tall stool beside another man, a thin, angular person dressed in the official countryman uniform of brown tweed. He had a shock of faded ginger hair that stood up in a wild halo around his narrow face. He squinted at me and then smiled widely.

"You must be Elsie's granddaughter!" he said, in a rich plummy voice that I always associate with BBC news readers. "I'd recognize the McCorrigan look anywhere! Your lot certainly do stamp the progeny, eh wot, old boy? I thought our lad Toby was the only one hereabouts but it looks like I was wrong!"

The last part he'd directed at Mr.Goodship who had the good grace to squirm uncomfortably on his stool. He smiled at me and shrugged slightly.

I shook the offered hand. His hands were thin and bony but very strong and despite his lack of tact, his face was kindly and I'm sure he meant no offence.

"Come on, come on! Get yourself a bite to eat! Our Edie's done us proud once again. There's some ham and egg sandwiches or if you'd rather, some bread and cheese. The cheese is made from our own sheep's milk and you won't taste anything finer. Edie made the bread fresh this morning. Oh, try this mustard, it's homemade as well and would go lovely with a bit of that ham on a doorstep of bread. There's tea in the big pot or coffee if you prefer..."

He nattered away, showing me to the table and putting a plate in my hand, giving me a guided tour of the offerings — most of which had come from his stock or farmland — and I was made to feel instantly at home. He wasn't at all like my experience of the London gentry.

Having filled my plate, I leaned against the table and munched away. Astrid and her friend — Sidney, they introduced themself as — were deep in discussion over the plight of pollinators and Mr.Good ship, Alfie and Lord Dummell were having a lively argument over the merits of a particular variety of seed potatoes. I could see that potatoes were a very divisive thing around Winkle.

Bracken had been made much of when she was discovered, lurking behind me. She and a lively Jack Russell terrier named Dennis and a yellow Labrador named Ethel were last seen tearing off out of the kitchen for a game of chase-me-round-the-yard. It was so good to see her happy and mixing with new friends. I'd left my coat hung on a peg in the mudroom, upending Murk in the process, who hissed grumpily and then stalked off out of sight. He hadn't materialized in the kitchen, which was surprising as he usually gravitated towards the food. I was secretly hoping he'd get lost in the warren of rooms and I could forget he'd accompanied us. I guessed it would take him a while to walk back across the moor. I checked in with myself and found absolutely no pangs of remorse over such thinking.

"...what do you think, Hazel?"

I blinked, startled from my Murk abandonment fantasy. Sidney was looking at me, quite intensely behind their glasses.

"I'm sorry, I was miles away," I stammered, blushing infuriatingly. I reached up a hand to casually check for smears of mustard. "What was the question?"

"Astrid and I were just discussing the plight of our pollinators. I said that much could be done if people would simply choose to plant native species of flowers in their gardens rather than exotic, trendy bits of things. Not everyone needs to run out and start beekeeping."

I nodded vigorously. Finally, a topic of conversation I could warm up to.

"Oh, absolutely, I agree. But the onus is on the garden centres to offer those sorts of plants, and to make sure they also account for the larval stages of the pollinators, which is why native species are always the best bet. I think it would be marvellous if local nurseries had entire sections devoted to native plantings. They could do workshops and offer design help. It's hard for people to know what to plant and if it's not readily available, you can't blame them for just choosing what's on offer. I think most people would be happy to do it if only they knew how."

I realized that the room had gone silent. I flushed again. Oh dear, what had I said? My social filters switched off entirely when it came to the topics that I felt strongly about.

Alfie broke the silence with a chuckle. He came over and put his arm around my shoulder and squeezed.

"That's the most I think I've heard you say in company since you were six years old, pet."

I blushed even harder.

"Sorry, did I say too much? Only it's sort of a pet peeve that nurseries don't sell enough native plants. People who want to plant them have to rely on growing them from seed and that's not always easy."

"I agree," said Astrid, leaning forward, "Do you suppose we could put together something to canvas the nurseries with? Maybe we should have an information session..."

Sidney jumped in and started suggesting other ideas. At some point a pad of paper and pen was unearthed from Astrid's bottomless bag and the three of us bent over it, while Sidney took notes and made mind-maps. Mr.Goodship came around the table and offered advice and soon it was more rounds of bread being sliced, someone going out to the scullery to top up the milk jug and the kettle put on the hob for a fresh pot of tea.

The afternoon passed in a blur of ideas and inspiration. We didn't get around to the Hedge until nearly three o'clock at which point I felt like I'd been friends with these people for years. I couldn't remember the last time I'd felt so at ease with myself amongst other humans.

Lord Dummell, or Dummy as he was affectionately known to his friends, I soon came to learn was a rabid conservationist. His state of perpetual pennilessness was due to the fact that any spare money was ploughed back into buying up parcels of land in the area as they came up for sale. He was trying to put a stop to all further development he said, in an effort to preserve the countryside. In addition, he was wanting to convert Rookery Farm to permaculture and already had committed to raising only heritage varieties of livestock.

Unfortunately, as Alfie told me in a quiet aside at some point during the afternoon, his vision often surpassed his bank account and he was constantly scrambling to make ends meet. His high energy and flamboyant demeanour made him into something of a caricature in the village and he was prone to 'fits of the nerves', as Alfie put it, which is when Edie was called in to soothe his ragged edges. At the heart of it, though, he was a man who cared deeply for the countryside and that made me instantly fond of him.

Finally, after a third pot of tea had been brewed and a large slab of a particularly rich and moist fruit cake, courtesy of Mrs.G, had been sliced into generous wedges and distributed amongst us, our attention was directed to the matter of the hedge.

Lord Dummell began the proceedings by outlining what he'd learned about the intentions of BMZ and its developer allies. According to his sources (he referred to them more than once as 'informants'), the company was fully prepared to invoke a land seizure clause that allowed for the 'reasonable economical and cultural advancements of a remote area'. That their purpose was entirely self-serving and ultimately destructive was apparently of little concern to them. At some point during his speech, I heard the sound of the door and turned to see Toby sliding in. He nodded brusquely and then turned his attention to Lord Dummell.

"But how will it not be obvious to the council that what they're doing is *threatening* the economy and culture of the village?" demanded Astrid. "We've gathered all sorts of information about how perfectly economically sound the village is already and furthermore, reams of information about the ecological importance of the hedge."

"It's true," added Sidney, "They've had no shortage of proof. Clearly someone in BMZ is greasing the palms of the council members for it to have come this far."

They said this with the righteous vehemence of someone who believes passionately in the conspiracies of the corporate world. I had to admire their convictions.

"Now, now," said Alfie, holding up a gnarled hand. "It won't do us any good to go spouting accusations about the place, even when we're right. What we need to do here is keep calm heads on us and make sure we do everything above board."

He gave the two teenagers a knowing look. The two of them shifted in their seats and Astrid dropped her gaze to her pad of paper where she began doodling pictures of sheep.

"Yes, my young friends," said Lord Dummell, speaking sternly. He'd put on a pair of half-moon glasses to read from his notes and he peered over them now like a disapproving but kindly headmaster. "As much as we all would love to be a bit more forceful in our efforts, we must be seen to be clear-headed and sensible or we will be dismissed as lunatics and troublemakers. Heaven knows, some of us already labour under those labels." He paused as a series of guilty grins spread around the table, one of them his own. "Which is why," he paused again, this time to turn to me, smiling beatifically, "which is why we must turn our attention to young Hazel here, who, like an avenging angel has swept into our lives at precisely the right moment to save the day!"

To my surprise and horror, there came a volley of clapping and table-thumping and even a few shouts of "Hurrah!" and I was left staring, in faint panic, at the beaming faces of my new friends.

Chapter Nineteen

It turned out that they were all delusional.

Somewhere along the way, they had got the idea that I had some special dispensation to solve all of their troubles, by the simple virtue of living in my Nan's cottage. It seems the role of Caretaker extended to single-handedly squashing the grasping efforts of corporate giants as well. According to their mass disbelief, I also had insider knowledge of the legal system. In addition, my giant trust fund (which, in the interests of full disclosure is neither giant nor even available to me in lump sums as it's dripped out to me in an embarrassing similarity to pocket money. I got along on what I'd been able to siphon away from Teddy's extravagance and the modest sum brought in from my books), would take care of any further expenses incurred by our assured victory. That last bit was suggested by Astrid and Sidney, who, bless them, obviously had romantic notions of what a trust fund was and how it might be spent. It was then explained to me that my pending luncheon with one Mr.Collins of BMZ would be the first step in our full-on assault with me at the helm.

They may have not actually said all that, verbatim, but that's what I heard.

As soon as that horrifying mess had been laid out for me, I quietly excused myself, claiming to have to use the toilet (several large mugs of tea and it wasn't an unreasonable fib) but then quickly slid out to stand, gasping for fresh air, in the cobbled yard. A light, misting rain — a clinging sort of mizzle — had started to fall but in the shelter of the yard it was almost refreshing. My head ached and I felt feverish. I was suffering the beginnings of a doom spiral brought about by the realization that I'd made these wonderful friends only to have to disappoint them and, in due course, because that's how these things always go, lose them. I leaned my face against the cool brick of the house, willing the clock to rewind so I could refuse the invitation to come in the first place. And, I berated myself, I would've done just that if that wretched Toby hadn't worked his strange charm on Bracken and therefore on me.

Speaking of Toby...

"You'll catch cold, standing out here without your coat."

He appeared beside me, holding out my coat. I hesitated, wanting to refuse any interaction with him but also realizing it would look extremely stupid to refuse my coat in favour of standing in the rain without it. I had the perverse thought that I should do just that, if only to prove that I wouldn't catch a cold. That was my contrariness reaching all new levels of idiocy.

I took the coat and put it on but said nothing. I put up the hood and shoved my hands deep into the pockets.

"It's a lot to take in, isn't it?" he ventured, positioning himself in front of me so I was forced to look at him. I despised that assumptive manner with a vehemence that surprised me. I looked into his face, channeling all that vitriol into my eyes. He blinked and took a small step back, blushing.

"I just meant that they got a bit carried away," he waved a hand in an encompassing gesture. "I told them that just coming here was asking a lot of you and that we oughtn't push too hard."

I remained silent, noting however, his observation about my being asked to the manor.

"I imagine they thought you were settling in so well among them...so it seemed natural to include you in the plans, that's all. And the young ones are all full of righteous rage so they tend to get carried away..."

He lapsed into silence. He stuffed his own hands into the pockets of his jacket and looked out across the yard. He frowned, as if thinking about something and then ventured a look back at me.

"Can I show you something?" he asked, tentative, "Only, I think it might help you understand how urgent things are for his Lordship. And for the rest of us." He added, "I think you know by now that this goes far beyond Malmont and Winkle."

The last thing I wanted was to see more evidence of how I was going to fail these people. All I really wanted was to go home and curl up in front of the fire with Bracken and my knitting. Hell, I'd even welcome Murk if it meant I could hide away in the quiet of the cottage.

I stifled a shaky sigh. The tears were percolating just beneath the surface.

"Fine," I said, not trusting myself with more words than that.

He paused, looking pointedly down at my feet.

Bloody slippers!

That was almost my undoing. Something that could have been a laugh or a sob erupted from my throat and I hurried back inside to pull on my boots.

I followed him across the yard and out through a crooked five-barred gate. We turned left and walked for a short while down a narrow, muddy path that was flanked on both sides by a yew hedge. I was glad I'd opted for my wellies rather than my more fashionable Doc Martens as the path got wetter and muddier the further we went. The yews formed a silent green corridor, muffling the sounds of our squelching and giving the impression of being out of space and time. Of course, for all I knew we were wandering into a parallel world. Nothing would have surprised me at that point and I was past worrying about the consequences, feeling myself slipping into that helpless surrender to circumstances that seemed the only reasonable way to survive them.

The path ended at another five-barred gate. This one was made of metal, rather than wood, and in far better repair. It was secured with a length of chain at one side. A blue plastic bucket stood next to it. An old feed sack was stuffed in the stop, covering whatever was inside.

Toby came to a stop at the gate. He turned to look at me, an unreadable expression on his face.

"There aren't many folk as really know everything of what his Lordship has been doing out here all these years. He does a fine job of acting the absent-minded aristocrat and, to be fair, he isn't at all good with the bookkeeping so it's not much of a stretch. But this place would be a lot different if he hadn't been doing the work he's been doing."

"Which is what, exactly?" I interrupted, suddenly weary past the point of civility, "I don't need you to convince me that this land is worth saving. I believed that long before I found out about any of this business with BMZ. I've known it since the first memory I have of it. What you all don't seem to understand is that this place – Winkle, my Nan's cottage — all of this is the only safe haven I've ever known, since childhood. I don't need convincing. If not for..."

I broke off then, the sobs bubbling up past the tight hold I'd had on them. I rummaged in my pocket for a tissue but came up with a wizened carrot end and a handful of dog biscuits. The biscuits I could account for, but not the carrot end.

"Here," Toby held out a large checked handkerchief which I took, too fraught and miserable to care whether or not I got snot and tears on a stranger's hanky. I blew my nose, loud and unladylike, mopping my eyes with the other end.

I didn't bother offering it back to him, but shoved it into my pocket and sniffed. I pushed several strands of my hair away from my wet face. I imagined myself to look the proverbial drowned rat. Between the mizzle and my brief breakdown, I was a sight.

"Sorry if I've upset you," he said, his voice taking on that honey-dripped quality that he used on Bracken, "You might not believe me but I do understand what you mean. This land pulled me out of a dark place not so long ago. I never spoke about it when we were kids, but things weren't very good for me before I came here. Then when..."

He paused, looking down at his hands where they rested on the top bar of the gate. He seemed to be deciding something.

"Anyway, after that summer when Corny, Lord Dummell got sent away, well, I went off the rails a bit. I think I went a bit mad. I never should've..."

"Left me behind?" I said, not caring about trying not to care.

There was a brief pause. I looked at him. He was gripping the gate with his eyes closed, breathing steadily. I recognized the technique. He opened his eyes but didn't look at me, his gaze off across the stretch of moor ahead.

"I never should've included you in the first place. It wasn't right. You had, *have*, a family and people who love you. I was just a hot-headed lad with a giant chip on his shoulder. It would've been a mistake."

I felt the ground shifting under my feet and a rush of heat flushing my face. He shouldn't have included me, was it? What right did he have to make that decision for me? Then again, people had been making decisions for me my entire life. Was I that feeble, even back then? I hadn't thought so. I thought that was the one time that I was in control of my life, of my destiny. I didn't say any of that out loud. I shoved the rising tide of hurt and indignation down and did my own set of steadying breaths.

"When I finally found Corny he told me to go back. He said I couldn't stay with him, that I was going to make things worse and something just snapped in me, I suppose. I'd had a whole life of people not wanting me and that just seemed like the last straw. What do you know when you're seventeen, aye?"

"I was only fifteen and I knew that I loved you," I said, surprising myself, but I wanted to hurt him, if only to make him feel the tiniest twinge of guilt. "You were wanted in Winkle."

He opened his mouth to speak then closed it again, looking down at his boots. He had one foot up on the lower bar of the gate. The silence stretched out between us and I waited. All he had to do was say he was sorry. All he had to do was admit it was a mistake to leave me behind, to leave me with the mess that my life became after he was gone from it. It was grossly unfair of me to think that, but that's what trauma does to you.

Eventually, he spoke.

"I took off then, went and lived in Aberdeen. I found a bit of work but mostly went stupid for a while, did some really stupid things. The rest of the world wrote me off but when the old man died and our Corny took over, he tracked me down and brought me back here and showed me that there's another way to be in the world, a way that matters, that does good things and I've not looked back."

I only half-believed him. It seemed like one of those trite redemption stories and I was just angry enough and suspicious enough of him to imagine that he'd tell me anything to get me on their side. Their full-on demands had unraveled me so they sent the handsome rogue to charm me onto their side, relying on our shared childhood and former affection to bring me back into the fold. They didn't take into account the enormous chasm that existed between us, one that he apparently didn't want to cross. Which was fine. I could just as easily forget him again.

In that minute, I hated what this whole ridiculous mess was turning me into. I've never been a cynical sort of person; I always intrinsically trust people, never quite being able to understand why anyone would lie to me. It's hurt me more than once, case in point, and given me the reputation of being gullible and without the capability to function in the dog-eat-dog world all around me. But it's who I am and in the times that it matters, my trusting nature serves me well. It leaves me open to wonder and prone to exclamations of delight over seemingly small things and I like that about myself. I'm easily enchanted and I'm glad of that. In my more generous moments, I consider it my secret super-power. In light of that, I tried to get a grip of myself and shake off the negative thoughts and suspicions that I knew (thanks to the efforts of my patient therapist) were only the result of my fear of failure, of disappointing these people who I'd come to view as not only friends, but as kindred spirits. My emotional baggage around Toby had no place in this and I firmly shoved it back where it belonged.

"If that's the case," I said, sniffling and unearthing the hanky again, "Then you can understand why I don't want to be a disappointment to them. They've all been so good to me and I can't bear to think that I'm going to let them down. Because I honestly don't think that I'm any more special than the rest of you. In fact, I'm probably less so because I left...I've been away for so long." I took a deep, gulping breath. "I should've fought harder."

He was silent after this, in my ragged-nerved opinion, very revealing declaration. I had a surge of panic that I'd misread the situation, but it froze me in position. I almost cringed, waiting for his response.

He turned and took the chain off the gate, bending to pick up the bucket. He took the piece of sacking off to reveal a pile of pony nuts. He smiled, a genuine smile that made me think of summer and wild roses and how when we were children it was all so much easier.

"You're here now, aren't you?"

We kept walking.

I'd harboured the hope that whatever he was planning on showing me would be just on the other side of the gate. Perhaps a flock of Lord Dummell's heritage breed sheep — the lambing pens, maybe. I was cold and shivery and huddled down inside my coat, the post-upset hangover leaving me in tatters. I was worried about leaving Bracken for so long. She might have thought I'd abandoned her. My thoughts turned to the idea of abandonment: Corny's abandonment of Toby then Toby's abandonment of me. How I'd abandoned Nan and Winkle and everything that mattered so deeply to me when I was young. Granted I didn't always have a whole lot of choice. My mother is a mighty force to be reckoned with and she made very sure that my time here ended before I could fully develop an opinion of my own about how much I needed to be with Nan. I didn't properly understand that until I was away for good. And really, with all of her benign manipulations, she made certain that I wouldn't have too many opinions in general. It was always just so much easier to go along with things. All at once I was thoroughly fed up with myself. I was so worried about letting other people down but really, I'd let myself down long before now. I wondered if there was a trite redemption story in the cards for me.

"Is it much farther?" I asked, muffled from inside my hood. It smelled faintly of Murk which didn't delight me in the slightest.

"Not sure," came the reply, "It depends on where they are. This time of day they're usually down at the stream for water. They expect a visit, so it's likely they'll be there."

"What exactly are we going to see?"

"In a minute," said Toby, turning to grin at me, "You'll see in a minute."

The ground began to slope slightly upwards towards a copse of scrubby trees. I tried to place where on the moor this must be but I was all turned around. I thought we'd gone west when we left the yard but the gloom and cloud had effectively blocked out the sun, making it hard to get my bearings.

"There!" said Toby, triumphant, his face flushed with the cold and climb. I scrambled up beside him to the crest of the hill. What I saw down the other side literally took my breath away.

Down in a sort of valley ran a thin line of water, the stream he'd referred to. Milling about on the banks of the stream, was a herd of ponies. But they weren't the typical scrubby native ponies that were usually grazed on the moors. Those ponies had a roughness about them, a hardiness that made them all shaggy coats and short, strong legs. Even from a distance, I could see that these were different. For starters, they were longer-legged and slightly more fine in their heads. They still had the thick manes and tails of a moor pony but there was a strange light to their coats, an almost iridescent shimmer, even in the dullness of the day. They moved with a fluid sort of grace that made me think of shoals of fish, sliding through the water.

I gazed, spellbound, then turned to Toby, my eyes shining with the beauty of them.

"What are they?" I breathed, because surely they weren't ordinary ponies.

"They're the last herd of Glencarragh," he said, his voice filled with reverent awe, "Bred for centuries by the moor-men from their own native ponies and the water horses."

"Glencarragh?" I said, trying to place where I'd heard that name before. Mrs.Goodship, I think, and the lemon drizzle cake. Although what cake and ponies have in common I'm not certain.

"Aye," said Toby, "It's an island off the mainland of Scotland. Wild place, full of storms and faery people." His voice dropped to a whisper, "My place."

I shot him a look, which he ignored.

"Lord Dummell, Corny's father, had them brought here after..."

Here, he paused, frowning. I could see unfathomable emotions flitting across his face — confusion? Sorrow? Anger? He cleared his throat and carried on.

"There wasn't anyone that could look after them and so..."

"Oh?" I said, "And do they have to go back? Will they find someone to take care of them?"

Toby shrugged, shifting the bucket to his other hand.

"There isn't anyone up there anymore who knows how to look after them," he said, "And there's no interest in learning, I suppose. They can be difficult, flighty and a bit wild. Not to mention, they don't have a use for them either. Their time has come and gone and these are the last of them."

"What did they used to do with them?" I asked, entranced by the antics of two of the ponies who appeared to be engaged in a mock battle underneath the spread of a large tree.

"Oh, a bit of this and that," said Toby, evasively, "It was so long ago that most folk don't bother with remembering. Come on, we can get a bit closer."

I had the distinct impression he was fobbing me off but at the same time, I was delighted to think we could see them up close. I desperately wanted to run my hands over their coats. I imagined it would be like sinking my fingers into silk or cashmere.

I slipped and slid down the hill behind Toby who apparently had far better footwear for walking down wet, muddy inclines as he strode with great, confident strides. About three quarters of the way down we were noticed. One of the ponies threw up his or her head and snorted, drawing the attention of all the others. Toby held up a hand, and I bumped into him as he stopped suddenly. He grabbed my sleeve and pulled me close beside him. He tugged me down into a half-crouch and I inhaled the smell of forest and old leather that seemed to hang around him.

"Hang on," he said, his voice a loud whisper, "Let her get a look at us. She's the lead mare. What she says goes, so if we want them to stay we have to wait for her to invite us."

"There's a mare in charge?" I whispered back, pleased for the herd dynamics.

Toby nodded, without taking his eyes off the attentive figures.

"They're all mares," he said, "the males were always too wild. There was only ever one person who managed to tame a Glencarragh stallion, but that really was a long time ago and it's mostly fallen to myth and legend. It might be a complete fiction, but I like to think the old stories are true."

"So what happened to the stallions, then?" I asked, almost afraid of the answer. Visions of the fates of male chickens in egg laying operations and other assorted gender cleansing practices in livestock husbandry flitted uneasily through my head.

"They go back to the sea," he said, his tone clipped and final.

I didn't get a chance to follow up on that because something shifted in the herd below. The lead mare blew loudly through her large nostrils and shook her head, pawing at the ground. The rest of the mares bunched together, moving in a circle around her, tails swishing and manes flying.

"Easy, lass," Toby murmured, slowly standing up. "There's my bright girl." He jangled the bucket of pony nuts. The mare's ears flicked forwards at the sound and then one flicked back, as if she was listening to something behind her.

I recognized his Bracken-charming voice and smiled to myself. That pony would be putty in his hands.

Suddenly in a froth of churning hooves and high-pitched whinnies the band of ponies exploded into a gallop. Tails over their backs they galloped off over the moor and out of sight. All that remained of their presence was a muddied bank and brown, foamy stream.

My heart sank.

"It's my fault, isn't it?" I said, surprisingly close to tears. I'd wanted to see them so badly but obviously I hadn't passed muster.

Toby shook his head, his shoulder's slumping.

"No," he replied, "It's hit or miss with that one. She knows I come every day and she knows I've a bucket of pony nuts and she'll happily hoover down great mouthfuls of them. But she's a fickle creature. Too much of the sea in her, I think. Back in the old days they used iron on their head collars, it made them more co-operative," That last part he spoke with a forceful bitterness that took me by surprise. I glanced at him but he was looking over the moor in the direction of the ponies. "I won't have that," he said, finally, "they need to be free to choose."

He turned to me, his face creased with a kind of sadness. He seemed generally hurt and disappointed that she'd run off.

"Still, it probably didn't help that I'm a stranger." I added, because now I wanted it to be about me, about my intrusion, and not because she'd rejected him.

"Maybe if I come another time?" I said, before I could think it was a bad idea. Which it was because it was all manner of presumption and intrusion on something that he obviously held as a special relationship. I could feel the heat rise up from my neck. I quickly moved on.

"Anyway, what do you mean about the sea? And the water horses? Is that another breed of pony that they have in Scotland?"

Toby reached out a hand to help me up. He held my hand a moment longer than was necessary and I was panicked by my indecision over whether to take it firmly back or let him hold on. He let go, but not after giving it a small squeeze. The sadness was still in his eyes.

"We'd best be getting back," he said, "I'll fill you in on the way. They'll be missing us at the house."

Long ago, the people of Glencarragh got it into their heads to breed their own native ponies with the faery horses that lived in the sea around the island. They thought that with a strain of faery magic in them, their ponies would be stronger, braver and, most importantly, more valuable. And they were right. They sold their faery half-breed ponies for vast sums of money to collectors and enthusiasts on the mainland. Because that was the catch — the ponies had to be taken away from the sea. Too near the ocean, they could become wild and unmanageable. On the other hand, too far away from their native place and they could weaken or die. Either way, they took a knowl-edgeable hand to manage them and those were in short supply. The life of a pony-man was one of solitude and isolation as the herds needed to be kept away from people and livestock for reasons of mutual safety. Not to mention, there were plenty of people on the island that didn't agree with what was being done. Fraternizing with the fae isn't universally accepted, so it seems.

At this point in his story, Toby became somewhat hesitant, his face carefully composed and his tone measured, as if he were trying very hard to simply recite the facts in a detached, business-like way, like he wasn't all that bothered, though it was patently obvious to me that he was deeply, deeply invested in the story of these ponies. I had a thousand questions but something made me stay quiet as he felt his way through that part of the story.

The day came when the last pony-man on the island was no longer able to take care of the remaining herd. The island itself had become less and less isolated, the reliability of ferries and the attraction of migrating birds and the starkly beautiful landscape brought tourists and day-trippers, ramblers and bird-watchers by the boat-load. It was harder and harder to keep the ponies away from people. The ponies had to be moved. And so here they were. Only now they were threatened again. If the proposed wind farm went through, thereby closing the Winkle portal, there would no longer be safe passage for them to the faery grazing land.

"Are we in the Otherworld now?" I asked, as we approached the yew tunnel. I looked around, trying to look for the subtle differences in vegetation that I'd seen when I visited Mr.and Mrs. Goodship's side of the hedge.

Toby laughed.

"No, no. Just a quiet bit of the estate land. We move them to the Otherworld for about two weeks a month, from the waning of the moon until it's full again. That's as much as we could negotiate for them and it seems to be enough."

"Negotiate?" I said, "Negotiate with who?"

Toby had waved off the question with a shrug. Not an I-don't-know shrug but a you-don't-need-to-know-that shrug. He was definitely of the belief that I could be easily fobbed off. Which, to a certain extent, was true. I was temperamentally obligated not to make a fuss or upset people, but there was something about those ponies that tugged at the edges of a long ago memory; a story of Nan's perhaps. I groped around in my memories for it but either it was never there or it was buried under the rubble of other things.

We rounded the bend and approached the gate. I grabbed Toby's sleeve, forcing him to stop. He looked at me with a strange curiosity in his eyes, like when you meet someone who seems familiar but you can't quite place where you may have known them from.

"What happens to the ponies if the development goes through?" I asked.

Toby's shoulder's slumped.

"Honestly, Hazel, I don't really know. Without the grazing, they'd not survive too long. It's their native land and waters that they need to do well; the NetherWinkle streams and pastures are just a reasonable substitute. I suppose we'd have to find a way to move them back to Glencarragh. But that would mean..." Again, that furtive look in his eyes. He shook his head. "No sense in fretting about it. We just can't let it happen, aye?"

Without waiting for a response, he climbed over the gate and disappeared into the yard, leaving me to scramble after him, my mind whirring with the implications.

He wasn't in the kitchen when I got back, having first taken a wrong turn in the maze of outbuildings before finding the door to the mudroom. The rest of the group was sitting, talking quietly amongst themselves when I walked in. For the second time, all conversation stopped and their faces turned to me. They were a mixture of doubt and hope, suspicion and gentleness.

When I left the kitchen, I thought I'd be looking for ways to convince them I was of no use to them, but something had changed during that walk to see the ponies. It was still far from solid in my mind, all still an ethereal tingle at the edges of my memories, but I knew that, for reasons more than just being able to be left alone to live my quiet, unassuming life, I needed to do something to help these people, this land. It no longer felt like an obligation but had become a necessity. I realized with a wry sense of irony, that that was exactly what

Toby had hoped for by taking me to see the ponies. I probably ought to have been incensed at being manipulated, but it didn't feel that way; I had a quiet belief that his taking me to see them was a genuine act rather than a strategic one.

"Right," I said, with what I hoped was bright enthusiasm, "Let's see if we can't get ourselves a plan together, shall we?"

Four faces broke into wide grins and an excited chatter erupted immediately. I pulled a chair up to the table and we set to work.

Chapter Twenty

I got a lift home from Alfie.

I sat in the front with him, and Sidney and Astrid sat in the back with Bracken and Murk. The latter had conveniently materialized when it was time to go home, leaping from seemingly out of nowhere when the car door opened and insinuating himself onto Astrid's lap. Of course, she thought he was delightful and was utterly charmed by his rumbling purr and tattered appearance. I glared at him, not able to conceal my irritation. He ignored me and carried on rubbing his cheek across Sidney's outstretched finger. Ha! I thought, if only they knew the true nature of the beast. Bracken had pressed herself on the far side of Sidney, trying to wedge herself between them and the door, so as to be as far from Murk as possible.

We drove mostly in silence, each of us lost in our own thoughts. The plan we'd put together seemed a solid enough one, without any hint of magical expectations. I'd been frank with them regarding my alleged fortune and surprisingly they took it very well. Perhaps I'd assumed too much of their interest in me to be based on both how I might fund the endeavour and my wrongly attributed magical capabilities. It wouldn't be the first time that my paranoid hypersensitivity had put thoughts in other people's heads. So, for starters, we were going the rummage sale route. In typical village fashion, as small villages all over the country had done for decades in aid of church roofs and children's outings, we were going to organize a spring fête to raise money for our legal defence fund; the foundation of our strategy being that there were legal grounds to block the sale and so that was to be the first avenue of attack. Lord Dummell had insisted, with a knowing glance towards the young people who refused to meet his eyes, that we toe the legal line. Hamish had pledged his expertise *pro bono*, but also said that we should prepare for having to engage a more aggressive sort of law firm to handle the inevitable response from BMZ and to consult on the legality of any and all supporting documents we could get our hands on.

That, apparently, was my department. Nan had purportedly been the one to hang onto those sorts of documents – it was, I was told, with shifting gazes and much clearing of throats – one of the duties of a Caretaker. I let that slide without comment. That was a conversation for another day. My immediate task was to locate these papers, which would apparently then direct me to the appropriate place in the county archives, all in search of some other mysterious document that made it an impossibility for the land to be sold. Under *any* circumstances. Of that, Lord Dummell was quite emphatic. Or at least, he then admitted, it would muddy the waters enough to slow things down. It all sounded very vague and implausible but no-one else seemed to share my concerns. I admit to having difficulty with uncertainty, but so as long as my friends were happy, I kept my doubts to myself.

In the meanwhile, we were all to be in charge of different aspects of the fête. I'd been assigned the garden displays - scouting up entries and the arranging of judges and prizes. While it was acknowledged that Alfie was the senior gardener amongst us, he'd been put in charge of the infrastructure – tents and tables and the finding of volunteers to put them up and take them down, so in light of my experience with floral arranging, the garden portion had fallen to me. I felt a strange and unexpected surge of pride when my name was put forward, so I didn't point out that my duties in Roger's flower shop were mostly of the administrative variety. Already my mind was leaping about thinking of categories and possible prizes. Because it was still early in the season, it would be things like flower and bulb displays and spring veg. I had visions of strawberry jams and rhubarb crumbles, perhaps a cookery challenge using only home-grown ingredients.

My fantasies of pea pod sculptures were interrupted by a tap on the shoulder from the back seat.

"Did anyone ever reply to your advert?" asked Astrid.

It took a minute for me to sort out what she meant. I felt a pang of something like fear when I realized she was talking about my lost dog notice. I glanced back at poor Bracken who was trembling ever so slightly. She wagged her tail tip when she saw me looking. Her expression was pleading. I think she would have preferred to trot along behind the car, or even run beside a quad bike, than be trapped in such close proximity to the cat. Murk had curled himself up on Astrid's lap, his paws folded under him in that self-satisfied way that cats have of being righteous in their comfort. He stared, unblinking, at Bracken who did her best to blend in with the door handle.

"No, actually," I replied, swallowing hard, my mouth suddenly quite dry. I gave a nervous laugh. "I'd honestly forgotten all about it. I just assumed that she was here for the duration."

Astrid smiled at me and nodded.

"That's what I think," she replied, "Besides, I'm sure if someone really had lost her they'd have tracked her down by now."

She turned her attention to the quivering dog, reaching out a fingerless-gloved hand to smooth her wiry eyebrows.

"Lovely girl, aren't you?" she crooned softly, "You're much better off with our Hazel anyway, aren't you lovey?"

I smiled at her, but it felt strained. I only hoped that what she said was true and that enough time had passed for anyone looking for her to have tracked her down already. She'd become such a part of my days, and I couldn't imagine life without her. Shoving that thought firmly out of my head, I went back to daydreaming about strawberry scones and bouquets of sweet peas.

I soaked for a luxurious hour, letting the difficulties and upsets of the day float away in lavender and eucalyptus-scented steam.

Once she realized that the announcement of bath wasn't intended for her, Bracken padded up the stairs and made herself comfortable on the bath mat. The longer I soaked, the more I began to believe that things were going to work out alright after all. My new friends and I would get the whole land development thing sorted – just a matter of tracking down the right documents it seemed – and then life could ease happily into a state of predictable rhythms and routines.

I let my mind drift ahead to summer evenings on the patio. I would enlarge it slightly to accommodate a bigger table so that everyone could fit around it. We could have a barbecue and make exotic cocktails to sip in the mild evenings, counting the stars, unsullied by the light pollution of the city, as they winked into view. I would grow some beautiful wildflowers and perhaps even some veg worthy enough to enter into the harvest festival in September. I'm sure the church still had its harvest festival; I remember it was the height of the village social season when I was small, Nan planning her raspberry harvest to catch them at their sweetest and juiciest for her cordials and pie fillings. It was exceeded perhaps only by the Christmas concert which, interestingly, was always held at the winter solstice; so as not to interfere with the carol performances at the big churches in the city, or so everyone told themselves. I often suspected and Nan insisted that the villagers were far more heathen than was ever spoken aloud. Apparently the vicar had no problem with that, so long as his flock was happy and the donations for the current cause rolled steadily in, then who was he to argue dates?

The vicar had been a regular visitor to Nan's back in the old days. He would come bearing gifts of marmalade and peach pie from his wife and would leave with a bottle of Nan's dandelion wine and a jar of her famous cold and 'flu formula. It was a sinus clearing concoction of apple cider vinegar and garlic and onions and however many hot peppers she could cram into the jar. The two of them would share a glass of parsnip wine, or maybe blackberry, and sit by the fire talking about village goings-on and other strange things that I couldn't quite remember. I was supposed to be in bed, of course, but I would creep down the stairs and sit there, shivering, listening to the rise and fall of their conversation. I'm quite certain that Nan knew I was there but she never let on. She once, very conveniently, left my favourite tartan blanket draped over the bannister.

I sighed, with fond remembrance, content with myself for the first time in a long while. Yes, everything seemed like it was going to be alright after all. I could clearly see the days unfolding in peaceful bliss.

The year and a day would pass in the blink of an eye and before I knew it, it would be official and well beyond the reach of my mum's machinations. I knew that as long as it wasn't all signed and sealed, I would be carrying a slight tremor of trepidation with me, but now that I had made some friends and had some purpose, I wouldn't be so likely to dwell on that fact.

"So I suppose it's a good thing that I've got all this stuff to think about after all, isn't it, my girl?" I said to Bracken, reaching down a prune-tipped finger to tickle her ears. She thumped her tail on the mat. She was another unexpected gratitude I now had. I couldn't imagine banging around this old cottage on my own. It still had a faintly detached feeling to it, no matter how well I tried to placate it with leaving Nan's things where they were and getting to work on the garden. It would take time, I knew, for it to welcome me because of course it didn't quite trust me yet, it didn't really know me, after all. Not as I am now, anyway.

"Right," I said, reluctant to leave the enveloping warmth to step into the cooler air of the bathroom. "I'd better get out of here before I shrivel up. I could murder a plate of beans and toast. Fancy joining me"

An exuberant wiggling bum was all the answer that I needed.

The next day was a designated home day. Straight after breakfast I did a bit of cleaning and tidying, trying to curry favour with the cottage. I wandered outside to the garden, knowing I had all manner of pressing work to do out there and would have much preferred to be doing it rather than grubbing about in the attic, but needs must and I promised to reward myself with a garden session if I found the papers I needed before lunch. So, averting my eyes from the wheelbarrow and the still half-mulched vegetable beds, I quickly snipped some daffodils and went back inside. Nan had always been one for having flowers indoors, she said it blurred the lines between outside and in, so I thought I might bribe the cottage with the offering. The bowl of narcissi that I'd bought on my first trip into the village were just beginning to wilt now and I planned on replanting the bulbs in the autumn. The autumn! Just the very idea of having future plans here made me giddy with quiet delight.

I had just put the daffodils in water and was about to head up to the attic when there was a loud knock at the kitchen door. Bracken started up her frantic yelping bark assigned to familiar persons, so I knew it wasn't anyone selling encyclopaedias. I opened the door to see Young Craig standing on the step, a bottle of milk and a carton of eggs in one hand and a small, lumpy paper bag in the other.

"Craig!" I said, in genuine surprise. Then I realized that I hadn't had my delivery early that morning. Craig's whistle had begun to serve as a second alarm, the dawn chorus being the first.

"Hello, Hazel, lass," he said, handing over his packages, "Them's fresh ginger snaps that me mum sent over for you. As a way of apology for being late with the milk and eggs this morning. Sorry and all that."

He looked utterly exhausted. His skin had a greyish cast and there were dark smudges, like bruises, under his eyes. He made a particular point of making a big fuss of Bracken who was snuffling around his pockets, in search of a bit of liver sausage that he always kept on hand for the doggy members of his delivery families.

"That's no bother," I said, "I wasn't out of either. Thank your mum for the biscuits, they smell gorgeous. They'll be grand for my elevenses!"

I smiled, genuinely delighted with the little gift.

"Are you alright?" I asked, studying him more closely, "You look positively wrung out. Would you like a cup of tea? Fortify you for the rest of your deliveries?"

Craig smiled, tiredness creasing his face.

"No thanks, pet," he said, "We've had a terrible few nights with a couple of the cows. We lost a calf last night and it's a bloody horrible business, if you'll pardon my French," he added apologetically.

He sighed and looked down at Bracken, gazing fondly into her shaggy face, then chuckled.

"I sometimes think I'm not really cut out for this farming lark at all. I'm too soft by half, and me old uncle'll tell you the same."

"Did you ever want to do anything different?" I asked, "Other than farming?"

"Oh aye! I always fancied being one of those landscape designers. You know, the ones that design gardens from nothing, like. Only I'd do it with wildflowers and water features and beehives and such. None of this poncy shrubberies and lemon trees and what have you. Real English gardens that were a bit of the wild brought closer. I was all set to start a training course but then me uncle took ill and well, the farm means that much to him and I couldn't see him fretting about it. Him and Auntie were ever so good to Mum and me when Dad left. I couldn't have it, you see, the worry would've killed him. I've some cousins – a lad and two lasses – they're older than me so you probably won't remember them, but none of them have the first inclination for farming. I was always the one who loved the land. Only things have gone in all the wrong directions in the last few decades and I can't get behind it all. As I see it, we need to go back to the old ways of looking after the land, back when we had a lot more respect for it than we do now. Old Dummy feels the same, but we're like a pair of Dodos, us. We're forever banging heads over things, trying to make it work. It's all well and fine to have these high ideas, but it's still got to pay its way, hasn't it?"

I think I might have fallen a little bit in love with him just then. I wanted to reach out and hug him but that likely wouldn't have gone well.

"But those are all fantastic ideas, Craig. And you don't need a training course for that. You've worked this land all your life, surely that gives you more knowledge than anything you could learn from a book. I love all of your ideas. Is there no way you could do a bit of that on the side? I'm sure Lord Dummell would be supportive and anything to help bring in a bit more money is bound to be worth pursuing."

Craig shrugged, straightening up.

"No, lass. I doubt I've either the time nor the energy. We've got to keep the livestock and the crops going to stay solvent. Already, Dummy has to make up the difference and he's barely two ha'pennies to rub together. There's an agreement that goes back for miles, y'see, the farm and the Manor are attached. The two families have been bound since William the Conqueror's time. All very honour and duty and such like. But it's more than a duty for the both of us. It's about keeping the land safe from the likes of that BMwhatsit lot who'd pull up hedges and bring in giant machines and robot potatoes. Though heaven knows how we're going to manage it all, even if we do keep that particular wolf from the door."

It all sounded terribly familiar. Like the plot of one of my novels — all we needed now was an attractive but destitute heroine to replace

Lord Dummell and a dashing cad who needed an heir to keep the estate in the family. I mentally shook my head. Old habits die hard.

"Still, though," I said, "Isn't it better to keep exploring alternatives to the conventional ways? Surely the way forward is in looking backward, to how things were done before. I'm sure Lord Dummell would be keen."

"Oh, aye," said Craig, brandishing the egg carton, "These eggs were laid by pedigree hens with bloodlines going back almost as far as old Dummy himself. And the milk is from aristocratic Jerseys with more credentials than your average brain surgeon. He's keen alright. We just can't compete with the big farms down the road. There's not many folk who want to pay twice the price for eggs than the ones they can get in the supermarket, just so they know the hens get to see the sunshine and scratch about in the grass."

I nodded, commiserating.

"Never mind my gloom, lass," he said, patting my arm as I reached out for my pedigree eggs. "There's no need for you to worry yourself about it. Something always turns up, aye?"

I gave a small smile. I certainly hoped it would; quite literally, thinking of my impending attic search.

"Right, that's enough natter. Mrs. Blenkinsop will be hopping mad if she hasn't got her bottle of milk in time for Coronation Street. Ta-ra, love!"

And with that, he was off again. Striding down the garden path and out the gate to his waiting van. I shook my head, amazed as always at the way village folk seemed to be able to quickly extricate themselves from conversation, right when it was starting to get interesting.

I wandered back inside, putting the milk in the fridge and the biscuits in the tin. No wonder Lord Dummell was so keen for me to find this paperwork. He must be terribly anxious about keeping the estate afloat, not to mention the other, more faery-ish concerns. Finding the papers and stopping the land sale wouldn't solve the problem of Rookery Farm, though. How on earth was he going to remedy that? More questions than answers, as usual, I thought. I shook it off; it was time to get to work.

I pulled an old shirt of my dad's over my dress, not wanting to get either my dress or my apron covered in attic grime and tucked my hair under a spotted kerchief then headed for the stairs. Pausing with one foot on the first step, I turned and hurried back to the kitchen, grabbed a handful of ginger snaps from the tin - for sustenance, I told Bracken's reproachful face — and headed up to the attic.

I returned from my mission, an hour or so later, covered in dust and cobwebs, aching all over from being bent double and parched with thirst. Bracken greeted me like I'd been gone for days. She hadn't been happy to be left behind but there was no way that she could've climbed the ladder up into the attic.

"I know, I know," I said, fending off her capering delight, "It was horrid of me to abandon you like that, how did you ever survive it? But look!" I waved a sheaf of grubby, slightly moulded papers at her waggling eyebrows. "I think I've found what we need! I'll have to phone Lord Dummell straight away. He'll be thrilled. But first," I paused to peel off the dusty shirt and the equally filthy kerchief, "first there must be tea!"

The phone rang just as I was collapsing onto the sofa with my mug of tea and another handful of gingersnaps. I groaned.

"I'm going to have to get us a cordless phone, Bracken," I said, unbending my stiffening muscles to answer the phone, "Surely the cottage can't object to a few modern conveniences." As if in response, the stairs creaked and the boiler ticked loudly. "Hmph! Well maybe just an extension for the cord, then. Hello?"

"Hazel? It's Astrid, how are you today?"

"Very well," I answered, amused by her formal telephone voice and manner, "And yourself?"

"Also well, thank you. I was just wondering if you fancied getting together with us all at the Forge this evening to go over our plans for the fundraiser? We thought we'd have a bit of supper and then compare notes on how we're getting on so far. You know, an exchange of ideas before we roll into action."

"Sounds super," I said, surprised at myself that I actually meant it. Two social gatherings in one week! It was an all-time record for me. "It'll give me a chance to share the good news. I found the papers we need in the attic!"

There was silence on the other end for a moment.

"Are you still there?"

"Oh my goodness yes!" she shrieked, laughing loudly. "Oh Hazel! This is magnificent news! What do they say? No, wait! Don't tell me. Bring them to the Forge tonight and we can all find out together! Oh Hazel. I finally feel like we might be on the winning side. This is the first bit of good news we've had for ages. See you at 6?"

With that, she rang off, the Winkle transition as abrupt as ever. I stood there for a moment, beaming at the phone like a simpleton. It felt good to be making a contribution.

I hobbled back to the sofa and flopped down with a sigh. Bracken jumped up beside me and nestled in against my thigh, resting her chin on my leg. She looked up at me, then back at the pile of biscuits, then back at me, her eyebrows twitching comically every time she moved her eyes.

"Oh, darling dog!" I said, reaching over and picking up a biscuit. I gave her the whole thing. "How wonderful to have your only worry be when you might next mooch a snack."

I sighed again and leaned back against the squishy cushions, my mug cradled between my hands. I was tired and dirty but utterly content. Things were definitely on the turn for the better, at long last.

Chapter Twenty-One

"Ye do know the bigger meaning of this, don't ye?"

Alfie stabbed the mildewed sheaf of papers with a knobbled finger. He looked around at the faces at the table. We'd finished our meal long since and were in the coffee, tea and afters portion of the program. Astrid and I were going to split a slice of cheesecake — not to be missed, according to my old friend Ernie — and Lord Dummell had opted for a bowl of chocolate ice-cream. I found that to be quietly amusing. It wasn't the sort of pudding you'd expect a peer of the realm to order. Then again, you also wouldn't expect the aristocracy to be eating big platefuls of bangers and mash with a rag-tag group of misfits either.

"I'm sure you're going to tell us," said Edie, patting his arm. Although not really an active member of the group, she considered herself to be part of the support system and was going to be absolutely indispensable in the planning of the fête/fundraiser. She had years of village gatherings under her belt.

"Aye, right you are I am," said Alfie. He was on his third pint. Edie had given him a Look after he'd ordered it but he blithely pretended not to notice. His colour was high and he spoke rather more loudly than usual but he was pure benevolence with it. "What this means, my friends is that our lass Hazel, here," he paused to beam, bleary-eyed at me, "that our lass Hazel, here has passed muster."

He glared around at everyone at the table, as if challenging anyone to argue with him. He had no takers in that department, although I was more than a bit confused.

"You mean I've passed a test with you all?" I asked, pleased but also a bit unnerved that I'd been tested against my knowledge. "I know I haven't always seemed like I was on board with all of this, but you must believe that I'm doing what I can to help. I just needed you all to understand my...well, my limitations."

"No, dear gel," said Lord Dummell, leaning across to fix me in his intense gaze, "There was never any doubt in my mind that once you knew what was truly at stake that we'd have your support. No doubt at all. What I believe our comrade Alfred is trying to say is that the *cottage*," He put a great deal of emphasis on the word and paused a moment, letting everyone catch up, "The *cottage* has approved of you. And if the *cottage* has approved, then it must mean without question that you will take up the role of Caretaker!"

A murmur of approval followed, along with raised glasses and mugs, toasting the apparent good news of this. I was still floundering with the idea of the cottage having approved of me.

"How can that be?" I asked, "I mean, I've been there for a while now and nothing seems to have changed. It doesn't really feel any different." I wanted to tell them how much that was bothering me, but I'd been afraid to admit it until just now.

"Hazel, pet," said Edie, smiling kindly, "If the cottage didn't approve of you then it never would've let you find the papers quite so quickly. That old place has a jealous heart when it comes down to it and is fierce in protecting its own. If it didn't think you were up to it, you'd have been weeks looking for those papers."

"I think the house has been grieving," offered Toby, "It hadn't any reason to welcome anyone when it was still grieving the loss of Elsie."

He'd been mostly quiet during the meal, exchanging a few quiet words with Sidney who was sitting beside him but not really joining in the general banter. He hadn't spoken to me at all, other than to nod a greeting. I imagine he was avoiding me because of the potential for uncomfortable questions. But he was wrong, I had no plans to delve into what he'd clearly put behind him. I'd forgotten it all once and I could do it again.

Lord Dummell nodded, his face solemn.

"Indeed, it was, my lad. You're right there. You couldn't expect it to take to you right away, Hazel, even knowing you as it did from when you were young. And I think we all feel a bit chastened for imagining you'd settle in quickly enough to feel ready to direct yourself towards our troubles right away. Of course proper time should have been observed. I do hope you'll accept my apology, on behalf of the whole village?"

I blinked, still trying to process what he was saying. That the cottage could've hidden the papers from me wasn't something I'd considered. When Nan used to tell me that it was alive, I didn't really believe it to have a *wilful* sort of existence. That it could have, and express, emotion seemed a bit far-fetched, even for my willing imagination. Then again, maybe it was because it was too wonderful a concept that I couldn't allow myself to believe it, lest it be taken away from me by someone less, well, willing. I'd had a lot of my beliefs bullied out of me at school; it was a minor miracle I'd held onto any of them.

"Well, I don't really know what to say," I stammered, feeling the heat of embarrassment rise up my neck. And it was true. I was both stunned and delighted and a tiny bit frightened. What then, did this all mean? Were there now definite expectations? I always knew I was going to stay on at Rookery Cottage but I'd never been firm on accepting the role of Caretaker. Surely there were more qualified candidates than me. I said as much.

"Not at all, lass!" exclaimed Alfie, hiccuping slightly. Edie glared at him and reached across the table to move his glass away from his elbow which was flapping as he gestured magnanimously. "You're the perfect choice, isn't she everyone? There's always been a McCorrigan woman as Caretaker, for all the years that we've been paying attention, anyway. It's only right that it comes to you. Just because your Da..."

"That's enough, Alfie," said Edie, removing the glass entirely. She beckoned to Ernie who was hovering in the periphery and asked for a mug of strong, sweet coffee. "You know you can't handle your lager like you used to.

"What was that you were going to say about Dad?" I asked. I was noticing far too many unfinished thoughts and ideas left dangling by my new friends.

"Nothing, pet," said Edie, "he only meant as to say that your da being born a boy and all that, broke the line of inheritance."

"Meaning?"

"Meaning that the role of Caretaker is theoretically up for grabs," said Toby, his voice pitched low, forcing everyone to be quiet in order to hear him. "It means that if you, as the blood heir, choose not to take it, anyone who fancies it and has at least a working knowledge of...things...can take the oath."

"Is that true?" I asked, looking around the table. Suddenly everyone seemed intrigued by their cutlery or the wine menu.

"Is it true?" I repeated, "Can someone else claim the role?"

Lord Dummell cleared his throat.

"Yes, technically that is true. But," he held up a long-fingered hand. "It's quite without precedent and not likely to be supported by the interested parties."

"Aye, but there are a few who'd be keen to step in, all the same," said Alfie, blinking down at his place setting. He fiddled with the salt cellar, spinning it around and around. "And they're not the sort of folk who'd do right by the land nor the folk who live on it. People-folk and otherwise."

I shook my head, my usual reticence falling away in the face of what was being said.

"Okay, will someone please explain this, clearly and succinctly. Who can and cannot be a Caretaker? I was under the impression that if I didn't do it, then there just wouldn't be one."

"Not at all, my dear," said Lord Dummell, "The terms of the original agreement were quite clear. There *must* be a Caretaker to hold the boundary between the worlds, steward the portal and ensure the continued health and safety of all the residents – human and non-human. There's a requisite transition period allowed, of course, following the demise of a Caretaker..."

"A year and a day," I whispered, it suddenly all becoming very clear. What I thought was a choice, wasn't really one after all, was it?

"A year and a day," agreed Lord Dummell.

"And if I don't do it?"

"Then it passes to the next candidate. The person named by the previous Caretaker always has preference, in the case of the natural line of inheritance being broken, with that named preference, traditionally, being a blood heir."

"And *is* there another candidate? Surely one of you would be much better in the position. You've lived here far longer than I have."

I looked around at the collection of faces. Once again, nobody seemed to want to catch my eye.

"It's not really like that," said Edie, breaking the silence, "It would be far easier if it were."

"What *is* it like then?" I prodded, trying to keep the exasperation and desperation out of my voice.

"If the elected person from our side can't or won't take on the role then it automatically goes back to the other side, to NetherWinkle." said Astrid, knotting and unknotting the corner of her napkin.

That didn't sound too bad, I thought. Perhaps one of the Goodships would do it. They were both lovely and everyone knew them already.

That thought must have shown on my face because Astrid shook her head.

"Not the Goodships," she said, "They're middle-grounders. They have a different job."

"Middle-grounders?" I asked. I could feel the beginnings of a headache creeping up the back of my neck, winding its clutching fingers around my forehead. I put my hands up and tried to massage my temples in an effort to ease the tension.

"They live on the middle-ground, the borderlands. NetherWinkle is in the in-between space that separates the two worlds," explained Sidney, "There's always been an in-between; it's like a buffer zone between the human world and Deep Faery."

"And Deep Faery's not a place you want dealings with," muttered Toby, "Not if you can help it."

"Quite so," agreed Lord Dummell. "The Goodships, and their delightful neighbours in NetherWinkle, are ambassadors. And these days, they very much have their hands full."

He reached across and took my hands down from my temples and held them firmly but gently between his own. His grip was cool but comforting.

"The truth of the situation, old gel, is that if you don't take on the Caretaker's role then it could go back to a denizen of Deep Faery and, like Toby said, they aren't the sort of characters that we want to be dealing with. In fact, if one of them comes into power, things could go very badly for our side."

Toby offered to walk me home and I didn't have the emotional energy to protest.

We walked mostly in silence. I, because my head was in that teetering place where if I didn't concentrate on settling down I'd be in a full-fledged anxiety attack by the time I got home and Toby, well, who could know what was going on inside that head?

After the great revelation and, in my opinion, ultimatum, the puddings and Alfie's mug of coffee arrived and conversation moved, albeit awkwardly, back to the topic of the fête. With only half my attention, I confirmed my duties and responsibilities, which Astrid helpfully wrote down for me. Which was just as well as I hadn't retained much past the point where I'd realized I'd definitely be letting the side down if I didn't stand up and accept the Caretaker's oath. Why couldn't they see that I wasn't at all the best option? Surely there must be another way? It was one thing to band together with my friends against an obvious threat like BMZ, it was entirely another to take on a lifelong responsibility for the care and well-being of every living creature on both sides of the Hedge. I simply wasn't cut out for that level of responsibility. I folded quickly under pressure and needed long recovery times between social engagements. How was I supposed to manage all of what was involved in keeping things in order?

"Penny for your thoughts," said Toby, breaking into my angst-ridden thoughts.

I laughed, without humour.

"Not good value, I'm afraid," came my automatic reply, then I realized what I'd said. "Ha! That's what I always say to my dad when he asks me that. Sorry, I don't know why I shared that. I don't mean to imply that you sound like my dad."

Good grief, I only get worse as the day goes on.

"Wouldn't be an insult," said Toby, with a small smile. "Your dad is one of the good ones."

"He is, he really is. Although that's possibly a slightly biased viewpoint."

We lapsed into silence again for a bit. The evenings were still a bit chilly and the air was tinged with the smell of the village chimneys. There were lights on in the windows of people's houses and I had to force myself not to look in. I'd done that ever since I was small, always curious about how other people lived, how they arranged their furniture, what sorts of things they hung on their walls. Still, it was a bit close to snooping, I suppose, and so I didn't want to be too obvious about it in front of Toby. He might get the wrong impression.

"Can I say something?" he asked, out of nowhere.

I laughed.

"I dare say you just did."

Toby gave a nervous sounding chuckle. Sometimes I wasn't sure who was more awkward, him or me. It was a strange thing to feel like the more at-ease person in a conversation. I waited quietly for him to continue.

"Only, I get the impression that you think you're not up for this whole Caretaker thing," he said, "And I wish you'd see it differently."

I took a deep, slightly shaky breath. I had to tread very carefully, not wanting to offend my new friends, but also not wanting to feed into their misinformed opinion of me.

"You're right," I said, "I *don't* think that I'm up for it, but probably not for the reason you imagine. It's not a case of me not *wanting* to help, it's a case of me not being *able* to help. In case you hadn't noticed, I haven't got the sturdiest constitution."

I tried to make light of it, but the truth was, admitting my mental health issues out loud always leaves me feeling like a failure. As much as people try to understand and not hold it against me, I always feel as if I've been weighed up and found wanting. In a cruel twist of irony, as a person who was inevitably going to let people down, letting people down is one of my worst fears in life.

"Who told you that?" he said, coming to a stop and so forcing me to do the same. I turned back to look at him. He was standing in front of one of the few street lamps, the orange haze of it acting like a backlight, casting him into shadow so I couldn't see his features clearly.

"What do you mean, who told me that? Nobody had to tell me, though plenty have over the years, it's just how I am. Isn't it obvious?"

I was rattled. I had no desire to undergo yet another critique of my personal flaws. I fought the urge to turn around and keep walking.

"No, Hazel," he said, his voice low and gentle, "It's not obvious. Not to the people who take the time to truly know you."

"Oh? And who's that then? Other than Alfie and Edie, I've only just met most of you."

"Not me," he said, his voice even, though his gaze was steady. I met it, then looked away.

"We haven't seen each other for years, Toby. A lot can happen..."

"A lot *has* happened," he replied, "Though I suspect that at your core, you're still the same Hazel Price I knew when I was seventeen."

I refused to look at him. I knew exactly what he was getting at and I wasn't going to let him take me there. That had been a long time ago and a hundred promises broken in between.

"Well, you'd be wrong," I said, finally catching his eye. My own eyes smarted with the effort of maintaining contact. "Sometimes life changes you and all you can do is your best, given the cards you're dealt."

"You don't remember, do you?" he said, reaching out to catch my coat sleeve. I pulled it away.

"Don't remember what? Although, by me having said that, I'd say it's a fair assumption that I've got no idea at all what you're on about. Can we please keep walking? Bracken will be wondering where I am. Actually, you know what? I can go the rest of the way myself. Thanks for seeing me this far, I can manage on my own from here."

I spun around and started walking, as fast as I could without seeming as if I was trying to walk fast. I heard the sound of his booted feet hurrying after me.

"Wait, Hazel! Please don't take on, I'm sorry if I've upset you again."

Who even *was* he? It seemed to me that I'd met at least three different versions of this man so far. There was the rude, hostile version that I met on the moor; there was the gentle, honey-speaker who charmed Bracken out of her terror and spun stories about faery ponies; and then there was the quiet, ruminative Toby who rarely spoke up but when he did it was with calm intelligence. Now here was this one. None of them resembled my memories of the boy I played with as a child. Or the young man who'd kissed me in the branches of an old hawthorn tree.

No. I put my hands up to my temples. The ache had suddenly begun to thrum with a new intensity. I felt myself wobble. I was finding it hard to take a proper breath. I started to feel the dread of panic rising. Toby put a hand out to steady me. I shook it off, immediately regretting that as it made me stagger slightly to one side.

"Here," he said, "Stop pushing me away. Just stand for a minute, let yourself get steady. Focus on your breathing."

I obeyed, past the point of trying to save face. My head was spinning and I felt as if I might be sick; my heart was hammering in my chest.

"Deep breaths," he said, his voice lilting into a sing-song, "Let it all go. Stop trying to control everything. You don't have to have all of the answers,"

I fought to get my breathing steady, trying to remember what I'd learned in therapy. I tried to visualize a square but there were black spots dancing in front of my eyes; I squeezed them shut, trying not to whimper.

"Steady on, lass. Think of Bracken. Fix her in your mind, everything you know about her."

I did as he said, without even questioning it. I thought of her red-brown coat, wiry but soft at the same time; her expressive eyebrows and the way she could tell me exactly what she was thinking just by the way she moved them. I thought of the way she'd greeted Young Craig and his bits of liver sausage just that morning. I thought of how she felt against me when she burrowed under the covers – warm and solid and safe.

My vicious stab of headache began to recede, my heart-rate slowed and the nausea subsided. I took great deep breaths of the evening air.

"Are you alright to walk?" asked Toby, after a few minutes.

I nodded, I just wanted to get home. He linked my arm through the crook of his elbow and started walking. I walked beside him, too shaken to object to the liberty he was taking. Besides, I needed to lean on him or else I would've fallen in a heap.

"Can I make you a cup of tea?" I asked, as Toby guided me through the door of the cottage. Bracken greeted us with her yowling bark and full-body wriggles of joy. I must have left a lamp on, because a warm glow greeted us when the door opened. I noticed that the interior of the cottage felt a bit warmer than usual. Obviously smooring the fire was helping to keep the chill from invading during my absence. It was nice to come home to a warmly lit room, rather than the cold, darkness that usually greeted me on return to the empty cottage.

"It's the least I can do since you propped me up all the way home. But surely you see now, don't you?" I looked into his face, willing him to understand, "You see why I'd be positively useless to you all?"

Toby sighed. He stood in the doorway, as if uncertain of what to do. His gaze shifted, glancing around the cottage and then down to his boots and then back over his shoulder towards the door. Then, as if coming to a decision far larger than whether or not to have a cup of tea, he shrugged and started to unbutton his coat.

"Aye, thanks," he said, "I'd love a cup."

I made up the tea tray and took it into the living room where Toby was sitting on the sofa. Bracken had joined him, all sins forgiven; it was if he'd never chased her within an inch of her life across the moor on a quad bike, threatening to thrash her with his sheep stick. Once again, I marvelled at the forgiving powers of a dog.

"I wasn't sure if you still like it the same," I said, pouring him a mug. I nodded towards the sugar bowl and a little creamer of milk. "I know I don't put four spoons of sugar in mine anymore." I'd rummaged in the cupboard and found my emergency stash of HobNobs. I made a mental note to replace them next time I went into the shops.

I passed him his mug and saw a smile quirking at the corner of his mouth as he looked at the tea tray. I immediately felt both foolish and defensive. I supposed he would see it as just another affectation of my trust fund.

"I always make up a tray, even when I'm on my own," I said, taking myself to sit in the chair by the fire. "It saves taking more than one trip." I added, somewhat unnecessarily. "Besides, Nan always made a tray so it makes me think of her."

My voice broke slightly. Good lord, I was falling apart at the seams this evening. At least I was showing my full range of feebleness. I hadn't talked about Nan with anyone in a long time and I've no idea what made me mention her just then. I cleared my throat and attempted to collect myself.

"Anyway," I said, hurrying to move past the topic of the tea tray and all that it might say about me. "I meant to say thank you. For getting me home. I've had the headaches for years, off and on. It happens when I get anxious. Which, to be fair, is fairly often. When they get really bad I basically fall to pieces. I think maybe it's just the stress and upset of Nan and the move and my mum and trying to get the cottage put to rights. But you really do see now, don't you?" I repeated. I had to make him understand. "You see why I have to think carefully about taking on the Caretaker duties. I wouldn't be any good to anyone if I kept collapsing into fits of the vapours the minute things got stressful."

Toby stared into the fire. He had that same expression on his face that he had when we were watching the ponies. He looked down at his mug then slowly leaned across Bracken to spoon two sugars and a dollop of milk into it. Exactly the same as when we were children. He stirred, for what seemed an interminable age, and then helped himself to two HobNobs. He gave one to Bracken straight away. Obviously he didn't heed the warnings about the perils of chocolate and dogs.

"I love these," he said, his voice quiet and his face pensive. He turned the biscuit around, examining its biscuit side and the chocolate before taking a bite. "Your Nan always gave me these when I stopped in for a visit."

"They were her favourite thing to offer people," I said, smiling at the memory. "If she didn't have a cake baked, of course. She always said the combination of biscuit and chocolate would appeal to everyone. They're still my go-to choice. I even keep..."

"An emergency stash in the cupboard," finished Toby, grinning at me. "I do the same thing, courtesy of your Nan's example."

I laughed out loud, delighted to think that Nan's influence had seeped into someone's life just as it had mine. It was these little details, the unexpected reminders of who she was and what she meant to people that made me miss her just a little bit less. It eased the ache of her absence, at least, because it meant she was never really gone; just so long as people kept emergency supplies of chocolate biscuits in their cupboards.

We munched happily for a minute. I relished the chance to hold an intimate memory of my Nan to the light with someone who wasn't trying to tell me how irresponsible she was or how she lived an unconventional and so therefore unsavoury sort of life. I was thinking of my mum, of course. I sighed. Pushing thoughts of her and her agendas to the back of my mind where I liked to keep them.

Toby broke the silence.

"I know I'm the last person you probably want advice from..."

"And yet you're going to give me some anyway?" I bantered weakly, wishing we could just keep sitting quietly drinking our tea.

Toby grinned, his teeth flashing white in the light of the fire. His hair stood in a tangled halo around his head and if I squinted my eyes I could imagine him at seventeen, wild-eyed and frantic when he learned Corny was being sent away. He'd been so angry, with none of the self-containment this adult version of him seemed to have. I wondered if it was genuine equanimity, or if he'd caged all those huge emotions that had only ever got him into trouble.

"Aye, well. Maybe it's not so much advice as it is an observation."

"Oh?"

Even worse. Having people point out and explain my faults and defects is one of my least favourite pastimes.

"You seem convinced you're not up to the task of being Caretaker," He held up a hand as I got ready to interrupt, "Whisht now, let me finish. You make a point of listing out your various nervous complaints and your being too busy to be a part of things..."

"I *am* too busy," I retorted, "I have a book to write, five even, and a garden to resurrect. And my nervous complaints, as you put them, are real and debilitating, not to mention professionally documented."

He gave me an appraising stare.

"I'm not questioning that you've suffered a bad time," he said, his voice barely above a murmur. The more quietly he spoke, the more musical it sounded, his island burr more pronounced. "Edie told me everything that happened with...with things in London and I'm sorry for it."

"Yes, well. Thank you," I said, stiffly. "Things have been difficult. For a long time, actually." I let the words hang in the air, willing him to pick up on the veiled accusation. It was half-hearted, though, and I'd given up on the idea of an apology for something that had happened more than thirty years ago.

He nodded and put his empty mug down on the table. He gave Bracken's ear a tussle and stood up, smoothing his hands down his corduroy trousers.

"All I'm wondering is if maybe taking on something like this," he waved his hand around the cottage, "and all that comes with it, rather than being more than you can manage, might just be the very thing you need."

Chapter Twenty-Two

In the flurry of social gatherings and near-emotional breakdowns, I'd completely forgotten all about Hobart Guthrie and his minion. The village meeting seemed a lifetime ago, a whole other universe ago, so much had changed since the evening I'd sat in the village hall feeling like an outsider.

"Hazel?" said the booming voice down the crackling telephone line. "Glenn Collins, BMZ here. I'm phoning about that lunch you promised me!"

I had the receiver cradled against my shoulder, my hands clad in muddy gardening gloves. I'd been trying to clear out an overgrown patch of nettles at the bottom of the garden. I didn't mind them being there, only they'd rather trespassed beyond what would be considered a reasonable amount of real estate.

"Mr. Collins, yes," I said, feeling a sinking sensation in my stomach, "Of course, I remember. It's lovely to hear from you." How easily the social fibs tripped off my tongue. Years of practice.

"How does today sound?" he said, "I know it's short notice but everyone has to eat lunch and I thought if we met at The Forge it might not be too much of an inconvenience to you." He chuckled with what I imagine he thought was a good-natured apology.

Of course, for most people, that wouldn't be an inconvenience at all, technically speaking. I was a short bike ride from The Forge and yes, I did indeed need to eat lunch. The trouble was that I was quite set on the idea of a salad sandwich and a packet of crisps perched on the edge of the leek trench. I had a lot of things I wanted to get done in the garden, which also happily allowed for the necessary daydreaming that fuelled my writing. It was multitasking at its most prolific and delightful.

I sighed, quietly, so as not to seem rude. I had no idea what he wanted to talk to me about, but if I could possibly get any inside information about the status of BMZ and their strategies, I supposed I ought to seize it. One for the team and all that.

"That sounds lovely, Mr.Collins.What time shall I meet you there?" I glanced at the clock. It was just going on ten.

"Brilliant! How about half eleven?" he said. "I know it's a bit early for lunch but I need to set off for Inverness this afternoon. I've got a crofters meeting to attend and need to catch a ferry."

"Trying to flog more of those robot potatoes?" I asked, before I could stop myself.

There was a brief silence and then a hearty chuckle boomed down the line.

"Yes, yes, something like that. You'd be surprised how reluctant folk are about the new developments. You'd think people in those far-flung and inhospitable corners of creation would grab every opportunity to improve their lot."

"Hmmm, yes," I said, biting back my thoughts on his robot potatoes and people in far-flung corners of creation. "Half eleven it is, see you then."

I rang off in true, abrupt Winkle style and groaned aloud.

Bracken trotted into the kitchen, having noticed my extended absence.

"Do you fancy spending an hour with Alfie?" I asked, pulling off my dirty gloves. "It looks like I have a lunch date with the world's most oblivious man."

In the end, I couldn't manage more enthusiasm than it took to just wash my face and hands and drag a brush through my hair. The latter activity had alarming results so I quickly scraped it into a messy bun — which, with my hair, the messy part is less an exercise in artful arrangement and more a natural result of recalcitrant locks and low effort. I added one of my knitted headbands to hold the stray bits in place. Along with my Liberty floral dress, purple tights and green wellies, I thought it spoke volumes about what I'd rather be doing with my day. It was, once again, a quiet rebellion. No doubt it would be wasted on Mr. Collins but it made me feel less like I'd surrendered entirely to social expectations.

He was already seated when I arrived, the small table strewn with piles of paper and a laptop. He seemed thoroughly engrossed in reading something on the screen when I made a point of bumping into the second chair to announce my arrival. The wooden leg scraped on the flagstones and the sound jolted him from his intense concentration.

His face split into a wide smile when he saw me and he stood up, dislodging one of his piles of paper, to shake my hand.

"Hazel!" he boomed enthusiastically, "So glad you could come! Sorry for the mess, I was a bit early and thought I'd get a spot of work done while I was waiting. No sense wasting a minute, eh?"

I smiled weakly, being entirely of the opposite opinion. I preferred to daydream in the surplus moments when waiting for things. There was an excruciatingly awkward interlude as I stood fiddling with the strap of my bag while he tidied up his piles of papers. I agonized over whether it would seem silly to sit down while the table was still covered but I also didn't want to seem nosey or that I was rushing him by helping to tidy it up. These are the sorts of blurred social lines that leave me floundering. He was apparently unaware of my tortured state as he stacked and shuffled before dropping the papers with a thud onto the floor beside him.

He looked up and beamed widely, his teeth a gleaming tribute to modern orthodonture. He pushed back his chair with a loud scrape, coming around to my side of the table and pulling out my seat for me.

"There! All tidied up! Sit down, sit down! Something to drink? I'm teetotal myself, just having a pot of tea. There's plenty of that, but maybe you'd rather have a glass of wine or something?"

"Oh, no thank you," I said, shuffling my chair forward, flustered by the display of gentlemanly behaviour. "If I drink wine now I'll be asleep all afternoon. Tea would be lovely."

He made a grand gesture of pouring out a cup for me, adding the milk and sugar as per my directions and stirring it with a flourish.

"There!" he said, "get that down you!"

He was an odd mix of bustling business man and old-fashioned courtesy, a combination that made me feel very off-balance. I could warm to the old-fashioned courtesy, not so much to the bustling business man. I reminded myself that none of it was likely to be real, only a salesman's glamour designed to lull an unsuspecting mortal such as myself into trusting him.

"So, you're probably wondering why I wanted to chat with you," he said, steepling his fingers and fixing me with the sort of expression I remembered various mental health professionals giving me. A combination of probing analysis and deep compassion, as if my every reaction had his fullest attention. It would've been pleasant if it didn't seem so contrived.

I nodded, raising my cup to sip the tea. It was the most delicious tea I'd ever drunk. Sometimes you're in such a state that a cup of tea has that nectar-of-the-gods sensation to it — at the end of a long and busy day, or coming in from outdoors when it's wild with wind and rain. This was a similar feeling; it tasted of wildflowers and warm summer days. I closed my eyes briefly, a thousand beautiful memories chasing across my mind.

"Lovely cuppa, isn't it?" said a voice that hummed with bee-song, "I always bring my own tea with me. I prefer it to that awful bagged stuff."

I felt myself jolt slightly, as if I'd been caught dozing off in the middle of a presentation.

"Sorry," I said, blushing, "I've been working in the garden all morning, I must be a bit tired..."

Again, that smile. It reached fully to his eyes which were a shifting shade of green then hazel then brown. I felt myself warm to him after all. He was clearly a kind and gentle sort of person who was simply doing his job. It was my utter aversion and disinterest in business-y things that made me feel off-balance, and not him at all.

"No need to apologize," he said, waving a hand dismissively, "there's nothing more honest than a good day's labour on the land, is there?"

"I've always thought so," I said, delighted with his kindness and understanding.

Just then Ernie brought us a menu. He grinned widely at me and winked, making me blush again, quite without reason. I am entirely too prone to blushing.

"Hallo again, love," he said, patting my arm.,"Everything alright?" He shot a glance at Mr. Collins, a brief flicker of annoyance crossing his face.

"Yes, thank you, Ernie," I replied, smiling. He was such a pleasant little chap. He beamed back at me, nodding.

He turned his glance to Mr.Collins, his manner shifting abruptly. His smile faded and he straightened his shoulders, no doubt attempting to heighten his small stature. He nodded stiffly and handed Mr. Collins the menu.

For his part, Mr.Collins pursed his lips and returned the stiff nod.

Strange atmosphere, I mused, taking another sip of the wonderful tea. Although not surprising, I supposed, considering that Mr.Collins represented the party wanting to tear down the Hedge and upset the quiet goings-on of the village. Then again, surely a move towards re-newable energy sources was exactly what we needed in these troubling times? Not to mention, the flood of Upwardly Mobile people who would be thrilled to come and spend their fortunes in The Forge on fancy pub lunches and artisan beer. I shook my head, trying to focus on the task at hand.

"I'll just have the Ploughman's," I said to Ernie, handing back the menu.

"Same for me," said Mr. Collins, beaming at me, "I'm going to count on Hazel having exquisite taste and will follow her lead."

He held up his menu without looking at Ernie and leaned across the table slightly. "I had many a childhood fantasy of being in an Enid Blyton story, eating picnics by the roadside with food procured from friendly farmer's wives."

My eyes widened and I was filled with quiet glee.

"Oh, me too!" I gushed, unable to help myself, "I used to wish I could go rambling with the Five. Bottled fruit and fresh cream..."

"...paste sandwiches and flasks of tea," finished Mr.Collins.

We both burst into laughter.

"That's why I like getting a Ploughman's Lunch," I said, 'it makes me think of those sorts of picnics...bread and cheese and pickles and all that lovely stuff."

Mr. Collins leaned back in his chair, his ever-present smile widening.

"I think we have a great deal in common, Hazel, don't you?"

I grinned, feeling entirely happy with myself. It had been ages since another person had been able to relate so well to my silly self. Roger, of course, knew me like that. We were best friends after all, and he knew all of my tragic backstory. An image of Toby flashed across my mind's eye, but not the Toby I'd recently met. He was younger, not much more than perhaps twelve. His hair was as ragged as it was now, his face streaked with dirt and tears after finding a fox killed on the road. Then seventeen year old Toby, with his wild, dark hair and crooked smile.

I put my hands to my temples, feeling a dull throb creeping behind my eyes.

I felt a warm hand on mine. A tingle of electricity shot up my arm, immediately dispelling the beginnings of my headache. I had a brief moment of wondering what I'd just been thinking about before remembering, yes, Toby. I frowned, shaking off the memory; why on earth would I want to be thinking of Toby? I turned my full attention back to Mr. Collins.

"There, that's better, isn't it?" said that soothing bee-song voice. "More tea?"

"Mostly he just tried to convince me that the wind farm was a good idea," I said, leaning back against Alfie's armchair. I was sitting on the rug by the fire. Alfie and Edie were in their respective chairs, Bracken dozing on the floor beside me. "He was very nice, not at all obnoxious with it. He even had some very convincing arguments. Still, when it comes down to it, I don't really understand why he thought I needed to be convinced of anything. It's not like I have a great deal of influence over the council. It's really them who decide whether this thing goes forward or not. It wouldn't surprise me if they decided in favour of it, though. I really do think that it could be good for the village."

The fire snapped and crackled with a comforting rhythm. Spring had arrived, that much was clear from the hedgerow and gardens, but the evenings were cool and slightly damp. I much preferred it that way, it meant I had the best of all worlds.

"Well," said Edie, exchanging glances with Alfie. She made a point of adjusting the shirt that she was mending where it was piled onto her knee. She leaned down to her sewing basket to retrieve a tiny pair of scissors. "I don't think it's as much he was trying to win you over to their side as he was weighing up the competition."

Alfie grunted, taking a slurp of his tea.

"Aye, pet. Our Edie's right on that score. They're a wily lot and obviously not above a bit of meddling when it suits them. Still, I can't believe they'd dare it."

"Who?" I asked, "Dare what?" I was getting the uneasy feeling they weren't simply referring to Mr. Collins' driving businessman ethos. "Do you mean BMZ? Obviously they have a corporate agenda, though I'm sure it's in the best interest of everyone involved. You can't run a business by constantly trampling on the people you're hoping to win over."

Alfie barked out a laugh and Edie smiled, shaking her head as she re-threaded her needle.

"As I said, up to their tricks."

I frowned and looked behind me at Alfie, who was also frowning. He cradled his tea mug in his lap, his lips pursed.

"Alfie?" I prompted.

"Oh, aye. Well," he cleared his throat, "That tea you mentioned, what that Mr. Collins gave you?"

"Yes?"

"Well, and d'ye also remember our Edie suggesting to you at the meeting that he and his gaffer weren't quite as they seemed?"

I cast my mind back to the meeting, remembering how it felt to be the interloper among such a tight-knit group. I recalled Edie muttering something about Mr.Guthrie being 'one of them'.

I nodded.

"Right, well what she meant was that he were one of *them*. D'ye catch my meaning?"

He gave me a searching look, his shaggy eyebrows raised in suggestion.

I blinked, not quite sure what he was getting at. It must have showed on my face because Edie chuckled and spoke up.

"For heaven's sake, Alfie. Stop being so mysterious. It's not as if she isn't already in the knowing of things."

She paused to bite her thread.

"What Alfie is trying to hint at, is that your Mr.Collins and his gaffer are from *Deep* Faery and he gave you that tea to try and charm you; he tried to fill your head with nonsense that would make you want to support the wind farm."

I blinked again. I must've looked like a stunned fish, my mouth hanging open and my eyes goggling.

"What? You mean he put a spell on me or something? Was that tea some kind of magic potion?"

I felt a rising flush of righteous indignation.

"Aye, well" said Alfie, his voice gloomy. "Nothing so obvious as a spell, more of a mild enchantment. Bit of a grey area, that, though 'tis a violation of all that's gentlemanly between Faery and our world, no doubt on that score."

"So now what?" I said, flushing with embarrassment that I could've been tricked so easily. Again, more evidence to my uselessness. I should've known there was something strange about that tea. I mean, I appreciate the power of an excellent cuppa but that one went to glorious extremes.

Edie made a soothing noise and gave Alfie one of her quieting glares.

"Don't worry, pet," she said, "It won't last. Not on you, anyway. A good night's sleep in your own bed and tomorrow you'll wake up knowing it for what it was."

"A violation!" I said, close to angry tears, "That's what it was. How dare they?"

I felt humiliated and also confused because I couldn't really remember what I was humiliated and confused about. Everything was folding in on itself. It was an alarming feeling.

"There's no need to fret about it, my lamb," said Alfie, leaning down to grip my shoulder, "And don't try to think your way out of it right now. You'll just get muddled. There's no blame in it, you couldn't have known. None of us thought to warn you, because we wouldn't suspect they'd try anything so underhanded in broad daylight, as it were."

"Alfie's right," agreed Edie, "We're as much to blame as anything. We've got too comfortable, that's our trouble. All those years with your Nan in charge and she kept them all in line. They wouldn't have dared try anything like this when she was alive."

I think Edie meant to be comforting, but what it really was was another reminder about how very much I didn't live up to my Nan's example. I gave Edie a weak smile and fought back the tears.

"You promise it'll be better tomorrow?"

"Aye, lass. Everything's always better in the light of a new day."

It was times like that when I missed my Nan with an ache that felt like it would swallow my insides. I would've liked nothing more than to pick up the phone and hear her comforting voice explaining how it truly wasn't my fault and that I hadn't let anyone down. It spoke volumes about the myriad ways my life had changed that I was, instead, talking to a raggedy ginger cat about what had just happened.

Murk sat on the hearth rug, in the very place that Bracken preferred, his tail curled around one paw, running the other across his misshapen ears in that annoying, self-satisfied way that cats do.

I tried not to seem impatient.

When you're ready then, I fumed silently. I'd just broached the subject of otherworldly interlopers and their nefarious tactics and he was being infuriatingly noncommittal about the whole thing.

Finally, after attending to his meticulous toilette, he deigned to speak.

"Assuming this were true," he said, blinking slowly, "And I daresay I'm not the one to either confirm nor deny, how would you feel about it?"

Biting back the sarcastic comment that instinctively rose to my lips, I smiled thinly, trying to exude patience and forbearance.

"I don't suppose I'd really given it any thought until now," I said, "One doesn't often come across the idea of faery people at large among the general populace. Nor, especially, those of the possibly malevolent variety at the helm of large, multinational companies. It's all a bit Twilight Zone, don't you think?"

"I'm sorry," said Murk, yawning widely. His teeth were a mismatch to the rest of his scruffy self, being clean and white and very sharp-looking. "I'm not sure I understand your reference. Twilight Zone?"

"Never mind," I muttered, "I suppose I *feel* as if it would be quite fine as long as there was no ill-intent. I mean, excluding faery folk from the mortal world would mean excluding people like the Goodships — so, no, I wouldn't want that. Though I daresay the idea would be unnerving to the average person."

"Precisely," said Murk, standing and stretching. He unsheathed his claws as he stretched, revealing them to also be long and very sharp-looking. Bracken whined and sidled closer to me. I absent-mindedly reached out a hand to stroke her wiry head.

"What does *that* mean?" I said, losing grip of my patience. He really was the most aggravating creature.

"It means, dear girl, that much like you humans, there are a variety of intentions, as you put it, at play here – benevolent and otherwise."

"Which means?"

"Which means," he said, strolling casually past the sofa towards the kitchen, "all that really matters is what those intentions are."

I bit back yet another retort, mindful of the fact he definitely wasn't going to give up any useful information if I resorted to sarcasm. It was killing me not to take off a slipper and lob it at him in Hamish fashion.

"Which is exactly what I'm asking you," I said, through gritted teeth. "I'm asking you, *are* those two men from BMZ really from Deep Faery and, if so, what do you suppose are their intentions?"

Then, unable to hold it back any longer I added,

"I would've thought that was a simple enough question requiring a simple enough answer."

Murk leapt onto the bench and picked his way through the collection of plates and mugs that had accumulated since the morning. The kitchen window was open, letting in the cool, night breeze. He paused, looking back at me.

"If that is the case," he said, rubbing his cheek proprietarily against the window frame, "you should have no difficulty in finding out."

As he disappeared through the open window, I could've sworn I heard him laughing.

It was Lord Dummell who finally told me what I wanted to know.

The morning after my frustrating conversation with Murk, I did the uncharacteristic thing of dropping by Malmont Manor without prior notice. I'd set off with Bracken for our usual morning constitutional on the moor and found myself heading in the direction of the rambling old estate. It was a long walk, but it gave me plenty of time to rehearse what I wanted to say.

"Hazel!" exclaimed Lord Dummell, opening the door widely and ushering me in. "What a lovely surprise. Oh, yes, and hello to you too, dearest Bracken. Dennis and Ethel will be delighted to see you. Come into the kitchen, will you? It's the warmest room and I've just brewed a pot of tea."

I paused to change into a pair of the community slippers then followed him down the narrow passage into the kitchen. It was just as I'd remembered it from my previous visit — warm and welcoming and delightfully shabby. There was a smell of something baking and a comforting waft of porridge emanating from the top of the Aga.

"Would you like a bowl of porridge?" he asked, bustling about with mugs and spoons. "I always have porridge on these cool mornings. Nothing like warming yourself from the inside out after coming in from the outdoors. I was just chatting with Toby about moving the new lambs and I've got the most glorious chill."

He rubbed his hands together vigorously, a huge smile splitting his aristocratic features. It would be hard to tell by looking at him, how old he might be, a life spent largely outdoors had probably weathered his face beyond his calendar years. Unlike many of his aristocratic peers, it seemed he'd always had a very hands-on approach to the running of his estate. I was filled with a sudden surge of affection for this dear old man, and a pang of sadness for the way of life he was trying desperately to hold onto.

"No thank you," I said, "Bracken and I had our toast and marmalade before we set out. But a cup of tea wouldn't go amiss."

"Splendid, splendid! There you are," he placed a lopsided mug down on the island where I sat, perched on the edge of a stool.

"That was one of Toby's school projects," he said, nodding towards the mug. "He never did enjoy the arts portions of the curriculum. As can be evidenced by the quality of his workmanship."

I grinned.

The mug had an unusual tilting aspect to it and there was something about the handle that didn't seem to allow for holding it properly. The glaze was a sort of muddy green colour with random white flecks. All in all, it was very reminiscent of what you'd find in the classroom on Parents Day. I thought it said something very telling about Lord Dummell that not only had he kept the mug all these years, but used it. I said as much to him.

"Ah well," he said, blushing slightly, "I've always thought of Toby as a part of the family. He's the closest thing I've ever had to a son of my own."

He cleared his throat loudly and pulled a large, paisley handkerchief from his waistcoat pocket and blew his nose with a loud honk.

I smiled behind my mug, feeling my own throat tightening. To be loved and treasured as a child seems to me to be the greatest gift anyone could receive.

"So, Hazel my dear, to what do I owe the marvellous pleasure of your company at my breakfast table?"

"Well, I was rather hoping you'd tell me everything you know about the faeries living in the village."

Chapter Twenty-Three

The day of the fête dawned bright and clear. The threat of yesterday's rain had moved off during the night and it seemed as if we were going to have a simply brilliant day. Despite my initial reservations about being involved with village affairs, I was pleasantly surprised to find myself with the butterflies of excitement trilling about my innards. I would say that I leapt out of bed, but that would be a bit of an exaggeration; it had been some years since I was capable of that, but in my mind I was leaping. Bracken and I clattered down the stairs with great enthusiasm which was quite out of character for us both.

There was no time for staring, bleary-eyed out of the kitchen window while the kettle boiled that morning, so while it was burbling away, I busied myself collecting up the various files and folders that I'd made to keep the entries organized and the lists of who had donated what as prizes. I had the completed thank-you notes for those generous souls and paper-clipped them to my donations list. The box of ribbons was waiting by the door. As far as I could tell, everything was ready.

Toby had offered to pick up Bracken and I along with the large box and I'd grudgingly accepted as I didn't fancy trying to balance everything on my bicycle, though had wrestled briefly with trying to decipher his motivation. In the end, I put it down to helpfulness and an effort at civility which seemed reasonable.

We organizers were meeting at the church hall for an early breakfast of tea and pastries, courtesy of Edie and the Goodships. They weren't coming to the fête as they didn't want to be accused of trying to exert influence — something to do with them being ambassadors of the Borderlands — but would be watching from the periphery neverthe-less and Mrs.G promised us bacon and egg rolls to fortify us for the day ahead.

"Right, Bracken-dog," I said, once my tea mug was washed and the kitchen tidied, "Time to get ready to face the day."

Bracken waved her tail and waggled her eyebrows. She knew some-thing was afoot as we'd missed our usual leisurely breakfast. I hadn't realized how much we'd fallen into such familiar rhythms until we'd taken an exception to them. I smiled at the thought, quietly delighted to know that we were truly settling in as a pair.

I took the stairs two at a time and quickly washed and dressed. I went with a blue linen dress over a pair of flowered leggings. And since my mum was coming, I pulled on a navy cardigan – the double attraction of it being that it was both hand-knit *and* from an op-shop. To add to its charm, I'd embroidered tiny daisies around the bottom hem to disguise several moth-related holes. I grinned into the mirror as I put my hair into two plaits and tied bits of white ribbon around the ends. I would complete the ensemble with my lovely green wellies and would be a vision of shabby country chic.

The sound of Bracken's yodelling bark told me that Toby was driving up the lane so with one last look in the mirror, to satisfy myself that I looked appropriately like a village fête organizer (flower and veg division), I flew down the stairs to meet him.

The village hall looked magnificent. Astrid and Sidney had done a wonderful job with the decorating. They'd borrowed and framed photographs of the Hedge and surrounding countryside from anyone that would lend them and had them propped up and displayed on all of the tables. In case of rain, we'd decided to let people put their handicrafts and store their baked goods, as well as the jams and preserves on tables indoors. That had saved us a bit of money on tent rentals as well as the stress of people getting upset if they thought the damp would negatively impact their pastry. There were posies of wildflowers — all from the hedges and laneways — in empty jam jars dotted here and there as well as a collection of presentation boards highlighting Points of Interest about the Hedge and its inhabitants.

I was reading a little blurb about hedgehogs when Astrid came to stand beside me. She was resplendent in black, as always, but her hair had been freshly blue-d and her scuffed boots had a shine to them. Her black-ringed eyes were glowing with pride.

"Do you like what we did with the stories?" she said, gesturing to the series of displays hung around the walls. "We alternated between natural history sort of information things and personal stories from various people of the village. We went around and talked to all of the old folk and got them to reminisce about blackberrying and picking wildflowers and haws and we even got Mrs. Abbotsford to give us her recipe for sloe gin!"

"It's absolutely brilliant, Astrid," I enthused, truly meaning it. "I think it's a terrific way to get people talking about the Hedge and the countryside in general. I think that the more people are reminded how much the village depends upon the Hedge, the less excited they'd be about all of the supposed 'benefits' of having the wind farm."

"We thought so," said Astrid, beaming. "It's all about the connections, really. If people feel like they belong, they're more keen to protect the things they belong to."

"True, very true," I murmured, smiling, thinking about how my own perception had changed in such a short time. I'd gone from wanting absolutely nothing to do with anyone or anything, to carrying a clipboard around a village hall whilst simultaneously drinking tea out of a chipped enamel mug and munching on a bacon roll made by a faerie woman.

"Hazel!" called Alfie. "Where are you, lass? I've got some people wanting to set up their flower pots!"

"Coming!" I called, grinning at Astrid who grinned right back. "Duty calls!"

The rest of the morning was a blur of directing people to the appropriate tables and getting cups of tea for my judges. With Roger's help, I'd managed to get a fairly well-known horticulturist from the city to come and judge the veg and cultivated flowers and a botanist from the university to judge the wildflower arrangements. It didn't really matter that neither one had ever judged a village flower show before, the sheer exoticness of them was enough to thrill and delight the entrants. And it was a day out in the country for the two judges, with plenty of tea and home-cooked food laid on, not to mention gratifying awe for their expertise.

I was surprised to find myself thoroughly enjoying the hustle and bustle and instead of feeling overwhelmed at the sheer volume of people cramming into the tents and the hall, I found myself exchanging excited chatter and laughter with entrants and visitors alike. Bracken, too, was in her element, being made much of by everyone who met her and getting more than a reasonable share of tidbits from everyone who passed by with a plate in their hands. Her molten eyes and jaunty tail-wave melted the heart of even the most strict of people.

I scanned the crowd, trying to see if I could spot anyone from NetherWinkle. Lord Dummell had told me that, although traffic had slowed right down since my Nan died, there were still a few regulars who spent a lot of time on this side of the Hedge. It wasn't an unusual thing at all, especially on holidays and at large public gatherings, for the faerie folk to be drawn to crowds of people enjoying good food and good company; they liked nothing less than a celebration and the happy energy that went along with it. Those were the amiable members of the population; the more troublesome folk, the ones who held to mischief and disruption, were less frequent visitors, but only because Winkle was a generally peaceful sort of place. Those types of faeries were attracted to a different kind of energy and it was generally considered a worthwhile effort to cultivate a positive atmosphere so as to keep their presence at bay. As for the two who glamoured themselves as Hobart Guthrie and Glenn Collins, they were of a type who spent quite a lot of their time in the mortal world serving their own, usually nefarious, agendas. Lord Dummell wouldn't elaborate, but I got the idea that they were something of a chronic thorn in the side of Winkle.

"Enjoying yourself?"

Toby sidled up beside me and handed me a mug of tea and a plate with a rock bun and a jam tart, balanced precariously beside a very large sausage roll.

"Oh, lovely! Thank you!" I said, shaking off my musings and gratefully taking the mug in two hands. "Can you hold my plate, only my hands are frozen and I need to warm them through."

Toby smiled and held up the plate like a waiter.

"At your service, milady."

I flapped a hand at his arm and he chuckled.

"Brilliant turnout, isn't it?" he said, looking around at the milling crowd. The loudspeaker announced that the pie judging would commence in five minutes — fruit first, and then savoury.

"It really is," I said, between sips of steaming tea. "I don't think we could've asked for better, especially as it was so last minute."

We stood on the outside edges of the flower and vegetable tent. The prizes had already been awarded and the entrants were mingling with the crowd, accepting either congratulations or commiserations. The botanist was deep in conversation with Lord Dummell, the two of them like peas in a pod with their tweeds and peaked caps. It had all gone very well and everyone was pleased with the outcomes. Alfie had won first prize for his early peas and a second for his spring onions. I had a deep and happy feeling that comes with a job well done. There had been far less stress and aggravation than I would've expected and now that my particular section was successfully complete, I felt like I could enjoy the rest of the fête. I said as much to Toby.

"Well, finish up your grub and we can go and have a look at the pies, eh? I hear Mrs. Thorpe's strawberry-rhubarb is a dead cert for first in Sweet Seasonals."

I grinned happily and wolfed down the last of the jam tart, licking a stray smear of jam off my thumb before I could stop myself. I'd lost all inhibitions by this point.

"Come on then," I said. "I'm sure Bracken hasn't had any leavings from the cake and pie category yet and she'll be getting faint with hunger."

"Aye, I thought she was looking a bit peaky, like," said Toby, looking down at Bracken with a small smile. There was a softness in his expression that seemed so very at odds with the first time I'd seen him looking at her. It was the sort of change that made me believe that forgiveness wasn't such a difficult thing after all. With an uncharacteristic impulse, I looped my arm through his and tugged him in the direction of the pie judging.

"Hurry up, or we'll miss our chance at witnessing the presentation of the winning pie. By all accounts, it's like a royal decree. Besides, I want another one of those jam tarts, it was fantastic!"

Laughing, he allowed himself to be towed away.

Chapter Twenty-Four

It turned out that we were too late anyway. There had obviously been a lot of pre-fête speculation about the Sweet Seasonals category as the hall was packed to the brim when we arrived. I half-expected there to be bookies set up on the outer edges, suitcases open and chalkboards on a stand displaying the current odds. Who knew the competition could be so stiff?

"Goodness," I said, as we squeezed into the hall, begging apology to those whose toes we inadvertently trod upon. Bracken pressed herself against me, clearly uncomfortable with the press of people. I looked down when I felt the first tremor vibrate against my leg.

"I'm going to have to take her outside," I whispered to Toby. The pie judge had just begun a monologue on the virtues of home-baked pies and a hush had fallen over the milling crowd. "There's too many people, it's making her trembly."

Toby nodded.

"Go on then," he said, "I'll make my way around to the WI table. That's where I got your jam tart. I'll meet you back outside. We'll still hear the results just outside the door, anyway."

"Come on, girl," I said to Bracken, taking hold of her collar. "Let's get you out of this crush, shall we?"

I led her through the crowd and out of the door. We'd both just breathed a deep sigh of relief when I heard a familiar voice.

"Hazel, darling! We found you! My word, what a turnout! Such a quaint thing, isn't it Roger?"

Roger?

"Hello, Hazel," said my best friend, pulling me in for a warm hug. "You're looking lovely."

"Oh, Roger, you're too kind!" exclaimed my mum, bustling up and patting his arm, affectionately. "She looks an utter sight! Hazel, my love, what are you wearing?"

"Hello, Mum," I said, my face flushing hotly. I allowed my cheek to be kissed before pulling back to look at the pair of them.

"Roger! What a wonderful surprise. I didn't expect..."

"I invited Roger to come with me as your father was held up at the last minute. I thought, who else to accompany me?"

"And you just happened to be in the neighbourhood?" I asked Roger, who had the good grace to smile in apology.

"Actually, I was," he said, his voice a gentle murmur in contrast to mum's almost shrieking exuberance. "I came up to see my sister. She just got engaged, you see."

He shifted, likely unsure as to how I would receive the topic of impending marriage. I refused to have my day ruined.

"That's lovely, Roger," I said, meaning it. I'd always been fond of his sister, Teresa. The two of them were very close and she'd been vis-iting Roger when things went thoroughly pear-shaped for me. She'd smoothly and calmly helped him navigate the fall-out, telephoning my parents and arranging for me to be seen by a psychiatrist. She'd sent me a lovely card and a gift voucher for Blackwell's when I was in Serenity Meadows. Unlike most people, she hadn't shied away from the fact I'd had a breakdown. "Mark, isn't it?"

"Yes, yes. They're a super pair. I'm thrilled to bits for them. You'll be getting an invitation, when the time comes. I do hope you'll come?"

He looked at me, hope and worry combined on his gentle face as he tried to ask me how I was doing without asking me how I was doing. Getting invited to a wedding, when one's own divorce wasn't quite final, was shaky ground. He was the only other person I knew who worried about upsetting people as much as I did so I smiled, reached out and took hold of both of his hands, giving them a quick squeeze.

"I wouldn't miss it for the world," I said. "Especially if you're in charge of the flowers!"

Roger grinned, the smile lighting up his whole face.

"Not like I'd have much choice!"

We laughed and it was suddenly just like old times, before any of the dramatics of the last year, before everything had changed.

It was at that moment that Toby reappeared, bearing a plate of jam tarts. The expression on his face started off as confusion and then quickly clouded over to his standard look of guarded suspicion. He stood, awkwardly, just outside our little circle.

"Toby, oh good! You're back!" I said, desperately willing my mother to not open her mouth. I just wanted the rest of the day to be as lovely as the first half but I had a nagging feeling it was all about to go terribly wrong. I willed her not to say anything offensive. "I'd like you to meet Roger, my..."

"And who might we have here?" said my mum, pushing herself forward in that way she does when she's trying to intimidate a lesser mortal. It usually works. That Toby towered over her diminutive five feet two did nothing to dissuade her from her superior position. "Are you one of the locals from hereabouts?"

"Mum!" I exclaimed, mortified, darting a look at Toby whose face was unreadable. His lips tightened and I saw him swallow. "It's Toby, Toby MacDierran? Surely you remember him from when I used to visit Nan. He's Lord Dummell's estate manager now."

That got her attention.

"Estate manager?" she repeated, arching a carefully pencilled eyebrow, "I had no idea there was a stately home in the area. Not one of the more well-known ones, then?"

Roger, bless him, stepped towards Toby and held out his hand.

"Good to meet you, Toby," he said, with a wide smile. He glanced quickly over at me and winked. I blushed maddeningly. "I'm Roger, close friend of Hazel's from London."

Toby swapped the plate of tarts to his other hand and shook Roger's hand, somewhat stiffly, and nodded.

"Here's your jam tarts, Hazel," he said, his voice gruff. He handed over the plate. "I've just seen Lord Dummell and need a word. If you'll excuse me?"

He nodded to Roger and gave my mum a forced smile before stalking off. I watched him go, unsure of exactly how I felt about him leaving. Roger must have seen my face. He linked his arm through mine.

"Bit of a dish, that one," he said, elbowing me mischievously, then, with a lowered voice. "You never told me he was quite so...rugged. I could fancy him myself."

I laughed and elbowed him back.

"Never you mind, mister," I said, squeezing him close. "He's definitely not your type."

It was lovely to see Roger again, especially after all that had happened over the months prior to my leaving London. I never got a chance to properly thank him for everything he'd done to help me during that horrid time. He'd been an utter rock when I'd gone through my breakdown. I know I hadn't been easy to live with leading up to that point — alternately raging and grief-stricken — but he bore it all with good grace. He visited me every weekend at Serenity Meadows and been steadfast in not letting Mum steamroll me into going back to London when I was discharged. For reasons that amazed both my dad and I, she always listened to Roger's advice. He was one of the few people who could rein her in. Anyway, it was lovely to be able to spend time wandering around the fête with him, showing off the things that I loved about living in Winkle. Mum kept her distance, pretending to be engrossed in the displays of hand-knits — because of course we all knew how much she treasured hand knit garments — no doubt imagining Roger was, at that very moment, convincing me to leave this wretched backwater and the mouldering cottage and return to the real world.

We were admiring the rows of jams and preserves when I felt a tap on my shoulder. I turned around to see Mrs.Trout, smiling fiendishly at me from behind her glasses. I took a startled step backwards and stifled a gasp. She really was the most terrifying of creatures.

"Mrs.Trout!" I said, recovering myself. "Lovely to see you (liar). Are you enjoying the festivities?" I couldn't help but get that dig in. Of course she would come to the fête, being the compulsive busybody that she was, and indeed, had insisted on taking part in the organizing, despite the fact we were raising funds to oppose her dear husband and his cohorts. My barb hit the mark and she flinched visibly before fixing her smile ever more firmly to her pinched face.

"Indeed," she murmured, in what I'm assuming she imagined was a demure and civilized tone. "It's always delightful to see the village coming together in a time of need. Even an outsider like yourself must be amazed to witness the sense of natural solidarity we've developed over the years together. Of course, that sort of connection can only come from knowing one another for so long. I don't imagine you witness much of that where you're from."

I watched Roger's face as she spoke. His eyebrows slowly arched upwards until they disappeared into his flopping mop of hair. His lips parted as if he was going to speak so I put a warning hand on his arm. He closed his mouth and smiled his most winsome smile. It was a shame to waste it on the likes of Mrs.Trout but I could see it affected her just a little as her own grimace faltered a touch. She studied him for a moment longer and then turned her attention back to me.

"There's a young man looking for you," she said, her tone changing to one I didn't quite recognize. "He's here about the dog." She glanced down at Bracken who sat patiently beside Roger, having decided he was a soft touch and would very likely be sharing the sausage roll that she knew was wrapped in a serviette inside his pocket.

I blanched and a cold feeling settled at the bottom of my stomach. My hand gripped Roger's arm involuntarily. He turned off his smile and looked at me, concern on his face.

"Oh, silly me," said Mrs.Trout, as she turned to leave, "I forgot to tell you, didn't I? I took the liberty of transferring your advertisement to the main post office branch in Westham. Of course they get far more traffic coming through there, being right off the motorway, and

I assumed that anyone looking for their poor wee dog would be more likely to call in there than our tiny little office. He's waiting over by the refreshment tent. I'll send him your way, shall I?"

She laughed a tinkling sort of laugh that didn't match the venom in her eyes as she turned away.

"Hazel, are you alright?" asked Roger, putting an arm around me. I leaned into him, my knees suddenly trembling. My whole body was trembling, and my stomach started to roil. I put a hand down to Bracken who whined and pressed close. Roger's voice sounded like an echo through the ringing in my ears.

"No," I whispered. "It can't be. Please don't let it be."

Chapter Twenty-Five

But it was.

His name was Steven Willis and he was a perfectly nice fellow. He and his wife, Marilyn, who stayed in the car, afraid to have got her hopes up, had adopted Bracken – or, Angel, as her name had been – from a rescue group in Scotland. They'd driven up to collect her and had stopped on their way home to have some lunch at The Forge (because they were the sort of Upwardly Mobile People who knew about Destination Eateries). Afterwards, they'd taken Angel (I kept wondering who they were talking about) for a run on the moor, thinking she'd like to stretch her legs before they set off again but something in the Hedge had frightened her and she'd run off. They searched the moor for hours but had to give up. They'd left their two year old little boy with his grandparents and had to get home. The rescue group had suggested they search populated places, imagining she'd want to seek out people to care for her. Evidently they'd been wrong and the Willis' spent ages looking in all the wrong places. Eventually, retracing their steps they'd run across the notice that Mrs.Trout had so kindly circulated to the Westham post office and that led them here.

I handed her over without a modicum of fuss. They had her adoption papers with an attached photo and it was unmistakably her; there was no point in hysterics, no point in pleading my case. I gave them her new bed (that she never used) and the leash that matched her collar as well as her bowls. Numbly, I told them that she was a bit nervous at first but that once she knew them, she'd be just fine and was the best of dogs. I waved them away, watching my darling girl's tail waving at the unexpected car ride.

I'd sent Roger and my mum away before I went back to the cottage to get Bracken's things, not wanting to feel the agony of Roger's empathy, nor listen to the it's-for-the-best speeches from my mum. I just wanted to curl up on the sofa and close my eyes. I wanted to put myself there, tucked under the blanket that I shared with Bracken, so that I could imagine that I was simply waking up from a very bad dream. I never did make it to the sofa.

Instead, Toby found me in a heap on the floor.

I stopped answering the phone and hid if anyone came to the door. Astrid and Sidney came by, several times, as did Alfie and Edie. Toby came every day. He knocked for a bit then called through the door to let me know everyone was asking after me and to phone if I needed anything. I appreciated their visits and phone calls and felt quite churlish to be avoiding them but I simply couldn't face them. I didn't have the strength to pretend I was alright but didn't want to break down in an awkward and embarrassing fashion in front of anyone. Toby saw the worst of it, when he found me on the day they took her away, and I had no intention of revisiting that level of vulnerability again.

There was more to it than losing my darling girl, though. Since she'd been gone, I'd found myself questioning whether being at Rookery Cottage really was the best place for me. My initial enjoyment of the fête and the hour or so I'd spent with Roger had reminded me that I could, in fact, function in society if I was motivated to do so and hadn't I done just that for years? Perhaps all I'd needed was a break from the hustle and bustle and to get away from Teddy. Perhaps, in future, as long as I scheduled in some down time — a regular weekend at home with my parents, for example — so that I could better manage my energy, then maybe I could cope with London life, after all. The truth of it was that I missed the libraries and the museums; I missed being able to hop on the Tube or catch a train for a weekend in Wales with Roger. We gave each other National Trust memberships every year for Christmas and had a series of favourites we went to over and over. Once, before things had become irreversibly complicated, we'd planned to spend an entire summer doing the "Trust Tour". It seemed very attractive all of a sudden. I'd spent hours cleaning and working in and around the cottage and it didn't feel all that much closer to being a home than it had when I arrived. And now, without Bracken's presence, the cold and emptiness seemed magnified tenfold.

My only visitor had been Murk. I would've preferred he wasn't there either, but I forgot to close the kitchen window and once he was there, it was easier to just ignore him rather than argue. As it turned out, he wasn't at all annoying during his visits, but sat quietly by the fire. I automatically dished out food for him, and poured him a saucer of cream, but we didn't speak. In a way, I suppose I found his presence something of a comfort. It was at least nice to have another living creature in the house.

After three days, occupied mostly with crying (at least I'd broken the crying embargo) and writing anguished entries in my diary, I decided I would benefit from some garden therapy and took myself out in the early morning to spread mulch into the appropriate places.

In my absence, the late spring weather had caused an effusion of change and growth in the garden. The daffodils and snowdrops were just going over, and in their place, several clumps of pinks were poking up along the edge of the footpath. That was one of the great joys of spending the first spring in a new place, seeing what was going to come up. I caught myself having that thought – the notion of a 'first' spring suggested there would be subsequent ones. I mused on the fact that only days earlier I was planning for the years to come. Now, I wasn't certain I'd be here to harvest the vegetables I'd planted. Thinking about it brought me back to the brink of tears again, so I forced myself to concentrate on the tasks at hand. The distraction of physical labour was a balm to my ragged nerves and broken heart.

I was so engrossed in my tasks that I didn't hear the sound of the shed door opening. Mr.Goodship's shadow crossing in front of me was what first alerted me to his presence and I almost dropped my rake in surprise.

"Oh!" I said, startled. "I was miles away, I didn't hear you coming."

I must have looked a proper sight as his face crumpled into concern and, worst of all, sorrow.

"Aw, lassie," he said, putting out a hand, his own eyes brimming.

"Please, don't," I said, hastily rummaging for a tissue in my cardigan pocket. "I can't bear it if you're sympathetic and kind. It only makes it harder for me to keep a grip of myself. It's funny, really, I haven't properly cried in decades and now I can't seem to stop. I've only just managed to get out of the house so let's talk about other things, can we?"

I scrubbed roughly at my eyes and blew my nose, attempting a bright smile which was more of a grimace.

Mr.G cleared his throat and nodded.

"Right you are, right you are," he said, handing over the basket he was carrying. "Provisions from the missus," he said, smiling. "She thought mebbe you hadn't been feeding yourself so sent along some bits that are easy on the stomach. Bit of leek broth and some oat and ginger biscuits."

I was nearly undone again. I nodded, wordless, and took the basket. I swallowed a few times and blinked hard before thanking him.

"That's lovely, thank you. Tell Mrs.G I'm grateful, would you? It means the world..."

I choked on a clog of tears so stopped talking.

Mr.G patted my arm.

"That's alright, pet. She knows. Now, how are you getting on with the papers you found? Have you made any inroads there?"

I shook my head.

"Honestly, no," I said, grateful for the change of subject, although gripped by a pang of guilt at my complete lack of progress and enthusiasm. I'd lost all my will to follow through. "I'd been so focused on getting the things done for the fête and then...well, I haven't been back to it since."

"Aye, I hear we raised a tidy sum for the defence fund," he said, chuckling merrily. "Our Hamish has put a call in to a chum of his that works from one of those fancy firms in the city. He says we can afford enough of that fellow's hours to make sure we've got our paperwork in proper order. All we need to do is search out the information that we need so that Hamish can draw it all up."

He looked at me, his eyebrows raised in a pointed expression. I couldn't meet his eyes.

"I don't know, Mr.Goodship, if I'm the best one for the job. I'm a useless lump at the moment and surely now that I found those first few bits, anyone can read them and sort out where we can find the rest of what's needed."

"Oh, aye lass, I'm sure you're right about that," he said, nodding, pursing his lips thoughtfully. He squinted up into the spring sunshine and then looked around the garden, at the budding pinks and the baby spinach and lettuces that I'd planted in the old sink. "But I'm of the mind that perhaps it's your place to do it, rather than anyone else's?"

He turned his gaze back to me and his merry blue eyes held something more in them than the casual way in which he'd spoken. I looked into their depths and saw an old wisdom there, deeper and more far-reaching than I'd ever known. I suppressed a shiver. It was easy to forget he wasn't human.

"Is it really, though?" I asked, voicing my fear, once and for all. "Is it really my place?"

Chapter Twenty-Six

In the days since Bracken left, I'd been trying – rather unsuccessfully – to find a new rhythm to my days. Everything up until that point had been built around our time together. Breakfast, followed by a turn about the garden, a session at my laptop to eke out some words, followed by a long walk before we settled in to more writing and whatever else needed doing. The weeks prior to the fête had been so full of organizing and to-ing and fro-ing that I'd forgotten how little I actually had to do.

There were the usual household chores to occupy me – cleaning and tidying and what passed as cooking. I baked things that I didn't have an appetite to eat, just to have something to fill the time, and with Edie and Mrs.G sending food parcels there really wasn't much call for any attempts at kitchening. I couldn't face tackling my manuscript; I still hadn't properly addressed the correspondence from Rhonda so had little enough enthusiasm for it up to that point and my current mood made it even less appealing. I was mostly caught up in the garden – the big work had been done and now it was a matter of waiting to see what came up. I had my few bits and pieces planted but all of my earlier enthusiasm had petered out. I knew the reason for it – and it was the reason why I found myself not entirely surprised when a knock on the door revealed Hamish, standing with a bunch of spring onions in one hand and a thick brown envelope in another.

"Mr.Reed, come in!" I gestured him through the door then looked out, wondering if Murk was lurking nearby. There appeared to be no sign of him. Small mercies, I thought, closing the door.

"I was just about to make a cup of tea, will you have one?" I asked, filling the kettle.

"Lovely, thank you," said Hamish, passing me the bunch of onions. "Not quite a bouquet of roses," he said smiling kindly, "but likely of a more practical use."

I chuckled.

"I absolutely agree. They'll go nicely in my salad for lunch," I said. "I'm over-run with lettuce and spinach at the moment. I always think it's unfair that all of the things for a really good salad don't come in at the same time. I'd love a nice tomato and a bit of cucumber, but they won't be ready for ages yet."

Hamish laughed.

"True indeed! And it's a sad thing to have one of those miserable tomatoes from the shop at this time of year. I don't know how they pass it off as proper food."

We spent the duration of the kettle boiling and the tea steeping discussing the state of out-of-season fruit and vegetables – admitting to fancying a strawberry in January but knowing it wasn't worth it – and then settled down onto the sofa to deal with whatever was in the envelope.

"I was sorry to hear of your wee dog getting taken away," began Hamish, frowning down at the envelope that he rested on his knee. "It was a real shame, that."

I nodded but decided against trying to speak as I still couldn't talk about her without blubbering. I was berating myself as ridiculous because really, it wasn't as if she'd died tragically or something. Still, it was difficult to imagine her anywhere other than here, on the sofa, eyeing up the plate of biscuits.

Hamish cleared his throat.

"Anyhow, lass. You'll be wondering why I'm here, other than for a cup of your lovely tea and to deliver my spring onions."

"I imagine it has something to do with that big fat menacing looking envelope," I said, trying to make it easier for him. I was resigned to bad news. It was becoming something of a pattern.

Hamish nodded and reached into the envelope to pull out a sheaf of papers. It was pages and pages of print, with a formal looking letterhead on the top page.

"I got this by courier this morning," he said. "I've only just skimmed over it, it's the usual legal rigamarole but I got the general idea."

He paused to take a swig of his tea. I could see he was trying to formulate his next sentence, he had that frowning look of someone who was wanting to put the words together carefully. I sat, sipping my tea, patiently waiting. I was in no hurry for further trauma.

"It seems that your mum wasn't convinced that your Nan's will was executed properly."

"You mean she doesn't believe she has to comply," I said, fully aware of how Mum's brain worked. If she thought something ought not to apply to her, she presumed there'd been an error made on someone else's part. "But you said you'd had it checked over and it was watertight."

Hamish nodded.

"That I did," he said. "And indeed it is."

"So what's the problem then? I presume there is one or you wouldn't have that frowny look on your face."

"If you'll pardon my asking, Hazel," said Hamish, crinkling his eyes in a kindly manner. "But have you spent time in a...mental health facility in the last while?"

I shrugged and drummed my fingertips against my mug.

"Yes, I suppose you could call it that," I replied, uncomfortable that it was worded that way. Serenity Meadows dubbed itself a Centre for Well-Being but I could acknowledge that it was indeed a mental health facility. "Things got a bit much for me, living in London after Teddy and I split up, so I went there for a few weeks. I spent time there when I was in my teens. I had some...difficulties...at school and whatnot and it helped get me back on track. My marriage wasn't the most healthy you see, and my nerves..."

I trailed off, suddenly wondering how much Hamish knew about Teddy. There weren't many people who knew all of the details but Nan knew and she might have confided in him. He nodded, his face filled with empathy.

"I understand," he said. "There's no need to go into detail. I'm just glad that you're safe and sound now and I can tell you that it gave your Nan a great peace to know you'd left the...situation."

I swallowed down a sudden lump of tears.

"I suppose it's nice to know that you know I'm not completely crackers," I said, forcing a smile. "So yes, I did spend time at Serenity Meadows and obviously you know why. What does that have to do with anything?"

"Yes, well, it's a bit awkward, you see. It seems that your mum has had one of your primary care psychiatrists sign a document which would possibly nullify the clause in your Nan's will that says you must live here alone for the year and a day."

"Meaning?"

"Meaning that she's trying to have it declared that you're not...mentally fit, as it were....to live here under those conditions. Ultimately, it's a way to be able to sell the cottage before the allotted time set out by your Nan."

I don't know what I would've thought of that revelation only a few days ago. I probably would've laughed and considered it just one more feeble attempt of Mum's to get me to leave. I would've phoned her and we would've argued. Then I'd get her to pass the phone to my dad and between us we would've sorted it out and it would've been just another story to share with Alfie and Edie over a mug of tea and a chocolate biscuit. That was then, though, and at some point all things had converged and all of the fight had gone out of me.

"Can they do that?" I finally asked, feeling the beginnings of another headache – no doubt brought on by stress and an excess of crying. I wasn't entirely convinced that my newfound ability to bawl was really that good for me.

Hamish smoothed his hands over the papers, his lips pursed. I don't know if it was something typical of all solicitors or just Hamish and his considered country manner but he seemed to weigh everything before he spoke.

"Well, they can certainly try. It would likely have to go before a judge for a final decision. I imagine there are precedents but this sort of thing is tackled on a case-by-case approach, for obvious reasons. I have no doubt that you'll be able to overcome it. We would simply find our own psychiatrist to assess your current condition. And, of course, we could also delay it long enough that the year and day would almost be up anyhow and the deed would be transferred to you. I'm happy to take it on, at no cost, of course, as I consider it part of my service as executor of your Nan's will." He smiled, warmth and kindness radiating from his every pore. "I think I speak for everyone in saying that we're not about to let you get plucked away from us again, just as we're getting you back."

I smiled at him, wishing I was deserving of his faith in me. Everyone seemed to have such high hopes that things could go back as they were; that me being here in my Nan's place would return things to rights and no-one need worry about the Hedge or the portal. And at some point, last week, even, I would've delighted in all of that and been happy to go along with the illusion. Or is that delusion? It's a fine line.

"Let's just wait and see, shall we?" I said, putting down my mug and standing up, abruptly ending the conversation. It was rude of me and I was inwardly horrified at my behaviour but I felt like I just couldn't cope with any further discussion on the matter. If he was put out, he didn't show it. He followed suit and stood up, smiling again. He reached across the table and patted my arm.

"Hang in there, pet," he said, "We'll get through this. It's just a bit of a hiccup, that's all. I'll hang onto this, if you don't mind. I can make a copy if you like?"

I shook my head.

"No need," I said. "I'd be bored to death before I got past the first page!"

Chuckling all the way to the door, Hamish departed.

I watched him walk down the path and go through the gate, pausing to smell a spray of hawthorn blossom that was overhanging from the hedge.

"It's just one more thing, isn't it?" I said, out loud, as I closed the door, forgetting that Bracken wasn't there to hear me.

Oh well, I supposed, talking to myself was a sure sign of my apparent nutterhood; I was validating the questioning of my mental fitness. How typically co-operative of me.

"I think, though, it might be the last thing."

Naturally, mum was delighted with the news.

"I just knew you'd see sense eventually," she practically crowed down the telephone line. I could imagine her beaming, then reaching for the pen and paper she always kept on the table. She'd be scribbling down a new 'to-do' list under the heading of Moving Hazel. "And you needn't think for a minute that you're not perfectly welcome to stay right here with Dad and I until we find you the perfect place. I hear there are some lovely new developments just along the road from Winkle, so you could be close to all of your new friends but without living in that hovel..."

I let her ramble on. I couldn't help but notice that she'd acknowledged I'd made friends and that keeping them was now an option. Bless her, but she changed her tune like she changed her handbags. Which is to say, quickly and without a backward glance. Still, it was something of a comfort to be thinking about the option of going back to their house for a while. Next to Rookery Cottage, it was my favourite place to be. The desire to feel at home was an almost physical ache at this point. Without Bracken, the cottage had lost much of the warmth it had been slowly gaining.

I sighed inwardly and glanced at the clock. I'd phoned Hamish to arrange a meeting before I'd rung Mum. There was no point in him continuing to work on counteracting my mum's plans around the will. My leaving voluntarily simply meant I'd have to find someone to keep the place clean and looked after until we could sell it. I felt a pang of something in my belly when I thought of selling. Maybe we could lease it out.

"Mum? Sorry to interrupt but I have to get going. I've got a meeting with Mr.Reed and really ought to have a bath and tidy myself up before I go."

This was true. I'd been remiss in the self-care department in the days since everything went horrible. Mum rambled on for a few minutes more about the charming appeal of barn conversions before I interrupted again and then quickly rang off. I caught myself smiling at the Winkle-ness of my abrupt end to the conversation before shoving the feeling down and heading upstairs to run the bath.

"Ah, lass. You can't mean it."

My heart broke a little at the expression on Hamish's face. His welcoming smile collapsed into such a vision of pure sadness that I almost couldn't bear it. I coped by not looking at him, instead I fiddled with the buttons on my coat.

"It's for the best, really," I said, firmly, "There's just no possibility of me being able to manage the cottage and the garden all on my own. I was deluding myself thinking I could so I've made up my mind and this is the most sensible option.There's so much that needs doing and I struggle with the day to day details of things, what with my absent-minded artist tendencies."

I forced a laugh and risked a glance up at Hamish. He looked as if he might burst into tears. I pushed on, averting my eyes away from his.

"Anyway, I just wanted to pop in and thank you for all that you've done as far as Nan's will and everything. And if you could recommend someone that might act as a caretaker until I can be permitted to put the cottage up for sale..."

My voice faltered at that part and I swallowed hard, pushing down the rising tide of despair at the thought of selling Rookery Cottage. I cleared my throat and blinked rapidly. I spun the lower button of my coat so tightly that it almost came off.

"Of course," said Hamish, coming to my rescue. "I'm sure I can think of someone who can look in on things," He paused and I looked up to meet his eye. He smiled gently, reaching across his desk to pat my arm, "If that's really what you want?"

I nodded, not trusting myself to speak, knowing he would very well catch me in a lie. Of course I didn't really *want* to leave, but there was simply no way I *could* stay. I was well used, by this time in my life, to doing things I didn't necessarily want to do but for which the more preferable alternatives were difficult or inconvenient or unreasonable. It was better for everyone for me to take the uncomplicated route. Depending on where you stood, this was one of those situations.

We exchanged a few more generic pleasantries and then I rose to leave. On impulse, I turned back as I opened up the door to his office.

"I'll stay on until the hearing, of course," I said, referring to the council meeting where the fate of BMZs application was to be determined. "I'm still going to find those papers, to make sure they can't go ahead with it. And I'll be staying local, so..."

It was a last effort to barter away my guilt. It would've been far easier for me to just pack up my things and go back to Mum and Dad's without another word but, with a burst of uncharacteristic courage, I chose to do the braver thing. It meant having to face everyone with my decision and that filled me with a gnawing dread. It didn't matter that I'd always been destined to let them down; it never mattered that I always *knew* I would disappoint people. Knowing it would happen didn't stop it from tearing me apart every single time.

I considered it fair and just punishment for my cowardice at giving in. Again.

From Hamish's, I went to the post office. I had a letter to post to Roger and I was all out of stamps. I uttered a silent prayer that Mrs. Trout wasn't at the helm but evidently karmic retribution doesn't delay. I was met with one of her alarming smiles as the door tinkled merrily open. Not for the first time, I mused on the contradiction of such a jolly, welcoming sound. She didn't waste any time.

"Miss Price," she said, folding her hands primly on the counter. "Wasn't it just a great thing to have that dog find its rightful owner? You must be feeling pleased that you did such a good turn at putting up that advert. Of course, it didn't really help just having the notice posted around here. Naturally everyone knows which animals belong where and clearly that one had nothing to do with the village. It was a blessing to you, and the wee doggie, I imagine, that I took it upon myself to move the notice where it would reach a wider audience."

She straightened her shoulders and smoothed the front of her cardigan in that self-righteous gesture known universally to the martyred and long-suffering.

I swallowed but said nothing, merely nodding.

"I need a stamp, please," I said, handing my letter across the counter. She frowned down at the envelope, turning it over to reveal the blob of sealing wax and took a breath as if to speak. "I've been assured that the sealing wax offers no trouble to the sorting machines, Mrs.Trout. I got that from a postmaster in London so I imagine it's reliable information."

"Hmph," she replied, opening up the drawer where the stamps were kept as she simultaneously placed the letter on the scales. There was no way it was overweight but I'm sure she was just doing the right thing by His Majesty's coffers by checking. "That's as may be," she said, staring at the scale, no doubt willing the reading to go higher. "But I fail to see the point in trying to complicate matters for the sake of vanity. Or whatever it is you're trying to do."

She glanced at the address.

"I was speaking with your mother at the...festivities... last weekend. Such a lovely woman, I remember her always as a model of decorum."

I smiled, biting back a diatribe in the defence of sealing wax.

"Is this the young man who accompanied her? An old friend of yours, I understand? Not your husband, though? I didn't realize you were married. Will your husband be joining you at Rookery Cottage? Or will you be moving on?"

The last phrase was punctuated by a firm stare, almost a challenge. She stood with her hand hovered over the roll of stamps, her head tilted to one side like a malevolent sparrow. I was never so overcome with the urge to do violence as I was right then.

"The stamp, please, Mrs.Trout? It's just that I'm in rather a hurry."

Her lips pinched tightly together in a line and she expelled a sigh, forcefully, through her narrowed nostrils.

"That will be 65p, please."

I counted out the money and then held out my hand to receive the stamp and the letter. She collected the coins but held onto my letter when I made to take it from her.

"There are some folk who imagine they can make their home in this village when really they're far better off living elsewhere. They don't really understand what it means to be part of such a tight-knit community. Winkle isn't for everyone, wouldn't you agree, Miss Price?"

I held tightly to my letter, giving it a firm tug out of her claw-fingered grasp. I let my eyes meet hers.

"I absolutely agree, Mrs.Trout. There really are some people whose attitude and behaviour make it simply impossible to get along with others."

The bell rang, I'd like to think a bit triumphantly, as I wrenched open the door and marched out into the morning sunlight.

My last stop that morning was the grocer. I'd been subsisting on tea, toast and donations for what seemed like weeks. There were enough greens in the garden to scavenge for a bit of salad and what I really, really fancied was a nice fresh crusty bun to make a sandwich. It was the first true inkling of interest I'd had in food since Bracken had gone and I thought I probably ought to capitalize on it. What I hadn't expected was Astrid on the till.

"Hazel!" she beamed, quite uncharacteristic from her usual at-work demeanour. She hopped down off her stool and started running my purchases through. A trio of buns and a packet of Hob Nobs. I'd expire of scurvy before too long, I thought. "Aren't these gorgeous buns? We used to have a fabulous bakery on the high street but the owner was elderly and no-one wanted to buy it when he retired. I still think someone could make a great living if it were to re-open. I keep after Mrs.Goodship but she won't have it. These come from the baker in Westham and we can't ever keep them in stock. People want fresh things, don't they? Why buy some artificial crap when you can have something that was baked just that morning? And without all the chemical rubbish they put in factory-made things."

Her chatter was a pleasant surprise. I hadn't realized how much I had missed human conversation. I loved my solitude, but every once in a while I surprised myself with how I found a great deal of enjoyment in the company of good people. That said, any good feeling was marred with guilt, knowing my plans and how they would likely go over with Astrid. She was so fiercely loyal and I considered the fact she'd not only allowed, but welcomed, me into Winkle's inner circle to be a great honour. I dreaded her finding out. For some strange reason, the opinion of this blue-haired, black-nailed teenager was important to me.

My reticence didn't go unnoticed.

"Oh, Hazel, I'm ever so sorry," she said, squeezing my wrist as I held out the money for my shopping. "I'm such a git. How are you feeling? It must be terrible for you, without Bracken, I mean."

Her black-rimmed eyes softened with sympathy and genuine concern. I felt such a toad. I shrugged, averting my eyes from her warm gaze. I hoped that she took my inability to talk as a matter of grief, rather than guilt. Which only made me feel even guiltier.

"I'm alright," I mumbled, stuffing my purchases into my bag. "It'll get easier, I suppose. Time heals all wounds and all that."

"So they say," she replied. "Although you can never say exactly how much time, can you?"

I attempted a smile. She was such a sweet girl underneath that hostile exterior. I wondered what made her think she needed that particular suit of armour. Then again, hadn't I a set all my own? Didn't we all, when it came down to it?

"Will you be coming 'round to the Forge later? We're having an informal strategy meeting. Only we didn't want to press you to come if you weren't feeling up to it. It's not like we've got anything new to discuss, it's just an excuse to get together more than anything else."

She grinned, transforming her face into a gentle sort of beauty.

"I think Alfie gets these things set up just so Edie'll let him go to the pub!"

I laughed at that, knowing it very likely indeed. It would be so lovely to be a part of it all, to feel that gift of great welcome and to be at home with them all again. I shook my head. I didn't deserve their kindness.

"I don't think so," I said, looking down at my hands where they were twisting the handles of my shopping bag. "I'm not quite up to being sociable just yet. Thanks for asking, though."

She nodded and climbed back up on her perch, narrowing her eyes at a couple of young women who had just walked in the door. They were decidedly not Winkle natives; designer sunglasses perched on their elegantly coiffed and highlighted heads, their profound-ly not-for-moor-walking high heels tip-tapping on the tiled floor. Astrid's black-painted lips tightened and she sighed audibly. Turning back to me she rolled her eyes dramatically.

"Tourists," she said. "You wouldn't mind them if they didn't just waltz in and out without really *noticing* the place, would you? They're never here long enough to belong, they don't give it enough time. What we need is people who come and stay, not just pop in for a hipster meal and snaps of the bluebells. Who could get excited about protecting a hedge that you haven't had a conversation with, you know?"

I smiled a small, guilt-ridden smile and scurried out of the shop.

"Are you feeling suitably wretched?" asked Murk, the minute I walked into the cottage. He was sitting on the arm of the sofa, facing the door, like a father who'd sat up waiting all night for his wayward daughter. I ignored him and walked into the kitchen with my bag of shopping. A large wicker basket sat on the table with a piece of notepaper propped against it. I knew without looking who it was from. I pretended not to see it.

"That won't make it disappear," he said, following me. "Mrs.Goo dship has an instinctive knowledge for these situations. I imagine she's trying to charm you back over to their side."

"I'm not *off* their side," I retorted, yanking the buns from the bag. "No-one needs to charm me anywhere. My feelings about the land sale and the welfare of the Borderlands and the Hedge haven't changed one bit."

"What about Heathcliff, then? Should I drop a word in his ear? Maybe he can convince you there's something more to stay here for."

I had an overwhelming urge to throw something at him. Instead, I made a point of opening the knife drawer and pulling out a large, snaggle-toothed bread knife. I was going to use it to cut a lettuce but he didn't have to know that. I turned to face him, the knife held aloft.

"Do not call him that," I said, enunciating each word, infusing them with as much menace as I was capable of mustering. "And do not presume to know anything about me, or my decisions. In fact, you should be applauding me for doing what I want for a change. Didn't you once point out to me how I was always living other people's versions of my life? Well, for once, I'm doing what I want."

I pushed past him and back through the door. Before it swung closed behind me, I heard him mutter, in a soft and almost kind tone,

"If only that were actually true, *mo chroí,* if only that were true."

Chapter Twenty–Seven

I planned to spend an hour in the garden before tackling my new book proposal. Garden time is a proven antidote for getting me out of my head, which had become a rather hostile place, and I needed to have my thoughts in order before I tried wrangling a convincing argument for Rhonda. She'd phoned me after I hadn't responded to the publisher's proposal and, after a lot of back-and-forthing, she'd told me to 'whip something up' and send it along. That was mostly optimistic, though, never one to burn bridges, she said she'd tell the original publisher that I was still thinking their offer over. It was probably a wise move on her part as I felt my enthusiasm waning in the wake of so much upset. I didn't *hate* my bodice-rippers; I just wanted something more of my own. I supposed I could work with a compromise of some kind.

Murk was gone when I returned from my lettuce hunting expedition and so I ate my lunch in blissful solitude. Only it wasn't quite as blissful as it might have been. The space that Bracken had occupied in my life was an aching void and I realized just how much I'd begun to depend upon her company. Murk was right, I *was* feeling wretched, just not quite in the way that he assumed. Of course, my brain was doing a good job of filling that aching void with guilt over deciding to leave the cottage. It made for a tumultuous inner landscape. Hence the prescription of dirt therapy.

As a first-line defence against the suffocating gloom, I took my after lunch cup of tea out into the sunshine. I sat, sipping contemplatively, nibbling on a slice of lemon drizzle from the basket that I finally admitted was there.

Mrs. G's note was short and simple.

"Thought you might need reminding what it all means. All our love, Mr. And Mrs. G."

The basket contained a large wedge of lemon drizzle cake, a bottle of Mr.G's dandelion and burdock, a dozen rock buns and a bunch of the cotton-top flowers that I'd later learned were called Sheep's Breath. Not a very glamorous name, to be sure, but very descriptive.

So Murk was right again. Mrs.G really did have an inkling of what I was planning. At first glance I wasn't really sure how lemon drizzle and rock buns were going to sway me, or clarify the meaning of my life. However, I'm well-versed in the fine art of navel-gazing and over-thinking so it wasn't long before I could see the profound meaning in these, the most simple of gifts: the gift of the land to be found in enchantment and simple, natural ingredients; the gift of heritage in the passing down and along of much-beloved recipes; the immense gift in the quiet act of service that's the preparing and sharing of food. No, the message wasn't lost on me.

It was all so obvious— how coming to live in Winkle, at Rookery Cottage, was the culmination of every childhood dream. And every adult one too, come to think of it. How many pages in my journal had I devoted to the imagining of this life? Living, writing, gardening, all in the place I loved best in the world? And now, in typical Hazel fashion, now that I had it, I'd decided to leave it all behind. It turned out that I actually *didn't* know what to do with my dream when it came true.

I was still mulling over the great unfairness of my dysfunction when a shadow passed across my sunny spot.

"Hamish told me that you're leaving,"

Just like that, no preamble. Why bother with introductory pleasantries when you can skip right to the point? I imagine some people might find that sort of directness to be charming. I found it discomfiting.

"Hello, Toby," I said, insisting on the introductory pleasantries. "Gorgeous day, isn't it?"

"Why?"

I squinted up at him. His face was in shadow, the sun behind him, illuminating his mop of unruly hair like a halo. I stifled a snort. Not so much the gilded version of an angel, I thought. He was more of the dark, Fallen variety. I felt the familiar twinge of inspiration and made a mental note to jot down the idea for a character. Paranormal romance is a big seller. That ought to keep Rhonda happy. That could be the middle ground, a stepping stone, as it were.

"Well," I replied, feeling impish after that revelation, "the sun is shining, there's hardly a cloud in the sky and the breeze is just enough to carry the scent of the apple blossoms but not enough to require a jacket. All in all, it's quite lovely. Tea?"

I motioned to my nearly empty mug. Some days were meant for more than one after-lunch cup and with the flash of inspiration I'd just had, I felt like I was halfway to getting my work done for the day. "I was just thinking of putting the kettle on again."

"No, I'm not planning on stopping," he said, gruffly. "Thanks, all the same."

I shrugged.

"You don't have to go," he said. "None of us want you to go."

I looked down at my mug, swirling the cold dregs in a circle.

"I *do* have to go, Toby. I was fooling myself, thinking I could live here. I'm not cut out for this life," I waved a hand, vaguely, in the direction of the cottage and the garden. "It was just a silly fantasy."

"According to who?" he said, folding his arms across his chest. I wished he'd sit down. I didn't relish him looming over me like that. It was an uncomfortably familiar arrangement and did nothing for my nerves.

"No-one," I said, not looking at him. "I just realized that sometimes the fantasy and the reality don't match up, that's all. Besides, it's not good for me to be allowed to isolate myself. I've a tendency towards spending too much time alone and since Bracken..." I paused to clear my throat then shook my head, ridding myself of the thought. "I'm better off having to be around people. It's too easy for me to slide into the life of a hermit. And not in a good way."

"But you're not on your own," he said, holding out his hand and counting off on his fingers all of the people I had around me. "It's not as if you're lacking in options. And besides, half the village would be at your gate if you said they could come around. And that doesn't even take into account the Borderlands. Once we get these bloody developers off our backs and you take over the Caretakership, the portal will be secure and you'll have all and sundry wandering through here."

"But that's not really what I want either, Toby. I came here because I wanted to live a peaceful, quiet life. I wanted to look after my Nan's cottage, I wanted to grow flowers and herbs and a few bits of veg. I wanted to write the stories I want to write, not the ones my agent says

I'm supposed to write. But how can I do any of those things when the opposite of them is what's best?"

Toby stepped out of the path of the sunlight and sat down on the edge of the leek trench, his face fixed in its perpetual scowl. He put his elbows on his knees and leaned towards me, furrowing his brow even deeper.

"What in the world are you banging on about? What's wrong with the sort of life you want? Seems to me that writing stories and gardening are the things you'd be best at. You were always scribbling away when we were kids. Do you remember that series you had about the talking hedgehog?"

I laughed, blushing. The Tales of Mr. Spikenard were my sad attempt at a combination of Beatrix Potter and Enid Blyton. I think I still had them somewhere, buried deep in a banker's box at the back of a cupboard in my parent's house.

"If only it were that simple, Toby, believe me, I'd be all over it."

"I don't understand why it isn't that simple," he replied.

"First off," I said, "Selling this cottage is the sensible option — let's face it, beyond its charming exterior I'm sure lurks a crumbling ruin in need of a great deal of care and attention, the kind which I'm not really qualified to offer. Secondly, I have to try and cobble together some sort of income because, believe me, my books may sell well but only enough to sustain me so I've no great pile of savings to fall back on should my decision to shift to...well, a different market, not pan out. So I'd need to find another way to support myself and employment opportunities are not exactly in abundance in Winkle. Thirdly, and I refer back to the second point of my books selling well. It makes absolutely zero sense to change my focus at this point because if I *did* insist on doing so, I'd likely lose my agent and so there goes my future income. Children's stories are a desperately hard market to break into and that's *if* you have a dedicated agent to pimp you around and mine is very close to dropping me because I don't want to fall in line. No matter which way I turn, I'm letting someone down. I just can't win. So you see, there's absolutely nothing to be gained by trying to make a go of it here."

Toby stood up abruptly.

"Well, then," he said, his tone clipped. "If that's really what you believe, then I doubt there's anything I can say to change your mind."

I tried to feel triumphant at having avoided further argument and need for justification but instead I was left with a hollow sensation in the pit of my stomach. I think that part of me was hoping he'd want to argue me around more. That hope, in and of itself, should've been a red flag.

"But what I will say, Hazel, is that I'm sorry that you can't see what's right in front of your face. And I'm sorry that you can't seem to let go of what other people might think of the choices you make because there's plenty of us who see life differently."

"That may be so, Toby," I replied, stiffly. "But what you aren't considering is that I'm not like you. I don't have the ability to just drop everything and everyone to go off and do my own thing, with complete disregard of others feelings just on a...a selfish whim."

There, I said it. The thing I'd been wanting to say for decades. The extremely large elephant was now dancing a jig around the room. There was a moment that stretched into eternity when neither of us was speaking. Hearing my therapist in my head, I breathed through the impulse to apologize.

"That's not fair, Hazel," he said, his eyes flashing. "You know well and fine that's not what happened."

"Do I, Toby? Do I really? Because from where I stand, that's exactly what it looks like. You got all full of self-pity and righteous indignation and buggered off, leaving the old Lord Dummell and Nan and…everyone else who cared about you…to worry and fret about where you were and what you were doing and if you were alright. You made a selfish decision that ended up affecting the lives of other people. A decision that hurt other people deeply. So as far as I'm concerned, no matter what we do in this life, no matter what decision we make, there will always be consequences. And whether there's ill-intent or just sheer thoughtlessness, someone is going to be affected. And I, for one, prefer not to be the kind of person who brings that sort of upset into other people's lives if I can avoid it."

"Is that what you think you're doing? Because as far as I can see, all you're doing is using other people as an excuse for your own cowardice." he said.

Shocked, I stood up. His words stung.

"What do you mean? How can you say that?"

"I can say it because that's exactly what it looks like, Hazel. You make it sound as if all you're thinking about is looking after other people but what it really is is an excuse to not do the thing that frightens you. Face it, living in Winkle, in Rookery Cottage terrifies you. You can't stand the idea of not being the best at something so you won't even try."

I stared at him, tears stinging at the back of my eyes. I didn't trust myself to speak.

He stared back at me for a moment, his grey flint eyes boring into mine. I remembered how I used to tell him that he was probably descended from the earth faeries…that he had stone coloured eyes and, in my ridiculous and elaborate childish imagination that meant he was an earth spirit. I have green eyes, so I'm a wood spirit.

The stone coloured eyes softened and his shoulders slumped.

"What happened to you, Hazel?" he whispered. "You used to be so fearless."

"*Life* happened to me, Toby," I snapped, "and you've no right to judge me when you don't know the first thing of what I've been through."

I threw the dregs from my mug into the radishes and started towards the house.

"That may be so," he said, almost too quietly for me to hear, "but I know your Nan was an excellent judge of character."

Whirling around I faced him.

"And what's that supposed to mean?"

He shrugged.

"Only that she wouldn't have laid this at your feet if she didn't think you could manage it."

My plans for working on my book went right out of the window after that conversation. I made myself the second cup of tea and went back outside. This time, though, I wandered down to the bottom of the garden to check on my peas. They'd been close to flowering last time I looked and considering the pattern of rain then sunshine, they'd probably burst into pod overnight. Sure enough, there was a generous offering to be had. I set down my mug and collected the little green treasure chests into the pockets of my apron. From there, as often happens in the garden, I moved from one little job to the next. I saw some weeds that needed pulling and then the honeysuckle needed tying up, then I remembered I wanted to scatter some cosmos seeds and trim the hydrangeas.

I'd heard somewhere that there are actually certain chemicals in the soil that help to lift your mood and that having both hands occupied stops your brain from dwelling on other things. So before too long, I'd forgotten the horrid exchange with Toby and felt my mind drift back to my book proposal. Was I really going to go through with it? And if I did, and Rhonda didn't want to pursue it, what then? Would I take it elsewhere? It would mean telling everyone that I didn't want to be Sally Applewood anymore. Or, at least, not *only* Sally Applewood. Was I brave enough to start all over again? Or was Toby right and my dawdling was all about needing to be sure the new direction would be a success? There was no guarantee of that, whereas keeping things as they were was something of a certainty and certainty was comforting.

Toby was right about one thing, I *was* fearless once. Or at least, I thought I was. I spent most of my childhood imagining I was a composite of every plucky girl character I'd ever read about. I was part Anne Shirley, part Jo March, part Sara Crewe, a good bit of Mary Lennox with a daring dash of George from the Famous Five. Although, to be fair, I rather preferred Anne's character of all the Five, even though I was supposed to find her domesticity an affront to the feminist agenda. I don't know when that all changed. Every time I try to pinpoint the exact moment when I surrendered to my fears and anxieties it slips away. Maybe I wasn't ever really fearless; maybe it was all just make-believe and the time eventually came when I ran out of the energy I needed to pretend I was someone other than myself, and that true self was timid and frightened, not brave or plucky at all. There's a fine line, I think, between trying to be a better person and trying to be a *different* person. I wonder if I'd confused the two.

"Penny for your thoughts," said Mr.Goodship, hunkering down beside where I'd sat on the path. I was half-heartedly trying to dig tufts of grass from between the stones when his shadow passed across my line of vision. It says a lot about how much calmer I was feeling by the fact I didn't levitate off the ground in shock when he spoke. Dirt therapy, indeed.

"You know," I said, smiling over at him, "If I could just increase the price of my thoughts ever so slightly, all of my money troubles would be over. Apparently, my thoughts are in very high demand of late."

Mr.G threw back his head and laughed his booming laugh. His beard wobbled with each breath. Who knew I was that funny?

"Well, lass. Perhaps that's just what you need to do, then," he said, wiping his eyes with the end of his beard. "Seems to me you've a habit of undervaluing yourself."

I grunted, stabbing at an emerging dandelion with my screwdriver. Nan hadn't believed in fancy gardening tools when the simple option already existed.

"Yes, I suppose you're right. Bit of a chronic condition, actually. Habits of a lifetime and all that."

I wiped my forehead with the back of my hand. The afternoon sun was warm and I'd been grubbing about for well over an hour.

"Mrs. G well?" I said, wanting to steer the conversation in a less daunting direction.

Mr.Goodship nodded, smoothing a gnarled hand through his beard. He stood up, knees creaking, rocked back on his heels and surveyed the garden.

"Aye, she's grand. Sends her best. Garden's looking well," he gestured back towards the peas. "Getting a good crop, eh?"

"Yes, very good," I said. "Feel free to help yourself, there's far more there than I can eat. I was going to put a Free box outside the gate anyway."

"A what?"

"A Free box," I said, surprised he'd never heard of it. "You know, when you've got a surplus of something so you set it out for other people to take. We used to do it at the community gardens in London. That way we weren't all planting the same things. I never had any luck with cucumbers or courgettes but I was excellent at basil and other herbs and my leeks and brassicas were generally quite good as well. Truthfully, though, my heart's always been with flowers and herbs. Oh, and fruit of course. But we had communal berry bushes and fruit trees, on account of them taking up so much space. We were quite limited with the space, so we had to make concessions to be sure as many people as possible could have a plot. It's nice having my own..."

I stopped, realizing what I was saying. I cleared my throat and attacked the poor dandelion with greater vigour.

"You know, you get a real sparkle to you when you talk about your garden," said Mr. Goodship, thankfully ignoring the obvious tack that the conversation could've taken. "You've definitely got your Nan's love of the green folk."

"Well, that may be so, but I still managed to be just contrary enough to spoil things for myself," I said.

"Oh?"

"Most people would have it that when we're growing our own vegetables that we're each trying to be more self-reliant," I said, "That's what the general message at the community garden was. Because of that, I was only allowed to plant a few flowers in our plot. Each plot had to be 90% edible. Of course, I managed to work around that a bit by planting edible flowers and medicinal herbs. But it was always a struggle and it took some of the joy out of something that should've been very beneficial. I lived in constant fear that the garden police were going to do a midnight raid. There were people on the committee that took it all very seriously. They'd make Mrs. Trout look like a pushover."

I grinned at the memory. That was another time when my convictions overrode my anxieties and aversion to conflict. I had managed to get the percentages shifted with the argument that we needed to attract pollinators to the garden.

Mr. Goodship chuckled.

"I don't doubt you managed to work around it, lass. Besides," he said, gesturing towards the garden gate. "I would've thought the idea of community was more to the point in yon London gardens. If everyone does the thing they do best and leave the other bits to the other folk as do them best, then it all comes together in the end and nobody does without. Wouldn't you say? I don't see as why each person has to do all of everything by their own self. Seems a bit silly really."

He reached over and patted my shoulder.

"Right, lass. I'd best be off. The missus sent me over to pick up an order of something or other from down the side street and I fancy nipping in to see if our Alfie can get away for a pint."

It was my turn to chuckle.

"Well, you'd better hope he's been behaving himself or else Edie won't let him out to play."

"Aye, right you are, lass. Right you are."

In a blink he was gone, just a blur of colour disappearing through the gate, leaving me to think about everything he'd said. He may not have said anything overt about my decision to leave, but it hadn't stopped him from trying to plant the seeds of doubt, not knowing that I was suffering a glut of doubt already. It was a good effort but all that talk about community and everyone doing the thing they do best was utterly transparent. Despite knowing exactly what he was up to, I felt the resurgence of great pangs of guilt. I gave myself a mental shake. It was pointless to agonize over it; the wheels were set in motion. There was no going back, so there was no sense in dwelling on it. To change my mind now would cause no end of fuss.

Chapter Twenty-Eight

The next morning I came to the grim conclusion that there was no avoiding another trip into the village.

After an evening of torment, I finished my book proposal and now had to take the fateful step and send it off to Rhonda. She was of the old school and preferred a hard copy, rather than email. I'd told her often enough that she could print things out herself if she wanted to hold them in her hands but she insisted she was far too busy. I secretly believed that she didn't actually know how to use her printer and depended heavily for her technological needs on a long series of tyrannized interns who left her employ deeply questioning their choice of career. Anyway, considering that what I was sending her wasn't anything involving bodices, buxom-kitchen-maids-turned-long-lost-inheritresses or roguish dukes I'd likely have to wait a while for her reaction and was secretly happy for the inevitable delay. Toby was probably right; I'm an incurable coward.

I got lucky in that Mrs. Trout wasn't holding court in the post office. A pleasant, middle-aged woman named Lottie was filling in. She was wearing the most gorgeous Liberty print house-dress type smock and we spent a happy fifteen minutes or so bonding over our love of vintage style and fabric. She sewed all of her own clothing from vintage patterns that she scoured the internet for and she even offered to whip me up a version of her dress. I was on the verge of an enthusiastic "yes" when I remembered that I probably wasn't going to be in Winkle for much longer so, instead, I forced a smile and made noncommittal noises. Just as I turned to go, she invited me to the next meeting of the Winkle Textiles Enthusiasts Club, an offshoot of the WI, I was to learn, which was essentially a drop-in sewing group. It sounded utterly marvellous. I was only an amateur with a sewing machine, sticking to very basic things, and would've loved some tutelage from more experienced people. I felt a second pang of something that I preferred not to acknowledge.

Waving goodbye to my new friend, I stepped out onto the pavement and headed for the elusive side street. I'd heard so many references to this mysterious avenue of commerce and I didn't want to leave Winkle without having investigated it.

At first I was disappointed. Lottie had directed me to simply turn right, then right again, which is what I did but instead of a quaint street of boutique delights, I found a rather nondescript blind alley. The first premises was the now-empty bakers and an old-fashioned hanging sign announcing *Tinker, Pickle and Trott* seemed to be the only active place of business along the whole road. There were several other storefronts but they all seemed to be closed up and peering in the windows left me none the wiser, as all I could see were dust sheets. Shrugging inwardly, I decided to investigate the remaining shop, though I had a sinking feeling that, by the name, it was a fancy delicatessen or something else with equal lack of appeal.

There was a set of iron stairs leading from the street up to the entrance of what I presumed were second floor flats and underneath those was a little wooden door painted a brilliant shade of blue. It was delightfully old-fashioned looking with a large cast iron knocker in the shape of a lion's head and a heavy latch in lieu of a doorknob. A small, hand-lettered sign declared, *"Tinker, Pickle and Trott - Oddments and Miscellany for the Discerning Eye"*, then taped underneath, a piece of paper with the words, "NetherWinkle resident discounts honoured here."

As I lifted the latch and pushed the heavy door open, a merry little bell sang. It was a far more welcoming sound than the bell in the post office, which had started to sound more and more like the toll of doom every time I had to go in there to face Mrs.Trout. I was immediately assailed by the gorgeous scent of honeysuckle, mixed with something that made me think of a combination of sandalwood and vanilla. I inhaled deeply, feeling my tensions melt as I looked around the funny little entrance-way. I had the immediate impression that I'd just stepped into a shop in Diagon Alley. I half expected to see a display of wands or a rack of robes.

It was bright and airy, more bright and airy than you would imagine for a shop tucked in an alley out of the direct sunlight. The floors were of a pale, oak that looked to have worn in places, suggesting heavy traffic, although the shop appeared deserted. An ancient cash register sat on top of a heavy dark mahogany table that seemed to serve as the check-out counter. A rack of postcards depicting Winkle scenes sat next to a three-tiered cake stand that held small bags of what were advertised as Dewbright's of NetherWinkle Aniseed Balls. I immediately dropped two bags of them into one of the conveniently placed wicker shopping baskets. A gift for Mr. Goodship.

"Just coming!" sang a voice from somewhere in the far reaches of the shop. "I'm just boiling the kettle. Make yourself at home, Hazel, pet!"

I smiled, heading for the nearest rack of merchandise and then paused.

Had the voice just addressed me by my name? Surely not.

I wandered over to the nearest display, which was a knee-weakening collection of notecards, writing paper and matching envelopes. There was a shelf full of fountain pen ink, right next to row upon row of coloured sealing wax. An old tooth mug held an assortment of feather quill-pens which I assumed were just for the aesthetic factor.

"No, quite the contrary, my girl," said a smooth, rumbling voice right behind me. I managed to stop myself from yelping out loud. "We have several customers who won't use anything but a feather quill for their correspondence. Very much the traditionalists. Then again, there are some things that can only be committed to the page in the old way, aren't there?"

The voice belonged to a ginger-haired, barrel-chested gentleman, with a beard *à la* Mr.Goodship, though far tidier. He was much the same size as Mr. G, but in the place of the outdoorsy-wear that Mr.G preferred, this man was dressed in a crisp, snowy white shirt, tucked into neatly pressed tweed trousers. A bright yellow waistcoat was buttoned across his robust torso and a rainbow-striped bow tie completed the outfit. A pair of steel-framed, half-moon glasses perched on his very prominent nose.

That's it, I thought. I've definitely stumbled into the Potterverse. Wait! Did he just read my thoughts?

The little man chuckled and held out his hand.

"Robinson Pickle, at your service," he said, sketching a courtly bow. I went to shake his hand but he intercepted me and turned my wrist to place a kiss on the back of my hand. His touch sent a strange, but not unpleasant tingle up my arm.

"I apologize for the thought-cunning," he said. "It's a simple parlour trick, I assure you. No real intrusion at all, you have my word upon it. You'll not find evidence of Deep Faery malarky in *this* establishment. That sort of thing is very much frowned-upon here on your side of the Hedge and we're all very, *very* respectful of that. We like to think of ourselves as ambassadors of NetherWinkle and, unlike some," he paused to sniff in a miffed way and smoothed his hands down his yellow waistcoat, "unlike some, we take that role very seriously."

I nodded and smiled benignly, as if I actually had a clue what he was talking about, still trying to sort out if the phrase 'thought-cunning' meant he'd read my mind or not.

"Excellent!" he boomed, as if quite satisfied that all was settled. "Now, while the tea is steeping, why don't you tell me what I can help you with?"

I spent a delightful two hours in Mr.Pickle's shop. It turned out that the Tinker and Trott in the name belonged to two other NetherWinkle folk who, for various reasons, felt it best to remain on the other side of the hedge. Those reasons were relayed to me with a knowing glance, an elbow to the ribs and an exaggerated wink. I found myself nodding and smiling again, resolving to ask Murk what that meant. It occurred to me that I would've preferred to ask Toby to clear that up for me, Murk not being likely to actually answer my questions, and felt a twinge of regret that we'd ended our last conversation so badly.

It soon became evident that the shop was far more than just a stationer. In addition to reams and reams of the most delicious paper (rich, creamy sheets of linen and cotton; crisp, crinkly parchment that I could only imagine being used to bind in a grimoire or something equally as magical) and row upon row of shelves containing every possible colour and consistency of ink (bright, shimmering pigments and smooth, iridescent tones), there was an entire section devoted to incense and candles. There were lamps - both oil and electric - and ornate wooden boxes to hold pens and writing supplies. And the books! Ohmygiddyaunt! The books! Leather-bound volumes with hand-tooled covers on all manner of subjects in all manner of languages, some of which were unrecognizable as anything you might come across in the earth's geography. In addition to those more exotic tomes, there was a gorgeous selection of modern fiction (modern meaning published in the last three hundred years) in all genres, including, I was somewhat embarrassed to see, the entire works of one Sally Applewood. When he saw me glance at the row of my books, he smiled widely.

"Naturally, we like to support our own," he'd said, rocking back and forth on his heels. "I've read them all and thoroughly enjoyed every last one."

"You didn't!" I exclaimed, blushing in disbelief, only just stopping myself from attempting to justify my choice of genre, excuse my writing style and every other impulse that arose whenever someone actually mentioned reading my novels.

He pursed his lips, frowning.

"Of course I did!" he said. "And why wouldn't I? A well-written tale is a great treasure and no-one has the right to pass judgement on what form it takes."

I blushed again, now because I felt I was being remonstrated by a stern headmaster.

"Indeed," he continued, "there have been many volumes over the years that have been dismissed as too superficial for serious consideration, only to be revealed as genius in the goodness of time. It's merely a matter of fashion and perception and whomever has deemed themselves an authority. I pride myself on reading voraciously and widely and I will not suffer the snobbery of literature in my presence!"

After that outburst, we'd retired to a little sitting area next to the cash register. A tray of tea things had appeared and we sat for the duration of several cups, chatting about all kinds of things from gardening to the works of Jane Austen; from Beatrix Potter and her incredible dedication to the Lake Country to the merits of e-readers. I was surprised to hear that he was very much in favour of them, citing the benefits of having digital books available and easily accessible in every corner of the world. I even told him all of my worries and strife about the Caretakership, Nan's cottage, changing what kinds of stories I wanted to write and how it might affect everything. All in all, it was the most enjoyable few hours I'd spent in a very long time. He was extremely easy to talk to, I had no sense of my being judged or criticized. It was very refreshing and I felt a great weight lift as I unburdened myself to him. Without actually giving me any advice, he raised several questions that gave me quite a bit to think about. He managed, in the span of an hour or so, to offer a clearer perspective on things than my poor, beleaguered therapists from Serenity Meadows had done in weeks.

Just as I was leaving — with a stack of gorgeous writing paper (off-white, recycled cotton/linen blend), a stunning new notebook (smooth, creamy paper with a beautiful illustrated cover by a Nether-Winkle artist) and several tester pots of ink (Salem Black, Crimson

Ghost and Glencarragh Violet to name but a few), a large beeswax candle and a packet of Borderland Brew (a special blend of tea that was guaranteed to delight) — he placed his hand on my arm and fixed me with a piercing glare.

"I know it seems untenable just now," he said, his voice far gentler than his gaze, "but this is where you belong."

"That's kind of you to say…" I stammered.

He held up his other hand and gave my arm a tight squeeze, sending that odd tingle up through my shoulder, making my scalp prickle.

"No lassie, 'tisn't a kindness at all. It's no easy life, holding the space between the worlds. There'll always be trouble and there'll always be sorrow, 'tis just the nature of the thing. But believe me when I tell you, the rewards are far beyond the trials."

All of a sudden a great wave of emotion swept over me. I felt my heart lurching in my chest. I had an ache deep inside myself, an ache that felt like grief and longing and every heartbreak I'd ever known.

He nodded slowly.

"Aye," he whispered, his eyes pooling with unshed tears. "That's about the feel of it, pet."

"What?" I croaked, shuddering under the weight of my feelings. "the feel of what?"

"The land without someone who truly cares for it."

I finished my shopping in a confused haze, going from Mr. Pickle's shop to the grocer. Considering my current mood and the fact that Toby would've surely spread the word by now, I was glad that Astrid wasn't on the till. As it was, the girl serving me kept giving me the oddest looks, as if expecting me to do something untoward. I looked back over my shoulder, wondering if there was some sort of criminal element lurking behind me in the line. I paid for my few bits of things and wandered, vaguely, back into the street. I stood still, clutching my parcels, momentarily having forgotten what else I had to do, when I turned to see Toby striding towards me, his face as black as thunder. That had the desired effect of jolting me out of my stupor.

"Toby," I said, somewhat pointlessly.

"Hazel! For heaven's sake woman, where've you been? Alfie and Edie are out of their heads with worry. They've had your bloody mother on the phone every half hour."

I shook my head.

"Whatever do you mean?" I replied. "I've just been doing some shopping."

I gestured to my bags.

His eyes widened as he reached for the green paper bag from Tinker, Pickle and Trott's.

"Hey!" I said, yanking it out of his reach as he tried to take it from me. "Careful! You'll rumple my paper."

He groaned and ran a hand through his hair, making it stand on end even more than it usually did. He had the look of a chimney sweep on the descent.

"The little bugger," he muttered.

"I beg your pardon?"

He shook his head.

"How long were you in with himself then?"

"Who? Mr.Pickle you mean?"

"Aye, him."

I shrugged.

"I don't know, a couple of hours. He's very interesting. We had lots of things in common, and he's very easy to talk to," I said, defensively, resenting the need to justify how I was spending my time.

"Why? What time is it?"

"Four o'clock," he said looking at his watch. He looked back at me and added, "Four o'clock on Tuesday."

I frowned.

"Tuesday?" I said, incredulous. "Stop having me on, it's Monday, you numpty. And I went in there just before two so that makes my estimate right. You've clearly spent far too much time roaming the moors. You've lost all sense of time."

"No, Hazel," he said, softly, taking my elbow gently as if I were an invalid in need of assistance. "You're the one who lost time."

I sat, disbelieving, in the chair by Alfie and Edie's fire, clutching a mug of tea in my nerveless fingers as I desperately trying to unravel what had happened to me.

"It's like that in there, sometimes," said Edie, handing me a tuna sandwich. "Here, eat that. Get a bit of protein into you, you're looking a mite peaky."

"Aye," said Alfie. "He doesn't do it a purpose of course. He's one of them that treads very lightly over this side of the Hedge, a real stickler for courtesies and whatnot. A grand old sort he is, from very clever stock but he's not too much of himself with it, aye? He's just as happy having a pint in the Forge and a game of darts as he is sipping the Solstice wine and banging on about his books."

"It's true, Hazel," said Toby, "Mr. Pickle is a great bloke but he has a sort of unconscious habit of slowing time when he's enjoying himself. He must've taken a real shine to you for that to happen."

I chewed a mouthful of sandwich and swallowed. I hadn't realized how hungry I was.

"Oh, we had the loveliest chat," I said, "And he took me all around his shop. What a marvellous place that is. It's like a bit of heaven in there, all of my favourite things. And he even stocks my books!"

I sighed, wistful at the thought of the shop and how it had made me feel to be in there. I had that slightly surreal, disconnected feeling that sometimes happens when you come home after a lovely holiday. Full of the good memories and not quite ready to return to ordinary life.

"And so he should!" said Edie, full of pride. Next to Nan, she'd always been one of my biggest encouragers. I wondered how she'd feel if I switched to writing different stories. Would she be disappointed? I couldn't bear that. Speaking of disappointment, it came to me suddenly that they all knew I was planning on leaving Winkle.

I had my first real wobble. Still, there was no sense beating around the bush, it had to be faced at some point.

"Listen," I said, staring down at my hands, feeling my chin start to tremble. "I know how you all must be feeling, like I'm letting you down by not staying on at the cottage."

The only sounds were the fire in the grate and a quiet bubbling coming from the kitchen. Edie had a pan of soup on the hob.

I cleared my throat, trying to dislodge the threatening clog of tears.

"And I *am* letting you down, I know that. But no matter how hard I try to do the best thing, someone is going to end up being let down. Talking with Mr.Pickle today was the closest I've felt in a very long time to feeling like I belonged somewhere."

I looked up at the faces around me, all of them so very dear in their own way. Even Toby, I had to grudgingly admit.

"I mean, you all make me feel like I belong but it's a bit different..oh dear, I'm making a complete bollocks of this!"

I sniffled and someone handed me a tissue.

"We know what you mean, lass," said Edie, putting a hand on my shoulder and giving it a squeeze. "Take your time, there's no rush."

I blew my nose and took a restorative gulp of tea.

"What I'm trying, so very terribly, to say," I said. "Is that Mr. Pickle seemed to really understand what it is to be *me*. For the first time, I felt absolutely comfortable being myself. I didn't once worry about what he was thinking about me. I didn't once worry about saying the wrong thing or making a mistake. I told him everything that was bothering me and he never once tried to tell me I was being unreasonable. We even argued about some things and it was bloody marvellous. Now, because of that, everything is just so very muddled again. I thought I knew what the best thing was, but he helped me to see that it's not quite as straightforward as all that."

My three friends exchanged an indecipherable look. I looked around at them, noticing them shift in their seats. Alfie looked down, refusing to look Edie in the eye. Toby was likewise uneasy.

"What?" I said, "what's going on?"

"While you were missing and we were all out of our minds with worry, we had a chance to think on the way we've all behaved toward you. The lads owe you an apology. As do I," said Edie, glaring at Alfie and then Toby.

"Oh? Whatever for?"

Edie opened her mouth to speak but Toby interrupted her.

"We've all been so bent on sticking it to BMZ and making sure we had our hand in, that we didn't take into account how difficult it must've been for you to come back to Winkle. It can't have been easy to walk into Rookery Cottage after all these years, and with your Nan gone. Especially after everything you've been through."

"Aye," said Alfie, "yon cottage can be a bit touchy, as I'm sure you've noticed."

I thought back to the coldness of the stone floors and distant, standoffish atmosphere, as well as the propensity for my knick-knacks to mysteriously fall off shelves and smash. I chuckled.

"Yes, well, I did notice it was different from what I remembered."

Edie smiled.

"Ah, it were the same when your Nan first took it over," she said, nodding at my raised eyebrow. "And she lived there her whole life, only not as the Caretaker until her own mam passed. 'S'truth, isn't it, our Alfie?"

"Oh aye!" he said, "She had a right terrible time with it. For months she was having to pick her washing up off the ground when there weren't even a breath of wind and re-light the lamps every time the cottage snuffed them out with one of its mysterious draughts."

He slapped a knee and laughed loudly.

"Eh! Do you remember the first time she tried to light the stove?"

"Do I?" laughed Edie. "It took her months to grow her eyebrows back!"

I stared at them with wide eyes. I couldn't believe what I was hearing. I'd only ever known the cottage to be a warm and welcoming place when my Nan was there. All things considered, I'd had it fairly easy.

"I thought it was just me," I whispered, the realization dawning on me that perhaps I wasn't quite so ill-suited after all. "I thought it didn't think I was, I don't know, worthy, I suppose."

"Aw, pet," said Edie, reaching over to pat my knee. "It must've been a terrible time for you."

She glared at the men again.

"See what you lot've done now?" she said, "Completely disregarded our poor lass and her struggles, never thinking how hard of a time she might be having, and her feeling like she'd not a soul to share it with. There you all were, going after her with your demands and accusations." She directed the last bit towards Toby.

"Alright, alright," said Toby, crossly, his face flushed like an errant schoolboy. "I think we know we've been thoughtless muttonheads, don't we, Alfie?"

"Speak for yourself, laddie," chortled Alfie, winking at me. "Speak for yourself."

Toby scowled.

"Ah, give over, Heathcliff," said Alfie, slapping Toby's knee and bursting into laughter at the look on his face at the Heathcliff reference. "Don't take on so! That's the trouble with you, always so serious about everything."

"Hmph!"

"Well," said Edie, rescuing the situation before Toby got any huffier. "What they're trying rather poorly to say, is that we're all very sorry for rushing you into this. It's a powerful lot to take in and we've barely given you room to breathe, have we? It's no wonder you want to tell us all to get stuffed and go back to London."

"It is a bit overwhelming," I admitted. "But everyone seemed to be so casual about it, like it was the easiest and most natural thing in the world for me to just step in and take over where Nan left off. It was all too much, and I felt like I wasn't up to the task. Then, with Bracken going and Mum's attempt to have me declared unfit...well, it was a case of an overburdened camel and a last straw."

"And now?" asked Toby, leaning forward.

I shrugged, my head still full of the new information and my heart still full of what had happened when I was with Mr.Pickle.

"I don't know, Toby. I really don't know."

Toby walked me home.

"It's different for everyone," he said, breaking a long silence. The light was just fading and the hedge rustled with the creatures settling in for the evening. There was a hint of woodsmoke in the damp air.

"Hm?"

"The shop. Mr. Pickle's shop. It adjusts according to who's in there. That's why it had all of your favourite things in it."

I thought about that for a moment, letting it sink in.

"Oh, he's registered with His Majesty as a stationer, for the taxes and whatnot — he's very conscientious about being a good citizen of Winkle. But beyond the basic stock, it'll vary according to who's in there."

"That must get very confusing if there's more than one person in the shop at a time," I said, grinning to imagine my ink pots competing with bags of flour or fishing tackle.

Toby chuckled.

"That's another funny thing," he said. "I don't think I've ever seen another soul in there when I've been in."

"What's in your shop, then?" I asked, grabbing his sleeve and bumping against him. I was feeling magnanimous, the effect of the shop was lingering. "Row upon row of corduroy trousers in every shade of neutral? Bulk bins of sheep dip?"

I looked up at his face in the dim light, expecting to see him grinning along with my little jest but his features were solemn. I prodded him with my elbow.

"I'm kidding, Toby. I'm sure your depths have been heretofore un-mined. I bet your shop is full of all sorts of lovely stuff, eh? Tolstoy and the collected works of Browning and Keats?

He smiled faintly and shrugged.

"Aye, something like that."

"Oh! I know!" I said, tugging his arm. "I bet there's a whole section devoted to..."

"HobNobs!"

We said it at the same time and burst into laughter, then quickly shushed ourselves as we walked past the lit windows of the last few cottages on the road.

"Come on, then," I said, holding up one of my parcels. "I'll put the kettle on and we can try out my new brew. Who knows, maybe we'll be instantly transported to NetherWinkle whereupon we'll have all manner of grand adventures.

"You're quite daft," said Toby, taking the bag from me. "You're actually starting to sound like you did when we were kids."

Chapter Twenty-Nine

T he offices of Westham County Records (Historical Department) are in the gloomy basement of a three-storey office building on the Main Street in Westham. The building itself is of Edwardian provenance and looks to have stalled there, in appointments *and* maintenance. The lighting is dim, which only serves to make the place look darker, clad as it is in dark panelling and oppressive oil paintings of long-ago bureaucrats. It wouldn't surprise me to know that it's haunted by the unquiet ghost of a downtrodden clerk of the Dickensian persuasion. Entering into the cramped reception area, I saw a tightly-permed, bespectacled woman perched on a high stool behind a towering desk, like some sort of malevolent, all-seeing bird. She looked down at me over her long nose and the rims of her glasses. Somewhere a phone rang and various bits of office machinery hummed and clanked behind her.

"May I help you?" she said, although her tone and expression suggested that was the last thing she wanted to do.

"Yes, please," I said, refusing to be cowed by her apparent disdain for the people she was being paid to assist.

"I need to do a search..."

"Time period?" she barked, looking pointedly at a large stack of leather-bound ledgers.

"Well, I...I'm not exactly certain," I said, rummaging in my satchel for the papers I'd found in the attic. "I have..."

"Young lady," she said, her voice pitched low so that I had to lean in towards her to hear. She smelled of a strange combination of euca-lyptus and parma violets. She wore an engraved name tag on the end of a long chain. Constance Waverley, was at my service. Or not, as the case may be.

"What you see here in these volumes is merely the indices of the last *fifty* years worth of documents. What you do *not* see are the volumes representing the entire collection of this office, which contains the last three *hundred* years of property deeds, marriages, births, deaths, land transfers..."

She was enumerating each item on her bony, beringed fingers.

"I don't have a date on my document," I said, interrupting her ode to bureaucracy. "At least, I can't quite decipher it. Maybe if you would just look..."

She held up her skeletal hand.

"Absolutely not," she said. "I am not here in the capacity of a reference librarian. If you don't know what you're doing, you'll need to make an appointment with our archivist. I can't have you pawing, willy-nilly through these valuable documents."

"Oh," I said, secretly relieved. "That would be fine. Very helpful, thank you."

She lifted a smaller, slightly more modern notebook down from a shelf behind her. Pushing her glasses up her nose, she licked her thumb and forefinger and started flipping the pages. "I'm sure there'll be something available the first of next month..."

"Oh, no! That's too far off, I can't wait that long," I said, my heart sinking. By the first of next month my mother would expect me to be moving into a modern flat in a fashionable district.

Her mouth pursed into a tight point.

I dug deep.

"Mrs. Waverley," I said, summoning up the most pleading tone I could muster. "I realize you're obviously a very busy person. You clearly have a great deal of responsibility here, as guardian of these extremely valuable documents."

Her face softened, ever so slightly.

"I was really hoping I could appeal to your good and generous nature and you'd find your way to squeezing me in a bit sooner? You see, I'm on a rather special, somewhat sensitive, assignment from Lord Dummell. A bit of family intrigue, you see. I can't really speak about it, but you know how it is with the aristocracy."

I was appealing to her innate snobbery.

She sighed noisily through her nose, but the corner of her mouth twitched almost imperceptibly into a smile.

"Sit down over there," she gestured towards a row of hard, uncomfortable-looking chairs. "I'll see if Mr. Wainwright can see you."

Mr.Wainwright turned out to be a dusty, dormouse of a man, thoroughly supportive of the stereotype of archivist and librarian. Dressed almost entirely in sand-coloured tweed, with sand-coloured hair and

a slightly sallow complexion, he was in great danger of being camou-
flaged by the faded beige paintwork in the tiny room which he called
his office. He scurried about, moving piles of paper and files from
one surface onto another, to make room for me at the long table that
spanned the entire room.

"I very much appreciate your seeing me," I said, anxious to keep in
his good books. "I know you must be very busy."

He snorted, a sound which came out as more of an indignant
squeak.

"Not particularly, my dear," he said, gesturing to me that I should
sit down. "I'm something of a liability these days, as far as the county
council is concerned. We're the last outpost, as it were, of paper records
that go as far back as ours do. Most things are computerized now and
it's only because of certain...complexities," he waved a hand at the piles
and stacks of paper, "that I'm kept around. They suffer me, but not
with good grace."

He tilted his head and smiled. There was a sadness in his pale,
watery green eyes. I was filled with the sudden urge to comfort him.
He seemed so very lost.

"I'm sure that's not the case," I said, wanting desperately for it to
not be so, but knowing it was very probably true. The main focus of
everything these days seems to be automation, reducing the need for
the human element. I hadn't given it much thought until that moment, but now the idea of losing people like Mr.Wainwright seemed
unbearable. There wasn't a computer in the universe that would have
the passion for preservation and history that the Mr.Wainwrights of
the world must have. As a writer and lifelong bookworm, I knew the
incredible importance of having people with a passion for the written
word in all of its forms. After all, I was the child who practically lived at

the library and considered the local librarian to be of demi-god status. I told him so.

He shrugged his hunched shoulders, and smiled beatifically, momentarily making him look like a beige tortoise. He was a shape-shifting woodland creature.

"Thank you, dear girl. It's kind of you to say, and does my heart good to hear it. Although, the truth of it is that it's the folk that make the rules and policies that have the final say in these things and most of them don't look past the balance sheets. Nevertheless," he said, shrugging again. "I'm here today and that's what matters. Now, how can I be of assistance?"

"I'm here at the behest of Lord Dummell," I said, pausing to see if that held as much weight as I hoped it would. Mr. Wainwright merely blinked. "Erm, a matter of some importance regarding the deeds and rights pertaining to Rookery Farm and the land thereabouts?"

Something flitted across his expression then. I pushed the papers that I'd found in Nan's attic across the table and he reached out a trembling hand to pull them closer. He paused, took a deep breath and took out a large handkerchief, polishing his glasses before putting them back on.

He frowned down at the papers, his fingers drumming on the table. I barely breathed.

"Very interesting," he said, his voice quavering slightly. "And you came to be in possession of these documents, how?"

He looked up at me, his watery eyes beetling with intensity through the lenses of his glasses.

"I found them in my Nan's attic," I said. "Well, my attic now, I suppose. I'm the new resident of Rookery Cottage."

I bit my lip and flushed slightly, feeling a stab of guilt at the half-truth. Then again, I reasoned with myself, I *was* still the resident so it wasn't *actually* a lie.

"I see, I see. And do you understand the relevance of these papers?"

"Well, I think so. Actually, to be honest, no, I'm not entirely sure what they mean. I can't say I'm very familiar with the language and the script…well….I was told that they would help us to block access to the forced acquisition of some land."

Mr.Wainwright nodded, frowning down again at the papers. "Yes, yes. The wind farm, I'm familiar with the situation. Terrible business. Very clever, though. They're getting craftier by the decade."

He sighed again and took off his glasses, rubbing his eyes before putting them back on. He leaned his elbows on the table and steepled his fingers.

"Miss Price," he began.

"Hazel, please."

"Hazel," he inclined his head, smiling gently. "I'm sorry to say that there's nothing in these papers that will help with thwarting the access that the developers want. These are merely agreements signed between the ancestors of Lord Dummell and the Talbot family of Rookery Farm. What it is, is a deed of trust, drafted some time around 1325."

He waved a hand at my expression of disbelief.

"Nothing terribly new or revolutionary there. Those sorts of things weren't uncommon during the time of the Crusades. I suspect a leading member of Lord Dummell's family planned to join the merry band of murderers and so left the estate in trust to the Talbot family, lest one of the heathens get a good shot in. Well, stab, I suppose that would be."

"So nothing that could potentially block the proceedings, then?"

I felt a hollow, sinking feeling in my chest and a tremor of anxiety knotted my stomach.

No, I thought, this couldn't be. We'd been so sure. How was I going to break the news?

Mr. Wainwright shook his head.

"Not in and of itself," he held up a hand, "However, " he continued, "There *is* reference here to another document which may be of some use. In fact, I'm quite certain it's the document that Lord Dummell was hoping to have access to."

"But that's good news, isn't it?" I said, clinging to this raft of hope. "I assume that it's here, in your records?"

Mr. Wainwright nodded.

I beamed at him.

"Fantastic! Now, do I have to fill out a requisition form or something? I'd be very happy to do that."

"Yes, yes," he said, "That is the usual way of things."

He paused and ran a finger around the edge of his shirt collar before clearing his throat.

"Unfortunately," he said, "the approval for access to this particular document must be granted by the member of council in charge of these things."

"Oh," I said, envisioning a bureaucratic wrangling that would stretch the procedure out even longer. I tried not to think about how much time I might have left in Winkle. I really wanted to see this through.

"How long will that take?"

Mr. Wainwright got up from the table and went to the door of his office. Opening it, he popped his head out and looked up and down the hallway. Glancing at his pocket watch, he nodded and then closed the door again, turning the lock.

I swallowed hard, my imagination suddenly running off with itself. Was he some sort of serial murderer? Were there bodies buried behind the stacks of dusty boxes? I managed a bright sort of I'm-not-concerned-that-you-might-be-a-nutter smile.

"The trouble with that, dear girl, is that the person in charge of those approvals is Mr. Abernathy Trout."

What happened next was worthy of the most well-executed of MI5 manoeuvres.

It soon became apparent that there was no love lost between Mr. Wainwright and Mr. Trout. The Honourable Abernathy was apparently spear-heading the attempt to have the Archives and Records office closed down to the public. He wanted the files and documents therein transported to permanent storage with the British Library, just like every other regional records office, and having restricted access on the pretence of preservation. It was as close as he could come to destroying the lot, explained Mr. Wainwright, bitterly.

"But why would he care?" I asked, bewildered but somehow not really surprised that a Trout was responsible for trying to ruin something lovely and worthwhile.

Mr. Wainwright tapped the papers on the desk.

"Because of these, dear girl," he said, his voice rising to an indignant squeak. "Papers like these represent the difference between that lot of heartless bureaucrats lining their pockets and the preservation of this fine land. These papers represent not only the preservation of the *land*, but of this community and a way of life that goes back hundreds of years. Not to mention the goodwill of our friends on the other side of the Hedge. A goodwill, I might add, that would be very much in our interests to maintain."

I felt there ought to have been a rising crescendo of orchestral accompaniment to his speech. I looked down at the papers, half-expecting to see...well, I wasn't really sure what I expected to see. Certainly not the mildew-spotted, barely legible scrawl that was there.

"Oh," I said, with a small smile.

"Now, listen here."

He then outlined a plan whereby there was a forgery of signature ("Trout has the penmanship of a trained ape") and a quick trip to the photocopy machine in the reception area ("That Waverley creature will be gone on her lunch break until 12:55pm exactly").

"But don't I need the original document to give to our solicitor?" I asked. "Lord Dummell seemed quite convinced we'd need the original."

"Not when you have this," he said, handing me over a rather official-looking form.

It was an affidavit stating the historical and cultural importance of the document in question and due to the nature of the extreme fragility of the aforementioned document, it could not be released from its protected archival conditions.

I grinned.

"Beats him at his own game, doesn't it? Did you know I was coming?" I asked, curious as to how he could've had this all planned out in advance.

Mr. Wainwright grinned, revealing a row of crooked, beige teeth, returning him to the role of a contented dormouse.

"Not this exact situation, dear girl. I simply like to be prepared in the event of a need. I've always fancied myself with a bit of flair for subterfuge and it will make my day to stick it to that menace, Trout, and his band of cronies. If they're going to get rid of me, I'm determined to get a few parting shots in. Besides," he added with a chuckle, "I was that fond of your Nan. She used to make a grand cup of tea and I'll never forget her kindness over the incident all those years ago."

"Incident?" I said, raising an eyebrow.

Mr. Wainwright coloured slightly and shook his head.

"Not important, just now," he said, turning to rummage in a drawer. "We've no time to waste if we want to thwart that wretched woman at the front desk. She guards that photocopy machine like it was a state secret. It'll be bad enough when she finds out someone made a copy without her knowledge. Oh aye, she keeps track. It'll have her head spinning for days. Desperate harpy of a woman, she is."

I stood waiting for about twenty minutes, which felt like an eternity, while Mr. Wainwright disappeared through a small door that led from the back of his tiny office.

"Sorry, my dear Hazel," he'd said, as he donned a pair of white painter's overalls and pulled on shoe covers, white cotton gloves and a shower cap. "We may not have the state-of-the-art hermetically-sealed conditions that these documents require, but I do my best to keep them safe from the ravages of your everyday pollutants. I'll have to ask you to wait here while I find what it is you're needing."

I nodded and tried to look at ease. The truth was, I was a ball of nerves. I was worried that the intrigue necessary to secure this paperwork would come back to bite us in the backsides. I knew from reading detective novels that all it took to destroy a legal case was a silly loophole of procedure. Surely, forging a document and acquiring evidence illegally qualified as a loophole of procedure? The rule-follower in me trembled at the thought but I had to admit it was also a bit thrilling at the same time. I was left with a churning stomach and an irrepressible grin.

Eventually, the door opened and Mr Wainwright re-emerged, a toothy grin engulfing his features. He held aloft a brown envelope in a triumphant gesture worthy of a sports hero.

"Here it is!" he squeaked. "Quickly now, get yourself to the photocopy machine. Do three copies of each page – there's three pages. Hurry now! Don't forget the gloves and handle the pages like they were spun gold!"

I grabbed the envelope (gently) and shot out the door and down the hallway to the main reception area. There wasn't a soul in sight. I glanced at the clock. I had ten minutes to get the copies and get back to the records office before Mrs. Waverley returned.

With trembling fingers, clumsy in their white cotton gloves, I unwound the string that held the envelope closed, cursing my nerves for the hundredth time. Carefully, I pulled the sheets of paper out, trying to hold them at the edges like Mr. Wainwright had showed me.

It was more parchment than paper, which is perhaps why it felt sturdier than I would've imagined for a document of such great age. I held each page gingerly in my fingertips, trying not to breathe on them, thinking with horror that I was getting corrosive gases all over the precious artifact. I should've borrowed a mask from Mr. Wainwright. According to him, the document had been drafted in 1239, three years after the Commons Act. If I'd had more time, I would've paused long enough to marvel that I was holding such an old document in my hand, and wondered about the people who had written it, who had commissioned it and who had kept it safe all these years. I was the sort of person for whom that level of deep historical connection was a sort of magic. Like old furniture and old buildings, the stories that were soaked into the very existence of them took my breath away. Imagine if they would have spoken! But, I hadn't the time for such fanciful musings. Besides, the document was written in an archaic form of French and I had only a schoolgirl grasp of the modern version.

I located the copy machine and prayed it didn't require a key or a passcode or had some other security feature. It wouldn't have been unexpected considering Mrs. Waverley's fierce policing of its use but then again, perhaps she had so much faith in her omnipresence that she felt safe not having one. There was a level of carelessness when one was that drunk with power. Happily, our particular dragon was sufficiently inebriated by said power to have not bothered with trifling security measures and I was able to make my copies. I put the original back into its envelope, tucked the copies under my arm and went back through the door leading to Mr. Wainwright's office. Just as the door closed behind me I heard the sound of someone coming into the reception area — it was Mrs. Waverley, haranguing some underling about checking the phone messages. It wasn't until I put my hand on the doorknob of Mr.Wainwright's office that I realized I was holding my breath. I let it out in a long, quivering exhale then marched through the door with my own triumphant grin.

I stayed for a glass of sherry and plate of shortbread with Mr. Wainwright. We thought it only reasonable to celebrate our little victory, our 'sticking it to the man' as he put it. It was such an apt statement, but so oddly out of character for such an old-fashioned little fellow, that I couldn't help but burst out laughing. He joined in and we were apparently loud enough to attract the attention of Ms. Waverley who came storming down the hall, burst into the room and demanded that we cease our joviality immediately.

Like a pair of disgraced schoolchildren we nodded and attempted to pull our faces straight, all the while feeling the laughter bubbling up.

"Ah, lassie," said Mr. Wainwright, wiping the tears from his eyes after the door slammed behind Miss Waverley. "I've not had a laugh like that in a long, long while."

I smiled at him, thinking much the same.

"But you know what makes my heart the most glad?" he asked.

I shook my head, reaching for another shortbread biscuit.

"It surely makes my old heart glad to know that we've got someone like you to look after things. I feel like all of my efforts into hanging onto this place, all the fighting to stay on and look after these bits of paper when it would be so much easier to just roll over and take their pay-out package and let it all go, well I feel like it's naught been in vain when there's a young lass like you to take over the job of keeping it all safe and looked after."

He smiled his dormouse smile at me, his eyes filling with tears behind his glasses as he reached across the table and patted my wrist.

My own eyes filled, but for a very different reason than his.

Chapter Thirty

"And this one, you'll find, is a very classic example of nouveau countryside," exclaimed the tall, willowy real estate agent. She gestured with a perfectly manicured hand towards the renovated cowshed, now named The Byre, according to the plaque on the wall, that stood on the edge of a freshly sandblasted cobblestone yard. The cowshed stood at right angles to the old dairy — now also an Upwardly Mobile Dwelling — and across from the original farmhouse which had been divided into three separate flats. The former stable block made up the other side of the square and managed to support four residences — two up and two down. All of them were grouped around the yard which the brochure boasted as 'community outdoor space' in which we were supposed to hold barbecues and wine-tastings and games of croquet. The croquet, of course, was to be played on the immaculately groomed grass of the "orchard", adjacent to the yard which currently sported only two living trees, the rest having been deemed too aesthetically displeasing to stay.

"The original windows were, of course, too small to be serviceable and so the architect took some artistic licence and reconfigured them to allow for the most natural lighting possible. Paired with the hand-tooled, artisan window frames and reclaimed glass you can see the result is truly magnificent. As you can see here, the original, artisanal stonework…"

I wondered to myself if I ought to be counting how many times she'd say 'artisanal' and did 'reclaimed glass' mean they got the windows out of a construction skip? Mum was making all of the required ooh-ings and ahh-ings so I allowed my mind to wander.

It was a lovely little cottage, I had to agree. Not quite as large as Rookery Cottage but it had the same old feel to it, if only on the outside. The inside was pretty much standard fare for modern living — shiny appliances, white plaster walls, hardwood flooring. Nice, but soulless. Still, there was a great deal of history soaked into the stone and timber that had survived the architect's whims; that it was the history of generations of cows, didn't escape my notice. I considered asking how they got the smell of dung out of the stone. A great deal of chemical treatment, I imagine. Whatever it took to sanitize the original purpose out of it.

I wondered what my dad would've thought of this place. Ambleside Farm Estate, by name. The original Ambleside Farm had been in the Smithers family for six generations, according to the brochure, but apparently the newest generation didn't fancy the vagaries of agricultural life and had sold off the whole thing for a whopping sum to a developer of these nouveau countryside dwellings. Apparently, they'd even filmed an episode of Escape to the Country here last year. I think he'd have been as sad as I was, walking through the scrubbed and polished door, given our mutual preference for maintaining things in their original state. His business favoured preservation over renovation and I knew he faced a lot of criticism – a lot of it from my mum – for not doing lucrative conversion projects like this one.

I couldn't help but think of Rookery Farm and Young Craig and how, despite not wanting to farm the way his uncle had, he had set those desires aside to keep it in the family. And now with the land seizure threatening, how would that impact the farm if it went through? The idea of the end of generations of farming, of relationship with the land, was a sobering thought. I stuffed down an annoying pang of guilt.

"Well, darling? What do you think? Isn't it just the absolute perfect thing? It's quaint and farm-ish so that should appeal to your tastes. But instead of being a rambling ruin, it's all fresh and modern. Perfect compromise, wouldn't you say?"

Mum was in her element. We'd spent the last two days traipsing from cottage to house to flat to renovated outbuilding. She'd struck up an immediate best-friends-forever relationship with the estate agent; Mindy was her name. I doubted that, but that was the name she was using. Her real name was probably Barbara or Eleanor but that wouldn't have suited her high-powered real estate tycoon image. Obviously, I'd developed opinions about Mindy/Barbara and her penchant for profiting from the rape and pillage of local culture and I was finding it increasingly difficult to keep those opinions to myself

But with mum it had been non-stop declarations of delight and paroxysms of perfection. She seemed terribly pleased with herself that she'd organized the viewing of these countrified properties, imagining she was being extremely understanding and supportive of my desire to live in a small village, away from the city. The fact that every single one of the places we looked at was about five minutes drive from a major roadway didn't count. Nor did the fact that there was no actual *village* to speak of as most of the houses were weekend or commuter homes.

Not only that, many of the properties had been reclaimed from their original purposes, thereby signifying the end of a long-held way of life. There was little to no resemblance to traditional country life in any of these places. A lack, I was coming to realize, that was more and more depressing every time I was made aware of it. Despite my desire for a hermit's existence, the village community was something I'd come to value very much.

"Yes, lovely," I said, trying my very best to mean it, I didn't want to sound ungrateful. "I wonder, though, when it gets damp, does the smell of the cows seep through?"

"That was entirely uncalled for, Hazel Price. The smell of the cows! Honestly! That poor woman didn't know what to do with herself. You know, sometimes I don't know why I'm even bothering trying to help you. I'm simply trying to make things easier, trying to reduce your stress around the whole matter. I really should just let you get on with it and you can move into some grotty old flat above a village chippy."

We were sitting in the Forge, having worn Mindy out. Well, that's what I assumed anyway, by the look on her face when Mum said we'd call it a day after my comments about The Byre. A mixture of relief and elation, is what I interpreted it as. Or maybe that was just how *I'd* felt at the prospect of calling it a day. I smiled and thanked Ernie for his delivery, then poured us both a cup of tea from the wonky purple pot.

"Have one of those coconut things," I said, gesturing towards the three-tiered cake stand that held an assortment of high-tea-like confections. "Ernie's wife makes them. With butter from Neth...with grass-fed butter."

Mum gave me a look which suggested she knew precisely where the butter had come from. She pursed her lips and made a point of not taking a coconut square, opting instead for the raspberry tarts. I decided not to mention that Mrs. Goodship supplied the raspberries. Which weren't actually raspberries but a NetherWinkle cousin of the raspberry that had a hint of honey and cloves in the flavour. Quite an otherworldly taste. Literally.

"Oooh! These are lovely," said Mum, dabbing the invisible crumbs at the corner of her mouth with a napkin. "What a delicate flavour! Anyway, as I was saying. Mindy comes highly recommended and she's taken considerable time out of her schedule to come around with us. She needn't have bothered, you know. She could just as easily have sent a junior agent. Apparently, she's very busy with a new development in Newcastle, a conversion of one of those horrid warehouses down near the docks. I really don't know why you have to be so very difficult."

She said the last sentence leaning towards me with what I imagine she thought was a withering look. All it did was remind me of how much more difficult I could be if only I said what I was thinking instead of what I thought she wanted to hear. I cleared my throat and helped myself to another coconut square, handing her another raspberry tart as I did so.

"I just didn't fancy any of them," I said. "It's horrible to think of all those lovely old farm buildings turned into hipster lofts and places for rich people to visit on weekends. Nobody that lives there even cares about looking after the countryside or preserving the community of the villages. All they want is a tax dodge or somewhere to throw parties that'll make their friends jealous. I bet none of them have so much as a windowsill herb pot."

"Not everyone wants to muck about in the dirt, Hazel. Some people are quite content to get their lettuce at Lidl. I'm surprised at you, passing judgement like that. Aren't you always banging on about being non-judgemental?"

She had me there. But I rationalized that some things were judgement-worthy and buying a house in the country just to show off to your rich friends was one of them.

"Anyway," she went on, sipping her tea daintily. "As I was saying. You'd do well to try and keep a more open mind, and be a bit more flexible. There's no such thing as the absolute perfect place."

"Really?" I said. "As far as I could tell we saw at least five of them, according to you and your friend Mindy."

"Hazel," she said, placing her tea cup down with a precise and deliberate movement. She paused to take a breath, no doubt preparing herself to explain to me the various ways in which I was being unreasonable. "What you need to keep in mind, is that all of those people who sold their farms or their cottages did so of their own volition. Not everyone has the privilege of having high ideals. What the buyer did with them after that was out of their hands. They were lucky to find a buyer, I'm sure, since many of them were paid a pretty penny for what really was just a rundown collection of smelly stone and wood rot. You have an unhelpful habit of falling into a state of nostalgia, Hazel. In a person of your...sensitivities, that can be a treacherous thing. Things just aren't like they are in your storybooks. Besides, the developers are to be commended for putting in the time and effort to preserve those 'lovely old farm buildings', as you call them. You of all people should understand the value of historical preservation. It's only the ground upon which this family's fortune stands. Which would have been worse? A refurbishment or demolition?"

With that, clearly rhetorical, question the subject was closed and we moved on to less confrontational things, like the new suit Dad had bought on his trip and how much Reenie Tyler paid for her haircuts, the exorbitance of which apparently didn't stop her looking like she'd been dragged through a hedge backwards. I paid attention as best I could and made all of the right comments and noises, but inwardly I was seething about how easily she dismissed the importance of caring for the land, not just the buildings on it. The ground upon which our family stood was about more than doing up old buildings and she knew that. If Dad were here, he'd have pulled her up on that one but she was counting on the fact I wouldn't fuss. It *was* more than just the buildings; what about the communities that had vanished? I looked around the Forge, seeing a few familiar faces, people I knew by name at least, and where they lived or who they were related to, even after only being here for a short time.

Outside, on the high street, were the shops I used, almost every day – even the post office with horrid Mrs.Trout had suddenly become dear. What about the treasure that was Tinker, Pickle and Trott? How would it be if Winkle were to be sold off, piece by piece, to indifferent people who just wanted the right to boast about 'their place in the country'? Add to that, the complication that was NetherWinkle.

I resolved in that moment, with even greater conviction, that before I left, I'd do everything in my power to make sure that the land access wasn't granted and BMZ was sent packing. It would be my parting gift to Winkle, for having shown me how much preserving these places mattered to me. Just because I wasn't going to live here myself, didn't mean I couldn't see the incredible value in it and the absolute need to keep it safe.

"Oh please, Hazel dear. Do *not* frown like that, it makes you look sulky and it's not at all becoming. Not to mention the wrinkles you're starting. Are you using that face cream I gave you?"

After promising to meet her the next day for one last round of house-shopping, I kissed Mum on the cheek and saw her into Wendell's taxi with a barely suppressed grin — she was going to enjoy her trip to the train station. I waved until they drove out of sight then breathed a monumental sigh of relief. Finally, I could breathe again. Checking my watch, I saw that I had time to stop in to see Hamish and deliver the papers. I realized I was excited to see the look on his face when I handed them over.

"Hazel! Come in! You're just in time. I've just this minute put the kettle on and Mrs. Finch has left me a pan of the most delicious smelling soup. Will you join me for a bit of something?"

I felt all of the tension of the past few days melt away in the presence of this lovely man. He was just so easy to be around and was the picture of comfort, standing there in the doorway in his worn tweed trousers and argyle pullover. He must have been working in the garden as his shirt sleeves were rolled up and he still had a pair of secateurs sticking out of one pocket. Despite the fact I was full of tea and coconut squares, I readily agreed to sitting down for a bowl of soup with him. No need to make my own meal now. The weight of that had been looming surprisingly large.

"So, what have you been up to?" said Hamish, pouring a ladle-full of fragrant soup into a carved wooden bowl. I recognized it as one I'd seen in Mr. Pickle's shop. "I saw you with your charming mother earlier." He smiled and winked, quite aware of how things were between Mum and I.

"Yes," I said, colouring slightly. I made a point of stirring my soup, avoiding his eyes. "She was taking me around to look at houses and things. You know, for when I move out of the cottage."

The kitchen clock ticked loudly and somewhere outside a lawn-mower fired up. Hamish pulled out a chair, scraping it loudly on the flagstones.

"I see," he said, settling into his seat. He passed over a plate with large, doorsteps of fresh, buttered bread on it. I took one, still without looking at him.

"And?" he prompted, getting up again to fetch the teapot. "Did you see anything you like?"

"Not really," I said. "I mean, there were some lovely places, all very nice and clean and modern."

"But?"

"But," I said, breaking my slice of bread into small pieces and dropping them into my soup. "Even though the buildings were old, some of them even older than Rookery Cottage, they'd been so done out and done over that they'd been rendered entirely, well, I don't know..."

"Soulless?"

I looked up at him, meeting his kind gaze.

"Exactly! They'd had all of the life scrubbed out of them. And there wasn't any sign of there actually being villages, as such. Just groups of houses where people lived. There's a big difference, you know. I hadn't realized that until I came back to Winkle. I had got so used to London; I mean, London is chock-full of people so you couldn't possibly expect to know all of them. And when you can't know all of them, I suspect at some point you don't bother trying to know *any* of them. At least, not the way people around here know each other, and, if I'm honest, I rather hoped it would be the same when I moved here. I just wanted to be left alone to look after Nan's cottage and write my books and grow some flowers and a bit of veg."

"Oh?"

"Well, it's what I *thought* I wanted..."

I stopped and stared down at my soup. There were large lumps of potato and carrot floating in the golden broth, speckled with bits of green and slices of spring onion. I bet everything in it had come from Hamish's garden. I spooned up a mouthful. Delicious.

"And now?" prodded Hamish, pouring a dollop of milk into his tea and stirring vigorously. "Has that changed?"

I sighed.

"Honestly, Hamish, I just don't know. Being here and being a part of this wind farm thing has sort of turned everything on its head. First, I get roped into being involved, then I find out about this whole Caretaker bit and the next thing you know I'm sending off the entirely wrong sort of book proposal to my agent and making illegal photocopies in some secret, underground records office!"

Hamish chuckled. It was a lovely sound but it didn't make my situation any less bewildering.

"I felt it was all too much. I *still* think it's all too much," I said, lest he think I was having a change of heart on that score. "I'm not at all suited to being in charge of things or being responsible for anything but myself because even *that's* a stretch at times. I *still* want to be mostly left alone and I *still* want a quiet, uncomplicated life where I can write stories and look after...well, have a little place to live with a bit of a garden."

I paused, a spoonful of soup halfway to my mouth as I was hit with an abrupt wave of misery. I became suddenly and completely aware that what I really wanted was to stay in Winkle.

Chapter Thirty-One

After our delicious supper of soup and fresh bread, Hamish and I took our refreshed tea mugs into his study to go over the paperwork. He'd been gracious enough to change the subject after my outburst and we'd spent the rest of the meal chatting about our respective gardens and how well the weather was turning. The subject of Murk came up but neither of us had seen him in a while and we both decided that was a good thing.

Settling into the comfort of the worn leather chair, I rested my mug on my knee and waited to see the look on his face when he read through the papers. I'd only glanced at them briefly since smuggling them out of the records office under my cardigan and since it was a whole lot of overwrought legalese and written in arcane French at that, it was even more undecipherable to me than modern, overwrought legalese. But apparently, to a person fluent in such bloated prose, it was the answer to all of our prayers.

Hamish carefully slid the papers back into the envelope and then swivelled his chair around to face the shelves behind him. On the middle shelf stood an old-fashioned fire-safe which he opened with careful deliberation. After putting the envelope in and closing the door, he swivelled himself back to face me and took off his glasses. His wise blue eyes crinkled at the corners as his face split into a wide grin.

"Hazel, my lass. You've done it. That, there," he waved to the safe behind him. "Is going to stop those grasping bastards in their tracks."

I hesitated, my hand poised over the receiver. Should I? It had been my first impulse when I got home from visiting with Hamish, but I was suddenly unsure of my welcome. Perhaps that was an impulse worth challenging. My life was fraught with enough current complications without dredging up old ones.

"Oh, go on," said a familiar voice from behind me. "You know you want to and besides, he'll be all tortured with not having spoken to you for days on end."

Murk.

"You're back," I said, gritting my teeth. "How lovely."

"Your sarcasm is wasted on me," he purred, jumping down off the worktop and twining himself around my ankles. I resisted the urge to send him flying across the room. It wouldn't technically be kicking him, merely helping him along with my foot. I could even make it look like an accident, pretend I'd tripped over him. If only I could be so horrid; it was like throwing slippers at him – completely ceremonial.

He continued, "I'm happily immune to your fickle human moods, which is to say, I couldn't care less how you're feeling. I do, however, care that your indecisiveness in phoning Heathcliff will delay your procuring me a plate of sardines. So, why don't you just ring him up and tell him all of the news then get on with getting me something to eat. I'm half-starved."

"That's a shame," I said, dialling Toby's number. Not because Murk had told me to, but because I was going to all along. That's what I told myself, anyway.

"What's a shame?" he asked, settling himself on the hearth, despite the fact there was no fire in the grate.

"That you're only *half*-starved. It might be better for all of us if the job had been finished."

"Hello, Toby?"

Who else would I be expecting to answer his phone?

"It's me, Hazel."

Good lord.

"Oh. Hello. Anything wrong?"

"No," I said, momentarily confused. Is that the only reason I should be phoning him? I quickly cast about in my memory for every other occasion that I'd phoned him and found I couldn't even remember if I had.

"Quite the opposite, actually."

To drown out the internal cacophony of self-recrimination, I launched into a lengthy description of my adventures with Mr.Wainwright and then my conversation with Hamish, all to the end of being absolutely certain that there was no way the developer could nullify the legislation.

"It goes almost as far back as the Magna Carta," I enthused. "Well, not really, but it carries about as much weight. There's no way they can legal their way around it, according to Hamish, not without a whole lot of research and applications for things that I can't remember but sounded like they'd be time consuming. *Very* time consuming. To the point of it not being worth the time or money, especially since there's an alternate site available. Hamish says it'll do the trick, the council will never go for it."

Silence on the end of the line.

"Toby? Are you still there?"

"Did you find anything?" he asked.

"What? I just told you what I found..."

"No, I mean when you went looking at houses with your mother. Did you find something suitable?"

My turn to be silent. My heart thudded painfully and I felt the familiar clench of anxiety in my stomach. Why, oh why did he have to bring that up?

"Um, no. As a matter of fact I didn't. We're supposed to be going out again tomorrow."

"Oh, I see. Well, good luck. And thanks for letting me know about the paperwork. That's great news, I'll pass it on to Corny. Bye, then."

He rang off and I stood there staring at the telephone wondering exactly what just happened.

"What happened is you're being kept at a distance. In advance of your leaving, you see? I dare say he feels no point in continuing on with your friendship, or whatever it is, if you're just going to abandon them all. And really, can you blame him? Poor mite has issues with being abandoned, you know. Humans are such fragile creatures."

I swallowed the rising lump of tears.

"No," I whispered, feeling thoroughly and utterly bereft for reasons that hardly made sense and to which I really had no right. "I can't blame him at all."

"Now," said Murk, running a paw across one ragged ear. "Instead of feeling sorry for yourself because, let's be honest with ourselves, shall we, it's entirely your own fault, why not get out the tin opener and see to those sardines?"

I tossed and turned most of the night before finally falling into a restless sleep just before dawn. The sound of my alarm blaring jolted me awake, bleary-eyed and headachey. I must have slept right through it because it was almost nine o'clock. I contemplated not bothering to get out of bed at all but as Mum was expecting me to meet her at the train station at half-past ten, I weighed the pros and cons of incurring her wrath. To cancel now would be viewed as a horrendous inconvenience, besides, I'd already booked Wendell to get me there. Mindy had another roster of possible houses and was picking us up in her car at the station. I had barely an hour to get myself ready.

I ran a bath, thinking it would refresh me. It didn't. So I clumped downstairs in my dressing gown to put the kettle on for a fortifying mug of tea. Happily, Murk appeared to have departed at some time in the night. Tiny miracles. My tea hurriedly slurped, I clumped back up the stairs to finish getting dressed. I made a point of picking out an outfit most likely to offend the sensibilities of my mum and also, by virtue of her upward mobility and power-suits, Mindy. A pale turquoise linen pinafore (thrifted) over a hand-embroidered vintage petticoat (thrifted then modified by me to cover up a stain on the hem); a white, crinkle-cotton t-shirt, (to complete my un-ironed look), a pair of purple and green striped knee-high socks and one of my hand-knit cardigans, in case it got cold. I may not have the courage to change my mind but I refused to go quietly. I briefly considered putting my hair in two plaits again but decided against it. That might be a bridge too far.

"Hazel! What in heaven's name are you wearing? Why must you insist on looking like an overgrown child, I simply don't know. However will people take you seriously when you're dressed like that?"

Rhetorical questions, none of them unfamiliar. I just smiled and tried to look admonished, while silently noting the win.

"Now, Mindy will be picking us up shortly but I wanted a word with you before she arrives. Dad and I were speaking and we've decided that any profits beyond the asking price of your new home that come from the sale of the cottage will go to you. Mindy has assured me that with some very slight modernizations and a nice, minimalist decor, we'll get a very good price for it. Now, how does that sound? A nice little nest egg to tide you over if the sales from your stories start dropping. Which, let's face it, is bound to happen eventually. It's just the fickle nature of publishing, isn't it? I really think you should consider finding more steady employment. What about the flower arranging? You could use the profits from the cottage to set yourself up. Oh! I know! What about you and Roger? He told me he was wanting to get out of London and go to work for himself. In fact, I said to him…"

I tuned her out. It was the same old thing; she had a knack of zeroing in on the things that mattered the most to me and making them seem unimportant, as if I were silly to have them mean something. The trouble was, it was all done with the kindest and most generous of intentions so one felt churlish for getting annoyed or offended. Bossing people around is my mother's love language. She shows she cares by trying to make everything perfect for her loved ones. The only flaw with that approach is that her idea of perfection isn't necessarily the same as mine. Or my dad's. I think he finds it easier to go along with things though I often found myself wondering if he'd ever rebelled and if he did, what it looked like. I smiled inside at the look on Mum's face in just such an imaginary scenario.

I was rescued from further suggestions on how to improve my life by the arrival of Mindy. Her shiny, silver Mercedes glided to a stop at the curb, causing heads to turn in admiration. She twinkled her fingers at us as we hurried down to the car, aware that every second of her time was spoken for. That's another thing I find unsettling about people like Mindy; they always make you feel rushed, like you should scurry to keep pace. Those sorts of people are especially hard on people like me, who are ever in a state of bumble at even the most pedestrian of paces. Life among Teddy's cronies was much like that; I always felt ten steps behind and three conversations out of date. It's one of the many reasons I love the company of my friends in Winkle, especially people like Hamish, Edie and Alfie, they're just so very restful to be around.

I shook my head. It was no use getting lost in the nostalgia of Winkle. I'd made my decision and had to follow through. There was far too much at stake now, all of this time with Mindy and my parent's plans to help me finance a new place until the cottage sold. I found I couldn't think of it as Nan's anymore. It made the whole thing too unbearable. Besides, the cottage had a mind of its own and would accept or reject anyone who lived there, regardless of their pedigree.

I redirected my attention to the conversation in the car. Naturally, I sat in the back seat and my mum in the front with Mindy. Mum held a sheaf of papers, the particulars of today's viewings, I presumed. She was rifling through them excitedly. She really was in her element. I couldn't help but smile at her enthusiasm.

"Oh, Hazel, darling. Mindy has some truly wonderful properties here! You know what?"

She clapped her hands together in glee, her eyes sparkling.

"I really do think that today is the day!"

Mindy tinkled a laugh, tossing her glossy hair back over her shoulder as she turned in her seat to look at me. She was flawlessly made up, but I could see evidence of tiredness in her eyes. I smiled, suddenly feeling sorry for her. What must it be like to be so driven all of the time? It must be a standard that's nearly impossible to maintain.

"What do you think, Hazel?" she asked. "Do you feel as if today's the day you find your dream property?"

I didn't want to disappoint her so I smiled wider.

"It just might be!" I replied, reaching across the space to squeeze my mum's fingers as she extended her hand.

Mindy turned around and expertly guided the car out of the station and into traffic.

My heart gently broke because, again, I already knew where my dream property was. But, in my usual way, I'd let my fear of not being good enough ruin everything. It was a self-fulfilling prophecy that had stalked me my entire life and I had no idea how to change it.

Chapter Thirty-Two

The phone shrilled loudly as I struggled in through the door. I had a collection of shopping bags tangled over my wrist, making it difficult to grab the latch. I muttered a few curses and then suddenly, the door sprang open, seemingly of its own accord.

"No sense trying to suck up to me now," I grumbled at the cottage. "Bit late for that, don't you think?"

Not expecting a response, I dumped my bags and grabbed the phone.

"Hazel? Jolly good, old thing. I was almost going to ring off. In the garden were you? Listen, we're marshalling the troops for a bit of grub at The Forge and a last-minute strategy meeting. Toby tells me you've saved the day and got us the papers we need. Bloody magnificent, darling gel, I knew you could do it. Seven o'clock sharp. We'd meet earlier but the youngsters have theatre rehearsal in Westham and can't get a bus. See you then!"

Lord Dummell. I suppose that steamrolling over me was easier than having to wade through my potential excuses for not going. He certainly had me figured out.

I glanced at the clock on the mantel. It was just past six o'clock. I thought longingly of my plans to curl up on the sofa with a glass of wine and the new book I'd just bought. Mum had treated me to a take-out from Bombay Delight in Eastham and I had my mouth all ready for a vindaloo. I sighed. I supposed it would heat up for lunch tomorrow. I felt a sudden pang as I'd just about said as much out loud to Bracken, before remembering that she wasn't there. How long before I stopped missing her?

I switched on the lamps in the living room and unpacked my shopping. I was only buying small amounts of things, not wanting to have too much to take with me to my new place. It was a strange way to live and I didn't like it one bit. Part of me was pretending I'd just phone my mother and tell her I was staying — I had it all planned in a vivid fantasy where Rhonda had been thrilled with my book proposal and had already accepted a six-figure, three book deal on my behalf. I was also far braver in this fantasy and took on the role of Caretaker as easily as I took charge of my duties for the village fête.

I was replaying the part where I picked up the phone to call Toby to tell him I was staying (not dwelling too much on why he'd be the one I called first) when the ringing of the actual phone almost caused me to drop the packet of shortbread I was holding.

"Jesus wept," I said, taking a shaky breath. "Hello?"

"Hello, Hazel."

Toby.

"Hi Toby," I said, mildly freaked out by the coincidence. "Everything alright?"

I spared a nanosecond to reflect on how we each seemed to assume that some crisis had occurred in order to justify a phone call.

"Sure, sure. I was just wondering if you wanted a lift to the Forge? You are coming, aren't you?"

I paused before answering. It wasn't exactly on his way to come by here and pick me up. What did that mean? Anything, or nothing? Was I forgiven? That was probably asking too much. Lord Dummell had probably put him up to it. They were probably driving together anyway.

"Well, considering Lord Dummell didn't bother waiting for me to respond when he phoned just now, I'd say that's a yes," I replied, with a noise somewhere between a laugh and a sigh.

Toby chuckled.

"Ah, that's just his way. He's always been a bit dubious of the modern technology."

We both laughed again. Lord Dummell thought any technology developed after the telephone to be greatly suspect and to be avoided whenever possible. Part of me could really get behind that philosophy.

"Are you sure it's not out of your way?" I asked, knowing full well that it was.

Toby snorted. I wasn't sure if it was a snort of derision or a laugh-snort. I was getting annoyed with myself for even caring.

"Of course it is, but the offer stands."

I resisted the urge to waffle, trying to guess his motives and to then act in the way that would best prevent misunderstanding or upset. I also resisted the urge to self-flagellate over how much I overthink everything.

"Well, in that case, it would be rude of me not to accept," I replied, keeping my tone light and friendly. Surely that couldn't be misconstrued.

"Indeed it would. See you at 6:45-ish, then?"

Without waiting for an answer, he rang off.

Well, I thought, putting the receiver back on the cradle, that's that, then.

Toby honked the horn at exactly 6:44pm. That was fine, because I'd been standing at the window watching out for him since 6:35pm. It was an old habit from the days when I got a lift to Brownie's with a friend's father. He was ex-military and had a gruff, terrifying manner and a penchant for punctuality.

I hadn't bothered getting changed. My designed-to-shock outfit wouldn't even raise an eyebrow amongst the Hedge Defence crowd, or anyone else in Winkle, for that matter. Except perhaps Mrs.Trout but even my feelings for her had achieved a sort of benign exasperation in light of my imminent departure. I caught myself wincing at the thought, then pushed it firmly out of my mind. There was no sense in allowing myself such silly flights of fantasy about staying. I'd made my decision and the wheels were in motion.

Scurrying out to the car, I wondered, not for the first time, why I always seemed to be finding myself in the position of scurrying towards someone else's expectations. But that seemed a far too deep and dangerous thought to be having as I was clambering into the ageing Land Rover that Toby drove.

"You look nice," he said, smiling at my stripes. "Did you knit that cardi yourself? It looks like something your mum would disapprove of."

I grinned, pulling the heavy door closed. It didn't catch so I had to open and close it again, twice. Eventually, Toby leaned across me and gave it a good heave. I tried not to inhale too deeply. He smelled of moss and soap and something faintly spicy. Sandalwood perhaps.

"Sorry about that," he said, wrestling with the gear shift. "The old girl has seen better days but she still runs like a top so we forgive her the aesthetic quirks."

There was a grinding of gears and we lurched away from the gate.

"You won't find me complaining," I said, struggling to put my seatbelt on. It was twisted impossibly and I couldn't seem to locate the end. "It beats having to walk. I've been on my feet all day. Um, does this seatbelt not work?"

Toby glanced over.

"Oh, no. Sorry about that, it's just a bit temperamental. I should've untangled it for you before we set off. There's a bit of a knack to it." he said, shrugging and turning back to the road. "I don't often have passengers, mostly just bags of feed and things like that. Can you just hold it in place for now? I'll fix it once we're stopped.

My silence prompted another glance.

"Is that a problem?"

I swallowed, trying to phrase my words so as not to sound like a total prat.

"Well, it *is* the law," I said, aiming for that light-hearted tone that so often eluded me. "I would hate for us to get pulled over."

Toby laughed.

"What? In the less than five minutes it takes us to get to the Forge? I can't remember the last time I saw a copper in Winkle."

I stared out of the window, holding the seatbelt across my body.

"You like to follow the rules, don't you?" asked Toby, a hint of mockery in his voice.

"Is there something wrong with that?" I asked, stiffly, every episode of childhood teasing and bullying bubbling to the surface in a surge of defensiveness. Being a rule-follower wasn't a popular stance in my school.

Toby shrugged, tapping his fingers on the steering wheel.

"That depends, I suppose," he said, expertly veering around a large pothole. I clung to the door frame.

"Oh? On what?"

"On whether the rules are there to help or hinder," he replied.

I let that sink in for a moment, searching for what he was really getting at.

"I mean, if you go along with what you're 'supposed' to do and it gets you where you want to be going, then I suppose it's alright. But if you follow along just because someone says you ought to, and not because it has any benefit, and maybe is even to your detriment, then I don't believe it's a good thing at all."

I snorted, most unladylike.

"Well that's a very anarchistic approach to life, don't you think?" I asked. "I mean if we all did only what benefited us then there'd be rather a lot of people getting trampled on."

"More than what get trampled on now because they're too afraid to go against the grain? How many folk do you think are living miserable, frustrated lives because they wouldn't take even a small chance on what they truly wanted for themselves? Plenty. Worse again when the chance comes to change and they don't take it. That doesn't make for a healthy world."

We pulled into the parking lot of the Forge. I could feel the burn of tears in the back of my throat. I felt suddenly very much that I wanted to go home, except I didn't know where that actually was, which only made things worse. I swallowed hard, staring down at my fingers where they were knotted in my lap, willing the tears to subside.

"Hey," said Toby, his voice soft and full of concern. He reached over to tuck a wayward strand of hair back off my face. "I'm sorry, Haze, I went too far. I'm an insensitive sod sometimes."

I sniffed and attempted to smile.

"Yes, you are a bit," I said, clearing my throat. "Though I'm feeble and overly sensitive so that doesn't help. I've had a trying few days, that's all."

I didn't specify what I meant and hoped desperately that he wouldn't ask for details. I couldn't bear having to talk to him again about leaving Rookery Cottage.

He squeezed my shoulder.

"I imagine that coming out to mingle with us rowdy lot was the last thing you fancied doing this evening?"

I managed a real smile that time.

"That's the understatement of the year," I said, "but only because I'm afraid I won't be very good company. Not because I don't love being with you all, because I really do. I've never felt more at home with such a rowdy lot."

Toby stared at me for a moment, as if considering saying something else but instead he pushed a hand through his hair and sighed.

"Right, come on then," he said. "Let us go forth into the fray, shall we?"

I nodded and pushed at the door. It was apparently as difficult to open as it was to close and I thumped my shoulder against it several times. Finally, Toby had to tug it from the outside, laughing when I tipped over as the door flew open. I fought down the familiar helpless feeling of being entirely out of my element as I looked up into his smiling eyes.

He held out his hand and I took it.

The strategy meeting was in full swing when we arrived. Alfie and Lord Dummell had evidently been warming the seats at our table for a good few pints before everyone else had filtered in. Astrid and Sidney were just coming back from the bar with tall glasses of orange juice, garnished with fresh slices and striped cocktail umbrellas. Edie was in deep conversation with Hamish, the menus they held clearly weren't being read.

"There they are! Jolly good!" boomed Lord Dummell, jostling Alfie's elbow. Alfie beamed with an air of lager-induced benevolence and I couldn't help but grin back at him. Dear old thing, he was going to be in great trouble with Edie but she seemed to be looking the other way.

"Hazel, love," said Alfie, patting the empty seat beside him. "I saved this seat for you, our guest of honour!"

"What?" I said, laughing as I sat down.

Lord Dummell leaned across, sloshing Alfie's pint with his corduroy-patched elbow.

"You're the heroine of the cause," he said. "Hamish was just giving us the details of your adventures in the county records office. Goodness, but how you managed that dreadful woman! She and Mrs.Trout could compare notes, I don't doubt! And our dear Mr.Wainwright, always a champion of things forgotten."

He raised his glass and stood, rather unsteadily, tapping a convenient spoon to get everyone's attention.

I blushed and tried to make myself smaller. We weren't the only ones in the bar-room and all heads had turned to the swaying aristocrat and his raised pint glass.

"To our darling Hazel," said Lord Dummell. "Long may she remember how much we treasure her and no matter where she roams, may she know that she always, always has a home in Winkle."

"To Hazel!" came the chorus of voices. I looked around at their smiling faces and felt a mixture of warmth and sadness. I was letting them down, quite terribly, and yet here they were, kindness and generosity itself, full of well-wishes and gratitude for the trifling contribution I'd made.

I smiled, shy and self-conscious.

"Thank you, you're all lovely. I really don't deserve..."

"Nonsense!" interrupted Alfie, squeezing my hand. "You deserve all of the wonderful things and more. Now, why not get that man of yours to fetch you a drink. Toby! I bet our Hazel would love a glass of Nether Winkle Heather Mead. Ernie tells me that they got a case of it in just yesterday."

Alfie winked at me.

"It's the 'under the counter selection', don't you know," he said, with a wheezing chuckle. "Can't have those hipster types getting wind of it, we'd be overrun with the buggers."

"Oh, Alfie," I said, tears welling my eyes again, this time from happiness, his reference to Toby as 'that man of yours' quite forgotten. "You're only the dearest thing in the world to me, I hope you know that."

He patted my arm again.

"And you to me, my lovely lass. You to me."

Several glasses of NetherWinkle mead and a hearty supper of vegetable stew and crusty bread and I was full of good cheer and sentiment. The meeting, such as it was, had been surprisingly productive. The date for the hearing had been set — fairly quickly, on the scale of your typical bureaucratic time-lines – and Hamish had gone over the approach he was going to take. It was quite simple: the paperwork I'd retrieved stated incontrovertibly that, due to a binding covenant between the family of Malmont Estate and the Talbot family of Rookery Farm, the land could neither be "seized nor sold" against the wishes of either party. Hamish explained that he was going to use the covenant to question the ownership of the land, thereby indefinitely delaying the proposed sale by compulsory purchase. Should the council decide to ignore the results of the village vote, BMZ would be in a position to invoke compulsory purchase against Lord Dummell's refusal to sell so we needed to make sure that wasn't an option either, hence the search for this old paperwork. Because it seemed that Malmont Estate had never been voluntarily registered, there were reams of paperwork that needed to be done and so the terms of the centuries-old covenant made the land surrounding both Malmont, Rookery Farm, as well as the boundary hedge which bordered the moorland, all the way past the hazel coppice and out to the main road as under its protection. As the current resident and caretaker of Rookery Cottage, I was required to witness the affidavit that Hamish had prepared to that effect. I saw that both Young Craig and Lord Dummell had already signed it. I had a bit of a wobble around the word, "caretaker" but since no-one else seemed to add any emphasis to it, and as it was written with a lowercase 'c', I didn't bring it up.

Once all the papers had been signed, another jug of mead was acquired and we raised our glasses for another toast, to Hamish this time.

"It's all gone so well, don't you think?" asked Astrid, coming to sit beside me once all of the talking and planning had been finished. Alfie had moved away to sit in one of the armchairs by the hearth. I half-expected him to be dozing off but instead, he and Sidney were debating the merits of various types of manure that might produce marrows of a prize-winning proportion. The theatre troupe had applied for an allotment and Sidney was in charge of soil amendment.

"I really think it has," I said, hugging myself. I was desperately tired and wanted only to go home and process the myriad emotions that were assailing me. "It's such a relief to know that things are going to be okay isn't it?"

Astrid smiled and nodded.

"Well, for now, anyway," she said, her smile fading slightly and a crease forming between her eyes. Her regulation black eyeliner was smudged, giving her eyes a bruised look.

"What do you mean? Surely the documents prove that any further attempts to develop the land would just result in years of expensive legal wrangling. That's not exactly a good business move for BMZ, especially as they have an equally, if not better, site already in contention. The Hedge is protected for at least another few hundred years now, I'm sure"

"Yes," she said, "I'm sure you're right. Excuse me, will you? I have to speak with Lord Dummell about something."

I waved her away, squashing down the tremor of unease that was rising up from my belly. I looked around at my friends, this time with a more critical eye. There were definite signs of strain on all of their faces, worry etched around eyes and mouths and dark circles of sleeplessness. I had been so busy fretting over my own worries that I hadn't paid close attention to how this whole business had affected these people who had become so dear to me. It really must have come very close — the Hedge and all that stood beyond it really had been in very great peril. I felt a pang of guilt — possibly because I'd only just redeemed myself by digging up the world-saving papers from Nan's cottage. I should've taken it far more seriously. I shook my head in an attempt to dispel the cloud of gloom that had settled on my shoulders again.

"You look like you're ready to go home," came a voice in my left ear. Toby stood, head inclined towards me, his eyebrows raised expectantly.

"Is it that obvious?" I said, grinning tiredly. I rubbed my hands across my face, stifling a yawn.

"Not to the average observer, I don't suppose," he replied, winking. "But to my well-trained eye…"

"And the fact I told you I was knackered before you even picked me up?"

The corners of his eyes crinkled in a not unpleasant mischievous sort of way.

"Come on, I'll run you home. I have to go back to the Estate to check on a couple of ewes," he paused, glancing over at Lord Dummell who was playing a game of darts with a trio of oddly dressed men who looked suspiciously like they might be of NetherWinkle origins. "I don't think His Nibs will be ready to go for a while yet."

"Those men he's playing darts with…"

"Aye, they are," said Toby, winking again. "They don't often come in here to socialize but they'd heard about the good news and popped in for a bit of a natter. Friends of Mr.Goodship, they are. Borderland folk. Good people. I only wish..."

He shrugged, waving a hand as if to dismiss whatever he was about to say next.

"Never mind that, now. Shall we then?"

"Yes, let me just say my goodbyes and I'll be right with you. Thanks so much, Toby," I said, babbling. "For everything. I mean, it's good of you to give me a lift and everything, and for all of you to be so kind, even though I'm..."

"Abandoning us? Aye, well. That's just how us Winkle folk are, full of the milk of human kindness. I'll meet you out in the parking lot."

I couldn't tell whether he was still being jokey or getting in a dig. His sarcasm was difficult to separate from his version of humour. I realized, with an uneasy lurch, that him understanding why I couldn't stay was important to me; I didn't like that it was important and I liked even less that he seemed willing to dismiss the whole thing without so much as a backward glance. I gave a small, uncertain smile that he didn't see because he was already halfway to the door.

We drove home mostly in silence. On my part it was because I was too much in my head and too tired to make conversation. As for his reasons, I could only guess. Perhaps his mind was already on his expectant sheep. The Land Rover shuddered to a halt outside the gate. With a firm shove, I managed to get the door open. I paused, one leg outside.

"Do you want to come in for a cup of tea?" I asked, feeling as if I should offer, although not really wanting to have to entertain anyone, least of all him and the confusion that surrounded him.

Toby grinned.

"Now wouldn't it just be the worst thing if I were to accept that invitation?" he said, his eyes glinting wickedly in the glow of the interior light. "The last thing you want is to have to make me a cup of tea and feed me HobNobs."

I blushed and opened my mouth to protest.

Toby reached over and cupped my burning cheek in his hand, making it burn even more furiously.

"Get yourself in, Haze. I'll see you later, aye?"

Nodding dumbly, I got the rest of the way out of the Rover and opened the gate. I turned back, hand raised in a wave but Toby was already turning the protesting vehicle around and didn't look up.

I sighed. With relief and something else I wasn't keen on examining. I reached my hand up to touch my cheek where he'd touched it then immediately put it down again.

I was being beyond foolish. I was leaving Winkle and that was that. That thought made me groan out loud. Mum had left me the list of the properties we'd viewed and I was meant to look them over and get back to her with a shortlist. She'd be phoning any minute, I was sure of it.

I walked slowly up the garden path, breathing in the clean fresh scent of the late spring air, and that of woodsmoke. I noticed the light of the lamps burning through the windows. The cottage really was pulling out all the stops. I shook my head, and muttered about too little too late.

I scanned the garden for evidence of Murk. One of his favourite tactics was to lurk in the shadows and then dash through the door before I could stop him. I was so busy trying to be sneaky that I almost jumped out of my skin when I walked through the door and found someone sleeping on my sofa.

Chapter Thirty-Three

"R oger?"

Roger, because that's exactly who it was, jolted upright. Fumbling for his glasses, which had slipped sideways, presumably when he'd dozed off, he was a caricature of dishevelment.

"Hazel!" he exclaimed, giving me one of his trademark thousand watt smiles. "Sorry to barge in like this, but the door was open."

"No it wasn't," I said, walking over to give him a peck on the cheek. "The cottage let you in. Tea?"

My extreme tiredness had evaporated at the sight of my dear friend. I hadn't realized how much I was missing him until I saw him again. Just like running into him at the fundraising fête, the sight of him felt like an enormous weight lifting from my shoulders. I know it wasn't the done thing to admit to, but Roger had always made me feel safe.

"I'd love a cup," he said, disentangling himself from the tartan blanket. "Where've you been? Night out on the town with our handsome gamekeeper?"

"Ha, ha," I said drily, "But as a matter of fact, yes. If you can call a communal supper and drinks with about eight other people at the village pub a 'night out on the town.'"

I filled the kettle and set it on the hob.

"Oh, and he's not the gamekeeper, for your information."

Roger smiled as he rummaged in the cupboards.

"You wouldn't have any..."

"HobNobs? Yes, over in the biscuit tin."

"A biscuit tin? Well, well, we are getting airs, aren't we? Used to be you kept them in the cupboard in their torn packet. When did you get so fancy?"

"Again, I say, ha-ha," I punched him lightly in the arm as he walked past. "It's Nan's biscuit tin. It makes me feel like she's here when I do the things that she used to do."

Saying that, a quick burn rose in my throat. I cleared it, fighting back the welling tears. I was obviously emotional from over tiredness.

Roger glanced over, a look of deep sympathy on his face.

"Oh, love," he said, crossing the space between us in two strides, folding me into his arms. "Go on, have a good one."

And so I did.

A short while later, my tears dried and my nose blown, we were sitting on the sofa, one at each end with our feet meeting in the middle. The tartan blanket was tented over our raised knees and we each cradled a steaming mug of tea.

"Sorry about that," I said, wadding up another tissue and depositing it on the coffee table. "It's been brewing for a while."

"I've always told you that a person of your sensitivities needs to have a therapeutic bawl at least once a week. To let off the pressure of...well, living in a world that doesn't appreciate your nature."

I nodded.

"You're right," I said. "I've been neglecting my cathartic crying regime. Though, to be fair, as I've only just regained my ability to cry at all I probably have a backlog."

"Tsk, tsk. See what happens when you up sticks and leave me," he said, poking me with his foot. "You fall to ruins."

I managed a feeble smile.

"But," he continued, leaning across the gap between the sofa and table to set down his mug. He reached out to take my free hand. "That might be going to change. What do you think about that?"

I frowned.

"Did Mum tell you I was moving back to London?" I said, making a mental note to phone her and tell her off. "Because that's absolutely not going to happen. As much as I love you, Roger, I simply can't cope with the city any more. I'll find somewhere close by, I'm sure of it."

"No, no. She didn't say anything like that. No, dearest Hazel, this is something entirely different and entirely unexpected."

He looked at me, his eyes sparkling

"Can you guess? No, you can't possibly. Try this idea on for size: What would you say if I told you that I was leaving the flower shop and setting out on my own? And even more exciting than that, I'm thinking of finding some premises right here in Winkle?"

I woke up to Roger singing over the sound of running water in the bathroom. For a brief moment, I thought I was back in his London flat. Roger was one of those desperate people who are unfailingly energetic in the mornings, even without excess consumption of caffeine. I would bet he hadn't even had a cup of tea yet.

The sunlight streaming in the window and the chirping of birds assured me that I wasn't in London, but safely tucked into my bed at Rookery Cottage. The window of Roger's spare bedroom in the London flat overlooked the building next door, with only a narrow alley to separate us. In days gone by I imagined there were clotheslines strung in between the buildings but that would've been against the tenant's code nowadays. The only sounds that ever came in that window was the wail of sirens or the radio blaring from the flat opposite. The elderly man who lived there had a fondness for loud, brassy, marching-band sorts of music. It was intrusive to say the least. I sighed and stretched, not wanting to dwell on life in London. It had eroded my health and well-being for long enough without revisiting unnecessarily.

I flung back the covers and slid my feet into my slippers. No matter how much warmer the days had become, the cottage floors were always cool. Before I could stop it, I had the thought that it would be welcome in the warmth of summer. I pulled on my dressing gown and padded down the stairs to the kitchen. Roger may have had a fondness for caffeine-free starts to his day but I certainly didn't. Besides, I was still somewhat bewildered by all that had transpired last evening. I'd given up trying to take it all in and Roger had shooed me off to bed, with promises of details come morning. The gist of it was that he'd met someone very special — Nathan, who was a chef at a sort of bistro cafe — and the two of them were madly in love and wanted to strike out on their own. Roger's big vision was a B&B combined with a small cut-flower nursery and café that catered strictly for lunches and cream-teas. If all went well, perhaps they'd branch out into larger scale catering and flower-arranging classes and the like. He was so full of enthusiasm and excitement that I hadn't wanted to raise all of my doubts about the idea. Wasn't it a bit sudden? What about the shop in London? He'd been managing it for almost ten years and they'd be lost without him, not to mention the loss of a secure income. And who was this Nathan fellow? What did he really know about him? Wasn't it moving a bit too quickly?

I filled the kettle and spooned coffee into the cafetière for Roger and tea into the pot for me. I was rummaging in the cupboard for a bag of porridge oats when I heard the distinctive rasp of Murk's breathing as he jumped down off the bench. Oh no, not now.

I stood up and said as much out loud.

"As opposed to when, I wonder?" said the wretched cat, twining himself around my legs.

"I'm thinking never would be a safe bet," I retorted. "I've got a friend staying for a bit and the last thing I need is for you to be hanging about giving him all the wrong impressions."

Murk raised the feline equivalent of an eyebrow, the effect produced by that and the combination of his ragged ear was alarming indeed.

"A man friend, is it then?"

"Yes and don't get any silly ideas. It's just Roger, my old flat-mate from London. And why am I explaining myself to you?" I raised my hands in despair. "Look, I'll give you a whole tin of sardines if you'll sod off."

"I might be persuaded," he said, his purr rumbling like an outboard motor, "if you were to throw in a bit of smoked salmon."

"I haven't got any bloody smoked bloody salmon, you beastly animal!" I growled in a snarling whisper, hearing the sound of water being let out of the bath.

"I think you'll find that Friend Roger put some in the fridge when he arrived last evening. Along with some other rather tasty-looking morsels that I couldn't help but wonder if you'd like to send my way? You know, just to make sure I don't get peckish again and have to come back. Repeatedly."

He cocked his head sideways and blinked slowly. I would've loved to throw my slipper right at his cheeky smirk. The bathroom door opened and I heard Roger walk across the hall to the spare room.

Murk's tail twitched ever so slightly.

"Fine!" I said, marching over to the fridge. "I'll put the sardines and some salmon out on the back step for you. But you're not getting any of the other stuff until I've had some too. Now go on, bugger off!"

I flapped my hands at him and he bounded nimbly up onto the bench and out of the open window, a suspicious cackling sound accompanying him.

"Who're you talking to?" asked Roger, coming into the kitchen. He was fresh and clean and smelled of something like vanilla. I sniffed.

"Do you like it?" he asked. "Nathan does a bit of dabbling in lotions and potions as well. He's developed a brilliant hand lotion for 'gardening hands' – which does just as well for 'chef hands' too. This is the vanilla-scented one. I brought you a bottle; just because you're a country person now doesn't mean you have to have country person hands."

He blushed at the mention of Nathan and my heart melted. It was so nice to see him happy, I hated to be the one to bring up all of the possible problems with his plan.

He cleared his throat and looked around the kitchen.

"Was someone here?"

"No, just me talking to myself," I said, casting a furtive look towards the kitchen window. "That's what happens when you live alone, I suppose! Now, kettle's just boiled. I'll pour the water then let's go back to the living room and you can give me all of the juicy details, yeah?"

Roger grinned and rubbed his hands together.

"Brilliant! Oh, and I've stocked your fridge a bit with some stuff that Nathan sent. He does these great breakfast rolls and he packed a couple for us to try. He figures we could sell them to the outdoorsy crowd – you know, the rambler types who want a bit of something to tuck into their packs."

"Yum," I said, meaning it. "Here, you carry the tray through. I've just got to pop into the garden for a second. There's this horrible stray cat that comes by and I feel sorry for the poor thing so put a bit of food out for it. I'll just be a minute."

"Horrible stray cat?" said Murk, from atop the leek trench when I set the saucer of sardines and salmon out for him. "I rather take exception to that. So much so, I might have to parade myself in front of your guest so that he can *feel sorry* for me, too."

"Don't you dare!" I said, putting my hands on my hips. "You do that and it'll be the last tinned sardine you ever eat."

Murk chuckled and jumped down to his saucer. He paused, twitching his long whiskers.

"Mind you listen to him, *mo chroí*. He might just have what you need."

"Oh never you mind with that!" I said, flinging open the door in exasperation. "You and your cryptic announcements. Honestly, you're like the plot of every fantasy novel I ever read as a teenager. 'Mysterious talking cat speaks ominous prophecy!' Just eat your sardines and sod off!"

"So that's the plan," said Roger, wiping his mouth with the corner of a linen napkin, also provided by Nathan. With the gourmet breakfast wraps (egg and cheese of an exotic variety, speckled with bits of green on a seed tortilla) and tiny bowls of chopped fresh fruit (pre-chopped by Nathan and then presented by Roger) I felt like I was on the set of a home and garden program. "What do you think?"

I stifled a burp and sat back against the sofa. The wraps had been delicious — simple ingredients but so fresh and artfully done and I would never have bothered to chop up fruit but it somehow tasted better that way. I imagined I would eat far more fruit if I had someone to chop it up for me. That was a strange and not entirely unwelcome thought that I nevertheless dismissed immediately. I cupped my hands around my mug of tea and dug around in my brain for the right words. I had all kinds of doubts, not the least of which was finding a premises nearby that could accommodate all the wants and needs of the budding entrepreneurs at a price they could afford.

"I think it's utterly bloody marvellous," I said, truthfully. "It sounds like just the sort of place I'd like to visit myself. Nathan's obviously an amazing chef and you've obviously got the whole flower thing in the bag so I really can't see how you can go wrong."

Roger clasped his hands together and grinned like a schoolboy.

"Do you really think so?"

I leaned over and placed my hand over his clasped ones, looking into his dancing eyes. There was a ghost of worry in them and I could see that he really needed the encouragement.

"I do, darling. I absolutely do. And I've never seen you so happy — you're positively giddy! – so with that to power you along, there's no hurdle you can't manage, I'm sure."

His smile faltered slightly and his forehead creased in a frown.

"What sort of hurdles do you think?"

I quickly waved my hand dismissively, not wanting to rain on his parade. He really had thought it all through. It was possible that I was simply jaded from having my own fantasy life blown to smithereens. I admired his enthusiasm, and envied his simple faith that everything would work out.

"Oh, just finding a suitable premises and all that. It might take some time to find exactly what you need, you know. Believe me, Mum and I have been scouring the area for places and there's a great trend towards these hideous conversions and 'weekenders' it would make you weep to see it."

Roger nodded, looking somewhat relieved.

"Thank goodness that's all," he said. "I was afraid there was some great and hidden secret lurking behind the hedges and picket fences!"

I spluttered, choking on the mouthful of tea I'd just taken. Roger banged me on the back at the same time as he tried to mop me down with his designer linen napkin.

I flapped my hand, leaning over to put down my mug. I wiped my streaming eyes and pushed my hair back from my red face.

"I'm alright," I said, "Must've gone down the wrong pipe."

Roger frowned, tilting his head.

"Are you sure that's all it is?" he asked. "You know I can spot you in a lie from a thousand paces so don't even try it. If there's something here that's going to interfere please just tell me. Oh god!"

He clapped his hand to his mouth, his eyes goggling.

"I'm SO sorry," he said, anguish written all over his face. "I never even *thought* to ask how you'd feel about me moving here. Is that it? Do you not want me here? Would we be encroaching on your turf?"

My eyes filled with sudden tears. Nothing could be further from the truth.

"Oh, Roger! You silly, silly man!" I said, sniffing loudly. "I can't think of anything I'd love more than to have you close by. Truthfully, though, I don't even know where I'm going to end up. We might not even be near each other."

The thought of that was a crushing disappointment. I felt the weight of it settling on my heart. Why, oh why did I have to be such an enormous idiot?

"I hadn't thought of that," he said, smoothing the knife-edge crease of his trousers. "I suppose I got caught up in the excitement and utter perfectness of it all and just imagined you'd still be here,"

He glanced around, smiling softly, as he took in the wonder that was Rookery Cottage.

"It's so you, isn't it, darling?" he whispered. "And there's still so much of your Nan here too. It's just oozing with character, with the history of your whole family."

His eyes filled as well, making mine respond in kind.

"You miss her terribly, don't you?"

I nodded, not able to speak.

"Oh, love. Come here, have another cry," he opened his arms and drew me in for a strong, comforting hug as I sniffled.

He kissed the top of my head and murmured, "Do you really have to go?"

I didn't have an answer, or at least not one I could say out loud, so I just kept crying.

"Halloooo! Anyone in? It's just me, Craig!"

I hastily scrubbed a tissue across my face and self-consciously tried to smooth out my hair. I must've looked an absolute sight. Roger evidently agreed.

"I'll go," he said, grinning. "Why don't you go and get yourself ready? I'm thinking we should join forces for our property scouting. We could pretend we're on Escape to the Country or something."

I groaned, thinking of my outings with Mindy that felt just like that, only not fun. Still, I far more relished the thought of looking at properties with Roger than with Mum, and it would keep her off my case.

"That's a lovely idea. Go ahead, it's just Craig with my milk I suppose. Oh, no I need to pay the man."

I looked around for my handbag.

"I'll get it" said Roger. "It'll give me a chance to ask him about how he'd fancy supplying the B & B. Nathan is very adamant about supporting the local farmers."

"Thanks, love," I said, squeezing his arm. "For everything."

"Oh now, don't you start blubbering again!" He laughed. "I'll have my pound of flesh, don't you worry. I might be camping out on your spare bed if I can't find a place. I've already given up the lease on the London flat."

I was left with my mouth hanging open as he went to see to Craig.

Well, I thought, I wasn't expecting *that*. He certainly hadn't wasted any time. What must it be like to be so sure of things? I let my thoughts drift back to Murk's cryptic pronouncement about Roger having something I needed; he had confidence and faith, for starters. I sighed. Bloody cat.

An hour later and we were beetling down the road in Roger's car. True to form, he'd packed us a picnic lunch so we wouldn't become faint with hunger and have to stop our search. I thought for the hundredth time how nice it was to be spending time with him again. I hoped beyond hope that he and Nathan could find something close to wherever I might end up.

"That Craig's a nice fellow," remarked Roger, glancing over at me. "He says he's running the family farm pretty much singlehandedly."

I nodded, rummaging in the glove compartment for the inevitable bag of humbugs. Roger always kept a bag on hand.

"Yes, Craig and his mum moved here when he was young and then when his uncle took ill, he stepped in to run the farm. It's a bit of a shame, though, as his heart really isn't in it these days. He told me once that he wished he could give up the livestock at least. He's like you, he prefers plants and flowers."

"Oh?"

I unwrapped a humbug and popped it in my mouth, savouring the perfect combination of mint and caramel. Humbugs were quite possibly one of the first world's best inventions. Along with HobNobs of course.

"Yes, I think he's a bit tenderhearted, to be honest, but he wouldn't dare give up the farm. He's very dedicated to the land, you know. And besides, it would finish his old uncle off, I'm sure, to leave the place. His family has been farming Rookery Farm for generations."

"Is that so?" said Roger, in a tone I recognized.

"What? What are you thinking?"

He shrugged.

"Nothing at all. I'm just trying to get a feel for the place, absorb a bit of the local culture."

"Hmph," I said, not believing him but knowing I'd be wasting my time trying to dig any deeper. "Where are we off to first?"

"I found a couple of listings on the internet," he replied, gesturing towards a sheaf of papers tucked in beside the gear box. "I thought we could do some drive-bys before I try to set up appointments. No sense wasting everyone's time if they're not suitable."

"Genius," I said, drily. "It's a shame my mother didn't go in for that sort of strategy. It could've saved us hours upon hours."

"You really haven't seen anything?" he asked, giving me a pitying glance. "Surely there must've been something that would do. There's some lovely properties around here."

I nodded, reluctant to admit that as fact.

"True..."

"Do you want to know what I think?"

"Is that a rhetorical question? Never mind, I know it is."

I folded my arms and shifted slightly in my seat to face him.

"I think that you're actually regretting the idea of leaving Rookery Cottage but because you've already said you're going to leave, *and* told your mum which then sparked all manner of maternal delight and planning, you're afraid to tell anyone you've changed your mind. Because let's face it, your mother will have several fits. Plus, to change your mind now would support your internal narrative that you're flaky and unreliable. Which, by the way, is categorically untrue and is a story given to you by persons which shall remain unnamed."

I shifted my position back to facing straight and stared pointedly out the front window.

"Well?" He prodded. "Am I right? I am, aren't I? Of course I am."

He let out a little yip and banged his hand on the steering wheel, turning to me with his thousand watt grin.

I scowled and pursed my lips.

"Bastard," I muttered, unable to keep from laughing.

Chapter Thirty-Four

"Hazel! Come in, pet," Edie's beaming smile was a balm to my soul. "Alfie!" she called back over her shoulder. "It's our Hazel," turning back to me, she gestured, "Come on, love. Get yourself in. What a lovely surprise. Cup of tea?"

Without waiting for an answer, she bustled off down the passage towards the kitchen. I took off my coat and hung it on the peg, remembering all of the times I'd done that when I was younger. I seem to remember that Alfie had added an extra set of pegs lower down on the wall, next to the row they had for their own grandchildren, for me and Toby when we came to visit. Which, during those glorious summers, was almost every day. I sighed heavily. I was at great risk of becoming extremely emotional. Just for a change.

The sitting room was warm and smelled faintly of chips. It must be egg, beans and chips night, I thought. Sure enough, Alfie was just mopping up the bean juice on his plate with a slice of bread. He sat by the fire with a tray on his knee.

"Aren't we awful?" said Edie, coming back in with a loaded tea tray. "Times have changed, haven't they? Gone are the days of sitting proper at the table while we eat. Mind you, we always have our Sunday dinners at the table, don't we Alf?"

"Oh, aye," said Alfie, with a grin and a belch. "Got to keep the standards up, don't you know?" He winked and passed his tray to Edie, who traded him for a mug of tea.

"I eat a lot of my meals off my knee these days," I said, reaching for the teapot. "I find it's far cosier to sit by the fire, or on the edge of the leek trench if the weather is fine."

Edie bustled about in the kitchen, the sound of running water and dishes clattering were a comforting backdrop to the murmur of the radio and the crackle of the fire. I took a sip of my tea then closed my eyes and leaned back in my chair, feeling the tension of the past few days easing slightly. How easy it was to be here, to be in the company of these people. It felt like a thousand homecomings every time I walked through their door. It was a different sort of comfort than that of my mum and dad's; theirs was a comfort of the familiar, but this, with Alfie and Edie, was the comfort of belonging. There was, I understood, a subtle difference between the two. The sound of Edie coming back into the sitting room brought me back from my musings.

"So how are things, lass? How are you managing?"

I swallowed hard. The weight of concern in Alfie's voice was almost my undoing. I sighed again.

"Oh, you know. A bit horrid, actually."

I managed a feeble smile.

Edie nodded her head and reached over to pat my arm. She glanced at Alfie who inclined his head towards me.

"Hazel, love. You know we've never interfered, like. We've always supported you, no matter what. I hope you've known that."

I nodded, momentarily burying my face in my mug of tea before taking a deep breath. I knew they'd have to be the first.

"I know that. And I can't tell you how much that means. I really don't have the words. You two are so very dear to me," I paused, swallowing the rising clog of emotion. "It would kill me to think I'd ever let you down..."

"Never, my lamb," interrupted Alfie. "You could never do such a thing."

Edie nodded her agreement.

I smiled.

"You're obviously blind to my flaws. I'm a chronic disappointment, I know," I replied in an attempt at humour. "But I appreciate it all the same. No, I'm fully aware that this whole business with Nan's cottage and me leaving it is a tremendous let down to you both. To everyone, really. And I feel horrid for it. You've all welcomed me back to Winkle, it's like I never left sometimes. I mean, this is all of my childhood dreams come true, isn't it?"

"We always hoped you'd come back to us someday," said Alfie. "You and Toby both, even though there isn't a whole lot for young people here in Winkle. But when Toby found his way back, we thought well, that's a start, isn't that right, love?"

Edie nodded.

"We knew the two of you belonged here. Our own youngsters never had the connection to this place that you two did — though we're glad they found their way to places and lives that make them happy. We wouldn't ever want to keep anyone here that didn't properly belong."

"No, that's not the Winkle way," agreed Alfie, leaning towards me in great earnest. "You see that, don't you? That there's a way of things here, a way of going on?"

I nodded. Because I did see. There were people here that truly belonged to the place — every member of the Hedge Defence Alliance for starters. And even people like the Trouts had a rootedness here as well.

"I know. I really do. There's a sort of natural order to things. I would never want to get in the way of that..."

"You could never do such a thing! So you just stop talking such nonsense!" said Edie, putting her mug down on the tray with a clatter. Alfie put a restraining hand on her arm.

"Don't you mind our Edie," he said, smiling affectionately at his wife. "She gets a bit het up over this sort of thing, don't you pet?"

"I just don't like people thinking less of themselves," said Edie quietly, "least of all our Hazel. You do that far too often.When I think of what that awful man has put you through..."

I flushed and looked away.

"Anyroad," said Alfie, giving her a warning glance, "As we'd started to say, we've never told you what we think you should be doing because we don't like to get in the natural way of things. But we've talked it over and it seems you dropping in tonight is a sign of some sort."

Edie nodded emphatically.

Alfie took a swallow of tea and then placed his mug on the little table beside his chair. He sat back and crossed his arms.

"We think you're making a terrible mistake, leaving Winkle and Rookery Cottage. You belong here. Your Nan knew that and that's why she left it to you instead of your Da and it's why she did her will like she did. I reckon she thought if she could keep your mam from selling it outright that you'd be happy to stick it out for the year and a day and realize that you were where you belonged. I don't think she'd ever imagined that you'd want to leave of your own accord."

I let his words sink in. The crushing weight of the inferred disappointment was suffocating, making it hard to breathe. I had tried not to think about the fact I was letting Nan down as well – to have disappointed her was the most wretched thing. I often wondered if she'd been disappointed that I'd made my life in London, though I know she would never have said as much. She'd put a lot of faith in me by giving me Rookery Cottage and, more than anything else, I wanted to be worthy of that. I also wanted to be worthy of my own dreams. I think that's what it ultimately came down to: did I feel worthy of my own dreams? Or did I want to carry on with the rest of my life making things easier for other people? I was finally free to do and be what I wanted for a change so why would I pass that up just to save a bit of bother? If people wanted to think I was flaky and indecisive then that's their business, not mine. I wasn't going to become confident and assertive overnight, there were bound to be wobbles. It was time to reclaim some of that fearlessness that I had as a child.

"Now don't you go taking on a load of guilt over what our Alfie's just said," said Edie, coming to sit on the arm of my chair. She put her arm around my shoulders and pulled me in for a sideways hug. "We don't mean to add to your burden but we felt we had to say something. We just don't think you're giving yourself a proper chance, that's all. That daft old cottage takes a lot of getting used to, no-one expects things to be exactly like they were when your Nan was there, so nor should you. And with everything else that's gone on in the last while, you can't expect to be at your very best right now. Nobody else expects that, either. And as for that Caretaker business, well, that's not something you'd be needing to do on your own, so don't let yourself be overwhelmed by it. You've got all of us looking out for you and more than happy to do so. You belong here, my love. You always have."

I leaned against Edie, feeling the solidness of her. Despite her diminutive size, she's always seemed so sturdy and strong to me. Immoveable in her convictions, unshakeable in her certainty of things turning out alright in the end. Everything I wished I was.

I cleared my throat.

"It's funny you should say that," I said, smiling through the tears that wouldn't be swallowed away. "Because the reason I stopped in was to tell you that I've decided to stay."

Edie poured me a glass of bramble and hawthorn wine. We'd left off the tea when Toby and Lord Dummell arrived. Lord Dummell brought the wine and Toby brought two packets of HobNobs.

"What else would we eat to celebrate?" he'd offered a quick smile at my expression. "Plus, they were all I could find on short notice. The grocer's long closed. I tried to get Astrid but she and Sidney are over at the pub in Westham doing the quiz. It's a big night as they're facing off against Eastham otherwise I'm sure they would've come. Oh, and Hamish said he might stop by as well."

Alfie had phoned over to the manor as soon as I'd told them of my decision. I wasn't sure whether to be glad or overwhelmed that my little announcement had turned into a party. But apparently, the news needed toasting. And I'd been toasted at least three times by Lord Dummell who was quite fond of his hedge-brew.

"Any excuse for a tipple," whispered Toby as he handed me a saucer with three HobNobs on it. "Whatever you do, don't ask him for the recipe. He'll go on for hours about it being handed down from generation to generation. *'It's an hedge heirloom'*, he'll say, with emphasis on the silent h's. And then he'll laugh and challenge you to say it five times fast."

I smiled fondly over at Lord Dummell. He really was a lovely man. His perpetual state of dishevelment only made him more endearing, although I suspect that was partly an act to throw off the unsuspecting observer. I was getting the distinct impression that there was far more to Lord Dummell than most people gave him credit for.

"Edie!" he boomed, raising his glass. "You wouldn't have a spot of something to put in my stomach, would you? I feel like this glorious brew is going straight to my old brain."

Edie laughed.

"Aye, alright," she replied. "I've got some sausage rolls I can warm through. They were going to be for our Alfie's dinner tomorrow but I daresay he won't begrudge you."

Alfie roared with laughter and clapped Lord Dummell enthusiastically on his tweedy shoulder. The hedge-brew was potent.

"Typical gentry," he said, "Taking the food out of the mouths of the poor folk!"

At that, the pair collapsed into fits of laughter.

"I'll give you a hand," I said, needing to get away from the bustle and noise. "Maybe I can make a few sandwiches to go along with the sausage rolls. I can't see them soaking up all of that wine."

I stood up and made to follow Edie into the kitchen when there was a knock at the door. I started back but Toby put a hand on my arm.

"Go on, get yourself a bit of quiet," he said. "I'll get the door. It might be Astrid and Sidney. I left a message on Astrid's phone."

I smiled gratefully and escaped to the relative calm of the kitchen.

Edie's kitchen was a study in domestic history. She was a staunch believer in that the old things were the best things and nothing anybody made these days either did the job properly or lasted any great length. And while I greatly enjoyed the convenience of modern toasters, I had to agree with her. The white Belfast sink was the original, as were the scrubbed oak benches that lined the walls. Alfie had mended and restored everything as the need arose and so stepping into the room was like stepping back in time.

Edie was in the process of putting the sausage rolls on a baking tray. There had never, nor ever would be, a microwave in this kitchen.

"Oh, hello, pet. Do you need something?" she asked, opening the door on the old stove. Alfie had tried to convince her to upgrade to a more modern version of the Aga but she insisted that she already knew this one's temperament so there was no point in changing now. It mostly meant that she was the only one who could use it for anything more than warming things through.

"No," I said, flopping wearily into a chair. "Well, other than a bit of peace and quiet. I came on the premise of making some sandwiches to supplement the sausage rolls but mostly I'm just trying to escape the party."

Edie chuckled.

"That were always your way," she said, busily taking plates down from the shelf. "Fill the kettle, will you?"

"Really?" I asked, turning on the tap to fill the huge kettle. "Do you think I'm a trial, Edie? Because I truly do feel like such a burden sometimes, you know? I mean, the way this whole mess came about, it's been a horrible waste of everyone's time and energy. I sometimes feel as if my various neuroses are too much for people to have to cope with. Teddy always said I was frustratingly flaky. I often wonder if he might have been right. I mean, haven't I just proven it? One minute I'm leaving and the next I'm staying. I wouldn't blame people for thinking I was unreliable. I *am* unreliable. Aren't I?"

I swallowed hard. I hadn't meant for all of that to come out. A huge tidal wave of despair rose in my chest, leaving me breathless.

Wordlessly, Edie took the kettle from me and put it on the hob. She took her biggest teapot down from the shelf above the sink and gave it a quick rinse. Still silent, she spooned tea into it and set it on a tray with a bowl of sugar and a small, beautifully painted jug of milk. I wondered if it was the work of a resident of NetherWinkle, the painted flowers seemed to almost be waving in an unseen breeze.

Thinking she hadn't heard me, I was just about to fetch a loaf of bread to begin making some sandwiches when Edie took my hand and led me back to the kitchen table. Gesturing for me to sit down, she pulled another chair around and sat facing me. Our knees were touching as she reached out and took both of my hands in hers.

"I'm going to say something to you now, my lamb, and I don't want you to take it in the wrong way. You know that me and Alfie love you as if you were our own. Heaven knows, your da was in and out of this house as much as our own lot when they were all growing up. We promised your Nan when she took ill that, as long as we were still breathing, we'd keep an eye out for you. No matter where you were."

I nodded, worry fluttering like a trapped bird in my chest.

"Now, we think the world of your da. Like I said, he was just another one of ours and your Nan was like a sister to me. God rest her soul."

Edie paused, squeezing my hands. She closed her eyes briefly, as if working herself up to something.

"Och," she said. "I'd just as soon get to the point. Your mam, now she's another kettle of fish."

I opened my mouth to agree but she held up a hand.

"No, pet. Just let me finish. Your mam is a good woman, I've no doubt in my mind of that. She loves you and your da to the ends of the earth and I know he feels the same. We never did figure how the two of them ever found each other — coming from such different upbringings like, but it just goes to show you that the folk that are meant to be together will find each other no matter what the obstacle."

She paused there and looked meaningfully at me. I blinked and said nothing.

Edie sighed.

"But the trouble with your mam is that she's never liked the idea of Winkle, you see? She's the sort of person that doesn't trust the things that she doesn't understand. And, to be fair, it's asking a lot of most people to understand the way things are, here in Winkle."

I nodded again. Edie had had plenty of exposure to my mum's feelings on Winkle and its inhabitants.

"Now, I know she's your mam and when you're a child, and even a grown adult, you think you have a duty to go along with the things she says. And let me tell you, it was the hardest day of mine and Alfie's life when you told us that you weren't going to be coming back to Rookery Cottage for your summer holidays anymore. But you're a grown woman now, lass. You had yourself a fine life in London, until things went poorly for you. Not to mention, you went through all of the awfulness with that husband of yours –- and let me just say that nothing he's ever said to you can be taken as a truth and that's just that. He was unforgivably cruel and the sooner you get shot of him for good, the better. So when I think of the courage it took to leave that life behind so you could look after yourself, I can't understand why you can't see it for yourself. And you've written all them books! You're a published author, for heaven's sake! As far as I can tell, it takes a strong and resilient sort of person to stick with that as a profession."

I smiled, thinking of the countless bars of chocolate and boxes of hankies required in response to every rejection and bad review, though none of them stopped me from writing. Not for long, anyway. I suppose I wasn't as feeble as all that.

"Aye, you can see that now, can't you? I think that a lot of what's troubling you, my love, is that you've been letting your mam tell you the story of how you are, based on things that happened long ago. I know she worries for you, it's what any good mother would do and I suspect she feels not a small bit guilty for having pushed you into things you didn't have the temperament for, never mind how she pushed you into the arms of that bloody man. But by trying to protect you, trying to keep you feeling like you can't cope, she's only making it harder for you to move on. Do you see that? And to do all that, *and* get you away from Winkle, a place she's never understood, probably seems to her like the best solution. The problem with that, though, is that it isn't really a solution at all, is it?"

Edie's much-beloved face wrinkled in concern. I could've wept for how much her words meant to me, in that moment and beyond. She was one of the very few people who had always taken me as I was. It was a great, great gift. And more than that, she was right. Of course, everything that she was saying were things that, on some level, I already knew. But hearing them from her somehow made them more real — and true.

I nodded and cleared my throat.

"Thank you, Edie. I know those two words don't even come close to expressing how I feel but they're all I've got for now. I hope you know how much I love you…"

And then the sobs I'd been squashing down all evening came shuddering to the surface.

When it came time for the party to disperse, and it had certainly achieved the level of party by the time the evening came to an end, I declined the offer of a lift home from Lord Dummell and Toby. After all of the excitement and high emotion, I wanted a peaceful, quiet walk home by myself. I turned off the main road and sighed happily as I started up the lane towards Rookery Cottage.

Dusk had set in and the evening chorus of birds was in full song. Various rustlings and squeaking emanated from the Hedge and the scream of a fox echoed from the distant forest. I smiled to myself, remembering a time when those sorts of noises would've made me flinch but now they simply made me feel welcome. It was amazing to me how quickly I could decompress with only a short stroll in the relative calm of nature. At the same time, it felt so wonderful to feel a part of the bustle of the human community in Winkle. I realized, after speaking with Edie, how much I'd held back from fully immersing myself in village life because of what I'd been assuming about my right to be there. No-one else but me had ever doubted that I would belong (well, other than Mrs.Trout but she had her own agenda, I was sure) and that I had a part to play in the saving of the Hedge. Edie was right; I was still playing out an old storyline that was no longer true.

A particularly loud rustle in the Hedge followed by a high-pitched shriek distracted me from my musings. I glanced over in time to see

Murk emerging from the undergrowth with something small and furry clenched in his jaws. I winced.

"You are quite horrid," I said, averting my eyes. "I thought you were above securing your own food in such a barbaric fashion."

"Hrmph," he mumbled through his full mouth, the glare of his yellow eyes speaking volumes.

I glared right back.

"Don't you dare bring that anywhere near my house," I said, turning to open the garden gate. It creaked a welcome. "I won't have you parading the spoils of slaughter on my kitchen floor."

I closed the gate behind me, without a backward glance, and walked to my door, which had unlatched itself and eased open. I grinned and walked inside.

A fire crackled merrily in the hearth and the lamps had turned on, making the whole place radiate warmth.

"Thank you," I whispered, still not quite used to the idea that I was speaking to a building.

"A cup of tea, don't you think?" I said, then bit my lip, remembering again that Bracken wasn't there to answer. I hadn't had a lapse in days, and thought I had sufficiently recovered from her sudden loss but apparently I hadn't. Perhaps, now that I was staying, I'd look into finding myself another companion. Life was just so much nicer with a four-legged friend to share it.

"What about me, then?" said Murk, pushing his way through the partially open kitchen window.

"Why do you let him in?" I said to the air, completely ignoring the wretched cat and his annoying habit of acting as if he could read my thoughts.

I filled the kettle and put it on the stove. I felt as if I'd drunk a gallon of tea already, but it was the ritual of making it that further soothed my ragged nerves. Which were clearly about to become more ragged as Murk settled himself in front of the fire and started to clean himself.

I continued to ignore him as I went about my tea-making business. I was absolutely not going to offer him anything to eat.

"Everything went well then, did it?" he inquired, "Got them all told?"

"I did," I said, stiffly.

"And they were suitably delighted, I suppose?"

"I suppose they were."

I assembled my tea tray and willed the kettle to boil faster. The last thing I wanted was one of Murk's smug commentaries.

"Excellent," he purred, tucking his forepaws under himself as he lay down on the rug.

I was immediately suspicious. He'd never passed up an I-told-you-so opportunity. I narrowed my eyes but said nothing. He was probably trying to lure me in. I refused to be baited.

The kettle whistled and I poured the steaming water into the teapot.

Still nothing from the hearth rug.

I tucked my book under my arm and carried the tray to the coffee table, making a point of not looking in Murk's direction.

As I settled myself down, a mug of tea in one hand and my book in the other, he began to purr loudly. I glanced over in time to see him open one eye and arrange his features in his peculiar grimace that I suppose passed as a smile.

"Just as well," he said.

I took the bait.

"Oh?"

Just then the phone started ringing.

"Because she's not going to be very happy at all."

Chapter Thirty-Five

The morning sun burned down on the back of my neck as I bent over the row of lettuces. I'd been up before dawn and wandered out to have my cup of tea on the wall of the leek trench just as the sun was rising. I had sat and sipped, listening to the morning birdsong and the bleating of far-flung sheep, wondering for the umpteenth time how I could have considered leaving this all behind. But then the memory of the conversation with my mother the night before came creeping back in and spoiled the moment altogether. So I went back into the cottage, changed into my gardening clothes and embarked upon a little dirt-therapy. I had weeding to do and some decisions to make about fixing the polytunnel if I wanted to grow some tomatoes. Which I did.

The creak of the shed door caught my attention and Mr.G emerged, carrying one of Mrs.G's baskets, which seemed to be full to overflowing with various jars and packets. I could feel my face split into a wide grin at the sight of him.

"Good morning, Mr.G," I called, raising a hand to wave. He turned, a look of surprise on his whiskered face.

"Hullo, lass. You're up and at it bright and early this morning, aren't ye?"

I chuckled.

"Yes, it's the best part of the day, though, isn't it?"

"Aye, it is that."

"Would you like a cup of tea?" I asked. "I've only had one so far and could do with another."

The little man frowned and looked down at his basket, then at the garden gate and then towards the cottage. Apparently this was a decision fraught with variables.

"I've got day-old currant scones," I said in a wheedling tone. "Nowhere near as good as your lovely wife's, I'm sure, but probably the best this side of the Hedge. Made by a gourmet chef, no less."

I tilted my head and grinned.

He shrugged and smiled back.

"Ah, go on. You twisted my arm. But if I get into bother with the missus for being late with my deliveries, I'll lay it right on your doorstep."

He winked, cheekily, knowing full well that Mrs. G would never believe him. He set down the basket and walked towards me, holding out his arm.

I laughed and tucked my own into the crook of his elbow. I only had to lean over slightly to make it work.

"Well, you can tell her that a generous blob of her blackcurrant jam was the only thing that saved the scones from being inedible. That should smooth any ruffled feathers.

We strolled down the garden path, arm in arm, as if it were a grand tour around a country estate. He paused frequently to remark on the state of the raspberry canes (much improved from my ruthless hacking), the quality of the soil (greatly benefiting from the manure Toby had brought me) and the great variety of colours in the mass planting of pinks (a happy accident of "augmented"seeds from the other side of the Hedge). I got the distinct impression we were in one of those time-altered states that the NetherWinkle folk seemed to fling about at their convenience but I didn't mind one bit. Any chance to stroll with a kindred spirit and chat about soil and manure and seedlings was one I wasn't going to turn down.

At the end of the path, I got him comfortably seated with a cushion on the trench wall then went inside to put the kettle on.

As I piled a plate high with the slightly old but still delicious scones, a dish of butter (from Rookery Farm) and a pot of jam, I heard the sound of voices drifting in through the window.

"Sodding cat," I muttered, assuming Murk had made one of his highly unwelcome appearances. But when I carried everything outside, I saw with surprise that it was none other than Roger, and he was accompanied by Craig.

"Roger!" I exclaimed. "You're back! I thought you weren't coming until next week."

I set the tray down on the table and went over to kiss his cheek.

"Hello, Craig," I said, "Is it delivery day?"

I turned to Roger, suddenly remembering how early it was.

"Wait! What on earth are you doing here at this hour?"

The pair of them laughed.

"Questions, questions," said Roger, wagging his finger. "Why don't you go and get a couple more mugs and we'll tell you every-thing."

"We?"

"Oh, and introduce me to your friend, won't you?'

He grinned cheekily and folded his arms.

I looked between him and Craig and Mr. G who were both suddenly very interested in the stone work on the leek trench.

I sighed.

More laughter erupted as Craig, grinning sheepishly, shrugged.

"I figured he might as well know the way of things," he said. "I had to fill him in. He's going to be doing business with the NetherWinkle folk after all.'

"What?"

"Mugs, darling!" said Roger, flapping his hand at my confusion. "We're gasping!"

"I can't believe you held out on me, you wretch," said Roger.

We sat swirling the dregs of our tea. Craig and Mr.G had left to attend to their deliveries and it was just the two of us and the birds.

"Well you must admit, it's not exactly the easiest thing to bring up in conversation, is it?" I said. "'Oh hey, Roger, guess what? There's a portal to the Otherworld in my Nan's shed and I'm often visited by faery creatures who bring me pots of jam and cheese pasties. And then there was the time I went into what I thought was a stationery shop for a half hour and came out a day later."

Roger chuckled.

"Hm, yes. I see what you mean."

I tossed a wadded up napkin at him.

"And speaking of holding out," I said, "What about you and Craig masterminding all manner of plans. When did you decide to talk to him?"

Roger shrugged.

"I popped in at the farm after I dropped you off the other day. He wasn't in but I had a word with his uncle – lovely old boy – and he invited me around for tea. I tell you, Nathan has a few things to learn from Craig's mum – she makes a rhubarb crumble that'd make you weep with joy. She says the key is cutting the rhubarb at exactly the right time. Something to do with when the swallows start to nest in the old barn or somesuch."

"Well, she would know, I suppose," I replied, reluctantly getting up to collect the detritus of our little impromptu breakfast party. "As I said, Craig's family has been farming here for generations. Are you sure they're willing to let you two turn Rookery Farm into a B&B? And what about Lord Dummell?"

"And a flower farm and market garden," he said, tossing the leftover tea into the leek trench. "Don't forget that part. I thought Craig was going to turn a cartwheel. We've got a meeting with Lord Dummell to iron out the details but he's absolutely delighted with the idea. He said with the extra income, they can hire someone to deal with the livestock if Craig decides he wants to step away from it when his garden design business takes off, which I'm sure it will. I think the old folk knew that Craig wasn't happy but they didn't want to say anything in case they were wrong. Besides, it's not the whole farm becoming a B & B, just one of the outbuildings."

"And *he* didn't want to say anything to them in case they thought he wanted to give up the farm all together," I said, shaking my head. "Such a silly thing, isn't it? Just think, if only they'd talked to each other they would've known how they were all feeling. Craig could've started his market garden ages ago."

"Hmmmm," said Roger, glancing meaningfully at me. "Funny how communication is such an important element to human relationships. Especially among family, eh?"

I scowled at him and picked up the loaded tray.

"Yeah, yeah," I retorted as I carried it into the kitchen. I called back over my shoulder, "What's it like being perfect, then?"

"Oh, you know," he replied airily. "Takes a bit of getting used to but I feel like I've mastered it now."

Roger stayed through the afternoon and helped me with my garden jobs. It was so nice to have someone helping me, not so much for the work as the company. We'd known each other for so long that we could work side by side in contented silence, only speaking when we needed to ask a question or request a tool.

For all his jesting, Roger knew my mum well enough to know how impossible she could be and why I always dreaded any sort of important conversation. Last evening's telephone call was just such a one and if she hadn't been the one to phone, I'm not sure when I might have summoned the courage to broach the subject. Avoidance has always been my strategy of choice.

"Hazel, darling," she'd begun, launching straight away into one of her instructive monologues. "Mindy has found three more properties for you to view and there's one in particular that I think ticks all of your mad boxes. It even has an outside toilet – it has an indoor one as well, of course - but also this bizarre thing called a 'composting loo' that apparently you can use to fertilize your trees. It sounds positively revolting but just the sort of thing you like. What time shall we pick you up? Also, while we have you, Mindy has drawn up the paperwork for conveyancing your Nan's cottage. Of course we can't really move on it until that ridiculous provision of the will is sorted out but I'm certain, since we have your full cooperation that it's just a matter of crossing the tees and dotting the eyes. And as I said earlier, Dad and I are happy to bridge you for your new home in the interim. So, what time then?"

Murk had sat the whole while my end of the phone had been silent, blinking sleepily on the hearth-rug. At that moment, though, he'd opened one eye and looked in my direction. Again, it was his approximation of a raised eyebrow and spoke irritating volumes. I had to admit, though, his being there and my wanting to prove him wrong, probably gave me courage I might not have normally had. I found it equally irritating that he very likely knew that and it's why he turned up in the first place.

"Actually, Mum," I said, my voice rasping slightly. I cleared my throat and tried again. "Actually, I was meaning to phone you earlier. There's been a change of plans."

It went much as I'd expected. Outrage and recriminations followed by expressions of deep and wounding disappointment. So much wasted time, what on earth could I be thinking and what was Mindy going to think?

What Mindy thought was precisely the very last thing on my mind but I didn't think it would have been helpful to mention that. I was proud of how I held my ground, though, glaring at Murk all the while, resisting the childish urge to stick out my tongue at him.

At last, in a fit of despair (I could envision her hands being thrown in the air), she handed the phone to my dad, who'd been alerted by her raised voice that something was amiss.

"Hello, love," he said, his voice with its soft burr that reminded me so much of Nan. "Bit of an upset, then?"

I managed a giggle. It was slightly hysterical but a giggle nonetheless.

"Go on," he said, "She's gone off to the kitchen – probably to take it out on poor Mrs. Bates."

"Say sorry to Mrs.B for me, will you?"

"Aye, she doesn't take any notice of your mum when she's like that. I expect Mrs. B can give as good as she gets."

"I'm sorry, Dad," I said. "I'm disappointing you both again, aren't I? I don't mean to be so flip-floppy, really I don't. But I just can't leave here. You understand, don't you?"

"Of course I do love. I never thought you'd actually leave. I knew it was probably adjusting to the idea of it all that was giving you a wobble. It's a lot to take on, Winkle is. Not to mention the other lot," he chuckled. "Is Mr. G still coming through the shed?"

"You mean you knew?" I asked, incredulous, "Why didn't you say?"

"Your Nan asked me not to," he replied. "And she was right. It's better that you sorted it all out for yourself. You've had people fussing and pointing you in all sorts of directions for too long now. You needed to find your own way."

I sighed, exhausted by it all but overcome by waves of gratitude that my dad, at least, was on my side.

"Will you..."

"Aye, pet. I'll smooth things over with your mum. She'll come around in time, you'll see."

"Do you really think so?" I asked. "Shouldn't she have come around when she met and married you?"

The other end of the phone stayed quiet for a moment before he replied with a sigh of his own.

"I expect you're right, pet. I suppose I've held out hope that she'd see things the way we do, but Edie always said that your mum has closed her eyes to magic. It's just her way and we can't really fault her for it anymore than she can fault us for the way we see things. Besides, you can't let your mum's worries and worldview stop you from having yours. You've your own life to live now and Rookery Cottage needs you. And so does Winkle. Both of them. How's that Hedge defence coming along?"

We chatted for another fifteen minutes or so about everyday things. I updated him on Roger's plan to leave the flower shop and how Alfie and Lord Dummell were concocting a plan to sell bottles of Hedge Brew to the unsuspecting public just as soon as they could find a way around the licensing laws. He rang off with promises to drive up at the end of the month when he got home from one of his business trips. A pub lunch and a stroll across the moor was exactly my idea of a good visit.

"Your father is a good sort," remarked Murk, as he yawned and stretched.

"Yes," I'd replied, not willing to go any further into conversation.

Murk strolled lazily into the kitchen before he'd looked back.

"Pity about what happened, though," he said, as he scratched at the door. It creaked open. "I'd have bet a lifetime supply of sardines that he would've beaten them. It would've saved a lot of this heartbreak, I don't doubt."

With that he'd slipped through the crack in the door, leaving me gaping in frustration.

I'd scowled after him for a moment longer, half-wanting to follow him out and ask for an explanation. But then I decided that was exactly what he wanted and refused to be baited. I was sure that he was being purposefully obtuse, very likely full of rubbish and I wasn't going to fall for it.

With Roger back off into Newcastle to stay with his sister (he was meeting Nathan there and was going to bring him back to see Rookery Farm), I had the cottage and garden to myself again. It had been a long but satisfying couple of days, the perfect antidote to the difficult conversation with my mum. I knew my dad would at least stop the flow of recriminations, but it was still going to be awkward for a long time. Seething resentment, disguised as cool detachment, was her weapon of choice. I was easy prey, given my years with Teddy and his similar tactics. I admonished myself as I felt the old spiral of unhelpful narrative starting in my brain — I had only to hold my ground and go boldly onwards. The best way to defy her was to simply get on with it. Easier said than done, was the phrase that came to mind; this was a bit bigger than my choice of cardigans, but I would do my best. If not for myself, then for Rookery Cottage and the land it served.

Just as I closed the tool shed door, I heard the distant ring of the telephone. Briefly, I considered ignoring it, but I knew it wouldn't be my mum as I had at least a week of the silent treatment coming so I hurried down the path and into the house, catching it just as it was about to ring off.

"Hazel?" boomed Lord Dummell. "Jolly good, thought I'd missed you old gel. Just wanted to pass on the message that we've been given a new date for the hearing. Miracle of miracles, they've had a scheduling mix-up at the old courthouse and we've been slotted in for Friday at noon. Unheard of expediency. But we won't look a gift horse, eh wot? I imagine the Netherfolk may have had a hand in but why shouldn't we play our advantage, wot? Heaven knows the other side would. Hamish is all set and will report for duty. It's a closed room so we're all going to gather, en masse, in the lobby. Bit of moral support, eh? Toby will fetch Alfie and Edie then come around and pick you up. I'm taking Sidney and Astrid and we'll see you there. Until then!"

The line went dead before I could get a word in. I just stood there grinning.

Chapter Thirty-Six

"What do you want, you wretched creature?"

A deep, booming purr rumbled in Murk's chest. It was shortly before 5am and I'd been awoken by the sound of his yowling outside my bedroom. I leaned out the open window and glared down at him.

"Is that any way to greet the day?" he said, running a paw over his tattered ear. "I would've thought you had some sort of sun salutation thing going on. You know, to keep up the positive spirit and all that."

"Funny," I retorted. "Very, very funny. Now is there an actual reason for this disturbance or is it just my day to be tormented?"

"As a matter of fact, yes, I do have a reason for being here. A rather important one," said Murk, huffily. "But I'd prefer we conversed in the kitchen. This shouting up at windows like a fishwife is simply not on." He stretched and made to walk towards the door before pausing and looking up again. "And for the record, I strongly resent your attitude. It would serve you well to show me a bit of respect."

I snorted and muttered something which would've made my mother's hair curl.

He was waiting for me when I got down to the kitchen.

"Why did you even bother with the whole window performance," I said, banging cupboard doors and turning on the tap with as much vehemence as I could muster. "You know the door would open for you. You could've saved yourself the bother and just walked in."

"What? And deny myself this exchange of witty banter?" he said, his tail curled demurely around his front paws as he sat waiting for his saucer of sardines which I, naturally, was dishing up for him. They'd been on offer at the larger supermarket in Eastham; Roger and I had stopped in there during our property tours and I'd come out with six tins of sardines and three of tuna, none of which I eat.

I banged the plate down ungraciously. He was the absolutely most exasperating animal. For the hundredth time I asked myself why I still pandered to his whims. I had six tins of sardines in the cupboard for heaven's sake!

"Because you're a kind and good-hearted soul, that's why," he said as he tucked noisily into his sardines. "You have a good heart and a soft spot for wayward animals, though, to be accurate, I only look like one of those. Also, you haven't quite sorted out whether I'm a person to be trusted so you're hedging your bets."

"Stop it!" I threw the sardine fork into the sink. "I do not appreciate your forays into my thoughts. I find it rude, intrusive and a gross invasion of my privacy."

"Are you angry because I'm right?" he said, smacking his lips. "Or because I can sense your thoughts. Which is different from reading your mind, by the way. That sort of magic is quite frowned upon. I'm merely a very observant person with a keen eye for human behaviour; a student of the human condition, if you will."

I sighed, realizing the fruitlessness of the argument. It was early and I hadn't yet had my first cup of tea. Definitely not a fit state to be verbally sparring with a talking cat. I took a moment to reflect that this was even a situation I needed to assess. The thought was a surprisingly pleasant one. There were worse things to have to contend with, I suppose.

"Right, now that we're both fed and watered," I said, "Why are you here again?"

I'd taken my tea outside. The benefit of being up at that hour was being able to watch the world wake up. I made a mental note to try and do it more often. I spread a blob of Mrs. G's blackcurrant jam onto my toast.

Murk leapt onto the edge of the leek trench and gave the toast and jam an appraising stare. I scowled and pulled the plate closer to myself.

"I'm here with a message from the people of Nether Winkle," he said, his voice low and solemn, with no trace of his usual lazy mockery.

"Oh?" I said, sitting up straight. I wiped the jam off my fingers on the edge of my nightgown. "That sounds awfully serious. Is everything alright?"

Immediately my mind starting turning over the possibilities – all of them dire. They'd heard that I was staying but decided they didn't want me after all. And who could blame them? I was clearly a flake who couldn't be relied upon. Perhaps my history of nervous breakdowns was making them doubt my suitability. Again, who could blame them? After all, I was the biggest doubter of my suitability.

Murk made a noise in his throat.

I frowned at him, realizing what he was doing.

He held up a paw.

"Anyone who's known you for five minutes would know what you're thinking," he said. "And you couldn't be further from the truth."

My shoulders sagged in relief. Until that moment I hadn't really considered how much being accepted by the Netherfolk meant to me. And I'd really only had dealings with the Goodships and Mr. Pickle so had no idea at all how anyone else might feel about me as Caretaker.

"A delegation arrived in the Borderlands two days ago," continued Murk. "There were representatives from three of the four Lands. It was unanimous among them that you are to be welcomed as Caretaker and given whatever aid you require to fulfill your duties."

My stomach lurched with nerves at the idea of "duties". I still had no practical grasp of what I was getting myself in for. I had attached myself to the idea that it was a largely ceremonial role.

"Well," I said, my voice squeaking. I cleared my throat. "That's very generous indeed and I feel very fortunate to be in their favour."

I groaned inwardly. Now *I* was channeling every fantasy novel I'd ever read. If I lapsed into High Elvish I'd have to check myself back into Serenity Meadows. A different ward, this time.

If Murk noticed, he didn't mention it.

"You must know, however," he continued, "That there are certain factions in NetherWinkle who don't believe the new Caretaker should be of human persuasion. It was hoped among certain *groups*, shall we say, that you wouldn't accept the role and so it would become a matter of designation. Evidently, there are several candidates waiting in the wings. None of them at all desirable."

"Ah, I see," I said, although I didn't.

Murk tilted his head and raised an inquiring eyebrow. I looked down at my mug.

"Hmm. Anyway, the matter is in hand. The transition is expected to be a smooth one but it's only fair that you are made aware of how things are. There have been skirmishes and scufflings in the Nether-Lands since before time began. We generally just let them get on with it. It tends to be self-limiting, if you understand my meaning?"

I nodded and made agreeable noises. I felt very much out of my element. This seemed to be some sort of formal declaration and I wasn't sure exactly how I was supposed to respond. Did I send a gift? Did I write a thank-you note? Did a return delegation need to be raised? I sighed, resenting having to admit my ignorance to Murk, but said as much.

Murk chuckled, the sound resembling the creaking of rusty gears.

"Worry not," he said. "When the time comes, all will be made clear."

And with that extremely cryptic announcement, he leapt over the leek trench and disappeared up the garden path.

The clattering of the estate's Land Rover preceded the blaring honk of the horn, announcing Toby's arrival at the garden gate. In my usual way of pathological punctuality, I was already standing waiting.

"Oh! Sorry!" he said, winding the window down. It got stuck part way so he raised his chin up to the gap to speak. "I didn't expect you to be there already, that's why I honked."

I blushed, for no good reason. Cursing myself inwardly, I flapped a hand and went to the back, passenger side door which Alfie was trying to tug open for me.

"Sorry again," said Toby, getting out and coming around to join Alfie. "This one sticks more often in the damp." He bumped it with his hip and then tugged back, but the door remained closed.

"It's about time his Lordship sprung for a new vehicle, eh, laddie?" chuckled Alfie. He was dressed in his Sunday best — a dark suit, circa 1979 with a dashing red cravat at his throat. His hair was bryl-creamed into a 1930's duck-tail and he'd clearly made free with his after-shave. My heart almost exploded with affection for him.

"Nowt wrong with it," grunted Toby, wiggling the handle. "Just a few cosmetic issues, that's all. Still runs like a top."

Just then, Edie's door opened and she stepped out.

"Never mind fighting with the silly door. We're going to be late. Just get in my side, Hazel, before those two eejits get themselves all covered in muck."

She shook her head at the two men, but she was smiling. She'd worn her favourite blue dress, the one she'd worn to my graduation and she still looked as lovely as she did all those years ago. I was filled with a deep appreciation for the quiet contentment of their lives. Toby thought nothing of having to drive a dilapidated Rover and it would never occur to either Edie or Alfie to buy new clothes when the ones they had were perfectly fine. Especially when they only wore them on 'high days and holidays'. I thought of my mum and her friends and their frantic obsession with keeping up with the newest fashions. I smoothed my hands down my vintage smock dress and allowed myself a little grin. These were my people.

I shuffled along the back seat and belted myself in. I was pleased to note that all of the Rover's seatbelts appeared to be functional. Edie climbed in beside me and the two men got back into the front. After a brief struggle with the passenger side door, Alfie pulled it to with a bang and turned around in his seat to look at us. His face was lit up with a beaming grin, his cheeks slightly rosy. He was like a schoolboy on a day trip.

"Alright my lovely lasses?" he said, eyes twinkling merrily as he rubbed his hands together. I glanced sideways at Edie who was tutting and shaking her head.

"Sit yourself straight and get your seatbelt on," she said to Alfie, who just winked and turned back around.

"Onwards, my lad!" he said to Toby, who was grinning as the Rover lurched into gear. "Onwards to victory!"

"Here you go,"

Toby handed me a styrofoam cup of tea.

"It'll probably taste like absolute shite but it's hot and it gives us something to do, yeah?"

I nodded and smiled.

We'd been waiting for what seemed like days.

Hamish had bustled into the courtroom at five minutes to twelve, winking as he went. It was now almost two o'clock and nothing so much as a murmur had come past the dark mahogany doors.

Lord Dummell had brought a hamper full of sandwiches and cheese pasties so we had an impromptu picnic in the lobby, much to the amusement of the bailiff. He'd looked so longingly at the pasties that Astrid had wrapped one in a serviette and taken it to him.

"Eeee! Thanks, lass," he'd said with a beaming grin. "I'll just put it by 'til my tea break. That'll go lovely with a nice brew, it will. Bless you."

Astrid returned to our little party, a small smile on her face.

"Buttering up the staff?" teased Alfie. "Think he'll put in a word?"

"Oh Alfie, leave her be," scolded Edie. "There's always room for a bit of kindness in this world. And despite her terrifying exterior, our Astrid is one of the biggest hearted folk in Winkle."

She'd grinned and elbowed Astrid and who smiled more widely.

"Edie's right," she said, passing around bottles of lemon squash. "I've decided there's enough aggro in the world and I'm not contributing to it anymore. Hazel and this whole business with the Hedge has shown me that there's no shame, and plenty of progress to be made, by being pleasant and gentle."

She'd looked around at the open-mouthed stares, a hint of her old defiance flashed across her face.

Toby was the first to speak.

"Jolly well said! Catching more flies with honey and all that, right? Let's drink to that, shall we?"

"To kindness!"

"To kindness!" We all echoed, raising our bottles and clinking with our neighbours.

I was still mulling over the deeper implications of Astrid's little declaration when Toby handed me the tea. A packet of lemon custards had materialized from Lord Dummell's picnic hamper and Alfie was passing it around.

"Do you think I'm feeble?" I asked, suddenly in need of an outside opinion. I knew what I'd say if I asked myself.

Toby laughed softly and shook his head.

"Of course not, you silly git. Why on earth would you think that?"

I waved my hand vaguely in the air.

"All of this," I gestured again. "How I handled it. Or didn't handle it, as the case may be. My flip-flopping and indecisiveness, my apparent inability to stand up to my mother. My wanting to run away from the best thing that's ever happened to me…"

My voice trailed off as I fully comprehended the enormity of what I'd almost done. How could I have ever wanted to leave Winkle?

Toby reached over and placed his hand on mine. It was work-worn and callused, but warm and strong. He gave it a quick squeeze.

"Quite the contrary," he said. "You've had a whole lot of big stuff shoved on you at a time when you really weren't in any state to cope with it. You've been unwell, you've lost your Nan and then here we were, practically bullying you into taking on a responsibility that you knew nothing about."

"No-one bullied me," I interrupted, but Toby raised a questioning eyebrow. I smiled.

"Okay, maybe it was all a bit overwhelming," I conceded. "But no-one ever made me feel like I had to do it."

"Maybe," he said, but I could tell he didn't believe me. "Anyway, I think you coped with it better than you've given yourself credit for. And all that really matters is that you've made your final decision and it's one you're happy with."

He frowned and looked worriedly into my face.

"You are happy with it, aren't you?"

I looked around at my friends. Astrid and Sidney were playing Snap with a pack of cards that Astrid had found in the bottom of her capacious handbag. Alfie and Lord Dummell were in deep discussion over something to do with sheep dip and Edie had pulled her knitting out. Her needles clickety-clacked in a soothing rhythm that marched in time to the ticking of the large clock on the wall. I couldn't think of anywhere else I'd rather be.

I turned to Toby and smiled, placing my other hand over his.

"I couldn't be happier," I said. "There's no..."

Just then the double doors of the courtroom burst open and several dark-suited people spilled out. It was a sudden confusion of briefcases and shiny shoes as I searched the group for Hamish.

Just then, he appeared. He looked slightly disheveled, his tie was crooked and there were bits of paper poking out of his satchel. But he was smiling.

We all gathered in a nervous cluster. We'd convinced ourselves there was no way we could lose, but what if we'd overlooked something? Edie shot me a worried glance. I reached out to hold her hand.

"Well, old boy!" boomed Lord Dummell. "Don't keep us all in suspense! What's the word?"

"Well, it was a long, hard argument," said Hamish, passing a hand over his tired features. "It wasn't nearly as straightforward as we'd thought. The other side had some convincing arguments." His shoulders sagged and he took a deep breath.

"But surely..." said Astrid, her voice a breathless squeak. Sidney put a protective arm around her shoulders. I felt Toby take my other hand.

"But not convincing enough!" said Hamish, his face splitting into a huge grin.

"D'you mean it's over?" I said, feeling my throat closing over with a clog of tears. "Is the Hedge safe?'

"For now and, with a bit of careful paperwork, at least the next hundred years!"

The lobby erupted into hoots and whistles. Astrid and Sidney took hands and capered a reel around the chairs. Our friend the bailiff came over and there was much shaking of hands and thumping of shoulders.

The din was enormous and I half-wondered if we'd be charged with disrupting the courts.

I suddenly felt my knees wobble so I made my way back to the chairs and sat down.

It was over. It was really over. The Hedge was safe and so were the folk of Winkle and Nether Winkle alike.

I took a great shuddering breath and burst into happy tears.

Chapter Thirty-Seven

"Astrid!" called Edie, weaving her way through the crowd. "We need more samosas!"

"Right!" replied Astrid, her face wreathed in smiles. Her blue hair clung in wet tendrils around her face as she pushed up her sleeves and disappeared through the door of the village hall towards the kitchen. I watched her go, amazed at the transformation from sullen, black-eyed teen to enthusiastic organizer and picnic caterer. She'd handmade ten dozen samosas according to her secret family recipe and they were going down like gangbusters. I'd seen several people trying to weasel the recipe out of her.

"Drink?"

Toby held out a paper cup of lemonade and I took it gratefully. The weather had come up trumps — I'd been assured there'd been no magical interventions — and it was gloriously sunny with only the hint of a breeze. I was sitting in the shade of one of the ancient elms, happy to simply watch the bustle and excitement from a distance.

"Ta very much," I said, swallowing a large gulp in a very unlady-like-like fashion. "It's a warm one, isn't it?"

"It is that," said Toby, smiling out at the people milling about the green. Residents of Winkle and NetherWinkle mixed in as if it were the most natural thing in the world. The landlord of the Forge was in deep discussion with a lanky, long-bearded man dressed in loose-fitting earth-toned trousers and a billowy-sleeved white tunic. Even Mrs. Trout was mingling; she was in a conversation with Mrs.G and a small, green-haired woman who appeared to have a goat on a leash.

"That's Barrington," said Toby, nodding towards the Forge's landlord, and his conversation partner.

"Oh?"

"He runs a small brewhouse in NetherWinkle. Fraser has been after him for years to supply the Forge but it was always a bit tricky with...well, things. I think he's hoping the spirit of victory will soften the old warlock's resistance."

I spluttered my lemonade.

"Warlock? He's an actual warlock?"

Toby grinned.

"Sure, why wouldn't he be?"

I shrugged.

"I don't know. I suppose I just expected...well, I don't really know what I expected. It's just, well, he looks like your garden variety New-Age, hippy yoga instructor or something. I can't say as I've ever given the appearance of warlocks any serious thought."

"What do you think warlocks should look like? Pointy hat? Silver stars and a long staff, perhaps?"

I glanced over at Toby who was trying hard to stifle the smile that was tugging at the corners of his mouth.

I reached over and swatted him.

"Don't make fun," I said. "This is all still very surreal for me. I was only just getting my head around Mr. and Mrs. G when all of a sudden there's a stream of odd looking people coming out of my shed this morning."

"Busy thoroughfare, isn't it?"

"Lord Dummell! You made it!"

"Absolutely, my dear gel. I couldn't miss the feshtivities, could I?"

Lord Dummell lowered himself to the grass with a great deal of groaning and creaking of joints. Somehow he managed not to spill a drop of his foaming pint.

"Barrington's finesht," he said, nodding blearily towards his glass. "Jolly chap brought two casks for the party and I'm making the behst of it. He's a terrible old tease, you know. Fraser has been badgering him for ages but the wily old sod won't part with any more than a few casks at a time. Ridiculous business, border politics and all that nonsense. Mayhap we can get that sorted now that this other mess has been cleared away."

He took a long draught of his ale, smacking his lips then belching with great appreciation.

"Bloody good shtuff, that."

He turned to Toby who was still grinning behind his lemonade.

"Now, Toby old boy," began Lord Dummell. His head wobbled ever so slightly as he peered into Toby's face. "We musht get our Hazel here acquainted with the goings-on in NetherWinkle. You know, get her up to shpeed on the you-know-what."

He winked at Toby and smiled beatifically at me before taking another swig of ale.

"Itsh not too soon to warn..."

"Potent stuff," said Toby, talking over Lord Dummell. "When he said he's making the most of it, I'm sure he wasn't exaggerating. That won't be his first pint of Barrington's brew."

I smiled, but my stomach had that familiar clenching feeling.

"What's he on about?" I asked. "Warn me about what?"

Toby waved a hand.

"Never mind that," he said, airily. "Just more village politics. The usual petty disputes that'll no doubt re-emerge now that the Nether-Winkle folk will be coming and going more often. Certainly nothing that needs to be discussed just now. Let's just enjoy the spoils of victory, shall we? Oh, look! There's Astrid back with more of those brilliant samosas. Shall I get you some?"

Without waiting for an answer, Toby sprang to his feet and marched purposefully off in the direction of the food tent, leaving me frowning after him.

Lord Dummell reached out a hand and patted my knee.

I turned to look into his lovely, odd face. His eyes were red-rimmed and he blinked owlishly, the slow and deliberate blink of someone who might no longer be in full control of their fine motor movements. My heart filled with sudden affection for this dotty old man.

"Never you mind, pet," he said, pronouncing his words slowly. I looked down at his other hand where the empty pint glass dangled. "It'll all come right in the end. I've every faith that you're the right man for the job. I told our Alfie that you'd get everything shorted out as shoon as poshible..."

I patted his hand, gently removing the empty glass. I rolled my cardigan into a pillow and put it on the grass, easing him down into a prone position.

"Why don't you just rest your eyes for a minute, Lord Dummell? It's lovely here in the shade and you look like you're in need of a little nap."

"Jolly good, old gel," he muttered, obediently crossing his hands over his stomach. "Itsh been a long road and I'm ever sho tired..."

His gentle snores started almost immediately. I slid his hat out from under his head and placed it over his crossed hands, then crept quietly away.

I found Edie sitting in the tea tent with Mrs. Trout. A giant Brown Betty steamed between them, along with a large plate of sandwiches. I paused, wanting to speak to Edie but at the same time not wanting to engage with Mrs. Trout in any way. I found it hard to believe that she'd be so forgiving of how things had worked out. After all, it was her husband's pet project to have BMZ come into the community. Surely that had represented a tidy kickback for them, so I was a tiny bit suspicious of the way she was joining in with the celebrations.

Swallowing my misgivings, I made my way towards their table, pasting a pleasant smile on my face.

"Hazel, love!" beamed Edie. She patted the seat next to her. "Sit down and have a cup of tea and a sandwich. I bet you've not braved the crowds for anything to eat, have you?"

I shook my head. I was holding out for Toby's expedition to retrieve me some samosas, though the sandwiches were very tempting. Any sandwich made by hands other than your own always tasted better somehow.

"You'll be needing to keep your strength up, young lady," said Mrs. Trout, fixing me with her beady-eyed stare, her head tilted slightly and a small smile on her thin lips. I imagine she thought she was being kind.

"Oh?" I said, sitting down next to Edie and helping myself to a cucumber and tomato sandwich. "Why's that then?"

Mrs. Trout shrugged, her bony shoulders hunched up to her ears making her look vaguely like a vulture. I made a point of looking directly at her, inviting her to continue. I didn't trust her one bit.

"Well, everyone knows that this business of the Hedge isn't quite so simple as a bit of paperwork. That's merely the tip of the iceberg. Tea?"

I nodded and she poured me a cup, sliding it across the table towards me.

She smiled again and dabbed the corners of her mouth with an embroidered napkin.

"Is that so?"

"Oh yes. I think you'll find that there's far more to contend with than a wind farm. In fact, I'd go so far as to say that the bigger trouble is yet to come. Now, if you ladies will excuse me, I have to get back to the Post Office. His Majesty wouldn't like to know that we were closed all afternoon for such an occasion as this. But, as you know, Mr. Trout and I are very community minded and I told him that we mustn't be seen to be sulking simply because things didn't go quite as we'd hoped. It's far more important that the health and happiness of Winkle is maintained, don't you agree?"

"Very much so," I replied, narrowing my eyes at her. "I can't think of anything more important than looking after the welfare of this village. On both sides of the Hedge."

Mrs. Trout winced visibly before sucking in a deep breath and pushing back her thin shoulders. She clutched her handbag in her long, red-tipped fingers.

"Indeed," she said, before nodding her head in a dismissive gesture and walking away.

"Horrible bloody cow," said Edie, with a vehemence quite unlike her.

I was mid-sip and almost choked with laughter.

She grinned and patted my hand.

"Never you mind, pet. She's just a bitter old bag and must be absolutely livid that we had our way. But like she said, she wouldn't dare be seen to be going against the village,"

Edie frowned and followed Mrs.Trout's departure with her eyes.

"Mark my words, though, she's not going to take this peacefully. I wouldn't underestimate her, she's as mean-spirited as they come but she's clever with it; spite dressed in a sugary coating."

An involuntary shiver ran up my spine. I stared after her but she'd left the tent.

"Those are the most dangerous types of all," I said, under my breath.

"What's that, lovey?"

"Oh, nothing,," I replied, not wanting to dwell on the unpleasantness. "I'm just wondering if I can have my dad's secretary send me a book of stamps in the post so I never have to go into the post office again!"

Edie chuckled.

"Not a bad idea, that. Now, how about another sandwich? Oh, hello! Look who's here!"

I had an egg and watercress sandwich halfway to my mouth when I felt two strong hands grip my shoulders and got a whiff of the familiar smell of Versace's Eros, Roger's latest cologne obsession.

"What's this?" he said. "I leave you alone for a few days and you're back to eating the food of peasants. Tomato sandwiches indeed!"

A big wicker basket appeared over my shoulder and was put onto the table.

"Good thing I packed extra. We need to show these provincials how we celebrate in the big city!"

I stood up and turned around and was immediately engulfed in a great, squeezy hug.

"Bloody good job," whispered Roger into my ear. "I knew you'd do it."

"I know you did," I whispered back. "Thank you for believing in me."

I gave him a tight squeeze and then broke the hug, stepping back.

"Edie," I said, "I'd like you to meet my very best friend in all the world, Roger Sanderson. Roger, this is Edie."

Roger grinned his trademark beaming smile and reached out to take Edie's offered hand. In true Roger fashion, he bent his head and kissed the back of her hand.

"It's a pleasure to finally meet you, Edie. I've heard so much about you from Hazel, I feel like we've already known each other for years. But I must say, Hazel greatly understated your youth and beauty."

He sketched an awkward bow and I just rolled my eyes as he winked up at us.

Edie burst into delighted laughter.

"Get on with you," she said. "You can't fool me. Our Hazel warned me ahead of time so you're wasting your talents on me."

Roger grinned and leaned in to kiss her on her offered cheek.

"Ah, it never hurts to try," he said. "Now, who wants to help me with this hamper? Nathan can't go anywhere without packing enough food for ten."

"Speaking of Nathan," I said, accepting a ham roll wrapped in brown paper. "Where is he?"

"Off charming the locals, no doubt," replied Roger, passing out little jars of chutney. "Last I saw him, he was haranguing your friend Astrid for her spice blend."

"Good luck to him," said Edie. "Our Astrid is no pushover. She won't give up her secrets easily."

"Hallo," said a voice, "Where'd all this grub come from? Here's me having stood in line for twenty minutes only to miss the last samosa and you lot are living it up with exotic sarnies."

Grinning, Toby reached across the table and shook hands with Roger, who was only a bit stiff in his return. Roger had become rather protective of me since the debacle with Teddy; his gamekeeper jokes aside, he viewed Toby with some suspicion. It was entirely unwarranted of course, there was no reason to consider Toby as anything other than an old friend.

"Sit down," said Roger. "Have one of our exotic sarnies, as you call them. Chicken or ham?"

I sat back and soaked up the moment. A collection of my favourite people, happy and chatting and eating delicious food. I felt completely and utterly at home. Whatever Lord Dummell had been talking about and despite Mrs.Trout's veiled threats, I truly felt like everything was going to be okay. At that moment, things couldn't possibly get better. Winkle was safe from development, which meant NetherWinkle was also safe. I would still have my mother to contend with, but I was well and truly committed to my life at Rookery Cottage and everything that went along with it. I was going to write what I wanted to write and if that meant I had to take a side job, then so be it. I was sure Roger could use the help. I was just enjoying the daydream of working with Roger again, helping him and Nathan build their business when a flurry of activity over by the lemonade stand caught the corner of my eye.

Half-expecting it to be Lord Dummell, awake and wondering where he was, I leaned back in my chair to get a better look.

Sidney emerged from a cluster of people and started towards the tea tent, everything in their body language spoke of agitation.

I felt my stomach clench.

Surely there couldn't be any upset already.

"Hazel!" They called, as they burst into the tent. They looked wildly around before I caught their eye with a wave.

"There you are! I've been looking everywhere. You've got to come with me, it's really urgent."

Their hair curled in sweaty tendrils and clung to their face. They pushed their glasses up their glistening red face. I scanned it for possible hints at what could be so urgent.

"What is it?" I asked, reluctantly getting to my feet. "Is everything alright? Is Lord Dummell okay?"

"What?" they said, faltering. They flapped an impatient hand. "Oh, he's fine. Still out cold under the tree where you left him. No, this is something that really, really needs your attention. Like, now."

They reached out and took hold of my arm and started tugging me in the direction of the lemonade stand.

"Sidney!" I said, breathlessly as I stumbled on one of the tent pegs. "Slow down!"

"Never mind that," they said, turning their head and grinning. "You'll be glad I made you rush in a minute. Here she is!"

With a shove, I was thrust into a cluster of people, standing around drinking lemonade. Blushing, I looked at them all, shrugging apologetically.

"Sorry," I said. "I'm afraid I must be having a trick played on me or something..."

I looked around for Sidney but they seemed to have disappeared. Then I caught sight of them ushering Astrid towards the group. Over the tops of heads, I saw Toby and Roger escorting Edie from the tent.

Oh no, I groaned inwardly. Surely they weren't going to do some sort of hideously embarrassing presentation or make me do a speech or something. A well of panic started to rise into my throat. I felt like a trapped animal.

"Miss Price?"

A vaguely familiar voice came from behind me.

I turned to look and saw a tall, sandy-haired man in a blue windbreaker. I tried to place him, he looked so familiar but...

"Sorry, I just went to take some lemonade to my wife. She's over by the apple bobbing with our son. He's not at all old enough to join in but he loves watching."

I must have looked very confused because he stopped talking and held out his hand.

"Steven Willis. We met a few months ago. You'd found our dog. Well, she was our dog..."

Bracken.

My heart lurched. I felt a stab of guilt as with everything going on, I hadn't thought of her in a few days. I had hoped it was a sign I was getting over the whole thing. Why did they have to come here? I didn't need reminding of the heartache. I swallowed and forced a smile.

"Yes, of course," I said. "I'm sorry I didn't recognize you right away. That day was a bit of a blur, emotionally, that is."

I choked off the words and swallowed again.

"And how is she getting on? I'm sure she's very settled by now."

Mr. Willis shuffled his feet and cleared his throat.

"Well, that's what I was hoping to speak with you about. You see, things haven't gone quite as smoothly as we'd hoped with Angel."

"Oh?" My throat felt very dry. I accepted a cup of lemonade from Roger who had appeared at my left elbow. Astrid appeared at my right. She squeezed my elbow and smiled.

"Yes, erm, well. I imagine you remember that she was a bit of a sensitive creature...very prone to startling and all that."

I thought back to the first time I'd seen her, a quivering heap of fur on the heather and allowed myself a small smile.

"Yes, not quite the bravest of dogs," I replied.

Mr. Willis nodded, his face pinched with a frown.

"Well, that didn't change when we brought her back to the city. You see, she hasn't coped well at all. The noise and the traffic...we feel as if she spends all of her days in a state of pure terror."

I felt a sharp contraction in my chest. Poor Bracken. But why did he feel he had to come all the way to Winkle to tell me that my beloved Bracken was miserable? And why on earth was Toby grinning from ear to ear?

"I'm sorry to hear that" I said, "Perhaps she just needs more time."

I looked around, helplessly, as the idiotically grinning faces of my friends. What on earth was wrong with them? Didn't they see I was upset?

"Actually," said Mr. Willis. "I got in touch with the rescue place — we wanted to explore all the options, of course, and we were prepared to do whatever we had to do to help her. She's just the loveliest dog..."

I gritted my teeth.

"I know."

"...and they suggested it was probably just her temperament and that maybe a life in the city wasn't the best option for her. They said they could take her back and try to place her in a country home."

"But," interrupted Astrid, her eyes bright with excitement "Steven phoned me first – he knew me from the shop when they first came to pick up Bracken – and asked me if I thought you'd consider it. Isn't it just perfect?"

My heart hammered in my chest and I could feel my face burning. I hardly dared to believe it.

"I cleared it with the rescue — they're very strict about that sort of thing," assured Mr. Willis, "So if you'd be willing, there's some paperwork of course..."

I could barely see. Tears streamed down my face and I was laughing and sobbing all at once. I couldn't form any words so I just nodded, my hands clasped to my mouth. There was no other option than the ugly cry.

Just then, a whiskery, shaggy eye-browed face pushed its way through the crowd, towing Alfie, holding onto the leash — the leash I'd bought — behind her. Her tail spun like a windmill and she was doing her shrieky yodelling bark.

"Bracken!" I whispered, kneeling down on the trampled grass.

She whined and wiggled and tried to crawl onto my knee.

"You're home."

Wait! Don't go yet...

I hope you enjoyed this book — it was my honour and privilege to share it with you.

If you *did* enjoy it, would you consider leaving a review? Perhaps you could recommend it to a friend or family member who might also enjoy it? Word of mouth is the most effective source of 'advertising' and any effort you can offer is deeply appreciated as it keeps me in tea and notebooks so I can write the next one. Thank you!

Have you read my other books?

The Tales of Glencarragh Series: Skelly, Wind Singer, Soul of the Sea, Sea Bride – available in ebook and paperback.

Acknowledgements

It's been said a million times by a million different people for a million different reasons, but it really does take a village. This book has challenged me in a multitude of ways and I wouldn't have crossed the finish line without a great deal of help.

Special thanks to...

The Nines – your unconditional love and support has kept me going when all I wanted to do was curl up in the corner and quietly dribble on myself – I love you guys!

Becky Grisell, Christianne Squires and all of the beautiful souls in the Light House...thank you for seeing and naming what I have such a hard time noticing.

Antoinette, Claire, Leanne and Sue – for agreeing to walk together on this wild ride called writing. You got me through the hardest bit on this one.

My family, always and forever.

About the author

Melanie Leavey was born and raised in the north-east of England before emigrating to Canada with her family at the age of nine. An aspiring hermit and passionate gardener, she likes nothing better than drinking tea and thumbing through a seed catalogue. She's fond of book-forts and notebooks with ink-crinkled paper.

A country mouse turned town mouse, she lives with her family on the Territory of the Haudenosaunee Confederacy, Fort Erie, Ontario.

Join her community of readers and writers and stay up to date with new releases at:

melanieleavey.substack.com